Unexpected Lessons in Love

Unexpected Lessons in Love

BERNARDINE BISHOP

JOHN MURRAY

First published in Great Britain in 2013 by John Murray (Publishers)
An Hachette UK Company

2

© Bernardine Bishop 2013

The right of Bernardine Bishop to be identified as the Author of the
Work has been asserted by her in accordance with the Copyright,
Designs and Patents Act 1988.

A CIP catalogue record for this title is available from the British Library

ISBN 978-1-84854-782-7
Ebook ISBN 978-1-84854-783-4

Typeset in Adobe Caslon Pro by Palimpsest Book Production Limited,
Falkirk, Stirlingshire

Printed and bound by Clays Ltd, St Ives plc

John Murray policy is to use papers that are natural, renewable and
recyclable products and made from wood grown in sustainable forests.
The logging and manufacturing processes are expected to conform to
the environmental regulations of the country of origin.

John Murray (Publishers)
338 Euston Road
London NW1 3BH

www.johnmurray.co.uk

In loving memory of my mother,
Barbara Wall

PART I
Gut Feeling

Chapter 1

S he was still in bed at eight, which would have been
unthinkable until the last two years. It was acceptable now
because she was ninety. She had been Sister Mary Vincent in
1939, then she had been Mother Mary Vincent, respectively
informally addressed first as Sister and then as Mother; then
she had been Sister Diana Clegg, and had simultaneously
forfeited, or been relieved of, the veil. Now she was Diana, or
Sister, or, to differentiate herself from other nuns in a context
where identification was needed, Sister Diana. She was accustomed to 'Diana' now, but it had at first been distasteful, for
Diana is not a Christian saint, and the name offered no star
to follow, unlike the resplendencies of Mary and of Vincent.

Married women change their names, or had in Diana's young
day. The change signified the start of a new and dedicated life.
She had welcomed setting aside the familiar 'Diana Clegg' and
had welcomed renascence under the name of Mary Vincent,
and not only because she loved both those saints. It was also
a rite of passage. She was no longer only the intense, tousled
Diana Clegg who had been good at hockey and bad at maths,
who had adored her mother and feared her father, who had
decided one windy day alone on the top of the South Downs
to be a nun. She knew she was not going to become a different
person, tempting though that fantasy was; but she had gathered
her whole self together and pointed the pieces in the one

3

direction, excluding other choices, in the name of love. When in her hard-working, habit-hardened forties she and her confrères had been instructed to revert to their birth names, she had taken it with grim humour, as a sign that she could only ever be who she had always been, and that God knew and accepted that, unaccountably loved it, even. Nevertheless one of her mottoes remained George Eliot's 'It is never too late to be what you might have been' and at ninety she was trying as hard as ever.

In a hotel bedroom in a small town two miles away from Diana's convent lay Cecilia Banks, not at all startled still to be in bed at eight. She reached for her mobile and texted: 'OK confêrnce niceish hotel will be seeing M M V this a m See you pm Rmember to feed Thor.' Her paper had gone down better yesterday than her laconic reference to the conference suggested, but her husband knew her and would know this. Participation in the conference had been her first professional reappearance since her operation and consequent retirement from regular work. Her first reappearance, or her only one? Time would tell. Her hand went to the colostomy bag. It was the first time she would change it, if it turned out that she needed to, away from home.

It felt about half full, and her fingers pressed the clayey substance through the smooth plastic. Her guts had worked overnight without her knowledge. She was used to this. It was one of the things that made excretion so different from excretion in her life up to the age of sixty-five and so different from the norm. She had reflected, well, I used to shit in the mornings; it must always have been during the night that the shit was funnelled unnoticed past this point near my navel where it now comes out.

The unhealed, perhaps unhealable, surgical wound hurt as she got out of bed. In the bathroom she considered not changing the stoma bag until she got home. It might be due a quiet day. On the other hand, she thought, beginning to remove and replace bags, it might unpredictably awaken, and be in full cry, or rather full chuckle and whisper, on the train. Anyway, it would be unseemly to share toast and marmalade with MMV, knowing that there was a portion of shit, albeit unseen and unsmelling, an inch from the tablecloth.

These were new decisions for Cecilia, as they would be for anybody, and she was still surprised that she had to make them. In one sense, as a practical person, she had in the past year got used to her changed body. In another sense, she knew that if her wrist was strapped to a lie-detector, it would register that she had no colostomy. Cecilia had been a psychotherapist for the thirty years before her forced retirement, invalided out of the profession; so she was accustomed to thinking about degrees of truth, of belief, of honesty.

And it was good to register that she had on a clean and empty bag when she embraced Diana, who rose to greet her, then sank back into her upright chair, beaming beautifully and still holding Cecilia's hands. Nuns are great hand-holders, remembered Cecilia. 'It's wonderful to see you, Mother,' she said.

'It's wonderful to see you, my dear,' said Diana, 'and looking well. You have been through so much since last we met.'

'I certainly have,' said Cecilia, noticing that Diana had heard and been pleased by 'Mother'. 'I know we have to call you Diana, now, but once Mother, always Mother. What a year. Two years, really, since the cancer was first diagnosed.'

She had got into the cancer absolutely at once, she observed. Perhaps no surprise, for she had always perceived MMV as a life and death person, fully signed up to both. So Diana heard the whole story, and occasionally said, 'My dear, what a story,' 'So what happened next?', 'How awful for you,' and 'Don't ignore the toast while it is still hot.' She was glad her hearing aid was working well, and indeed she thanked God.

5

These two went back a long way, for Cecilia too had undergone her tousled intensities, and also had felt impelled to enter religious life. When she arrived at the convent with her suitcase, Mother Mary Vincent was novice mistress. Though at that time relatively inexperienced, Diana knew enough not to have a lot of trust in Cecilia's vocation. Cecilia was too much inclined to adoration of the senior nuns, particularly the novice mistress; and Diana did not hold with such adorations. Cecilia scorned the recreation hour, and was to be found kneeling in the rain before the garden *pietà*, and Diana, torn from reading *Middlemarch* aloud in the common room, had to seek her with a brolly. Cecilia had imposed fasts on herself, and other acts of supererogation of which Diana disapproved. Theory and intuition told Diana it was better that Cecilia should realise she had made a mistake. When that time came, they had an emotional parting and had kept loosely in touch through the decades.

When Cecilia arrived home, home being London, she found Thor in but Tim out. Almost before putting her bag down, she looked for a note from Tim on the kitchen table. There was no note, not even in the places he sometimes put a note where no one in their senses would be likely to look for it. His text in answer to hers in the morning had merely said: 'Glad all went well. See you later.' She put the kettle on. Next she checked messages on the home phone, and heard other voices but not his. Then she unpacked the overnight bag, to whose ordinary things, including her paper for the conference, had been added for the first time colostomy supplies. Then she turned her full attention to Thor, who had been asking for a response all along. Thor at least had greeted her whole-heartedly, with purrs and self-stroking round her feet, and she could not let him go longer unthanked. The cup of tea would have to wait.

She loved it when Tim was in when she got home. She

could hardly believe he didn't know this, but perhaps he didn't, or didn't remember it. It was so different, after all, from anything he might feel, or so Cecilia thought. The sense of being alone settled on her. She loved Thor, possibly more than she loved Tim, though it depends on what you mean by love; but the sense of sustaining presence offered by Thor was limited, however much attention he was paying her. Tim only had to be sitting at the computer with his back to her, groaning a distracted greeting, and the world was an unfrightening and adequately populated world. She had been admired and perhaps celebrated at the conference, and the conversation with MMV had induced even exuberance. Now she was deflated and tired, a lonely, elderly woman with a colostomy and a sore bottom, having a cup of tea with the cat on a grey Sunday afternoon in London.

One of the answerphone messages had been from her son Ian, and he had asked her to ring him back. She did this now.

'Mum, I've got tons to tell you. Are you sitting comfortably?'

'Yes,' said Cecilia, who remained standing. Sitting was less comfortable than standing, but she could tell that Ian was in no mood to hear about her state of health. It was unlike him not to enquire: something must be up.

'Well, I'd like to come over, because all this is rather long and complicated for the phone. But I can't come over without talking to you, so . . . OK. Tim's not there, is he?'

'No.'

'OK. Do you remember Leda?'

'Yes, of course.'

'Well. Because you disapproved of her so much, and of course I saw why, I didn't tell you things. She was pregnant from me, insisted on having the baby, and the baby was born. Are you there? Sorry to be catching you up with so much so quickly, but the moral for you is, don't disapprove too much and you will get stories in digestible instalments.'

'Of course I'm here. But stunned. Well, catching up.' Cecilia was remapping her world. She had a grandchild.

'Leda had lost interest in me, and I in her, and but for the baby I would have faded out completely. She is a lot madder, as well, voices and everything now. Of course I've been giving her money and coping with her decision not to have an abortion, and I was there at the birth. I've registered the baby and everything. But that's irrelevant. I'm sticking to the headlines, and I haven't got to the banner one yet.'

'You were there at a birth,' Cecilia couldn't help interjecting. 'And it didn't even show in you whenever it was I next saw you!'

'Mum don't be silly, remember I've reported from Afghanistan, I knew you'd get distracted by that. It's nothing after what you see.'

Cecilia was disappointed. 'When was the baby born?' She didn't like to ask if it was a boy or a girl in case that also wasn't a headline.

'Couple of months ago. It's only tiny. But this is the important thing. It was left literally on my doorstep in the night. I'll read you the note.' Rustling. '"I have been called away, and I shall never come back. Cephas and you must live together. That is what has to be, as you well know. You will see the packet of his food and you can buy the same. Some say I am dead and perhaps I will be. Waters easily close above a head." Then there's a bit I can't read. Then, "You will never see me again." Well, that's not very good, is it?'

'No.'

'Well, of course I phoned her number, and have been phoning all day. I've rung the police. I'm rather stuck here because of Cephas. I don't know why he's called that, she wanted me to register him as Julius Perdito and my surname, so that's what I did.'

'You've been through so much, and I didn't even know.'

8

'Well, you were ill, and the whole saga's so mad, and I don't want Tim to know, though he'll have to now. What I want to do is get a taxi and come over and leave Cephas with you. I can't look after him, possibly. Of course I'll see him, often I suppose, at yours. I'm so sorry, is this all right? Otherwise he'll have to go into care.'

'Might Leda reappear?'

'Well, she might, anything's possible, she might be at home not answering the phone. I'll go round and try to find out once you've got Cephas, but I won't be surprised if she doesn't reappear. She's got much madder than she was when you knew her.'

'I hardly did. Only that extraordinary evening.'

'She's been talking lots about the sea and suicide. She doesn't call it suicide, she calls it offering her breasts to the deep. That's why she decided she shouldn't breastfeed, because her breasts were bespoken by the deep.'

'Darling, what a time you've had.'

'But for Cephas I would have been history for her and she for me. Immediately. Within a few weeks. I don't like mad people, nor babies, actually. Both are scary. Luckily for me, Leda didn't like me much. I think she took against me as an evil force. It would have been easy to extricate myself.'

'Yes, and I thought you had.'

'Yes. Well, I want to get in a taxi and come over.'

'Of course. Do you love Cephas?'

'No, I'm much too worried. I need to offload him. Mum, I've got other things in my life. Yemen the day after tomorrow. Fatherly feelings didn't stir at the sight of him. Nor since. I wanted Leda to have an abortion, but I could see the thought of that was making her madder. I don't love her or him. What if he's as mad as his mum? Of course I'll always pay for him, and I have been. He's of no interest to me, and I'm hoping he will be of interest to you.'

'He is.'

'Good. I'll be over in half an hour. You'd better warn Tim.'

Left to herself, Cecilia had good reason to reel. But diagnoses of cancer and the threat of its recurrence had immunised her against reeling. Nor did she phone a friend, or attempt to track down Tim, though both impulses were there. Instead, she considered her task, her difficulties with it, and her resources. Tim. Tim would be all right about this. The house. She and Tim slept separately now, and the baby would of course have his cradle in her large bedroom. She and Tim were both retired, and, like a lot of retired professionals, had quite a lot of energy left, and were more afraid of being bored than being over-occupied. It was very important that Leda should know where her baby was, but managing that could safely be left to Ian.

It was Sunday, so there might be a crisis about baby milk, and for the first time Cecilia felt a physical qualm. A packet had been mentioned in Leda's note, but would that see them through until tomorrow? And what about a bottle, and ster-ilising equipment? Then there was the matter of Cephas himself. How much harm would have been done to him, or how much good would he have been able to extract, from his time with a mad mother? And what if Cephas became attached to herself and then was snatched away from her, either by Leda or by cancer? The adrenalin customarily prompted by answering a new and sudden challenge began to subside. This was indeed a grave responsibility. Should she have accepted it so readily? But what choice had she had?

She tried to bring to mind Ian's early life and the routines she had presumably become reasonably proficient in. She had been married to Gerry then. She had of course been young, and was not practical, brave or calm. Things should be easier now. With luck it might count for something that she had studied child development, and done an 'infant observation' as part of her training. Also, forty years ago, she had no doubt spent time hankering for a fuller life, for happiness, for fun, for freedom; such aims troubled her no more. Gerry's philandering had also been a source of anguish. Poor Ian. She was in a better position now to take on a baby than she had been at twenty-four. But that was nonsense – she tired more easily; she was at least something of an invalid, she had long taken undisturbed nights for granted. Nature did not give you babies at her age, and no doubt wisely.

She must make sure Ian saw the baby often, very often, and, once he didn't feel trapped, he would be able to begin to love him. This must be a major, though at first covert, objective for Cecilia. She must never lose sight of this, however much she might at some distant but imaginable point want to keep Cephas herself. For the first time in her ponderings the likelihood of her love for Cephas hoved explicitly into view. This made her think of Thor, and then of how he would be about Cephas; and her spirits fell again. Not only would Thor dislike Cephas, but Cecilia would have to conceal the fact that this raised divided loyalties for her. What grandmother preferred the cat?

There was a commanding ring at the door and she opened it to Ian, with a carrycot in his hand. He put it down on the floor of the hall, fairly gently, and embraced his mother. He was grim, tense and determined, facing an emergency. He turned to go into the kitchen.

'Darling, you'll have to bring him in with us.'

'Oh. OK. He's asleep, I think. We can leave him . . .' But he brought him in.

Cecilia couldn't resist now, though she knew it would be more diplomatic to concentrate entirely on Ian. The carrycot was on the kitchen table. In it was a muddle of shawls, a baby-milk packet, a bottle, a couple of babygros, the *Guardian*, a label with letters cut from newspapers saying Julius Perdito Forest, aka Cephas. She parted these things and underneath them saw the little face.

'Oh. He isn't asleep,' was all she could say. The baby's eyes were wide open, looking back at Cecilia with a considering, curious, wise expression, his mouth moving as he sucked his lower lip in and out. Cecilia felt startled, almost found out, by his gaze. She had been anticipating him as a wonder, a problem, a project; his little face, as he slightly moved his head to get a better look at her, told her firmly, though without accusation, that he was a person.

The impulse to pick him up was too strong to resist, though Ian was tutting for attention, and Cecilia felt the extraordinary, always unexpected weightlessness of a new baby. She put his face to hers and swayed. Tears came to her eyes.

'OK, Mum, you've bonded,' said Ian. 'But there's lots we've got to talk about, I've got to get over to Leda's, I've got to phone the police, then I've got to meet someone. Sorry to be pushed for time. Don't think I'm not grateful.'

'Make sure Leda knows where Cephas is,' said Cecilia.

'Yes, of course. If I can't get into her flat I'll leave a note. I've written it already in case. And I'll tell the police. And if she goes on being missing the police have said they'll list her. They'll break in, of course.'

'Does Leda have a social worker?'

'No. She didn't really seem mad at the antenatal clinic. I know because I went with her a couple of times. I hounded her on the phone from abroad to go to her appointments, and I think she often did. When she was giving birth she passed for normal, or so it seemed.'

'How could she have?'

'She's white, middle class, educated, stylish, beautiful. Would anyone look further? Anyway, they didn't. She was in hospital only a day. She's very healthy. The weirdness of her calling me Caliban was lost on the nurses. They ended up calling me that too, thinking it was my name.'

They both laughed snobbishly in spite of themselves, Cecilia still swaying slightly, and feeling Cephas's lips moving against her cheek. He might be getting hungry.

'What about food?' she said.

'Yes. He's had three meals already today. And there's a bottle in his cradle. And a bit of food.'

Cecilia's imagination boggled. 'Did you prepare the feeds?'

Ian looked sheepish. 'No, Marina did. It's Sunday so we couldn't buy this sort of stuff, but all her friends are having babies, and she phoned round and got three disposable bottles, and she fed him. One not much more than an hour ago. We didn't want to use the powdered baby food or you would have been left in the lurch overnight.'

'Are you and Marina properly together now?' If Ian hadn't been at this moment profoundly in her debt emotionally, something neither questioned nor commented on by either of them, this enquiry might not have been dared.

'You could say yes, but don't get the idea we could have Cephas, we don't live together yet, if we ever will, and it's much too soon to . . . And anyway our lives aren't like that. Then she had to go to work, but we're seeing each other later.'

'I'm very glad about you and Marina,' Cecilia slipped in seriously. She was never sure that her comments counted for nothing, though Ian liked them to appear so; and Marina, who had been around for years, she liked and approved of. 'Didn't Marina fall for Cephas?' she ventured.

'She coped in her nice businesslike way, and yes of course she liked him. Not as much as you do, though.' At this moment Ian looked tenderly at his mother holding the baby. He smiled. 'I must go,' he said. 'When will Tim be in?'

'Soon, I should think.' She had heard a text come through during the conversation and was looking forward to checking if it was from Tim.

'Now you are OK, aren't you?' said Ian. 'I'll phone tomorrow and come round in the evening if meetings don't go on too long. I'll phone anyway and see if you need me.'

He went. Cecilia removed a hand from Cephas and steadying him against herself checked her phone. Tim. Home in twenty minutes.

Cecilia looked at the beautiful little face, her hand behind the dark-haired head. Cephas looked back at her, and a frown flitted across his forehead. His mouth was moving still, as if absorbing something, and his eyes intently met hers. Mine is the wrong face, she thought, and he knows it.

She held him more closely, so that for the moment he needn't look at her. What she wanted now was to be able to offer him a bottle. But she couldn't make one while cuddling him. And she couldn't put him down. Meanwhile she felt two things. One was love. It was a love she had not chosen or expected. It had quietly but completely claimed her. She had no choice but to submit to it. It was as well she felt it, in the circumstances, for the other feeling was loss. But for the love, the sense of loss would have been overwhelming, and she would have acted on it. She could and would heartlessly have made a case to Ian for Cephas going into care. Even in the shadow of the love, the sense of loss was severe. In the year since her operation and her retirement, she had lived a life of leisure. That life had been difficult, in many ways, fraught with pain, fear and novelty. But she had gradually come to enjoy it, even to revel in it. She had no doorbell to answer, no timetable to keep, no need to go to bed at night or get up in the morning. It was a selfish life, and it went unquestioned by Cecilia and her friends that it was right that she never had to make much effort; and she was mostly regarded as rather brave and wonderful although she did almost nothing. Now she would be tied to a schedule more demanding and involving than the busy practice she had for years been used to. She shrank from the future.

It was not only this sudden, new love, she thought, walking steadily up and down the kitchen, Cephas held close. It was the old love too. It was the love for Ian, a scarred and seasoned forty-year-old, rather than a pristine love, but equally unnegotiable; and it made it impossible for her to say no to him. This realisation made her feel both proud and ashamed. She knew that, hidden behind the conversations on the phone and in person that they had just been having, there had been a familiar emotional semaphore – from him, the gesture of need; from her, that of availability. It was true that he wanted to offload Cephas, but he would repine and ultimately rebuke her if he could not offload him on to her. Putting the child into care was a card in his hand, but he knew he would not really have to play it. *Are you going to put me first, as ever? Yes.* That had been the semaphore exchange.

And now she heard Tim's key. He came into the kitchen wearing full tennis regalia and prepared to be apologetic. Then he saw Cephas.

'Hullo hullo hullo,' he said, 'Who's this?'

'Ian's son. My grandson. Your step-grandson. Cephas.'

'I didn't know . . . Did you tell me . . . Ian . . . Have I forgotten something?'

'No. It's as much of a surprise to me. The greater surprise is that we are to look after him. At least at the moment.'

Tim came over to look at him. Cephas looked back at Tim. Tim put a finger in the clutch of a tiny hand. Tim was initially rather pleased, as Cecilia had known he would be. He liked an emergency. He liked rising to an occasion, and for this there was ample scope in the mixing of the feed, for which there were instructions on the packet which he read aloud and carefully followed; the sterilising of the bottle and teat by boiling, and the eventual cooling of the milk to blood heat. All this was new to him, as he had no children of his own, and he approached these tasks without recognition, nostalgia or dread. Cecilia loved his painstaking competence, and it came into its own now as she had hoped it would.

However, it was rather slow, and Cephas was crying before Cecilia was able to offer him the bottle. Cecilia hated to see his alert, intelligent and approving expression break up into the red wrinkles and oblong mouth of screaming. Thor had been asleep on a chair all this time, but the screaming sent him out of the cat flap. Cecilia had pangs about Thor. What could he suppose Cephas was? She hummed and danced and talked, and chivvied Tim, and then the bottle was ready, and to her relief Cephas was eager for it.

'She hasn't spoilt his appetite, whatever else she has done to him,' she said, but not aloud, for Tim had not yet heard the details.

Chapter 2

I an took a taxi to Leda's flat. Two things gnawed at the self-esteem that had taken time, trouble and achievement in the outside world to build up. One was the relationship with Leda. As a fling it had lasted only two weeks. But why had he done it? He had not been blind to her nuttiness. He had overwhelmingly fancied her, but why hadn't he thought it through? Of course drink was as ever a factor. But why had he assumed she was on the pill, rather than checking it out? Whatever her answer to such a question, it might well have been fantasy or poetry, but all the same . . . Marina had been working in Gaza at the time, but that was no excuse either. If he had wanted a flingette, there were other people he could safely and discreetly have had one with. Marina had been stoical but displeased about the Leda story, and more so with its development into a pregnancy, then a baby story. She had not made a fuss, but only because such fusses were beneath her, not because it hadn't hurt. And unfortunately it had brought up the baby issue for her afresh, as the biological clock ticked.

So he had lost his head for a fortnight. Lots of people do that. Surely that was not so bad. Ian's mind was often full of excuse and bluster, based either on the notion of other people being at fault, or the notion that his faults were no worse than the average. But underneath the bluster the gnawing continued, perhaps not only from his self-esteem, perhaps also remorse of conscience. The wish to live a good and honourable life was strong in Ian. As the uninterested father of a pregnancy, he had been exemplary, and everyone had thought so. He had suggested termination as tactfully as could be. Failing there, he had provided a new flat and rather large sums of money. He had tried to locate Leda's parents, a hopeless endeavour, with only Leda to supply facts, and Oubliette being an unlikely surname. He had been present at the birth and taken responsibility in a way the nurses thought remarkable.

'If only all the fathers we see were as kind and sensible as you, Caliban,' the head midwife had said.

He had kept an eye on things in the last month, sometimes from Afghanistan, and had persuaded Marina and encouraged other friends to telephone and drop in. He had been surprised and relieved that Leda's mothering did not seem by the sound of it as chaotic as most of her life. Not that he was a judge, but friends who were parents had reported favourably. You have to give her a chance, this may be the making of her, motherhood does strange things to people: that was the tone friends took. However, he was thinking of installing a nanny or au pair if Leda would have it; but now this had happened.

Ian was glad. He felt guilty for hoping he was rid of Leda, but so it was. Insofar as he was concerned for Cephas, which was not far, he knew Cephas would be all right with Cecilia. If Leda did not reappear, the story was satisfactorily in the out-tray, for him.

For him. But that was the trouble, the other trouble. What about his mum? She was ill, she was sixty-five, and she had been enjoying leisure for the first time in a hard-working life. Marina had pointed out these prosaic facts to Ian this morning, and he had been suspicious of the ease with which he countered them, with talk about Cecilia's being ill but better, probably cured; and how she must be longing to be a grandmother, as all her friends were grandmothers. It was difficult for him to feel guilty towards his mother, because of his lifelong feeling, corroborated by her, that her resources were his resources. But he could see, in the cold light of day, and especially as his problem was neatly solved, that in the space of two hours he had changed her life, and not necessarily, from her point of view, for the better. He knew that she could no more have refused to take care of Cephas when he asked her than water could refuse to run downhill. He had flagrantly used this.

But was that wrong? Think of the new love and new life that had unexpectedly entered her uneventful, narrowed existence. Surely that would be good for her and happy for her. Wouldn't it keep her young? It might even stop the cancer coming back. Ian loved to think of himself as a benefactor, and to be a benefactor to his mum was especially welcome.

Then at last he faced the question of Tim. He did not look forward to a moment in his imagination when he picked up the phone and it was Tim: 'Look, what are you doing to your mother? She is exhausted. We can't go on like this.' Then, man to man, Ian would feel deeply ashamed. But that moment would not happen. It would not happen, Ian registered sombrely, because Cecilia would hide fatigue and stress from Tim precisely so that Ian would never have to take that phone call or ones like it. Cephas might well be a ray of sunshine in Cecilia's life, but when he was not one, she would have to pretend to Tim that he was, and this would add to the strain on her. Ian did not want to entertain this truth, but he endured it.

He thought about Tim. Many stepfathers could not be trusted to accept into the household their wife's baby grandchild. Tim had qualities that would render this bearable, perhaps even better than bearable. One such quality was general goodwill towards the world. Another was the itch for something to be happening outside the common run. Another was that the sense of entitlement, of rights and proprietorship, of a home as a castle, was negligible in him. And another was his tendency to switch off, which, if he had a newspaper, book or computer to hand, or was playing tennis, would mean that the presence of a baby would scarcely enter his consciousness. All these qualities had been ones that Ian had mocked at times, sometimes with the guilty complicity of Cecilia; but now he was grateful for them.

Cecilia and Ian had been alone from when he was five to when he was fifteen. It had been in those ten years, if not also before, that the unwritten constitution had been drawn up between them. It had been difficult for Ian to accept Tim. But for the same reasons as Tim would not object to Cephas, Tim had not made life difficult for Ian. Moreover it had not occurred to Tim that Ian might make life difficult for him. That was not the sort of thing Tim thought of. If he considered advantages and disadvantages that he represented for his stepson, it would have been to think that it would be nice for Ian to have a bigger house to live in and more money and security. The two of them played tennis together, watched television thrillers together, and their link accounted for Ian's A levels in classics and maybe his continuing academic competence. Meanwhile the bond between Cecilia and Ian was unchanged, albeit complicated for both by bedroom arrangements and by speculations about what the other was feeling or minding or, indeed, enjoying. Before the year was out Ian had his first girlfriend, and curiosity and bereavement became two-way between mother and son, until, on the surface at least, a new version of ordinary life established itself.

Leda's flat was the ground floor of a nice grey house in a Victorian terrace. Ian did not have a key. There was no response to the doorbell. Ian listened. Absolute silence within. He rang the bell of the flat above, and Liz, the slightly known neighbour, came to the door.

'Do you know where Leda is?' asked Ian.

Liz had no idea. She thought she had seen Leda and the pram sometime yesterday, Saturday. But had she? It could have been Friday.

'If you see her, can you tell her the baby's at my mum's? I'll give you the phone number.' They did that.

Liz was getting intrigued, but was to be frustrated by Liz's immediate departure for the police station.

~

Diana Clegg had another conversation to face on that Sunday. It was not a conversation with an old friend, as at breakfast time. It was with someone she had never met before. This had been the letter:

Dear Sister Diana Clegg,

I hope you will forgive my writing to you.

I need to explain. My name is Clare George. I am thirty-two. I am the adopted daughter of Robert and Rita George, who I believe you know, or, at least, Rita, Mum to me. Mum died of cancer in January, and that was awful, but that is not what I am writing to you about. But I am sorry if I am the first to inform you, and if you knew her well enough for this to make you sad. I am writing to you because when Dad and I were going through letters and things that she had never thrown away, I found two letters from you. The first was a date in 1978, obviously answering a letter from her, which I think must have asked for advice, because your letter was saying you advised her to adopt, and give an unfortunate child a good home. That was me! The other letter from you was dated 1981, again obviously in answer to one from her, and you said you were very glad that she had her lovely little girl and you must have enclosed a medal or rosary or something because you refer to that enclosure.

When I was going through these things with Dad I was stunned by something he said, which I had never known or been told before. I was not adopted until I was two! I have no way of finding out where I was adopted from, or how things were done in those days. I can't remember a time when I didn't know I was adopted, because Mum and Dad told me. But where I was adopted from, or why so late, I have no idea. I had always thought of myself coming out of the hospital into Mum's arms, but perhaps I spent time with my birth mother. There are no documents in Mum's things and Dad is completely vague, and I can't bully his memory further, specially now. I am an only child, by the way.

I wrote enquiring about you to the address on your letters of long ago and got an answer giving me your present convent, and telling me you are now known as Sister Diana Clegg. So that is how I now address you. Mum's letters are signed Mother Mary Vincent, so I hope this is correct. I wonder if I could possibly come and see you to talk about all this.

Yours sincerely,
Clare George

Of course Diana had responded, and they had fixed a day. The appointment was today, at teatime.

She did not still have the two letters from Rita George whose existence Clare's letter showed, nor did she remember the name. Memories were hazy. She had written so many letters, and done so much advising and congratulating and condoling, over seventy years; it was hard to keep track. This would be thirty-two years ago. She pondered. Her guess was that Clare needed to talk. That was the important thing. Probably Clare did not really need answers. So Diana waited, with two shop cupcakes and four biscuits and a pot of tea, in the same room in which she had seen Cecilia that morning. She did not have to wait long.

Clare liked Diana immediately, although she had not expected her to be so old. The neat white hair, the thinness, the lovely smile, the warm papery little hands.

'You remind me of my lovely granny,' said Clare. 'Dad's mum. She's still going strong. In Hastings.'

The young woman who sat down opposite Diana was slight and fair with long hair and pretty, casual clothes.

'Good,' said Diana. 'That's a good start.' She adjusted her hearing aid and emitted a quick prayer on its behalf. There was a silence, in which she poured tea. Then she said, 'My dear, first let me say again I am so sorry to hear about your mother.'

'I could easily sit and cry,' said Clare. 'But I won't. Thank you. And yes, that cake looks lovely. Thank you. Well. There you were at the time I was adopted, you and my parents, all in the Hastings area. You have moved, but they never did, and Dad is still in our same house.'

'Yes. Go on.'

'What I know is who adopted me. I now know I was two at that time, not nought, as I've always supposed. I don't know anything about an agency I could have been adopted through, nor anything about my birth mother. Or my natural father. I wonder if there are any details, however insignificant, you might know that might help me. There are no other documents that go back to that time, you see, in what Mum has left – just these two letters from you. You are the only link, for me. I hope you don't mind.'

'What I do mind,' said Diana, 'is that I am afraid I won't be able to help you.'

'Did you ever meet Mum? And would you have her side of that correspondence?'

'I'm afraid I haven't. I've been moved twice since that time, and been abroad for quite long periods, and I don't save letters unless there's a special reason. I have been trying to think whether I met a Rita George. It's possible we just corresponded. The name doesn't ring a bell. I'm very sorry. But my sense is that what is perplexing you most, what has stirred you to get in touch with me, is the two years at the beginning of your life that you know nothing about.'

'Yes. And I've been thinking about it. I can't bear to think that Mum hid something from me. I imagine she told me I was adopted when I was about four, you know, that there are two ways of getting a baby, and one is you want one so much and there is this baby whose real parents couldn't look after her, and so on. Listening to that, I would have assumed I was a tiny baby when this happened. And I never asked for details. She knew I was two but didn't think to make it part of the information. She didn't deny it. She just didn't mention it. Perhaps she didn't like it because it could have felt as if it made me less hers. In my teens I got a bit interested in my origins, and there was another adopted girl in my form, and we made finding out our origins a sort of pseudo detective story, then we lost interest in it. Once at that time I asked Mum if she could tell me anything about my real mother and father. She looked upset and put her arms round me' – Clare was crying now – 'and said, "You mean your birth mother and your natural father. We are your real mother and father." And she was quite right! And they were wonderful parents. We had a home my friends always wanted to come to – two parents who loved each other and both loved me. I have been incredibly lucky.'

'Yes. So we're clear it's nobody's fault that you don't know anything about your first two years.'

'Yes. And I wish Dad hadn't said anything now. He assumed I knew, I think, or that it didn't matter. Or both. It wasn't said like, you know, an old secret slipping out.'

'You mentioned your dad's memory in your letter as if it was unreliable. Are you sure he was being accurate about the two years?'

'Oh yes, quite sure. I know Dad.'

The conversation continued, and the two made a link. Diana had made links with countless people down the years, many now dead; and she did not remember them all, let alone their names, which did not mean that the link had not been real at the time, or had not persisted over years. Clare talked with warmth and joy about her childhood, her school, her big dog, holidays by the sea, sailing with Dad, singing with Mum – she sang Diana a song and cried again; and the fact that Dad had quietly saved all those years so that she wouldn't have a university debt. She said she was an accountant like Dad, with a good job in a good firm, and lived with her partner David in Hackney in a flat they co-owned. She talked of her mother's death, and the fact that Dad and she had been able to keep Mum at home, and both had been there when Mum died. It was a good conversation and went on until the bell went for evening prayer. Diana invited Clare to join the nuns in the chapel, but Clare thought not.

'Can I come again?'

Of course she could, and 'I will pray for you, my dear.'

~

Helen Gatehouse was sitting at her desk. Besides the things desks have to have on them, such as her laptop, pens and paper, it was cluttered with a coffee cup, a whisky glass half full, cigarettes and an ashtray, also half full. She looked at the paragraphs she had written yesterday. She changed a few words. But the whole thing was wrong.

The day had begun badly. She was woken by a phone call from John, saying he was so sorry but he couldn't come round this evening after all. She felt deflated and had not been able to keep the whine out of her voice. And had his excuse been true? She doubted it. And she had not been able to keep the cynicism out of her voice, either. She had never changed, she thought. She was a difficult, demanding woman, and that was why she was alone in her sixties.

But in the past, ever since she was twenty-five, she had been able to write. Whatever had gone wrong, there had been a novel to work on. She had been able to rework her losses and calamities in fiction, and in doing so had distanced them. That faculty had seemed as native to her as having a body. Was it going to desert her now? If it was, how could she live what remained of her life?

Something else about herself that she had relied on without question or mistrust was her health. She herself did not call it health, for healthy people do not have a word for it. She smoked, drank, ate too little or too much, sunbathed, took no exercise except what was involved in getting from place to place, and was fat. She took her body for granted like a warrior his horse. She assumed it would come through battles neither shot nor lame, and so it did, and on it went. And her body had let her down now, too. While she thought it was cantering cheerfully towards seventy, it was in fact stealthily developing a carcinoma. She found this almost impossible to believe, and besieged the oncologists with questions about whether her results could have got mixed up with someone else's.

Thinking these thoughts, and worrying about whether the naturalness of her writing had absconded along with the naturalness of her body, she deleted a paragraph. She thought again. Perhaps fictionalising the devastation of a colostomy into the devastation of a breast enhancement gone terribly wrong was simply not going to work. Perhaps the colostomy had better be a colostomy. But she had never had to be so rawly autobiographical before. She sighed deeply and lit a cigarette. Surely she couldn't have drunk half a glass of whisky already today. She took another sip.

It was a year after her operation that Helen first met someone else with a colostomy. She had learnt that there are sixty thousand people in the UK who have one, but she knew, or even knew of, no such fellow sufferer. Of all the versions of cancer that are hearsay among non-medical people, it was the version Helen had always dreaded the most. She was not alone in this, and had to watch a mirror image of her own shock and disbelief on friends' faces when she told them.

From the moment she had been diagnosed with bowel cancer, it had been borne in on her that she was going to be a person with a colostomy for the rest of her life, if she survived; and she could hardly bear it. Survival didn't seem worth the price. One of the nurses knew someone who had run the marathon with a colostomy, and several nurses and doctors mentioned the Queen Mother. Athletic feats and royalty had no part in Helen's internal pantheon.

Some people in the hospital ward with her were eventually going to have their colostomies reversed. Helen's cancer was too low in the gut for reversal to be feasible, and that had been obvious to the oncologist from the first. He had offered no false hopes. Her anus was now obsolete for all time, but it remained vestigially in place. Some people in the ward had had a length of colon removed and the snipped ends joined up. They did not have colostomies and were regarded in the ward as the lucky ones. They were going to be normal again, further cancer permitting, and were not being advised to think about marathons and the Queen Mother. However, some of them were referred for post-operative chemotherapy, and this always sounded a note of gloom. Helen was not one of these. She had had two courses of chemotherapy before the operation, to shrink the tumour. At that period she had been obsessed by and petrified of hair loss, but on the drug she was given that had not happened. After the operation, as soon as she could stagger about, she was discharged, with a bag of medication and a list of outpatient appointments.

One of the outpatient appointments was with the stoma nurse, and it was in the stoma nurse's waiting room that Helen and Cecilia met. They were sitting opposite each other. Both of them, either because they were a novelist and a psychotherapist, or causally the other way round, were interested in watching people. Cecilia had been playing the game in her mind of guessing which, of pairs of fellow waiters, was the patient, and which the companion or minder. Neither she nor Helen had a companion or minder. Helen was playing the game in her mind of guessing who was worse off than herself from the point of view of cancer, and who better. When their eyes met, both smiled.

They might not have got into conversation had the crowd in the waiting room not thinned, so that they could start to pass the time of day without being overheard. After a short chat about having to wait for so long, and why that should have to be, and why Hyacinth, the stoma nurse, had this tendency to overbook, they introduced themselves by name. Both knew of the other. Helen was mildly famous, and Cecilia had read two of her novels, as well as having heard her name from the couch, and was very interested, even enthralled, to meet her. A friend of Helen's had been a patient of Cecilia's, and Cecilia Banks had become something of a household word in that group of friends. It pleased Helen to square the familiar, disembodied name with a person, and a person she immediately liked. Each was delighted to recognise and to be recognised. They were about the same age. To say the encounter passed the time in the waiting room would be an understatement. They did not know then that they were to be friends for life, but a glimpse into that future would not have astonished either.

They agreed to have a cup of tea when their appointments

were over. Cecilia's appointment was first, and she said she didn't mind waiting that bit longer for Helen afterwards.

'Did your appointment go all right?' asked Helen in the café. Of the two she was the more excited to have met someone else with a colostomy. She had consciously longed for a colostomy friend in a way Cecilia had not, possibly because Cecilia had a family, though not at this point a grandson; and Helen didn't. Helen was lonely anyway, and cancer and the colostomy had made the loneliness worse. In this initial conversation and many subsequent ones, they considered all aspects of their shared predicament and learnt the details of each other's stories. Helen couldn't help being pleased that in some ways her new friend was worse off than herself.

Cecilia had been diagnosed with anal cancer, which is usually curable by radiotherapy and chemotherapy. These she underwent, and Tim had accompanied her to appointments at which he marvelled and complained about the amount of radiation she was being subjected to. Cecilia minded this too, tutored by Tim; but what could she do? You take the advice the doctors give. The cancer had apparently been seen off, but after a year recurred *in situ*, to medical amazement; and there was nothing for it but what was ominously called a salvage operation. This had left Cecilia with a colostomy and without an anus, not even an anus Helen ironically called an ornamental one. Cecilia's pelvic floor remained wounded because of the damage done by the radiotherapy to the healing powers of the skin. So Cecilia lived with discomfort, sometimes pain, in a way Helen did not. But Helen lived with fear and horror in a way Cecilia did not.

Chapter 3

The first weeks were wretched for Cecilia and Cephas. His beautiful little face worked as he gazed back at Cecilia. He cried. It was a desolate wail Cecilia had never heard and did not remember from Ian. She shushed and rocked with great patience, and walked him up and down every room in the house and in the garden. She talked to him.

'I know, I know, I know. You miss Mummy, you don't know where Mummy is.' It was not in her character or training to attempt to distract people from their proper pain, so the two of them were miserable together. Sometimes she cracked. 'It's bloody awful, I know, but you are just going to have to make do with me now. Get used to it. All you can do is get used to it.'

She bought a sling, which was exciting because they had not existed when she was a young mother, and it left her hands free to get the next bottle without having to put Cephas down. On the whole the bottles were Tim's department, and he kept a neat, well-sterilised row in the fridge. It was only when these had run out and it was the cold dead of night in the kitchen that Cecilia had to make a feed from scratch. Thor watched from a crouching position. Cecilia kept Thor and Cephas apart. She did not want Cephas to get a traumatic shock as well as everything else. She bought a cat net for the carrycot. She was sorry for Thor but seemed to have decided that, like her, he must rough it for the moment. Tim was detailed to make a fuss of Thor, but it was not the same. Nothing was in the smallest degree the same. Cecilia was used to broken nights, but broken only by the restless workings of her own mind and body. She became dead tired, and, as Ian had foreseen, concealed this from Tim and from friends. She did not want Ian pilloried. Friends were interested and helpful. Helen, with her writer's block, now named as such, was in the thick of it.

Ian came when he was in England, but at the moment this was not much. He bought a magnificent pram and wheeled it round to Cecilia's. It took up nearly all the room in the hall. He left thick piles of twenty-pound notes on the kitchen table, although so far there was not much to spend them on. He was paying damages, rather than maintenance. He had done the same with Leda. Cecilia had hoped that Cephas would show signs of recognition when he saw Ian, and that Ian's presence would offer Cephas some continuity with the past. This was not so, or not obvious. But, as Cecilia had hoped, Ian became fonder of Cephas now he had no worries about him. Cephas began, in a small way, to be Ian's own. Ian held Cephas above his head and turned him this way and that, stamping and making noises. This could stop Cephas whimpering, but once he was sick on to Ian's face. Nothing was easy. Cecilia asked Ian if he had any photos of Leda, though she doubted whether Cephas's eyes would make sense of a photo. Anyway, there were none. As 'Missing Persons' advertisements for Leda began to appear in streets, Cecilia would stop the pram beside one, take Cephas out, and try to get him to focus on the face. Once she thought he felt something, a pang or a memory, and she held him very close and spoke to him. Being the wrong person, that was all she could do, so that is what she did.

It was not all terrible. Sometimes, after a feed, when he was not too windy, his eyes met hers, and she thought he was trying to smile. He had not smiled. Perhaps he had smiled at his mother. His mouth worked a bit, opened and went over to one side, but the smile did not spread to his eyes, which remained perplexed. Her smile, of course, was all over her face. At those moments he seemed to be taking her in, not as the right person, that was impossible; but as a new person.

Once or twice Ian brought Marina. The first time, Cephas scanned her young and pretty face hopefully, and then his lip trembled. But he was interested. Marina on her side found Cephas enchanting. She was captivated. Cecilia was privately rejoicing as she watched, as if in the presence of something that might bode well; and was even more delighted when she saw a look of quiet pleasure on Ian's face.

There were plenty of bad nights. Sometimes Tim was recruited. But this had to be rationed in case he took against Ian. There was a bad night when Cecilia had decided not to recruit Tim and she had tried everything – winding, walking, singing, the TV, an extra bottle, an extra nappy change. Nothing would stop Cephas's angry yells, and the backward thrashing of his strong little body. Cecilia sat down with him on her knee and began to cry. Suddenly she felt movement on her other knee. It was Thor, who had leapt silently on to the lap that until recently had been his unrivalled place. Thor had never been so close to Cephas before, and Cecilia felt she should push him back on to the floor at once, what with claws and germs. But there was silence. Cephas had stopped crying. Cecilia looked down. Thor was looking curiously into Cephas's face, and Cephas looked intently back. Their faces were about the same size, the baby face, and the furry, whiskery, black and white one. Thor's face, though recognisably a face, had a cast too unfamiliar to Cephas for him to see it as yet another version of the wrong face. Thor began to purr, and gently to trample Cecilia's lap. He reached his head forward and touched Cephas's nose with his own. He licked Cephas's cheek. Cecilia was tense. Should this be allowed? Cephas was panting with excitement. He reached his hands out. Thor placed a soft paw on one of the little fists to hold it down so that he could get on with licking. Cephas's open mouth went a little to one side and then, full in Thor's face, he smiled, smiled completely, his eyes full of intimate encounter.

'Since when,' said Cecilia, next day, recounting to Helen what had happened, 'he can be enticed to smile regularly. He smiles at me, at Tim. We only have to smile. It makes us feel blessed. He'll smile at you when he wakes up.'

'The cat must be the only one who doesn't smile at him,' said Helen, who was inclined to deflate other people's magical moments, and dreaded stories about grandchildren, which were increasingly common in her circle of acquaintance.

Cecilia understood this, and wanted to change the subject, but was too wrapped up in hers to find another, more weighted in Helen's direction. After a moment she said, 'Well, spring is certainly in the air today.'

'My first spring with a stoma,' said Helen. 'Do you use the opaque bags or the transparent ones? Hyacinth prefers the opaque. I think she feels they are more ladylike.'

'I've got both,' Cecilia replied. 'I used to use the transparent ones, but I'm moving over to the opaque.'

'I've got some opaque ones,' said Helen, 'but I find them very difficult to position. You can't be sure you're getting the hole over the stoma.'

'That is a bit tricky,' agreed Cecilia, the older hand. 'But there's something nice about not having to see shit whenever you see the bag.'

'I know,' said Helen, and there was despondency in her voice. 'Imagine me getting undressed with John, supposing such a time arrives again, and behold, clinging to my ample midriff was a lump or at best a smear of shit visible through the shiny plastic front of the bag. What then?'

Cecilia could not immediately think of an answer. She liked the way Helen put things. 'How's the novel? John wouldn't matter if you were writing.' Cecilia always played down John, not having seen evidence that there was hope for the relationship.

'Blocked,' said Helen. 'I think it's going to have to be an overtly stoma novel. I can't find a way to symbolise a colostomy. I thought plastic surgery gone wrong might do it – but you don't choose, or save up money for, a colostomy, so that's too radical a difference. But then readers are sure to know I have acquired a stoma. Why else would one write about it?'

'It's conceivable you could have researched.'

'A likely story,' said Helen.

'Something I find which is odd,' said Cecilia, 'is that when everything is going well, within its limitations, about my body, the stoma acting regularly enough, and the wound not hurting too much' – she did not add 'and the night not too sleepless', because that would have hinted at the Cephas topic again – 'I feel the sort of satisfaction, self-satisfaction, I used to sometimes get a surge of when I was well, when my body really was in good nick. That shows me you can make something of anything. You know, you lose your house in a tsunami and you find yourself laying a little tablecloth in your canvas shelter. Humans must always have been like that.' Cecilia was more globally minded than Helen, who was pursuing her own thoughts, and had never been health-conscious enough to think of being in good nick.

'What do you do,' she said, 'when the bag fills up and gets heavy in a social setting? – out to dinner last night, in my case. Quite difficult to chat normally when you're afraid the bag is going to come adrift, or pop.'

They both laughed. Cecilia said, 'Sometimes when it's full and pendulous, it feels like an extra breast.' She was catching Helen's way of talking about colostomies.

~

Clare visited Diana again. She came several times. She liked Diana. With Diana she could talk about her mother and father as much as she liked without feeling boring, or obsessed.

Diana had thought it would be rather nice to be in the garden when Clare next came. The sun and the blossom were out. But of course, it turned out to be too cold and too windy, and they trailed in again, Clare carrying the tea tray.

'It was nice seeing the garden, though,' said Clare, as they sat down. 'Dad is a great gardener. A mown lawn and spring flowers – your garden reminds me of home. I miss not having a garden in Hackney.'

'Did Mum garden as well?'

'A bit, but not so much. No, she did. But she didn't keep at it for hours as Dad did. "Now that's it for today," she used to say. And we would go in.'

'When you were little.'

'Yes. And then she would make a lovely tea. Rather an idyllic childhood, really. I never minded being an only child. And living in the same place all the time, which I think is nice. Mum and Dad bought the house when they got married and lived in it ever since. Dad still lives there. Dad is still working, which is just as well, or he would be incredibly lonely, because he misses Mum all the time. He says he hears her voice. Death is cruel, isn't it?'

'It is indeed,' said Diana, but there were theological implications in the turn the conversation had taken that neither thought it was the moment for.

They talked about Clare's job, and the probable psychological meanings of her following in Dad's footsteps professionally; of whether Dad really liked David, who was also an accountant; of how pleased Clare had been with David's demeanour on his two visits to Mum's bedside. Then Clare went back to worrying about her first two years. 'They are a gap in me,' she said.

'Need they be a gap in you?' asked Diana. 'Can't they just be a gap in time? You are you, aren't you?'

'I'm not sure. I'm always trying to remember, to find my earliest memories. Some of them might belong to this prehistory. But which? I remember a sunny garden, but that must be home, I think.'

'You probably can't remember that early,' said Diana. 'You lead me to think of some lines from *The Tempest*:

> *Do not infest your mind with beating on*
> *The strangeness of this business, be cheerful,*
> *And think of each thing well.*

'Something like that. However, easier said than done.'

Clare was not interested in the quotation, and was too at ease now with Diana to feel she must be polite about it. She went straight on, 'I'm afraid you'll think I'm not grateful for Mum and Dad, or not satisfied with them. But I really would like to know something about my birth mother. David gets a bit bored with all this, so I've stopped going on about it to him. But it's not getting any less important to me.' She began to cry. 'I keep thinking about how wonderful my parents are. I had a big birthmark on my forehead – I've seen it on the earliest photos, and they got the best possible specialists to remove it. It was removed completely, you can't even see where it was. Lots of things can go wrong with that sort of operation. They got the best. It's only recently I worked out it must have been private, and I asked Dad. But they never said a word about what it had cost. And they could have been put off having a child with a birthmark. Well, they wouldn't have been, because they were them. They were so good.'

'It doesn't sound as if whoever looked after you before did anything about the birthmark.'

'No, I know. That's the only shred of evidence I've got about the character of my natural mother.'

'If, indeed, it was she who looked after you.'

'Yes. More likely I was in a care home or fostered. I've researched children's care homes in the Hastings area, and phoned up and enquired, even. But I've got nowhere. There are lots and lots of websites but all you seem to get is other people searching, some of them the parents. It's over thirty years ago now, and procedures were different then. I find I prefer to have fantasies about being with my natural mother, but that could be because it makes a more interesting mystery.'

So they talked until the bell went for evening prayer. Clare left, but not before taking Diana's hand and saying, 'Sister Diana, I feel as if there is a hole inside me.'

'I hope and pray it can gradually be filled,' said Diana, grasping Clare's hand with both hers. She tried not to let her eyes be hinting, 'Filled with the love of God,' but, after all those years, it was hard to stop them.

The matter of the birthmark had a way of coming back into Diana's mind, particularly when she was in silent prayer. She had long since given up thinking of thoughts during prayer as 'distractions'. Distractions from what? God was quite beyond comprehension, and she did not want to invent him in order to have someone to feel she was in the presence of. Her feeling was that prayer is a passive, not an active, enterprise, though alertly passive if at all possible; and she sometimes said that, as prayer was not within her powers, she prayed because if she didn't pray she would think she could.

~

Spring. Ian and Marina marked a day of sunshine and a little warmth with a drink outside their usual pub.

'It's freezing,' said Marina, 'and blowing a gale. But it's spring. That's always encouraging.'

37

'It's not freezing. You've been in hot countries too much. Look, people are in T-shirts.'

'Young people always are, if it's not snowing.'

'Young people? You are young.' He looked affectionately at her charming, intelligent face.

They talked about work and sipped their drinks. 'Shall we have dinner?' They decided they would, and chose a restaurant, a short walk from the pub. They were old friends and their routines were established.

Sitting at the restaurant table, after choosing their food, 'Any news of Leda?' Marina asked.

'No. The police are looking.' He paused. 'I don't think you understand how incredibly ashamed I am about all that.'

'Tell me, then.' This was not Marina's favourite topic, but she had not been able to resist bringing it up, and the angle on it Ian now introduced seemed better than many.

'Of course I fancied her, and of course I'd had a few drinks, and then it was one thing after another. But I knew – I knew pretty soon – that she was completely nutty. Why didn't I stop pursuing her when I realised that? I must be a very silly person. Not only silly, to have such a nonsensical fling, but stupid, to get her pregnant. At the party where we met, she said she was at the *New Statesman*. Why did I believe that? And then I suppose I thought she seemed nutty merely because she was drunk. Though she wasn't, very. And anyway, I didn't think. I thought nothing. What would you say about this story if it was hearsay, gossip, if you didn't know me? The story of a complete idiot. Who would imagine it was a story about a forty-year-old?'

But Marina was disposed to be benign. She preferred this version of events to the one prefaced by Leda's being unbelievably beautiful. 'Stuff happens,' she said.

'And I'm guilty and ashamed in another way too. It's this: I don't care what's happened to Leda. I'm glad she's disappeared. That's terrible. I don't care if she's jumped off Beachy Head. I think I had become frightened of her. Now she's gone it's like living in a house that isn't haunted any more.'

'She may turn up,' said Marina. She could afford to say this now Leda was so clearly no threat to her.

Ian shivered and groaned. Their food came. Ian was forty, Marina thirty-five. Both were good-looking and confident. Both were television news reporters and good at their job. They were never accosted in the street nor remembered by name, but people sometimes took a second look, trying to place the face. They had been something of a couple, with interruptions, for about five years. Friends and parents wondered why they didn't settle down together. But of course they were each abroad so much. She loved him more than she thought it good for him to know. He took her for granted, and did not ask himself about love. He was never happier than when he was with her, but hadn't taken note of this, nor inferred anything from it.

There was a lot to say about work, and the people they worked with, and they said some of it. Then Ian reverted to the former topic.

'And then there's the guilt and shame about offloading Cephas on Mum,' he said. 'I don't know why you haven't taken me to task on that. Yet.' He spoke of this emotion for form's sake. He did not feel it, because of the character of his relationship with his mother.

'It's your relationship with your mum,' she said. 'It's not up to me to judge.'

'I feel so bad, though of course also intensely relieved, to have got off scot-free. You haven't given me a hard time about it, and Mum is holding the baby. I earn good money so the expense doesn't matter. OK for Ian.'

'You've been decent. You stood by Leda as best you could,

39

worried over her, took a flat for her, a lot of people wouldn't have done as much.'

'I hope they would.' But he knew they wouldn't.

'They wouldn't. It's only because you're nice that you think they would.'

He let that pass. 'And Tim. I don't know what to say to him. It's a ludicrous situation. I can't meet his eye. I arrive at Mum's and he's sterilising the bottles, sleeves rolled up, industrious, thorough.'

'He's been very good about it.'

'He has. His virtues help, and so do his faults.'

'I see what you mean.'

There was a silence, while he reflected, and she studied his face. Then he said, 'What an incredible fuss. How can it be? A few fleetingly, stupidly longed-for, disappointing fucks, and you get this upheaval of lives – Mum's in this case, and a whole extra person on the planet, who may live a hundred years. Perhaps I should have put him into care, he would have been adopted straight off probably, been part of unknown people's lives, and we would all have forgotten the whole thing by now.' He looked at her and saw her eyes on him. He smiled. 'Unlike sensibly longed-for, undisappointing fucks.'

'I'm glad you said that,' she said.

Although she readily said in her heart that she loved him, and in his heart the matter did not arise, he watched her as she made her way to the loo, enjoying the way she moved through the tables, noticing things about her hair and body, wanting to kiss her when she paused to exchange a word with the waiter. He watched her more closely than she would have watched him, and there was a speechless and joyful smile on his face as he watched, a smile not unlike Cephas's smiles. And the next evening, as he packed for Tel Aviv, he was to stand motionless and entranced in front of his television, watching her say her piece against a background of gunfire and running figures, an anxious eye checking that she was wearing her flak jacket. He was to rerun the item twice on iPlayer, his face alight with admiration and fondness.

~

In a house in St Leonard's, near Hastings, an elderly man with a good face was opening the french doors on to his garden. Spring had come. He had known spring would hurt him when it came, because she had loved it so much, and had loved their garden in the spring. And there the garden was. The blossom was out, and the lilac, and spring flowers beginning in the borders. He made a mental note to mow the lawn this evening. Now that the evenings were longer this would be possible, when he got back from work. It did not matter if doing things without her broke his heart. He must still do the things – take the train to work, come back to the empty house, sometimes draw breath to call her from the front door, then let the breath out with her name uncalled. One of them had to go first, he thought, and he was glad it was her. He had been able to see her through. Last spring she had been well enough to sit in the garden in a wheelchair and dead-head the roses. Now he was alone. People were being very kind.

Having had a look into the garden, he relocked the doors carefully, and began to think without hunger about breakfast. She had often asked him to take care of himself when she had gone. He wanted to do it for her. On the piano in the room he passed through on his way to the kitchen were pictures of Clare at various stages – Clare with her dog; Clare on a sailing boat; Clare in a mortarboard and gown; and a wedding photograph of Rita and Robert George, forty-five years ago. In every wedding photograph there is a tragedy, Robert George now said to himself, for he did not think in terms of divorce, nor of love growing cold – that one of those two happy people is going to die before the other, and the only consolation for the one left alive will be that the other will never have to suffer this pain.

Chapter 1

'What did you feel when you were told you had cancer?' Helen asked Cecilia.

They were actually able to sit in the garden, though in coats. This suited Helen as she could smoke, though she tried not to. Cephas was in his pram. Cecilia had bought a second more voluminous cat net for the big pram, and Thor had found that it served him well as a hammock. His heavy black and white body bowed the netting almost, but not quite, on to Cephas's blanket, and he looked down at Cephas through the mesh. Cephas could be heard gurgling happily in response.

'I was so horrified,' answered Cecilia thoughtfully. 'It was a question of whether my body had been betrayed, or whether my body itself had betrayed me. I felt too sad for my body if I thought of it as betrayed, so I think I preferred to think of it as the betrayer. It was as if I had imagined my body was a nice hard-working donkey, ageing but willing, and it was suddenly revealed, like a moment in a horror film, that really it was a crocodile. I asked the doctor if he could estimate when the cancer had begun. More than a year. Maybe several. So all that time, going about my daily life . . .' She fell silent. 'What about you?'

'I was horrified too,' said Helen. 'But I felt something much more like, You can't possibly mean me! I thought the scan had got mixed up with someone else's, or the biopsy had been wrong. It sounds as if you could at least believe it. I couldn't. It took me ages to believe it. I still don't.'

'I know what you mean.'

'I know people get cancer all the time,' went on Helen. 'But getting cancer myself showed me I had secretly looked down on them. I didn't even feel triumph over them, I'd been too complacent for triumph. But when I knew I had cancer myself I felt demeaned. I had become one of the pitied, the contemptible. I couldn't believe it.'

'I think I know what you mean. Do you think a lot of people feel like this?'

'Yes. Whether they know it or not.'

'It's good to realise,' said Cecilia, 'that one had that mindless health-snobbery. That at least is something I don't have any more. I suppose the fact that I've learnt something from having cancer means I do believe I have got it.'

'It's a difficult thing to believe.'

'It brings up questions. What is the body, in the self? We take it for granted. A lot of the time we take health for granted. When we have a headache we say we have a head. When a throat is sore we say we have a throat. Quite a lot of people have backs. It's as if we feel these parts of our bodies don't exist if they are not assailed.'

'Yes,' said Helen, interested. 'Did you have patients who got cancer?'

'Two. Both were treated and got better. I'd understand more about what they went through, now.' They were silent, then Cecilia said, 'Do you have envy?'

'Of the well? Of the untouched? Of the unconsciously contemptuous of me? Oh, all the time. Very much so with the doctors and nurses. Do they think they are invulnerable? I think they do.'

'Perhaps they have to, in their job.'

'I often feel like a wicked witch, wanting people to get cancer.'

44

'Are you glad I have it?'

'I'm afraid I am.' They laughed.

Tim came into the garden. He was never sure whether to stay and be one of the party when Cecilia had her friends, or whether to disappear. He was secretly rather sociable, so it was a dilemma. He usually fell back on offering coffee or tea, depending on the time of day, and he did now.

'Tea?'

'Why not?' from Cecilia, 'Bliss,' from Helen. Tim joined them for that, but soon went back into the house.

'Do you envy him?' Helen asked.

'Often, yes. His wellness is so effortless. I don't want him to get cancer, but I would rather like to see him have to worry about himself. Have a qualm about a mole, say.' They laughed again.

'Do you get frightened any ache and pain is the cancer coming back somewhere else?' asked Helen.

'Oddly, no. I have become relatively unfrightened by cancer now that I actually have it. I was always off to the doctor, before, with things I thought might be cancer. I don't have that dread any more, so it must have been dread of the unknown.'

'I see. I wish I was like that.'

'Well, you never feared cancer. I did. But the fear was of cancer as a nameless dread, a spook, a horror. Now it's just an everyday matter, and it's lost its terror.'

'Though what you would feel if a scan said . . .'

'Yes! True.' They talked about when their next scans were due.

Then Helen said, 'I'm worrying about not being able to use the opaque bag. Hyacinth asked me if I would like to learn how to flush out the stoma. A stoma enema. Of course I said no. But the advantage is that you don't have to use a bag at all for a certain period after flushing because you can be sure the

45

gut is empty. Perhaps I shouldn't have been so shocked by the suggestion.'

'But I can see why you were. Are the worries about the bag to do with John?'

'They are. He asked me what stomas look like. Horrified fascination, I suppose.'

'What did you say?'

'I said exactly like a labrador's arse. John likes dogs. Do you think that's about right?'

'Yes,' said Cecilia, struck by the parallel.

It was the fact of Helen's daytime leisure due to the writing block, and Cecilia's need for daytime companionship due to Cephas, as well as their shared plight, that had brought these two together so quickly. Helen was a person for rapid friendships and sudden discardings, so the speed of her closeness to Cecilia was not unfamiliar to her. Cecilia was one for long-term friendships, and she didn't reckon to lose touch with people who had once been friends. She found the rate at which Helen had become an intimate surprising as well as pleasant and amusing. Life that year as winter turned to spring, as her unhealed wound still hurt, as she toiled or rejoiced over Cephas, would have been much harsher for Cecilia without Helen's almost daily visits. Helen's lugubrious humour cheered Cecilia up, and the fact that she could still become essential to someone, to Helen, solaced her somewhat for her lost occupation. Helen was the more vociferously grateful for and dependent on the relationship. Cecilia tolerated cancer and colostomy with more fortitude than Helen did. Helen's rhetorical desperation brought out a compensatory calmness and resignation in Cecilia, and this they both drew strength from.

Cancers and colostomies were not their only topic. The next day, when Helen dropped in, Cecilia was writing a letter.

'One doesn't often see this, these days,' said Helen, indicating envelopes and stamps.

Cecilia stopped writing. 'It's a letter to a nun,' she said.

'A nun?'

'Yes. I keep in touch with her and I wanted her to know about Cephas.' She looked at Helen and said: 'I was going to be a nun once. I entered, as we call it, but exited after two years.'

'Good heavens! Please tell me more.'

'Well, I decided with the novice mistress that I didn't have a vocation. Came out, and a year later was married. Perhaps that proves I did not have a vocation.' For Cecilia this revelation was a ceremonial moment within the growth of a friendship. She was glad to see that Helen took it seriously. Cecilia went on: 'So I keep in touch with that novice mistress from time to time. I called in on her recently on my way home from a conference. Imagine: I thought that day was going to be recorded in my mind as the first day I did anything professional after my operation, or the day I saw Mother Mary Vincent after a five-year gap. But it wasn't. It was the day we got Cephas.'

Helen was incapable of this reflection, because the name of Mother Mary Vincent had arrested her mind entirely. 'Was she ever anywhere near Hastings?'

'Yes. The convent I entered was there. Why – do you know her?'

'Yes I do. My goodness. Look, this is obviously a turn our relationship has taken in which we exchange deeper autobiographical confidences.' Helen was silent and absent for a full minute, which was not her usual way. 'But I won't tell you right away how I know Mother Mary Vincent, I have to digest the surprise first. I haven't thought about her or heard her name for at least thirty years. But will you tell her you know Helen Gatehouse and give her my regards? She might remember me.'

～

47

Diana received quite a large number of letters every day. She liked her letters, and always answered. After the post arrived, at sometime in the morning, she collected her letters from the pigeon-hole designated for her, and took them to her room. She opened them all, slowly, not without certain arthritic difficulties in the fingers, and placed the envelopes in a pile for recycling. She then had her letters at her disposal, adjusted her reading glasses, and picked them up one by one.

The fifth was from Cecilia.

Dear Diana,

It was lovely to see you, and I'm sorry I've left it so long to write. Something extraordinary happened in my life that evening. I had to adopt, or take on long term, an unsuspected grandson of two months. Imagine! But I was very happy that my son Ian entrusted this to me, and Tim has been wonderful about it. The baby's mother had run away, it seems, and so far has not returned. It is a very odd story, but all is well. I thought you would like to know, and anyway, I know I wanted you to.

It is amazing to be back in the world of nappies, feeds, wakeful nights and the baby clinic, at sixty-five, but I am coping all right. Ian is ~~wonderful~~ all he can be with his important commitments.

I have made a new friend also with a colostomy, and I have just heard that she knows you. What a coincidence. Her name is Helen Gatehouse and she asks to be remembered to you.

Next time I see you I hope to bring Cephas, as the baby is surprisingly called.

Best to you all,

Love,
Cecilia

It was not Diana's way to call a halt until she had read all her letters. But when she had done so she fished Cecilia's letter out of the little stack and reread it. She was, of course, surprised by the principal information Cecilia had given her, and prepared to feel wonder and delight, as well as, more privately, a raised eyebrow. But what detained her most was the name of Helen Gatehouse.

Helen Gatehouse. She knew it rang a bell. But what was the bell, and from where did it tinkle? She thought carefully, and evoked an impression – she did not know how – that this person was mildly well known. She felt as if she had seen that name in the not too distant past, and that then that name had already rung its bell. Where might she have seen it? In *The Tablet*, among the reviews, or the letters? A name mounting a campaign for women priests, for example, or for the restoration of the Latin Mass? Memories stirred, but nothing clicked tight. There not being a statutory patron saint of memory, she prayed to St John the Evangelist, who on Patmos remembered so much, and was able so usefully to retrieve both significant and insignificant details.

Lunch was sociable that day, for they had a young Polish priest staying. He was improving his English, and posed a question. He addressed it politely to everyone at his table – Diana; a younger nun (young in the convent meaning sixty); and a charming novice, who was not destined to stay long. He had seen a notice by a fishing lake: 'No keep nets permitted.' Now how did that injunction work, grammatically? He had understood that 'No' in that sense was incorrect, that you would not expect to see 'No walk on the grass', or 'No pick the fruit'. If he was wrong there, and 'No keep' was OK, why then the word 'permitted'? Perhaps it meant on the contrary that it was OK to keep nets.

The younger nun weighed in, saying that keep-nets should have been hyphenated. It was a compound noun. They all agreed that this made sense. The younger nun warmed to the topic, and said that most compound nouns were made up of two nouns. But keep-nets were an exception. As examples of the norm she thought of chair-covers, and the novice piously put in altar-breads. Diana suggested carthorses.

The younger nun tried to think of helpful examples constructed like 'keep nets', with a verb and a noun. This was more difficult. But soon she proudly came up with 'think tank'. The novice said nothing, for she had thought of 'blow job'. 'Guard dog' was suggested, but it was agreed that the 'guard' of 'guard dog' could be seen grammatically either way. The young priest and the younger nun talked semantics between themselves now, and Diana turned to the novice.

'My dear,' she said, 'am I right in thinking there is something called Google?'

'Yes,' said the novice.

'Can you do it?'

'Yes, it's easy. I can teach you, on the computer.'

'It's not to learn how to do it, it's to look up a name.'

'Ah. What name?'

'Helen Gatehouse.'

'Oh, but I've heard of her. She's a novelist.'

'A novelist.'

'In fact there's a novel by her in the library,' said the novice. 'There's only one shelf of novels, as you know, but she's got one there. Rather surprisingly.' The novice was often attracted to that shelf, neglected and forgotten by the nuns, who now got their recreational fiction, insofar as they wanted it, from TV.

After lunch Diana made her way to the library. Once there, she realised she had brought the wrong glasses, and went back to her room for the other pair. It was all good exercise, she thought. Helen Gatehouse. She found the novel: *Poor Harvests*, by Helen Gatehouse. She carried it to a reading stall and sat down with it.

There was an inscription on the flyleaf, which Diana read, tilting the page towards the window, through which some spring sunshine was appearing and disappearing. 'To dear Mother Mary Vincent, an inappropriate but heartfelt offering, in gratitude, Helen Gatehouse. Photograph enclosed.' Diana opened the book and looked at a page or two. She could see why the author deemed it inappropriate for a convent, and did not believe that she herself had bothered to read it, though she could be perfectly certain she would have written her thanks – at least, she would have if she had had an address. Reading on, she was surprised that the book had survived in this library: the waste not, want not convent ethic must have collided with the purity of heart one, and been victorious.

At this moment, as Diana closed the book, something fell out. Annoyingly, she had to stoop from her sitting position to pick it off the floor – a laborious exercise. It was the photograph. She put the book on her lap, whence it slid off at once, and that would be dealt with later. She held the photograph in both hands, turning it this way and that in the beams of sunlight. She saw that it was a photograph of a very good-looking, smiling young woman, with a confident manner and plenty of fair hair. In her arms was a baby. Diana was no expert, but the baby looked about the same age as the gardener's youngest great-grandchild, who had just had a first birthday. The child was looking at the camera with a watchful, unsmiling expression, and gripping her mother's neck with a little hand. On the baby's forehead was a red birthmark.

～

Tim Banks was not as passive nor as wonderful as his nearest and dearest hopefully thought he was. In fact he was worried and tried by the Cephas situation. But he was in a difficult position. He couldn't very well interrogate Cecilia on her intentions or on Ian's, supposing she knew them, because Cecilia had had such a hard time with her illness, and in a different way was having a hard time now, suddenly being a baby's main carer. Tim certainly didn't want to make life more difficult for Cecilia. He was used to being inclusive, accepting, easygoing, nice, and, on the whole, giving in to his wife. But now wistfulness was just under the surface. Everything for Cecilia now revolved round Cephas. Not only did Cephas come first with her; she expected Cephas to come first with Tim. And there was some justice in this: a baby should come first. But Tim chafed. He had recently mentioned to Cecilia a trip to Fez, which they had discussed a few months ago as a possibility, and she had been horror-struck. He had held his tongue, but were they never to go abroad again?

On the surface things were going well. Once Cephas had settled down, he had turned out to be an easy baby. That was his character. He slept through nights. Tim and Cecilia's cleaner Eva, a nice Rumanian girl, now came three times a week instead of once. It had been envisaged that she might be something of a childminder, and she would certainly have preferred that, for, like everyone else, she adored Cephas; but Cephas always wanted Cecilia, and Eva did the shopping and cooking. Cecilia acted as if there was no long-term problem, and Tim, at his computer or tennis court, was able to forget the existence of the problem. Indeed, he was being groomed into forgetfulness of it. And winter had turned into spring.

But when he remembered to, Tim worried. Had Cecilia thought seriously what she was letting herself in for? Did she think about the future – making the house toddler-proof; choosing a primary school; puberty? He suspected she took one day at a time. And yet one day could not be taken at a time, even for Cephas's sake; he was attached to Cecilia, and to Tim, not to mention Thor. Was this indeed to be Cephas's home until he left for university, or for whatever other unknowns his life would hold? And if not, how would Cephas cope with another separation? He had had one already. And how would Cecilia cope with a separation from Cephas, or the idea that he was being put in care? She would certainly be in no mood for Fez.

Tim cherished a daydream that Cephas might be adopted. There were plenty of nice young couples who wanted a baby, and Cephas was still a baby. The nice young couple would not be being expected to take on a two-year-old. There would be plenty of potential adopters for a Cephas. It would need organising, of course, but that would be the easy part. The emotions would be the difficulty. Even mentioning the idea to Cecilia had proved impossible so far.

Tim's sex life with Cecilia had been important to him. That was gone, perhaps for ever. Cancer had robbed him of that, and he had been good about it. Cecilia's care and companionship were important to him as well, and cancer had left him them so far intact. If Cephas was going to rob him of them, he supposed he would have to be good about that too. When a filling had come out of his teeth yesterday at supper, Cecilia had taken no notice at all. Usually she would have exclaimed sympathetically and today reminded him about the dentist. Tim had not been conscious of having any rights, where his marriage was concerned, but now that the marital rights he had never had to think about were being everywhere infringed, he suffered.

The worst, from Cecilia's point of view, had she known it, was happening: Tim was growing critical of Ian. Tim could not speak to Cecilia about adoption, nor about realistic fears for the future – what if Cecilia was to die of a secondary cancer? She seemed to have forgotten about that – but, surely, Tim could speak to Ian.

Tim emailed Ian.

Ian. Next time you come over to see Cephas, could I have a private word with you? Perhaps we could go to the pub. Love, Tim

The time came. Cecilia was slightly surprised to see the two men in her life going off to the pub together after Ian's visit, and, Cephas on her hip, she watched their backs recede out of the sitting room window. It had seemed to be Ian's suggestion, so she did not sense trouble. Perhaps Ian felt his contact with Tim had been fading, and wanted to renew it. Ian did, after all, owe Tim a big thank you: Cecilia readily conceded this, in spite of her deep feeling that Ian had every right to make any demand. So she watched them. Ian was the taller, but only because Tim was stooped. There was something about their body language as they walked shoulder to shoulder that Cecilia did not quite like.

Ian and Tim sat down with their beers. The pub was the local Ian remembered well but had not been to often since he had lived with Cecilia and Tim. He associated it with after-tennis drinks with Tim and perhaps with their partners if it had been doubles. More ominously, Ian now remembered their visit to the pub the day after the weekend he had made Cecilia and Tim go away for his twenty-first birthday party, and his friends had trashed the house. Ian did not like to feel unequivocally in the wrong with Tim: he had felt so then, and perceived that he might now. Ian had let Tim pay for the beers, having in the first place reached for the money himself. Tim was the senior male and Ian realised uncomfortably that he himself must defer. It might help the situation, thought Ian, if Tim felt he was the silverback, not an animal either of them had in fact ever imagined Tim to be.

'How do you see the future for Cephas?' asked Tim, a prepared opening.

'Well. I'm very glad to have a chance to talk to you about it,' answered Ian, a total opposite to the truth.

'Good. Well?'

Better throw himself on Tim's mercy. 'I just don't know what to do. Mum didn't want him to go into care. I can't look after him. I'm abroad three-quarters of the time. What can I do?' Throwing himself further on Tim's mercy: 'What do you think I should do?' All along, the 'I' had gone against the grain. He would have preferred 'we', which of course is what Cecilia would have said.

'Might the mother come back? What is the position on her?'

'The police have been looking for her. She is a missing person. And' – this was a difficult moment for Ian, because his image of himself with Tim was of a man of the world, which the confession that he had slept with a nutter challenged – 'and I doubt if she would be in a fit state to look after a child.'

There was a silence, in which Ian felt found out, embarrassed and cross, and Tim felt righteous without wanting to. The silence said to Ian that this was his mistake, his problem, and he had to solve it. The silence brought home to him that he was forty, and should have acted like a grown man. His cheerful and unexamined notion that Tim would quite like a baby around the house now seemed to him ludicrous. It crossed Ian's mind to try the man-to-man helplessness of 'You see, she was just so beautiful!' but he rejected it, wisely, as Tim was the last person in the world to be excited into a nudge and a wink about irresponsibility.

'I want to help you,' said Tim. 'But how can I, for the best? You've thought of adoption?'

'Wouldn't that kill Mum?'

'I don't think so, if she knew he was going to a good home.'

'He's not a kitten.'

'That's exactly the trouble, he's not a kitten. And the more he stays with us, the more attached he'll get to us, especially to your mum.'

'I'm afraid it's happened already. Both ways.' Ian felt he had very few cards in his hand compared with Tim's cards, but Cecilia's love for Cephas might be one.

'Yes. Perhaps we should have talked about this earlier.'

'Perhaps we should,' said Ian. But he knew that it had been a safe gamble on his part that if Tim bearded him about Cephas at all, he would beard him too late; and Ian might now be able to play a led-up-the-garden-path card. This was still up his sleeve.

There was another silence. It was the most difficult conversation Tim had ever had. He had been brave to venture it. He struggled on. 'I think you and Cecilia should have a talk about adoption, perhaps with me there, perhaps not, whichever you prefer.'

'I don't think she'd like it. He's had one separation already. He might feel abandoned. She might be afraid of further trauma for him.' The word 'abandoned' was a card Ian had not known he had. Tim did not want anyone in the world to feel abandoned.

'OK,' said Tim, 'I don't think we can get much further tonight. However, four other points.' These had been prepared. 'No chance of you getting married, I suppose? No one would have to feel abandoned if you and a wife were looking after the little chap, and Cecilia went on seeing him in a grandmother role.'

'My girlfriend – you know her, Marina, is in the same job as I am.'

'What about a full-time nanny? In your house?'

'I've looked into the fees for that,' said Tim. It was a lie, but he was probably right anyway. 'That is strictly unaffordable.'

'Third point. Are you absolutely sure Cephas is yours? Cecilia has stepped in as a grandmother. She doesn't have a duty to him otherwise. There's a lot about loving him for your sake, you probably realise that.'

'Oh I'm afraid there's never been any doubt about that.' Ian was embarrassed again, because the question touched afresh on sex with a nutter. Tim on his side felt that the third question he had asked Ian had been unpardonably cold and hard.

They had another beer, bought by Ian, and though each felt guilty towards the other, they managed to talk of other matters, the tennis club, Libya and, rather poignantly, Fez. Ian had not noticed that Tim had only brought up three of his four final points. Tim had not been able to face voicing to Ian the question about Cecilia's reduced life expectancy, with regard to her and Cephas's future.

Off went Ian, to give a version to Marina on email of the conversation. Tim went home. There he found Cephas naked and kicking on a blanket in front of the fire. Cecilia was kneeling beside him. She dragged her eyes from Cephas to greet Tim. 'Supper!' she said. But she could not move. Cephas was waving and kicking, breathing hard, his expression purposeful and eager, the speed of his actions increasing and decreasing as Cecilia smiled at him. She did not say 'Isn't he wonderful?' because she was aware Tim would have been pleased if supper had been on the table. 'What did you and Ian talk about?' she asked.

'Well, the future for Cephas.'

'Good heavens!' Cecilia's head turned fully to Tim. 'His idea, or yours?'

'Mine, originally. But he was glad to have the conversation.'

Cecilia knew this had to be a false impression of Tim's. 'But I thought we were all right,' she said feebly, hearing a wail in her voice.

'All right to bring up a child from scratch, ourselves, at our age?'

Put like that, it did not sound realistic. Cecilia was well aware of her danger from cancer. Cephas began to whimper as the kicking and waving was no good when not accelerated by her smiles. She smiled falsely at him and turned back to Tim. 'We can't talk about this now,' she said. 'The supper's in the oven, I'll put Cephas to bed and we'll eat. You can dish up.'

But of course Cephas did not settle, and the carrycot containing him had to be brought into the kitchen where Tim had made preparations. Cephas clearly felt his kicking time had come to an end a bit too abruptly, or had been concluded amiss, and cried until Thor leapt on to the cat net and purred at him through the mesh. What with this, supper, their elderly love of harmony, and a programme Tim wanted to watch on the Minoans, the topic was shelved. But it had been broached, and both Tim and Cecilia were disconcerted.

Chapter 5

Helen's house was small, but convenient and pretty. Her bedroom had a shower room adjoining it. This shower room she now called the stoma toilet. No one but she used it. The stoma kit lay in easy reach on shelves. When Helen had come home with her stoma, after the operation, organising the stoma toilet had been a way of trying to take control. Tears had run down her cheeks as she devised places for the bags, the wipes, the sprays, and put them neatly away. She grieved, she raged; but to have something as horrible as a stoma toilet in her life was better than the alternative, which might mean she didn't have everything to hand for the horrors of bag change. She was accepting the stoma, because there was no alternative, but she was corralling it. She felt that this had been one of the few realistic steps she had taken before she met Cecilia, and she was proud of it. She had done it alone. Since she had been friends with Cecilia, everything had been easier, and she had not been alone. The stoma toilet had been achieved in loneliness and bitter misery.

She was now in the stoma toilet, changing the bag. Helen had not recognised what Cecilia said about a full bag being like a third breast. But Cecilia was thin and Helen was fat, and their bag changes were more different consequently than either of them realised. Helen had fixed a mirror at midriff level on the wall of the stoma toilet. Without that, she would never have been able to see the stoma, or form the opinion that it was identical to a labrador's arse. When she did not wear her bra, a breast hung down over the stoma and concealed it. That was hopeless. With a bra, a hillock was created that she could not see beyond. Thus the mirror was an essential part of her equipment. There was also the problem of creases. The stoma nestled between two rolls of fat. It was necessary to part them with her fingers. The bag's adhesive preferred a flatter surface. She wanted to cry but she could not allow herself to cry, needing her contact lenses so that she could position the bag. Instead of crying, she moaned and swore, and occasionally shrieked. She asked in wonderment: 'How have I come to this?'

She wanted to stick an opaque rather than a transparent bag on today, because John was coming. Probably nothing would happen, but, in case it did, she must be wearing an opaque bag. A transparent bag revealed any shit that might be inside it, gleaming through the clear plastic. An opaque one, if fairly empty, looked inoffensive, though very odd.

And who knew but what she would need to change the bag again before John came? The antics of the stoma were impossible to predict. This she thought as she left the stoma toilet and sat down at her desk.

She looked at a few stray paragraphs she had written.

The day the bandages came off, Marly was advised not to look at herself in the mirror. There was a lot of bruising still and that was to be expected. It was good to have the bandages off and she could get at her mouth with a cup of tea or a glass of wine. Two days later the surgeon came to see her again and gave her the same advice – wait a few days more. But that evening, after a few extra glasses of wine, she insisted that the nurse bring the mirror. It was held up in front of her, and she wished the face – presumably that of the nurse holding the mirror – would get out of the way so that she could see herself. Then she realised there was no nurse holding the mirror. The face she was looking at was her own. She had had her face for nearly fifty years. But now she did not recognise it. The eyes stared with a wide-open look, at once aghast and haughty, the cheeks were sunken, the nose askew. It was not only that her face was ruined, nor even that it was the face of someone else. It was that her face could no longer express who she was.

Then another bit:

'Hi,' called out Max, coming in with flowers. 'Bandage off day. All will be revealed. But why have they made you wear a mask?'

Why had they put a mask on her, Max wondered. He put the flowers down. What a foolish idea, to cover her face with a mask instead of bandages. He supposed the face was not ready to be fully exposed to the air yet and this was a compromise.

'Don't look,' she said. 'If you look you won't see me any more.' Then he understood. She was looking at him with a fixed, cross-eyed expression of shock, hauteur, a hint of vulgar amusement. He had never seen such expressions on her face before. He had never known she could harbour such peculiar combinations of emotion.

Helen sighed, and lit a cigarette. She had not yet found the language into which her horror about her colostomy could be effectively translated. She felt she could do with a drink, but she would be drinking later, so had better wait.

She accepted the existence of the writing block again, telephoned Cecilia and chatted, then sat in her small garden, exposing her white legs to the sun, and reading the paper. She heard John's ring at the doorbell.

She had met John at a publisher's party. He was about fifty, so over ten years younger than her. But they had got off together at the party and had met since. He was married, and their affair, such as it was, was secret and unsatisfactory. This was the first time they had seen each other since the operation. He had been very taken with this big, confident, heavy-drinking, well-known woman, and flattered by her attention. Helen always needed someone to have sex with, and as she got older and fatter, she had to lower her standards. However, she liked John. He was gentle and quite funny. It didn't matter that he was scrawny and short, and made her feel enormous, because they never had to go out together. She knew he found it difficult to reconcile himself to seeing her again, after having to imagine her body under the knife and defaced with a colostomy, particularly as a colostomy was a lifelong fear of his own.

They kissed lightly and she brought him into the garden, picking up a bottle of wine and glasses en route. 'There's no food, by the way,' she said. 'If you want any you'll have to get a takeaway.' Helen could be daunting when she feared rejection, and John, who had thought he was invited to dinner, mumbled something submissive. The wine soon took the edge off his appetite.

'So how have you been?'

'Absolutely dreadful. I never imagined anything like this could happen to me. I haven't been able to write, it's been awful.'

'I thought of you.'

'Not much sign of that. The only good thing has been my new friend.'

Helen told him about Cecilia and the colostomy meeting, and the baby, making the story interesting. Helen was both critical of Cecilia and supportive of her, and where Cecilia only ever saw Helen's supportive side, the criticisms could crackle a bit to an outsider.

'She must be completely mad to have taken this on,' she said. 'But she behaves as if it's perfectly normal for a woman of sixty-five with a cancer that could return, though the surgeon thinks he got it all, to take full charge of a baby, presumably for ever.'

'Is there a husband?'

'Yes, very much in his own world. And Cecilia protects him from Cephas, the baby. I go round often – they live near – and I love Cecilia. She has saved my life.'

John thought she looked accusingly at him through the cigarette smoke. To shift the ground, he said, 'How can a child be called Cephas?'

'I don't know. It's the psychotic mother's choice. Be a darling and get another bottle out of the fridge.'

He came back and poured. Luckily it was a screw top. Helen was not a wine snob. 'I can't imagine you liking being round a baby,' he said. 'I wouldn't have thought babies were your thing, or you would have had one, sometime.' Possibly he was retaliating for the takeaway and its implied accusation.

Helen had nearly told Cecilia a memory that had been stirred by the mention the other day of Mother Mary Vincent. The earth had been loosened painfully around that memory, and the wine, less painfully, shifted it further. 'I had a baby,' she said.

'What happened to it?'

'I had it adopted.' Tears came, to the detriment of the contact lenses. John had a tissue, and she dabbed. 'I never talk about it. It was over thirty years ago.'

'Between *Poor Harvests* and *Nest for a Cuckoo*?' he said cleverly, his heart sinking to see her cry. He knew she loved her novels coming into a conversation, and he had a gift for accuracy.

She smiled all over her face for the first time since he had arrived. Her smile reminded him that they had been lovers, and he looked conscious.

'Ah yes,' she said, reading his thought, but remaining friendly, probably because of the wine. 'Is all that in the past?'

'I have had time to think,' he said. 'Mine isn't an open marriage, technically, you know. You've been a secret. It's not great.'

'Of course it's not great, but we always knew that.'

'Yes. But I mind it more, now. The joy would go out of a frolic in the hay.'

She liked sex being called that. It made her feel young and foolish. 'Well,' she said, 'I expected that. What hurts is that I think it's about my body.'

He was silent. Then he was brave. 'Well,' he said, 'you know I'm a hypochondriac. A colostomy makes me scared and puts me off. It wouldn't everyone.'

'I hope not.'

'What does the bag look like? You told me what the stoma looks like.'

'Well. Suppose you had been writing letters in the nude, and a buff envelope had got its adhesive edge moistened and got stuck on to your abdomen. Not much worse than that, if the bag is the opaque sort, and empty. If it's full, it's like a buff envelope with a letter bomb in it, I suppose.'

They were both laughing now. 'I don't know which is more unlikely,' he said, 'someone writing letters in the nude, or, these days, someone writing letters at all.'

'Yes,' she said, 'though I saw Cecilia writing a letter the other day.' Her face became clouded and abstracted as she thought of the recipient of that letter. 'Never mind,' she said. 'Are we drinking too much?'

Another bottle. 'It's only wine,' she said. 'Can you imagine how awful it is to have a colostomy?'

'Well,' he said, 'I've thought about that, since what's happened to you. The fact is I don't find shitting much fun either. I get constipated, and hard stools aggravate my piles, then there's blood, and that aggravates my hypochondria. I have thought there would be something to be said for a colostomy. Also, before he died, my dad was doubly incontinent. With a colostomy, he would only have been singly incontinent.'

'That's a thought,' cried Helen. 'And what if I live to my

64

mother's age, ninety-two, that's if the cancer doesn't get me – I might be glad of a colostomy then, or my carers would.'

'If we have any carers by then,' he said.

They were getting more and more unbuttoned. Helen talked at length, rather boringly, though not so to hypochondriac ears, about the difference between transparent and opaque bags. 'I'd be scared to use the opaque bags,' said John, 'you would never see your shit, and what if it was black, from a cancer higher up the gut? You wouldn't know.'

They had the takeaway in the end, and ate it in the house, as the evening had become chilly. They were both cheerful, he relieved, she resigned. 'Pity if we can't still be friends,' he said.

'Well, we could be. I could be friends with you and Joyce. You could tell her you've met me, she would be interested, I could take you out to dinner, as the old and rich one. Though how I'll stay rich if I can't write, I don't know.'

'You will write,' he said, 'I know it.'

So they left it there, never in fact to see each other again.

~

Cecilia thought, in some ways rightly, that she was a very accommodating person. But she tended to assume that in the things that mattered to her most, she would get her way. She had married two men whose characters helped her confirm this view. Jerry had not been faithful, and this had caused her pain; but after a few years he had left her, and this had fulfilled a deeper wish. She had been much happier as a single mother among other single mothers, in Islington in the nineteen-seventies, supported partly by Jerry and partly by small ad hoc jobs in Ian's primary school, than she had been when eclipsed and put to work as a superwoman by the flamboyant and devious Jerry. Tim let her have her way in most things. In part this was because she could usually convince him, and this without deliberate manipulation, that her way was their way;

or because she was able to blind him to the fact that any way was being taken at all. Then if he had the mental and physical things about him that as a single person he relied upon, life could happen around him without his taking issue. He could enjoy and even relish its tapestry as a background. His parents had had each other in old age, and had died discreetly and demurely, giving as little trouble as possible to Tim and even less to Cecilia.

Cecilia had become responsible for her mother, in her mother's difficult eighties. Tim had taken for granted that this was a shared commitment, and had often been better with Cecilia's mother's distress, disability and restless desire for a loved one to be with her than Cecilia herself had been. In this Cecilia did not know that she was getting her way. She would have been astonished if Tim had not assumed without a second thought that he would visit his mother-in-law when Cecilia was too busy. It had been a matter of course for him that he financed Cecilia's psychotherapy training, and, indeed, that had been a good investment. But her enterprises and duties were his enterprises and duties, as his were not hers, but neither of them adverted to this. It was not very easy to see. If Tim had had a child by a previous marriage, Cecilia would have been a good stepmother, and would have enjoyed it. But Tim had very little baggage on which her devotion to his duties and aspirations could be tried. Fez could have been an example, but neither of them had discerned it as such.

Cephas was not going to be slipped into her and Tim's life, as she had always been able to slip in a dinner party, a new sofa, even the ground floor of the house being taken over as her consulting quarters. Cephas had been spotted by Tim as too big for that easy compliance. Cecilia was shocked and alarmed by Tim's questions to Ian, and thrown into the ignoble task of devising strategies to nullify them; but at a deeper level she admired Tim for what he was trying to do, and for the voice he had found. That did not mean she was going to listen to that voice. Against this reluctant admiration there was a dull ache that belonged to the feeling that had Cephas been Tim's grandson Tim would have felt the imperatives she felt.

Her best hope for Cephas was that Ian would reclaim him, and that there should be a wife or girlfriend, preferably unemployed, in the house with him. They would live near by. That was Cecilia's private daydream. Cecilia regretted Marina being in the same work as Ian, and abroad half the time. She had been charmed to see how well Marina got on with Cephas, and that he accepted her, with no more than a sidelong glance to check that Cecilia was in view.

If that private daydream was not going to materialise, Cecilia could see no alternative to looking after Cephas herself, backed up, as ever, by Tim, and visited, as much as possible, by Ian. Cephas had settled, was attached to Cecilia, was very much a person with his own loves and opinions now, and Cecilia was happy that she had pulled him back from the likelihood of irrevocable emotional damage. Cephas could not be taken away, except by his father, and even then his grandmother would have to be in constant attendance, at least at first. An elephant in the room was Cecilia's health. As Helen had told John, the surgeon believed he had eradicated the cancer. But cancer is cancer, and you never know, thought Cecilia, arraying Cephas in an adorable red stripy babygro that Marina had bought for him. Marina would be visiting later, and Cecilia wanted her to see Cephas wearing her present. Cancer is cancer. To get ill and die had been a poignant enough prospect for Cecilia before the advent of Cephas; now, for his sake, it tore her heart.

Ian and Marina arrived in the afternoon, both in England at the same time, and high-spirited on account of it.

'We don't see each other enough,' Ian had said, 'that's the trouble.' The use of the word 'trouble' might have expressed a sense that the relationship was not getting enough room for growth, a growth that would now have been natural to it. This interpretation was not something Ian consciously knew, but Marina did, and silently liked the word 'trouble'.

Cephas was in his best mood, having eaten and slept and woken not too recently. He looked intently with wide, alert eyes and smiled and kicked his feet against each other in the new babygro. 'Can I take him round the garden?' said Marina, and off they went, she picking her way carefully down the steps, talking to him as she went. Both Cecilia and Ian watched her, Cecilia with hope and calculation, Ian with unthinking pleasure. Marina loved Cephas. She had not loved a baby before, so the new love was a wonder. She loved him because he was Cephas and she loved him because he was Ian's. He seemed to look more and more like Ian, as his little face began to form. Together Marina and Cephas studied a rose bush. Spring had certainly come. She showed him a rose, a bud, and something that was going to be a bud. He was finding it an exciting trip.

'Tim?' asked Ian.

'Tennis.'

Ian relaxed. 'So how's it going?'

'Day to day, well.'

They talked of the fact that Eva now came three times a week, of the delicious meals Eva cooked and that Tim enjoyed them, of the recent visits to the baby clinic and how healthy Cephas was, of the introduction of solid food into his diet. Ian offered more money, as he always did; but this was not needed. The moment came when ordinarily they would have drifted into the international situation and Ian's latest assignment, but instead of letting this happen, Cecilia said: 'What will we do if my health breaks down?' She had rehearsed this way of putting it.

'Do you mean cancer?'

'Well, yes, of course.'

'Look, Mum, what did Mr P say? He said very clearly, with me in the room, that he had got all the cancer, and he was very pleased. OK, so it's tough that you've got discomfort from the surgical wound, but you are clear of cancer.'

'He said he was almost sure he had got all the cancer. He actually said surgeons can never absolutely promise anything.'

'He did say that, but obviously only to cover himself. You could see exactly what, with all his experience, he actually believed.'

She was silent, pleased. 'But—'

'No, Mum, but nothing. You've had two scans since the operation, or is it three—'

'Two.'

'Well, two, and they've both been absolutely fine. Your chances of a hale old age are now exactly the same as they were before you came down with cancer. Think of it like that.'

Cecilia liked to think of it like that. But after a pause, in which she looked at Ian's intelligent, attractive face, lively, as often, with polemic, she said: 'But should I think of it like that in relation to someone so precious as Cephas? Should I ever have said I would have him?' This was a difficult question to frame, and she was looking to Ian more for absolution than realism.

'Has Tim said anything?'

'Well. He's expressed concern.'

'Tim is perfectly all right with the situation. His life is virtually unchanged. You do all the care for Cephas, I provide the money. You could have more help, of course, any time, if you needed it. If you're saying Tim thinks you're going to die . . .' This was cruel to Tim, and Ian knew it.

'Not thinks. Takes into account.'

'It's not in the evidence. Remind him of that. Thoughts about you dying are because Tim is a – because for all his virtues Tim has a gloomy old sod side to him, and we all always knew

69

that. Look, why did Tim retire without a professorship? Pessimism, excessive caution, seeing things as risks that aren't. Same thing now.'

Cecilia proudly and very privately compared these qualities with the qualities in Ian that had instigated and furthered his own career.

Marina and Cephas came in from the garden, both pink and happy, but Cephas whimpered when he saw Cecilia and held out his arms to her. She took him, smiling at Marina, and they did not comment. Marina produced a rattle the shape of a rabbit she had bought for Cephas, which he liked, but not quite so much as the paper bag it came in. Now it was the turn of the international situation to come up, and then Tim came home, victorious at tennis, and made tea, which included Rumanian cake, much appreciated.

After they had left, Helen dropped in. 'A tea party,' she exclaimed.

'Only Ian and Marina.'

'Oh, the broody Marina,' said Helen, who had often overlapped visits with Ian and Marina. 'Can I have a piece of that cake?'

Cecilia did not quite like 'broody'. It gave her private daydream too vulgar a currency. So she said nothing.

Helen went on, chewing: 'All over with me and John.'

'All over? Helen!'

'Yes. And I don't even mind. We had a nice evening together and we'll probably stay friends. But nothing else. That leaves me with the question of where I will turn for sex. Maybe I should ask myself the deeper question, do I still want sex? Or rather, do I need to hustle for it? If it comes it comes, I could see it like that.' She was pensive, while Cecilia, listening to Helen, rattled the rabbit and smiled with Cephas. 'And I've got goo coming out of my virtual anus at the moment, which would not be exactly an aphrodisiac. Should I see someone about that?'

'The GP would be the person, at this stage.' They had the same GP practice, and the relative merits of the different doctors could be a topic. 'But I remember Hyacinth's colostomy book said something about that being normal from time to time. Not that it applies to me, without even a virtual anus.'

'I couldn't bear to read Hyacinth's ghastly colostomy book, with that handsome middle-aged couple on the cover, standing healthily on a hillside. It made me cry. Not because I wanted to be them, but because it was so awful to be plunged into a world where such an abhorrent couple were a good advertisement.'

'Did you see the bit in the book where it said it would be a bad idea to use the stoma for sex?'

'No! Did it? That's enough to put one off sex for ever.'

Chapter 6

Diana pondered what move she should make. Should she write to Clare and say she had stumbled on a possible clue as to her birth mother? Or should she contact Helen Gatehouse, via Cecilia possibly, and say she knew someone who could be her daughter?

With a quick prayer to St John the Evangelist, who had become her patron saint of memory, she sat down and looked at the photograph of the young woman, Helen Gatehouse, with the child in her arms. As she stared at the face of the woman, something stirred. It had been in the Hastings days. A young woman had come to see her, yes, it was after Diana had published an article in *Encounter* on Christ in the poems of Emily Dickinson. The woman – Helen Gatehouse, indeed – had been working on Emily Dickinson. She had seen Diana's article. The memories moved on. It had been distressing. Yes. The young woman had spoken suddenly of herself. She was about to have a termination of pregnancy. Diana had suggested she think again, and they had talked. Helen had cried, Diana remembered, and said she could not look after herself, let alone a baby. Diana remembered talking about adoption, and what a wonderful thing it was to be able to give a baby to a couple who wanted one. She did not think she had seen Helen again.

She needed to take advice. After Mass the next day, she indicated to Father Reg as he began to sweep out of the chapel that she would like a word. They sat down together in the little room off the chapel in which he was served his post-Mass cup of tea and biscuit, and the nun who brought the tray hobbled off to get similar supplies for Diana.

He listened attentively while Diana explained. She had become acquainted with a young woman, an adopted child, who had formed letters from Diana to her mother, recently dead ('God rest her,' said Father Reg, automatically), and her mother's death had aroused the young woman's interest in who the birth mother was. The young woman had mentioned the successful removal of a birthmark after adoption at the age of two. Coincidentally, or could it possibly be providentially, Diana had realised that she might be able to piece the story together, by means of memories and of a birthmark in a photograph. Should she bring the two, possibly birth mother and daughter, together? Diana gave Father Reg this account without mentioning any names or offering any unnecessary details. Then she waited for what he would say.

'Isn't it always best that people should learn the truth?' said Father Reg thoughtfully.

'There may be very painful things, on both sides,' said Diana. 'But I agree with you, and it is not my truth, it is theirs, theirs to know, certainly not mine to withhold. Do you think I should write to the daughter first, or the mother? Or write or speak to the daughter, whom I know well, indicating how she could get in touch with the mother?'

'But don't forget there may be no connection between them,' said Father Reg. 'You are already calling them mother and daughter, but it's a presumption. Birthmarks are not so rare. The only plausible link seems to be that you all lived in or around Hastings at the time, so the lady could have put her child in local care, say the Crusade of Rescue, and a local couple could have adopted. That may have happened.'

'The dates match. But I don't even know that the lady, the

older lady, lived in Hastings. I do know she came to see me, but that doesn't mean she came from around here. And it would be cruel to the younger lady if this were a false trail. If I say nothing, she will get over this wish to trace her past.'

'I would utterly trust your discretion,' said Father Reg, who had known Diana a long time.

It was all very delicate. A letter to Clare would bring a visit from her immediately. Would it be right to show her the photograph? The photograph would tell her something about the two-year gap, but was the photograph the best way for her to discover that? Wouldn't it be better to leave an explanation to the birth mother, if and when they met? But Diana had heard of birth mothers who did not want anything to do with their natural child. There was a new family and the baby from long ago was an intrusion. That could happen. She did not want it to happen to Clare.

She waited a couple of days to see if further thoughts occurred to her, and in that time Clare wrote and booked another visit, to which Diana responded briefly in the affirmative. She could tell Clare what she knew, and hear from Clare what she would like to happen. That was the best way. As for outcomes, they must be left to God.

It was possible and even pleasant, this time, for Diana and Clare to have tea out of doors. Two elderly nuns and an aged gardener looked after the convent's very pretty garden, and it was in its spring prime. It had a summer prime too, but the spring prime was more wonderful, coming after winter. A tea tray had been brought out and Diana sat at the garden table, her hearing aid at pitch point, waiting for Clare and praying.

Clare arrived and sat down, all pleasure to be there, appreciation of the garden, stylish clothes, and regret at being two minutes late. Diana's eyes were not good, but she saw at once, now that she had studied the photograph, that this young woman was Helen Gatehouse's daughter. There was the thick fair hair, the confident stance, the cast of features. Diana found this moving, and looked down for a moment, so that the tears should not be visible.

'Have you had a good journey, my dear?' she asked.

'Traffic. That's why I'm late. A sunny Saturday – people are bound to be out and about.'

'Will you pour the tea? My hands are getting less steady.'

'Oh! Are you OK?' Clare poured the tea, but also looked closely at Diana, whom by now she loved. She could see that something had happened to disturb or excite the old lady, and her first supposition was ill health. This meeting had been initiated by Clare, unsummoned; so she had no reason to anticipate developments in her own story.

'Thank you. Please have one of those cakes; they are rather nice. Thank you. Yes. I have something to tell you, to consult you about.'

Diana proceeded steadily with the facts and put them all before Clare. She did not mention Helen's name at this point. She touched on her own contact with Helen, but not that Helen had intended to terminate the pregnancy. Then she handed the photograph across the table to Clare.

Clare had been riveted by the account she heard, and stared intently at the speaker throughout. Her very first feeling was of relief that nothing was the matter with Diana. Then she settled down to making herself mistress of the facts.

'This is all Hastings, isn't it?' she said. 'You were at your congregation's branch there, Mum obviously came to see you . . . No, that's the wrong way round. This woman,' pointing at the photograph, 'came to see you, pregnant. You suggested adoption if she couldn't keep the baby. That was that bit. Then at some point later, say two years later, Mum came to see you, perhaps to talk about not being able to have a baby, and again you suggested adoption.'

'Yes. But the only connection between the events is the

75

baby's birthmark. Is that enough to make us take the link seriously?'

Clare didn't understand for a moment. 'Oh,' she said, 'this is me all right. It's exactly the same as the photos of me as a baby. Not as an absolute baby, but as a baby of two, which is as far as the albums at home can go back. And the earliest photos of me have this birthmark, exactly the same size, shape, place. I'll bring you one.' She was silent, staring at the photograph. She turned it over. 'May I?' But there was nothing written on the back. Diana thought to mention the novel and the inscription, but waited. 'She must have sent you this,' went on Clare, 'to show you she had kept the baby after all. But she didn't. She did and she didn't.' She was silent, and Diana said nothing. 'You don't know who she is, do you?'

'Her name is Helen Gatehouse,' said Diana.

The name rang no bell for Clare, who was not a novel-reader. She went on looking at the photograph. 'Helen Gatehouse,' she said dreamily. 'Well. She does look very nice.'

'And very like you, my dear.'

'Goodness, I'm sorry for not saying this before,' said Clare, coming out of her reverie. 'Thank you so, so much. This must have been a lot of trouble for you, however you made these discoveries. And thank you.'

'No trouble,' said Diana, a bit huskily.

'And do you think she's . . . still alive?'

'Yes, she is.'

Diana was wrong if she had thought that Clare would precipitately want to meet Helen. Clare was not going to decide yet what to do with her new information. She established with Diana that, if she wished to send a letter, Diana would have a way of conveying it. But at this point she did not wish to. She would talk to Dave, she would talk to Dad.

When the bell was soon to go for evening prayer, Clare said, 'I feel a bit better about the two-year hole in me. The

76

photograph has helped, somehow, and you have. I'll think what to do. What's the point of meeting her? It would be hard for both of us. And I'm not sure what Mum would feel. I'll talk to Dad. No, I don't want to take the photo, or not this time.'

A minute later, holding Diana's hands, Clare said, 'I think it would be – small-minded somehow – to make a detective story out of it and harass this woman – Helen – about why she kept me for two years and why she got rid of me. I don't remember her face at all. Mum's face is always with me. You have been such a help. See you soon, if that's all right.'

Diana said a warm goodbye, and, as there was a minute, trudged through to the front to wave Clare off. She noticed a freedom, a grace, a lack of constraint, which seemed new, about the way Clare walked to her car, waved, smiled, threw her bag on to the back seat, jumped in, waved again and drove off.

~

Ten days later, Diana received the following letter from Clare.

Dear Sister Diana,

First in case I forget to say this at the end of the letter I want to thank you again for all your kindness, thought and no doubt prayer about me and my life.

I have talked to Dave, and I have been down to see Dad, and then the two of us saw Dad and the three of us had a good talk, me and Dad crying, of course – not all the time!

So this is the decision. I do not want to meet my birth mother. I know who my real mum is, and that is enough. It's not that I'm afraid, it's that it's not needed. I am afraid, of course, but only in the sense of embarrassed. We thought about the possibility in all sorts of ways – just me; me and Dave; me and Dad; all three of us. And we all thought not. We all agreed on this.

Could you very kindly write to her, and say I am fine, and thirty-two, and an accountant, and have Dave, and we'll be getting married in the autumn (would you be able to come? Please try) and, most important of all, of course, tell her that a really lovely couple adopted me thirty years ago and I had a happy childhood with generous and loving people – all she could have wished for me. If you like, tell her the birthmark was entirely removed, she must have noticed it! Please don't give names, let alone contact details, I know you never do unless you decide to. Nothing ever slips out with you!

That's it really. I don't want to lose contact with you! Please let me come again before too long.

Love and thanks,
Clare

Diana wrote back:

Dear Clare,

I have your letter and will carry out your instructions. I am impressed by your decision, made in concert with your very best advisers. If appropriate, please give them my regards, and tell them I am glad you have two such men in your life.

I doubt if I will be up to coming to the happy occasion in the autumn, but tell me when it is, so that our Mass can be for you and David that day. My thoughts and prayers will be with you.

Indeed they are so today. I am sure you know that I should be very happy to see you any time.

Yours in Christ,
Diana CCHJ

That went with the post on the same day. The following two letters took a little longer. Diana had, of course, already answered

Cecilia's letter announcing the arrival of Cephas, and Cecilia and Diana had had one further exchange in the intervening time.

Dear Cecilia,

I hope all goes well with you and with Cephas and other members of the family. You have my very best wishes and prayers

In the post tomorrow, if the post is what it ought to be, you will receive a letter from me to Helen Gatehouse, your new friend, care of you. I need to get in touch with her and this is my best method. I hope you do not mind. I would do it otherwise if I were able. But you will handle the matter with your usual tact, I may be sure.

I would like to hear from you soon. You mentioned bringing Cephas here one day. If so, let it be soon – the garden is looking so beautiful.

Devotedly,
Diana CCHJ

Then came the difficult one.

Dear Ms Gatehouse,

Thank you for sending me your regards through Cecilia Bunks. Indeed I remember you.

I have a message to give you from someone who is important to me and has every reason to be important to you. She is a young woman of thirty-two, beautiful, successful and happy in her life. She was adopted at the age of two by an admirable couple who were childless. She became their beloved, though I do not think their spoilt, only daughter.

I was able to link this individual with the child in the photograph you sent me with your novel Poor Harvests, *nearly thirty years ago.*

Your natural daughter wants you to know that all is well with her. She is an accountant, and will be getting married in the autumn to a young man who sounds entirely suitable. She has decided that she does not wish to try to get in touch with you.

She thinks you might like to know that the birthmark on her forehead was removed, leaving no trace.

I am aware, of course, that this letter will come to you as a shock. But I hope it is a pleasant shock. Do write to me if you wish, but I am not at liberty to give any further details.

I am treating this matter in the utmost confidence. Of that you may be sure. I have had to use Cecilia's address as a go-between but she knows nothing of the content of this letter.

Yours,
Diana Clegg (Mother Mary Vincent) CCHJ

Chapter 7

Cecilia was intrigued to receive her letter from Diana. It was typical of MMV's scrupulosity that she ensured her letter of preparation to Cecilia would arrive before her letter of substance to Helen. She trusted the post, thought Cecilia, more than a modern person might.

Cephas's teeth were coming through. There were dashes of white on his pink gums, the larger ones slightly serrated. He gnashed and dribbled and bellowed. Thor could still calm him, purring though the mesh of the cat net. Cephas could direct his hand to hold the cat net now, and white paw and pink fist would meet in a moment obviously happy for both. When Cephas lay on the floor or a sofa, Thor might curl up beside him, their heads close.

'Is Cephas Thor's kitten or his mother?' Ian asked Cecilia.

'His kitten, of course,' said Cecilia stoutly, speaking up for Thor's adulthood; but it raised a question.

Cecilia, Marina and Eva thought Cephas was being very brave with his teeth. Tim, Ian and Helen thought he was making a lot of fuss. He chewed his rattles, his hands, teething rusks.

'It must be so strange for him,' said Cecilia, 'to find these hard things in his familiar mouth.'

'We've all been through it, I suppose,' said Ian.

'Yes, but so many things that are universal are awful,' said Cecilia. 'Death, for example.'

'Fair point,' said Ian.

Tim said: 'Isn't there something you can put on the gums?'

'Yes,' said Cecilia, 'and we've got it, and it's on.'

'Of course if he dribbles all the time,' said Ian disapprovingly, 'he'll wash it away.'

'This stage won't last long,' said Cecilia, the peacemaker, though she was tired, for the nights were broken again.

The surgical wound in Cecilia's backside was still very uncomfortable. Some days it hurt more than others. She had stopped hoping that it was getting better. The pain level varied, but there was no steady trend towards improvement. That had been a disappointment, but as a disappointment it had taken shape so gradually that it had not been fully palpable. Then Cephas had come and had swept so many other considerations away. When Eva was in charge, or occasionally Tim, whom she did not like to ask to babysit often, Cecilia went to the GP, or had an appointment with the surgeon or oncologist. It always seemed to be the same – the wound could not heal as it should because of the radiotherapy. She could not help wondering what had become of her vagina. She could not get a straight answer to this question. Mr P, being a surgeon, talked of vaginal reconstruction by plastic surgery. Cecilia did not want further surgery unless as a matter of life and death. Until the advent of Cephas, she would have thought more than twice about that even in those dire circumstances.

Because she was an energetic woman and her general health was good, and because she could afford help, and because, once he had settled, Cephas was relatively easygoing, she had not been worn out by having to look after a baby. But for the cancer, she would still have been working full time. All these thoughts came into her mind as she assessed how she was doing, physically and in terms of morale. This was the day Diana's letter for Helen was to be expected. Cecilia was in the garden, with Cephas on a rug. She had neglected the garden, this spring. But still, it looked very pretty, in sunlight.

Helen appeared before the post arrived, and Tim let her in, telling her Cecilia was outside. Helen came through the house and down the steps, heavily but gracefully. Cecilia was, as always, pleased to see her. They smiled at each other, Helen sat down. She settled comfortably and lit a cigarette. She had to make the most of garden cigarettes at Cecilia's, for she was not allowed to smoke indoors, on account of Cephas.

Helen said, 'I've made an appointment to see Hyacinth. Do you find the stoma gets constipated? I do. After a colostomy there's nothing psychological, emotional, about shitting. You know – you've got the house to yourself, you're relaxing, having a cigarette, looking at an old photo album, say, clearing out a cupboard – and lo and behold, you want a shit. There's nothing like that, post-colostomy, to get your bowels working. Whatever that was must have been situated in the bit of gut that's been removed.'

'Hyacinth will probably say you don't drink enough,' said Cecilia. Seeing Helen's look of incredulity, she added, 'Fluids, I mean.' They both groaned quietly at the familiar mention of fluids, then Cecilia went on, 'Some people give their stoma a name.'

'A name? Like what?'

'Well, Thomas, I suppose. Wendy.'

'Good Lord. I'm sure men don't.' Helen tried it out. 'Wendy's a bit sulky today. Thomas is a bit noisy. But why does Hyacinth tell you interesting things and not me?'

'She doesn't. It was in the colostomy book she gave us.'

They laughed ruefully. Then Helen said, 'I've been playing with a new idea for my stuck novel. I thought I might have something from the point of view of a stoma nurse. A character based on Hyacinth.'

'Why would that work?'

'Knowing so many colostomies, fat people, thin people, men and women, new recruits, old hands, people who hate it like me, stoics, stoics like you. And it's an angle on colostomies that doesn't involve having one. You could feel triumphant in that position. Or immune. Or benevolent. And why did she choose the job?'

'Her mother had a colostomy.'

'You see? She does tell you the interesting things!'

They laughed, Cecilia pleased, at first sight, by what Helen had said about her novel. A fictional point of view involving a calm nurse, rather than a ravaged person, argued a process where a certain distance from horror was becoming possible for Helen. But then, again, thought Cecilia, the situating of subjectivity in the Hyacinth person could spell unconscious denial in Helen that it was to herself, inexorably, that this awful thing had happened. Helen's horror of colostomy had brought out a balancing insouciance in Cecilia. But even Cecilia was sometimes overcome by evidence of digestive processes so denatured as they both had to endure, and changing a bag could be for Cecilia, as well as for Helen, a frightening moment of truth. But Cecilia had her backside to deal with as well, and for her this took some of the lurid light off the colostomy. At least the colostomy did not hurt.

Kicking and trying to get a piece of grass into his mouth had taken Cephas's mind off his teeth, but now he began to whimper, and Cecilia deemed that he was getting cold. They trailed indoors, Cecilia with Cephas, Helen with his parapher-nalia, where Cecilia made a pot of tea, Cephas on her hip. When Helen had her cup of tea, Cecilia found the baby sling and put Cephas on her front, now with practised hand. She thought 'Wonderful inventions, these slings,' but did not say it, to spare Helen.

It was at this moment that Cecilia heard the day's post slithering through the front door, and then the sound of Tim

84

coming out of his study to pick it up. She remembered what would be in store for Helen, if the post were what it should be. Tim came into the room with some letters.

'Two for you,' he said to Cecilia. 'One from the hospital, I think. And one for you, Helen.' Tim liked Helen. He found her amusing and rather vaguely thought that she was larger than life.

Helen was astonished, Cecilia not surprised at all, and Tim took the arrival of an outsider's letter on his doormat with minimal curiosity. He withdrew to his study with his share of the post. Cecilia watched Helen look at her envelope, be puzzled, and begin to open it. She saw Helen read the letter, and heard her gasp. Then Helen put down the letter on her lap. Then she picked it up and read it again. Cecilia waited quietly for Helen to speak.

'Thank God I'm with you, to get this,' said Helen, and read the letter a third time, Cecilia still watching and still quiet. Helen looked up at Cecilia and said nothing. Then she got up and handed the letter to Cecilia.

Cecilia read it, surprise and excitement all over her face. Then she came over and put her arms round Helen's shoulders. A hug was impossible, because of the sling. Cephas's nose pressed briefly against Helen's big bosom. 'Helen,' she said. Then, 'Why didn't you tell me?'

'I would have, in the end,' said Helen. 'It's just such a difficult bit of my life. I never talk about it. Little did I know, when I asked you to remember me to your nun, that this would come of it.'

'Tell me the whole story,' said Cecilia. 'Wait. Another cup of tea and a slice of Rumanian cake.'

They both settled, Cecilia standing for greater comfort, swaying to keep Cephas soothed; Helen sitting, collecting her thoughts, stimulated in spite of herself by the prospect of recounting. But then she was too much choked with emotions to begin.

'I've got to say something first. About the letter. Of course I'm really happy Clare is all right, even very all right, but why doesn't she want to see me? I would certainly want to see her. Now I've got that reaction out of the way' – she flapped her hand, but her face said the pain hadn't been so easily dispersed – 'I can begin.

'Late seventies,' she said. 'Me in my late twenties. I went to live in Hastings with a ghastly man I was in love with. He was doing a PhD at Sussex, and we lived in a little house by the sea. I loved the house at first – a funny bit of stained glass in the front door, entwined fish, I think, all blue and red, and a sweet little wisteria growing up the back. We were both writing, and at first it was OK, though needless to say not the idyll I had expected. He was a drinker, an alcoholic, I think. Terrible moods. Then, heaven knows how, I got pregnant. I had an IUD, but it must have come out. Of course I knew I had to have an abortion. Gordon, who was that awful sort of man who is a patriarch at heart without being remotely parental, said he wouldn't mind having a baby. That decided me. I certainly wasn't going to look after a baby that would be a feather in his cap without him taking any responsibility, which would have been his style. When I mentioned money he came round spectacularly quickly to the idea of an abortion. He had no money anyway, except a grant – we were living on mine. I went through the interviews and examinations and booked the abortion. It was all settled. I was going to go in the next week.

'Meanwhile I had read an article in *Encounter* or some such, on something or other I was working on at the time, and I saw it was by a nun who lived in Hastings, so I arranged to see her, to discuss the article. That was your nun, Diana Clegg, aka Mother Mary Vincent, the author of the letter you are holding. In the course of our chat – she was very nice – I burst into tears and said I was pregnant, and it was the first moment I knew I minded, though to be truthful not much, about having to have an abortion. I did mind of course – I mean I knew it was a solemn thing. But I was in such a hurry to be rid of this new problem, I didn't mind what I did. But this nun went on about adoption, and having the baby, and giving it life, and making a childless couple happy, so heaven knows why, I cancelled the abortion, and went ahead with the pregnancy.

'As time went on I enjoyed the pregnancy hugely. Surprising, isn't it? I was incredibly well, and loved having a huge tummy without it meaning I was fat, and adored feeling the baby move. It was one of my happiest times, actually. Gordon was OK once he knew it was going to be adopted. I finished my novel – *Bitter Harvests* it was called, or Something or Other *Harvests*. Then I had the baby, and after all that I couldn't part from it. I revoked the adoption, which was already half arranged. Completely arranged, probably. So I brought the baby home, called her Clare, breastfed her, a wonderful experience, I must say.

'Gordon was furious, drinking more than ever, gave up his PhD, blamed me. I had said I was going to have an abortion, he said; I had said I was going to have it adopted. And now he was landed with a baby. Him landed! He did nothing. Mum came down to help me. He was horrible to her. He was the sort of man that if something's bad already he makes it worse; if it's good he spoils it. By this time I really hated him and we had rows. You know what I can be like. Well, you don't, but I can. Anyway, he moved out. After that I had the cottage to myself, breastfeeding Clare, tired and happy. It was winter. I didn't miss writing because of the breastfeeding. We did it all the time. I had an open fire. A dreamy time. Mum came again, once Gordon had gone.'

'So from then on Gordon was out of the picture.'

'Yes. And a few years later I heard on the grapevine he was dead – unsure whether it was suicide or an accidental overdose. But he had gone out of my life and Clare's already.'

'So what happened next?'

'I suppose you could say I got fed up with it. This is the bit I am really ashamed of, not of getting pregnant like an idiot, that can happen to anyone, nor of falling in love with a shit, which can also happen to anyone. I got incredibly lonely and bored. I had no idea how to look after a child, and no interest. The breastfeeding hadn't made me bond with her, but only with breastfeeding. Even that I went off. I wanted to get back to writing, and I couldn't, because of her. I had always had men and I wanted a new one. I began to hate the house, every room. I tried to make friends with the neighbours but there weren't any suitable ones, and none I could dump Clare on. I had no friends. I didn't have a car.

'It became a ghastly life. I couldn't bear living in Hastings, having moved there only because of Gordon. I wanted to move back to London. My life had always been here. But because I couldn't write, not from writer's block at all, just the bloody baby, I had no money. That was another worry. And I got a wonderful offer to be creative writing resident for a term at a university in Philadelphia, with massive pay and immense fun, and I had to say no. I might as well have had my legs cut off at the knees! And then the baby had a red birthmark. She didn't have it at first, she was pretty at first. This birthmark began to appear and grow and it was big – bright red – on her forehead. The health visitor said it would go away. But it just got bigger. That was so difficult for me! You know what I'm like about the stoma. The stoma has reminded me of that birthmark sometimes – something horrible you don't expect to see, and nobody else has to have.'

'You poor girl,' said Cecilia. 'And all on your own with it.' She would not have been able to be sympathetic to Helen if she had not known, from Diana's letter, that Clare had made it into happy and secure adulthood, and had been a loved child.

'So I struggled on. Then I realised I could take Clare to

stay with Mum. So I did that. She stayed with Mum in Sheffield for short bursts. Mum gave up work. You and Cephas have reminded me sometimes of that. But Dad was a bit of an invalid already, not at all like Tim. I was so ashamed, and my brother and sister were angry, and kept ringing me up to ask when I was taking Clare back, and saying didn't I know Mum had her hands full with Dad's heart. So I took Clare back, birthmark redder than ever, and then I couldn't cope again, and I was drinking on my own at the kitchen table in that horrible little house in Hastings.'

'Perhaps we haven't got to this bit of the story, but how did MMV link you up with Clare?'

'I don't know. That's a mystery. What I do remember is that I sent MMV one of my novels as a thank-you – not that I felt grateful – and a photo Mum had taken of me and Clare in Sheffield. I don't know why I wanted your MMV to think it was happy families, but I suppose I must have.

'Cecilia, you just have to accept, some women aren't maternal. You know that. You know that, by the awful things that sometimes happen to the babies when some mothers and babies are left alone together. I would never have killed Clare, obviously, but I can understand it. Maybe poor mad Leda was afraid of doing it.'

Cecilia was thoughtful. She said nothing, holding Cephas tight and safe.

'You're not horrified, are you? You're not going to stop being my friend?' cried Helen.

'No, and no. But I'm appalled by what you had to go through. And Clare too, if I'm honest.'

'Then there came the time when I took her up to Mum's again, never mind what Marj and Harry said, and I left her there for quite a few weeks. Even a couple of months, maybe. Mum would ring and say she thought Clare missed me, and when was I coming, and Marj and Harry did their usual complaining. But in those weeks I got myself to London, and met Maurice, and you know about Maurice: it was the best relationship I have had, and the longest. He helped me move to London. Before long I had moved in with him. All this happened very quickly. I wanted to start afresh with no baggage, with Maurice, so I decided at long last to put Clare up for adoption. I went and got her from Mum – she didn't want to leave Mum, and Mum cried too, but it was the best in the long run. A childless couple who wanted a baby, just like MMV had said. That was the only hope for Clare.'

'Clare wasn't a baby, though, any more,' said Cecilia.

'No, but I told the social workers, or whatever they were, and the children's home in Hastings that she was up for adoption.'

'You can't be sure that will happen, just by saying so.'

'No, but it did, as we now know.'

Cecilia sighed deeply at her friend's recklessness and callousness. 'Yes,' she said, 'it did, as we now know. Helen, how have you felt about this all these years, not knowing?'

'Forgot, buried it, and thought of her adopted and happy. I didn't think of her. I'm sorry. I know you hate this.'

'I do. But I certainly don't hate you.'

'Thank God for that. The children's home people were very nice. They said I should come in and visit her. She didn't want to see me, and after I had properly moved to London with Maurice I didn't have time to go to Hastings any more. The couple of times I did go, there were letters and prezzies for Clare from Mum – that was touching – letters – "Darling Clare, you left your teddy, I have put it in a big envelope for you," etc. "Love and kisses from Granny." Which the women were supposed to read aloud to Clare, I think. I don't know if they did. She wouldn't have understood anyway.'

'How old was she then?'

'I can't remember, one, one and a half.'

'She was adopted at two.'

'How do you know?'

'MMV's letter says so.'

Helen reached for the letter and looked. 'Oh yes. That's the whole story. Maurice and I were together for the next ten years – more. It was the most settled time of my life. I wrote *Nest for a Cuckoo* and two other novels. They were wonderful years. Well, I have had some happiness.'

Cecilia thought coldly that sometime she would have to ask what *Nest for a Cuckoo* was about. Or she could get it out of the library. The title was suggestive of its being a rendering of the story she had listened to, but the nature of the rendering would probably be surprising.

Cecilia was angry with Helen. Helen used novel-writing as exorcism, Cecilia thought. It was not that Helen was incapable of guilt and remorse, but that she could write it out of her consciousness. Via her novels, she could bypass the sorts of agonies that help other people grow up. Her novels, Cecilia thought, were first-aid kits, or anaesthetics, ministering to their author's injuries. Other people's injuries, inflicted by Helen, thus need not matter. Cecilia saw Helen as a big baby: no wonder she could not love her child. Cecilia was speechless because she felt unforgiving towards Helen. However, she didn't want Helen to know how upset she was, so she got busy with Cephas. For the first time she was not disposed politely to protect Helen from the full impact of Cephas's importance.

Helen went out for a cigarette. Cecilia walked up and down, Cephas on her hip, talking to him. With an aching heart, she was assessing the damage to Clare. First few months not too bad; breastfeeding successful; happy mother at that stage. Never mind the quarrels and Gordon disappearing. Mother fed up; birthmark; a mother who did not like to look at her infant. Drinking mother. Unhappy, frustrated mother. Cecilia felt intensely distressed. Then grandmother: good relationship, too little of it; interspersed with bad times when returned to mother. Then some weeks continuously with grandmother, then torn away from grandmother (Cecilia winced), and put in the care of strangers, professionals, kind, no doubt, but, oh! how did they seem to Clare? Stability there, however; other children. Then the adoptive couple.

A very bad first two years, full of separation and of not being responded to. Cecilia was deeply critical of her friend. However, Helen had actually had the baby, and there was something lovable in that. In the teeth of both impulse and convention, she had decided to go ahead with the pregnancy. Cecilia could see Helen's rash courage and optimism in that, her strength and confidence, and could feel affectionate towards her again. Cecilia thought about Helen's pleasure in feeling the baby move, and in breastfeeding. It was clear that Helen could revel in the baby as a physical experience of her own, but the baby as a separate person was beyond the scope of her tolerance. Cecilia sighed. Helen was right in saying she was not maternal. But there was a gleam of humour and acceptance in Cecilia's eye towards Helen when Helen came in from the garden.

'Don't hate me,' said Helen. 'I've trusted you.'

'Yes, and I don't, and you were right to,' said Cecilia, sincerely.

'Well,' said Helen, sitting down cheerfully again, now the fact was established that she had not fallen out with Cecilia, 'another subject. I would very much like to meet Clare. Why doesn't she want to meet me?'

'We don't know why,' said Cecilia. 'We only know she doesn't.'

'Yes, but what about me? I do want to meet her. It would be such an interest for me to have a grown-up daughter. I need a new interest. Specially now I have probably had to give up sex. It would take my mind off the colostomy.' Helen was only partly mocking herself.

Cecilia was irritated afresh. It was the frivolity she found

92

hard to bear. 'Helen, she is not your daughter. You gave her up. She is this unknown couple's daughter. Don't find a way of contacting her. Don't pick at her until you get her to say she'll meet you. Don't arouse her curiosity with your charm. Don't leak it to her that you are a known novelist. Don't seduce. Leave her be. She has had a hard enough time.'

'You're right, I suppose,' said Helen, doubtfully, startled and displeased by Cecilia's plain speaking, cowed at the prospect of her disapproval, irked by a reprimand when she had expected a giggle. 'It seems a shame though.' And in her mind a secret scheme was already taking shape.

~

Meg Gatehouse, in a care home for old people in Sheffield, was trying to get her cup of tea. It had been put within her reach, but it was proving hard to get hold of. Her hand was entangled in the shawl that lay on her knees. A finger was difficult to extricate. It was not the sort of thing you called someone to help with. It was something you persisted with. Persisting was more difficult than it had used to be. It was easier now to want to cry out 'This bloody thing!' or simply to give up trying. But she felt she was within a whisker of her cup of tea, and it seemed worth persevering. Eventually she managed, and carried the trembling cup to her lips. She did not mind its being cool.

Pleased, she looked round the day room. The sun was coming in at the window, and the plants on the windowsills obviously needed watering, but that was another of the things you didn't point out. Perhaps if Marj came this afternoon she might do something surreptitious to them. Meg continued to scrutinise. Ken was in his chair and so was Kate. Sally was not in hers. There were rumours that she was not well. Meg did not look forward to another death. You would expect people to get stronger in the spring, thought Meg, but that did not seem to happen. Ah well, thought Meg, it is because we are all so old.

She finished her cup of tea, and, now it was empty, made no attempt to replace it on its saucer. That would be asking for trouble. It could stay on her lap. In the area of the room where Ken and Kate were sitting, the television roared and flickered. It was presumed, rightly, that residents were deaf, and, perhaps wrongly, that this was a reason to turn the television's sound up. Sometimes Marj went over and turned it down. Possibly Marj might visit later. Meg could not remember what her daughter had said. Harry would not come, she knew that, because he and Pippa were away for the week. Why? Where? Meg could not remember. But Marj might come.

Tony was being wheeled in. He was brought to his usual place a couple of yards from Meg.

'Company for you!' said Teresa.

'Be good, the two of you!' said Gemma, with mock suggestiveness.

They were nice girls, in their attractive uniforms, and Meg was glad to see them. 'Good morning, Tony,' she said. He tried to murmur a greeting, but moving from his wheelchair to his chair was too preoccupying.

'Nice day,' said Tony to Meg, when he was settled. Meg agreed. She liked to exchange words, although because of deafness, and in Tony's case dementia, you could not really call it a conversation. In the day room's folklore, Meg and Tony were special friends. Meg accepted this, and, when she did the crossword, read out the clues to him. She spotted the paper now.

'Teresa,' she said, 'be a darling and turn up the crossword for us. I should have a pen somewhere.'

'Will do, here you are,' said obliging Teresa, 'and I'll relieve you of your cup at the same time.'

It took Meg a long time to grasp the newspaper effectively and hang on to her pen. 'Person imitating another, five letters,'

94

she read out slowly. She did not expect, nor get, a reaction from Tony.

'Mimic?' called Gemma across the room.

But it was no good. Meg could not write the word in its squares. Her hands were too trembly this morning, and there was not a firm enough backing to the newspaper on her lap. She would do the crossword with Marj if she looked in this afternoon. Meg dozed.

Chapter 8

I an was corralled with other journalists in a hotel in Tripoli. He was wondering if there was any way he could slip out illicitly and get a feel of things. His BlackBerry buzzed and he looked at it, hoping the message might be from Jon, having had the same idea, and thinking the two of them together might manage something. He saw Leda's name come up. This was not the first email he had received from her since her disappearance, but such emails were infrequent enough normally to cause a frisson and immediate engagement with them. But now he was too involved in what he was doing, or what he was not being able to do, even to read it. He tagged it for later, and texted Jon.

So it was that he did not actually read Leda's email until he was home, unpacking in his flat, having texted Cecilia to say 'Safely landed at Heathrow', and Marina to arrange to meet. Even then, when he saw Leda's name among the emails, he did not read her message at once, but made a quick call to the relevant police station to say that he had heard from her. The 'Missing' posters had long since disintegrated, and all that remained now of the rather desultory search for Leda was the request from the police to Ian that if he heard from her, he should routinely let them know. Now, still standing, with his bag not yet unpacked, he read the following:

I am writing to tell you to stop reporting wars. You MUST stop doing it. Reporting wars is what creates war. You are guilty. You have caused civilian deaths. Never report wars again. I am telling you this from a higher authority. I am also telling you this from myself and from posterity. As you know, you are never allowed to answer my emails, and I reiterate that now. But if it was allowed, I would ask you to remind me who is the father of the baby on your doorstep. I am told it could be a number of people. Perhaps different individuals fathered different parts of his body. I am told that is possible. Even you may have a hand in him, for whatever reason. Never try to trace my whereabouts. I am not in your country. I serve the wind and the rain now. NEVER report war again.

Ian felt unease creep over him after reading this. The unease was not dispersed by unpacking his bag and making things shipshape in the flat, which he usually enjoyed; putting the washing machine on for the clothes from his trip, which was also liable to give him a quick stab of satisfaction, and showering, which should have been a pleasure. Having finished these now joyless actions, he sat down at his desk and reread the email on the bigger machine. Most of these themes he had met already in Leda's messages. The wind and the rain were familiar, as was the injunction not to report war, and the embargo on Ian's emailing her. But she had never mentioned Cephas before. Ian had grown to assume that she had forgotten his existence. Now she mentioned him, and in a very odd way.

Was there doubt about Cephas being Ian's son? The passage in the email seemed to imply this. Bonkers though the passage was, and fantasy-ridden though the ideas that had given rise to it no doubt were, it unavoidably expressed a certain vagueness about the identity of Cephas's father. Ian searched his memories. Could Leda have been seeing someone else? He had had no reason to think so. He and Leda had been together every night. It had never occurred to him that during the brief period of his and Leda's intensities, which had presumably given life to Cephas, any other man could have been on the scene. At the beginning of all this, Ian would have welcomed that possibility, as a more complete way of offloading Cephas than the one he had devised. But now, Ian felt not only crestfallen, but, yes, almost heartbroken, at the thought that he might not be Cephas's father.

Or was he quite wrong to see in Leda's email anything rational at all? Should he discount as a communication of any moment the painful passage in it, as completely as he discounted her view that reporting wars caused them? But then why had this chilling unease crept over him? Until he read those words, he had been rejoicing to be home, to be seeing Marina that evening, and yes, tomorrow to be visiting Cephas. Cast into doubt and dejection, Ian envied, as lost for ever, the self that had breezed into his flat, dumped his bag, phoned the police. He felt he would never regain that confidence, that innocence of doubt. It was a confidence and an innocence he had not known he had, until he lost it. That confidence, that innocence, had been like health, unnoticed until taken away.

He looked in his diary. Yes. Marina had been away working. There had been a fortnight in which he had spent nearly all the time with Leda. He could not think it possible that she had fitted in another lover in that time, that time immediately after which she had started missing periods. So he would be mad to take her message seriously. But he could not shrug off his unease with reason. Reason helped, however, and he felt able to get on the computer and do some work.

Working, he had a thought that hit him with a thump whose reverberation ran from his head to his feet. What if she had already been pregnant when they met? What if he had been a cover-up? Or what if she had not yet known? It was possible that when they met at that ill-omened party, she was already pregnant. And knew it? Whichever. That didn't matter. He was not taking a moral inventory of Leda, but trying to re-establish his own untroubled certainty. He could sit no longer but stood up and walked about the room. He was sweating.

It would be unbearable to tell Cecilia that there was doubt about Cephas's paternity. Cecilia had accepted and loved Cephas as a grandson, bone of her bone and flesh of her flesh. She had turned her life upside down for him, feeling and acting in every way as a grandmother. She had loved to watch – or imagine? – resemblances to Ian coming out in him. What sort of a let-down would it be for her? Ian couldn't think about it. He wanted to talk to Marina about what was happening to him, and he intended to. But there was a great reluctance. He realised he had felt proud to be a father in Marina's eyes. He had loved to see her adoration of Cephas, adoration of Cephas as part of him. He had not known he had these prides and pleasures. He knew now.

He met Marina outside their pub. She looked beautiful. Slightly windblown from hurrying, smiling delightedly to see him, jeans, shirt, loose light sweater. She saw something was wrong for him, but also saw that a smile of pure joy beamed out of his face when he saw her. He took her in his arms. It was a big hug for a public place.

He got drinks and they sat down. 'I have so wanted to see you,' he said. She was astonished to suspect tears in his eyes. Now he would not let go of her hand.

'Tripoli?' she said, happy, but mystified. 'Work? What's wrong?'

'Look at this,' he said, 'if you don't mind.' He held his BlackBerry towards her. She took it and read Leda's email. He watched her, loving to see her concentrate, attend, think.

'Does she often send you this kind of thing?' asked Marina, not taking her eyes from the script.

'I've had four or five in the time, and all I've done is alert the police, as they instructed.'

'Do you always get upset?'

'Never.' He was relieved that Marina had not seized on the difficult passage of the message as the obvious source of disquiet. 'You see, she's never mentioned Cephas before.'

'OK. And now she does. To say utterly batty things.'

'Is that all it is?'

'Don't you think so?'

'Don't you think . . . Isn't she making out I might not be Cephas's father?'

'Only in a mad way. It's the maddest bit of the email. With people having different fathers for different bits of them. She's talking about her own fragmentation, no doubt.'

Ian liked 'no doubt'. It struck him as a slightly old-fashioned usage. How could he habitually have noticed so little about Marina? He said, 'I like "no doubt".'

She didn't understand. 'Yes,' she said, 'because you have been in horrid doubt. Well, don't be. This is a mad email, in future delete them unread.' She deleted it and handed the BlackBerry back. 'There,' she said.

He was glad and curious that she had taken such a liberty. He said, 'Thank you,' and looked at her.

'What?' she said, looking back at him, blushing slightly under his gaze.

'Just . . .' He stirred and started to talk about choosing food, which they did, staying at an outdoor table. 'Has it ever occurred to you that I don't appreciate you enough?' he said, leaning across the table to lift a lock of hair away from one of her eyes.

'Not exactly,' she said. 'One doesn't think that sort of thing about oneself.'

'I know you've got parents in Woking, and a sister younger than you,' he said. 'But I've never met them. You have met my mum, you know her well. I don't know anything about your family.'

'Except that they exist.'

'Yes. Will you tell me, if not now, sometime?'

'Yes, whenever. But funny you should say this now, because I've been worrying a bit about Mum Dad's got emphysema, but he's not been too bad. It's bound to get worse. So there's that. And because I'm always abroad I hardly ever get home.'

'What about your sister? Does she get home?'

'Much more than me. Mum always says I don't need to come, and that I am so busy and important. She has News 24 on all the time, even when I'm at home, in case she gets a glimpse of me. And she worries. I went for the day yesterday.'

Marina did not say that she only visited her parents when Ian was away, but so it was. He might suddenly want to see her.

'I shan't do this job for ever, you know,' she said.

So they talked about work. After half an hour she said, 'We can still talk about work, you know, if I stop doing it, because I know all the places and all the people.'

'Yes.'

Why had she had to say that? He was not sure. Was she afraid she was not central to his life? But she was central. She had been for years. He admitted this to himself now, for the first time.

'My place or yours?' he said later.

'Neither, I've got to prepare for Kabul.' Then she saw his disappointment. 'Mine,' she said, 'so that I can start homework at five.'

'It would be so much easier if we lived together,' he said.

Her heart bounded. 'Easier,' she said, 'but would there be disadvantages?'

'To me?'

'Yes. Your commitment thing.'

'My commitment thing,' he said, laughing, and putting the

phrase in self-mocking inverted commas, 'has outlived its shelf life.' Then he said, 'What time do you go to Kabul? I was hoping you could come and see Cephas with me tomorrow. Seeing him is much better when you're there.'

'Is it?' She had not known this. Both were happy.

'I feel so much better about the paternity thing now,' he said. 'Thank you for being so reassuring.'

'You can get paternity test kits now,' she said. 'You could try it – to make certain.'

He wished she had not said that. When she saw his face fall, just a little, she also wished she had not said it. But she knew there was a part of her that wanted, not so much that he should not be Cephas's father, which she was sure he was, as that he should be a bit worried. She had seldom known him shaken, and he was more shaken this evening than she had ever known him to be. Uncertainty, insecurity, the fear of loss, seemed to favour his affection for her, and curbed the lordly way in which he habitually took her for granted. She had never seen him as disconcerted as he had been this evening. And she had never felt so close to him, nor sensed how much he wanted to be close to her.

The next day they were at Cecilia and Tim's together, the exigencies of Marina's timetable permitting a brief morning visit.

'How's everything, Mum?' asked Ian. 'I don't worry about you cancer-wise, as you know, but what about the unhealed wound?'

'Still there, still hurting. Nice that you ask.'

Ian was silent. Was it the hard truth that he did not appreciate anyone he cared about? Surely it was to be expected, rather than 'nice', that he would ask how his mother was. But, actually, he seldom did. This was partly because he didn't want to think that Cecilia was in pain as she ran about on Cephas duty, thereby making it his fault. But it was also because he was not good at bearing in mind speculations about how things might feel to other people. This brought him back to the thought of Marina, who was walking Cephas in the garden, wondering whether he noticed that more roses were coming out.

'Have you ever thought I take Marina too much for granted?'

'Yes,' Cecilia said.

'Hmm.'

'I've worried you were going to let her slip through your fingers,' Cecilia dared to add.

'My God, that would be awful. But it wouldn't happen.'

Cecilia said nothing, to let the enormity of the possibility sink into Ian's mind.

Tim looked round the door in his tennis gear. 'Goodbye,' he began to say to Cecilia. Then, 'Oh, hullo, Ian, you're here.'

'Game, or match?' asked Ian, who did not want Tim to be tempted by deeper topics.

'Just game, this morning. Marina here?'

'In the garden.'

Tim looked through the window on to the garden. 'Do tell her she must take a bunch of roses if she would like to,' he said. He didn't understand that she was not examining the rose bush entirely for her own interest.

'Not this time,' Ian said. 'But thanks. I'll tell her. She's off to Kabul this afternoon.'

Tim took his leave.

'He's all right re Cephas, isn't he?' asked Ian, in an undertone although Tim's car had already been heard starting.

'Yes. I think so. He knows there's no alternative. Cephas doesn't fall heavily on him, you know.'

'Do you mean he does on you?'

That was not what Cecilia had meant to imply, and she was chagrined. 'No, not at all,' she said. 'I didn't mean you to think that.'

In the light of this exchange the question of paternity made an unwelcome re-entry into Ian's mind. It was a terrible, overwhelming thought, to him, as he sat looking at Cecilia. The doubts were nonsense, of course, as Marina had said. He tried to shrug them off.

'What's the matter?' asked his mother at once.

'No, nothing is.'

'You're worrying about whether you take Marina too much for granted.'

'Yes, a bit. Oh, here she comes.'

Marina was walking up the steps from the garden, carefully, Cephas alert and friendly at her shoulder, Thor in attendance. 'I think he knows more roses are out now,' Marina told Cecilia. 'He was pointing as if he was counting. He was chatting away. I'm sure he knew.' Both Cecilia and Marina thought Cephas a genius. Marina went on: 'He laughed when he saw Thor, really laughed. I haven't heard him laugh before and it was wonderful.'

'Yes, he laughs now,' said Cecilia.

'Now he's got so much hair, proper hair,' said Marina, 'he's looking more and more like Ian.'

'Should we cut it yet?' Cecilia asked Marina, risking the 'we'.

Marina was pleased with the 'we', but vetoed the cutting. 'It's so lovely as it is,' she said, kissing the little head.

Soon Ian and Marina had to leave. 'I'm taking you to Heathrow,' said Ian.

This was unusual, and Marina was pleased. Ian raised an eyebrow towards Cecilia and smiled smugly. They left.

Driving back from Heathrow, Ian looked at himself and his life, not sorrowfully, but without his usual jauntiness. He wondered at his good fortune, rather than presuming without thought that it was what was due to him. He had a mother who had accepted parental care of his unplanned and unwanted child without demur, and a complaisant stepfather. He had a girlfriend who had forgiven him immediately for an affair, and who loved the child of it. And he didn't seem to have said thank you to anybody. And another piece of good fortune was fatherhood, unearned and unsought, for which it was harder to decide whom or what to thank. But this last reflection led to something ugly, tucked out of sight on the floor of his mind, and better ignored if cheerfulness was the criterion — the pateri-nity test kit.

Chapter 9

S oon after this Diana received a letter from Helen. It was handwritten in a flowing, rather italic script.

Dear Mother Diana Clegg,

Thank you very much for your kind letter. As you may well imagine, I have been enormously concerned all these years about what happened to my daughter. So to know that she was adopted and has done well is a huge relief. I thank you and I thank her for these welcome tidings.

I would like to come and visit you if I may. I am very free, so please indicate any time that would suit you.

With many thanks again,

Yours sincerely,
Helen Gatehouse

The arrangement was made, and Helen, in carefully chosen clothes, and with a squeaky clean colostomy bag on – not opaque, but that could not matter at a convent – boarded the train.

She had not told Cecilia about this venture, knowing that Cecilia would disapprove. Helen was not a person to want to explore the disapproval of someone she respected; she bypassed it, as if it were no more than a physical obstacle in her path.

And here she was on the train, planning how to make it impossible for Diana Clegg not to give her Clare's contact details. After she had been successful, Helen thought, then she would tell Cecilia.

The desire to know Clare had grown in her mind since she had received Diana's letter. She had told no one – yet. The time would come when she could introduce her daughter to friends; but better that friends should not get wind of her now. It was unusual for impulsive Helen to have a strategy, but she had a strategy about this matter. She saw herself as the glamorous, liberating fairy godmother in the life of a young person of narrow aspirations. Without knowing it, she had decided Clare's adoptive parents were worthy, industrious and boring. She wondered if she would meet them. She thought she probably would, in the end. Possibly they might get drunk together. That would be the best way. Nearly everyone, however conventional, likes a good drink when it comes down to it. Under Helen's auspices, Clare might see sides of her strait-laced parents she had never suspected.

Helen had not been so excited about a project since her last novel – not the present, stalled one – had got going. Or perhaps the last time she had been as excited as this was when her most recent serious love affair had started. Life had a zest, a meaning, a continuity, and recent days had also had this character. This Clare business had gone deep with her, she thought. She was sleeping less, but not feeling tired; and her dreams, though she could never remember them, felt full of magic, recognition and beauty.

She had worried a bit at first lest Clare be angry with her. But then she realised that Clare could not possibly learn anything about the first two years of her life from anyone but herself. Helen was the custodian of that struggle, with its different stages and phases, and need not tell Clare more than she saw fit. She could not, of course, masquerade as a perfect mother, or why should the adoption have happened? But she could present her loneliness, her pennilessness, the disappearance of Gordon, the frustration of her writing life, in such a way as to evoke sympathy, not condemnation.

She looked out of the train window, seeing fields and trees go by. The account she had given Cecilia of the beginning of Clare's life was a true account, she thought. She had described it more coherently and straightforwardly than she ever had to anyone else. To other people she had selected sections, for self-deprecation or even humour, and forged anecdotes. She had not done that with Cecilia. Going through the story with Cecilia had hurt. So it must have been true. But there was something Helen had not said, and this she had never told anyone.

Helen visited this forbidden memory now. She had gone to Sheffield to fetch Clare, and to bring her back to Hastings, to Hastings for the last time, because by then she had already partly moved in with Maurice in London. She arrived at her parents' house. Clare, by then a toddler, put a finger in her mouth and her arm over her grandmother's lap when she saw Helen. Helen could still see that picture in her mind's eye. Then Clare buried her face in her grandmother's lap. Helen went over to her, cooing a greeting, and Clare shrank away. Clare batted Helen's hands away as best she could and tried to anchor herself to her grandmother. Both Helen and her mother tried to make light of this. There was an attempt to laugh it off, in which Dad joined. But the next morning when Helen was wrestling Clare out of her grandmother's arms to take her home, the screaming brought the neighbours in. The taxi was waiting. The trip back to Hastings was managed somehow, with a furious, anguished Helen and a heartbroken child, and the next day Helen took Clare to Social Services. Or the children's home. Somewhere. 'Have her adopted,' she said, and left. That was the end of it. Then the happiest decade of her life began, the one with Maurice, the one in which she wrote three novels, her most successful ones.

The truth was that Maurice was not set against having Clare. Helen was frank enough, now, to remind herself of this. He was at that time too much in love with Helen to be set against anything. He had a child of his own, of primary school age, whom he looked after at weekends. It was Helen, not Maurice, who was averse to starting the new relationship burdened with her child.

She thought back to that dreadful night in which this incomprehensible, alien baby, as lively as a fish trying to escape a net, scarlet and streaming with tears and snot, her birthmark redder than her face, lay on the floor and howled for her grandmother, kicking Helen with hard little shoes if she came close. In desperation Helen rang her mother to get her to talk to the child, thus advertising to both parents her helplessness and humiliation; but the voice on the telephone did no good. She herself howled down the telephone to Maurice. Finally the child fell asleep, sobbing still in sleep, and Helen covered her with a coat and went to bed herself. She lay awake and planned what she would do with the child in the morning. Even then she knew she was punishing her mother, and taking revenge on Clare. But she did it. And it had been, as she had hoped, for the best.

She sighed, and prepared to get out at the next station. Everyone makes mistakes, she thought. Everyone does wrong things. But not everyone, she thought, has on their conscience retaliation against a child, rejection for rejection, and herself thirty. She could not make an anecdote or a joke out of that.

~

Teatime at the convent, and Diana's hearing aid primed and prayed for. She hadn't attempted to be in the garden; it was too breezy. So she sat waiting in the little room where people were entertained to tête-à-têtes with the nuns. The tea tray was in position. Clare had been in this room with Diana, and so had Cecilia.

When Helen came in, large and lively, grey suit, floating silk scarf, large smart handbag, effusive gratitude, Diana was struck by the likeness to Clare. Both had a lot of fair hair, and were noticeable women. There was an air that they shared. Clare was slim and Helen fat, but the latter's well-cut clothes concealed anything unsightly. Diana marvelled briefly about family resemblance. She could not tell whether or not she recognised in the woman now in front of her the person who had come to her all those years ago to talk about Emily Dickinson and to cry about being pregnant. If there was some recognition, it had been confused by the much greater acquaintance with Clare.

Diana risked pouring the tea herself, and her hands seemed to be up to the task. She did not want to appear helpless in the eyes of this affable and high-spirited woman, who might well want to turn helpfulness into domination. Diana had a premonition that she might have to work hard to hold her own in this encounter, and she wanted to start as she hoped she would go on.

'You know why I am here,' Helen began. 'I want to thank you in person for letting me know about Clare. I am so happy to know that the adoption worked out well and that she is managing life so splendidly.'

Diana nodded. She was disconcerted for a second to hear Clare named, and hoped the name had not inadvertently slipped into the letter she had been so careful about. Then the true explanation flashed into her mind, and she was at ease.

'I'd like to tell you a bit about what actually happened,' said Helen, and Diana smiled agreement.

Helen proceeded to give Diana a version of the year and a half in which she had looked after Clare. She thanked Diana profusely for encouraging her to reverse the decision to terminate. There was a hint, which Helen hoped could not fail to appeal to Diana, that carrying and bearing life had been a spiritual experience. Considerable heroism on her part was meant to be read between the lines of her account of her relationship with Gordon and its ending. Helen had guessed, perhaps rashly, that nuns can easily be turned against men. The dark days when she began to rely on her mother to look after Clare were depicted, and her father's heart condition exaggerated somewhat, to rule out what might be perceived in the other's mind as options for childcare. She knew that Diana had heard about Cephas, and the possibility of grandmothers as long-term mother-figures might be too much in her mind. The moment came when there was no alternative but to have Clare adopted, and this Helen had bravely and unselfishly put in hand. Helen's two visits to the children's home were gently augmented, and she could not resist presenting herself as having vetted and continuing to observe, with approval, the behaviour of the staff to the children.

Diana felt sympathy, and had been responding with nods throughout the narrative. Helen was surprised when Diana's first reaction was: 'I just want to clear something up. You talk of putting Clare up for adoption. But the truth of the matter is that you were putting her into care. She was adopted, as we know. But she might not have been. I wonder whether the word "adoption" got lodged in your mind to sugar the pill for you. "In care" is rather more frightening.'

'Well, you talked about adoption yourself!' said Helen. 'That was your word.'

'It was indeed,' agreed Diana, not wanting to say that her idea had been adoption at birth. She felt Helen's defensiveness, and foresaw possibilities of discord, but from what quarter she did not yet know. She sat quietly.

There was a silence. Then Helen said: 'You may not be

surprised to hear that I should very much like to be in touch with my daughter. In fact, I was wondering whether you could supply her contact details.' Helen hoped the word 'supply' would camouflage the emotion in the request.

'My dear, I am sorry that you should be disappointed,' said Diana, 'but I am not free to do that.'

'Why?'

'Clare has not given me permission. In my letter I passed on to you the messages she gave me for you. There are no further messages. I am sorry if you hoped for more.'

'But how can that be? How could someone not want to meet their birth mother?'

Diana was silent. She was not going to be drawn into generalities about the adopted.

Helen was shocked at how indomitable this fragile old thing had become. She appealed. 'But surely you see how much it would help me to meet her. And her to meet me, I should think. There are fantasies on both sides, probably, and we could clear them up. I know it would help me on' (she risked it, although it was florid) 'my spiritual journey.'

'She has her parents, you must realise that,' said Diana, who saw no reason to mention Clare's mother's death, 'and her past with them, and her full present life. She has made it clear that she has no need of a meeting with you. We have to leave it at that.'

'But I can't!' Helen exclaimed, impolitic with disappointment. 'I absolutely can't. If you knew how much I have been looking forward to this moment. It is the only good thing to happen to me since I got cancer.' Helen knew this was beneath her, but she was ready to try anything, now.

Diana had assumed Helen had been touched by cancer, from Cecilia's mention of a colostomy in the letter in which she told Diana she had met Helen – a fateful letter, as it had turned out. So it was not a shock, but Diana was sorry. After a minute she said, 'You look very well, I am glad to say. I hope it has been successfully treated, as we hope Cecilia's has been.'

There was a silence. Then Helen said: 'I think there may be a legal issue. I think it may, nowadays, be against the law not to give information about natural parents and their children.' There was no response from Diana, so Helen added: 'I wonder what you think about that.'

'Nothing at the moment,' said Diana. 'We would have to wait and see, if you were to take it that far.'

'I'm sorry,' said Helen. 'I didn't mean that. If you won't give me her details, at least give her mine. Will you do that?'

'She knows your name. That is all she knows from me, and all she will know.'

'But it's her right to know! Why should you have the power to keep us apart?'

Diana thought this was a good question. But she also thought that if Clare wished to – what was it – Google? Helen's name, she could, and presumably would be able to get in touch with her by some means connected to that. Diana was pretty sure Clare would not be moved to do so, but she could, at any time, if she wanted to. Helen at this moment also thought of Google. But what good was that if Clare did not want to get in touch with her? She felt powerless.

'Just tell me her surname,' said Helen. 'You know that it was I who gave her the name of Clare. Surely I am entitled to know my own child's surname.'

Diana found this emotive utterance embarrassing rather than seductive. 'Well, my dear,' she said, and this was disingenuous to say the least, 'all this must have brought you very close to your own mother.'

'I've never been close to my family!' wailed Helen. 'Dad's dead, Mum's in a home, my brother and sister don't like me. I thought Clare . . .' Her voice tailed off.

Diana was silent in the hope that the purport of what Helen

had just said would resonate in her mind. When she thought she had left enough time for that, she said: 'She must have been glad to hear about Clare.'

Helen was taken aback. 'I haven't told her,' she said.

Again Diana was silent, and with the same intent. Then she said: 'I take it you will?'

'Yes,' said Helen. 'Yes, I must.'

It was a sadder and wiser Helen who got on the train to London. Now she was not only thinking about Clare, but also about Mum. She had not been to Sheffield for over a year. Before the cancer, which now served as a wonderful excuse, she had visited her mother at six-monthly intervals, six-monthly intervals that could extend to the best part of a year. Marj and Harry lived in Sheffield. Let them visit Mum. There were grown-up grandchildren, most of them local to Mum. There were even a few great-grandchildren now. Mum was well provided for.

It had not occurred to her, she realised now, looking out of the train window and wishing there were still smoking carriages on trains, to let her mother know that Clare was all right. Mum had simply not come into her mind. Why not? She had been deeply involved in Clare's infancy. Why shouldn't she know? Partly, Helen thought, it was her own bitter and, it seemed, abiding resentment of that scene in Sheffield thirty years ago that had brought the neighbours in. Let her mother be written out of Clare's past as retribution for that. Partly it was because Helen had been so taken up with the excitement of herself and Clare as a magic duo that she thought of no one else. Helen faced these reflections.

Then she thought about her family. Since adolescence she had wanted to get away from them, their narrow horizons, their conventional outlook, their lower-middle-class aspirations. She was the eldest of three, and had always liked to think of herself as the rebel. Marj and Harry had married local people and had families. Helen had come to London and written novels and had lovers. The fact that she felt that in her mother's eyes she was the all-conquering one, the exciting one, and secretly the favourite, had made the failure to be all-conquering about Clare the more excruciating. She was in her own mind the independent one of the family, but Marj and Harry had never depended on Mum in adult life as she had at that time.

She sighed. All this was very painful. (But was there a novel in it somewhere?) She thought of Mum's phone calls and letters to her, asking after Clare, her careful recording of the address of the children's home, and her sending carefully wrapped presents 'from Granny with love'. Mum would have visited Clare herself, and must have wanted to, Helen now realised; but she could not leave Dad. Helen sighed again.

She went back to thinking about Clare, and the collapse of her hopes there. It was possible that Clare would have a change of mind or heart and find a way to be in touch. Helen would be watching her post and email. But she knew from the demeanour as well as the words of Diana Clegg that it was unlikely. Helen was used to picking herself up after losses, and was beginning to do so already about this severe one.

She thought of her mother's letter to her when she had heard about the cancer. Helen had written to tell her, and had let her know about the operation in prospect. Helen had never answered her mother's letter, and had not been in touch with her since. Marj and Harry had both rung to commiserate at first, which had not been welcome; and once, in the intervening months, Marj had rung to ask her how she was. Marj had said Mum wanted to know. Sitting on the train, staring out, longing for a cigarette, Helen was entering a state of mind that would lead to going to Sheffield to see her mother as soon as possible. It would be fitting to tell her face to face the good news about Clare.

When she got home she cried and had a drink and looked for the letter her mother had written when she heard the cancer news. At the time of receiving it, Helen had ridden roughshod over her response to Mum's careful, shaky handwriting. Now she let herself see it, and feel its meaning. Meg Gatehouse had written:

Dearest Hennie,

I was so sad to get your letter. I can't believe that you have got cancer. But they can do a lot for cancer these days. I hope you are in good hands. I will be thinking of you all the time. I do hope the operation is not too bad for you, my poor darling. You know Marj had an operation on her breast and she is quite all right now. We are all thinking of you. Make sure you let us know how you get on. Don't think of troubling yourself to come up until you are quite better. But when you are, I will love to see your bright face again. I would come down to look after you but I am very limited now.

Love,
Mum

Helen cried some more and had another drink. She did not ring Cecilia because there was too much to say for a phone call, and they would be seeing each other soon. She checked her emails to see if Clare had got in touch. She thought about the irony of having hoped for a glamorous relationship with a new daughter, and finding, instead, a drab relationship with an old mother.

∼

Ian found 'paternity tests' on Google, and sent off for one of the more expensive. Marina was still abroad. He had not told her he was going to do this. He had not told anyone. If the answer came back positive, or negative, or whatever would mean he was the father, he need not tell anyone. He would tell Marina what he had done when she got home, but only as a kind of joke, or a 'silly me' story. He looked forward to that moment.

He had rehearsed in his mind how he would feel if he was not Cephas's father. The unhappiness he foresaw, and the dilemmas he would confront, had made him wonder whether it was better not to know. Certain friends of his who had put themselves in harm's way never had HIV tests, which always astounded him. Now he felt he understood. Uncertainty was not pleasant, but better uncertainty than the feared truth. The intense relief – the reprieve – of a good result: was it better, on the emotional scale, than a bad result would be bad? The problem for Ian was that he could not stop himself from wondering. Once his paternity had got into his mind as a question, he had not been able to get rid of it. He could wake up cheerful in the morning and then he would remember. The thought dogged him, like a crime committed, or an intimation of cancer. He would never be carefree again until he knew. But if the knowledge went the wrong way, what would he do? At this point in the obsessional round his mind went back to the beginning. 'I needn't think about that because it won't happen.' And he would begin again.

So the 'paternity test' was the solution. Sometimes he cursed the fact that such a thing had ever been invented. If it had not, he would have had no alternative but to live with his unquiet mind, and his unquiet mind would presumably have healed itself with time. Or perhaps not. He might have been a person whose life was ruined. As he sent off for the kit, and waited for it to arrive in the post, he often thought about other men who might be availing themselves of this new facility, and how different most of their circumstances presumably were from his. Either they would be trying to disown the baby a woman was implicating them in, or retrospectively testing the fidelity of their partner. Ian did not want to disown the baby, the contrary was his only purpose; and whether Leda had or hadn't deceived him interested him not a jot.

There was an element of secrecy, of the surreptitious, that bothered Ian when he went round to Cecilia's with the kit in a small rucksack. Of course there was much in his life his mother did not know; indeed, he had not told her about Cephas's birth at the time it happened. But he was not aware of having actively planned to deceive her before. He had never had to. Now he would have to think of a ruse for being alone with Cephas that would not perplex her.

She was delighted to see him.

'So early! I was just going to push Cephas round the block to get him off to sleep,' she said. 'Now you can do that, and I'll make coffee.'

Fate had played into his hands. Cephas lay drowsily on his back under his blanket in the depths of the enormous pram. His hands were palm upwards by his ears. Ian and Cecilia looked at him.

'His arms are awfully short, aren't they?' whispered Ian. 'If I lay with my arms up beside my head my hands would be miles away.' He waved his arms to demonstrate.

'He's meant to be like that,' said Cecilia.

Off went Ian, pushing the pram. He came to a side road and went down it until he got to the porch of a building that did not seem to be frequented. He pushed the pram into the porch. No one was about. He quickly removed the rucksack from his back and took the test kit out. He had left within easy reach the four swabs which the instructions destined for Cephas's mouth, for this moment. Luckily Cephas found it amusing to have the swabs inserted into his open, smiling mouth, and speedily but gently rubbed against the inside of his cheeks. When all four were done, Ian put the equipment safely away, closed the kit box, put it back in the rucksack and replaced the rucksack on his back. It was as if nothing had happened.

Now Ian walked slowly to restore Cephas's sleepy mood, and by the time the big pram was in Cecilia's hall Cephas was asleep.

'Can you take the pram into the garden?' said Cecilia. 'It's better for him to sleep out of doors.'

'An old wives' tale if ever I heard one,' said Ian, taking the pram down the broad, shallow steps to the garden without too much jolting. 'You don't usually do this, do you, Mum?' Cecilia was following.

'I easily can, but Tim does sometimes. I'm just going to fix the cat net.'

This she did, and Thor leapt into his hammock.

'Is that OK?' asked Ian, looking at the cat swinging gently above the baby, purring at the sleeping face.

'Perfectly OK.'

Ian sent off the completed test kit when he got home.

Chapter 10

It was the first time Cecilia and Helen had had a conversation since Helen had been to see Diana.

'I knew you were going to do something like that,' said Cecilia. 'There's no stopping you.'

'There is, and your MMV did it, when she refused to give me contact details for my daughter. All I know about her is her first name.'

'Clare.'

'Yes. I gave her that name. Is that all I am to know of her?'

'Seems so. But that's all right. She has her parents. And she has every reason to be grateful to them.'

'You're so moral.'

'I can't help it.'

They laughed. Cecilia's annoyance with Helen had evaporated when she realised that she was accepting defeat, and was resilient about it.

'All I'm left with,' said Helen, 'is the hope that Clare will want to track me down.'

'You check your emails every few minutes.'

'I do.'

They could hear Cephas's and Eva's voices upstairs. Cephas had developed a liking for housework. But the conversational ease downstairs afforded by this would not go on indefinitely, and Cecilia's undivided attention was time-limited. Helen never thought of these constraints; Cecilia always did, and hoped Helen would be able to say enough of what she wanted to say before other needs prevailed. So Helen described the conversation with Diana. Cecilia learnt the details of how Diana had been unpersuadable. And then she heard how Diana took it for granted that Helen had passed on to her mother the news of Clare's happy fortunes, and that Helen had been seriously shocked with herself to realise she had never thought of doing so.

Then Helen was pensive, and said: 'I have understood something important. When Clare was little, I was jealous of her relationship with Mum. I didn't tell you this, when I told you what happened, but I always wanted to come first with Clare. Well, I always want to come first with everyone, don't I? I wanted Clare to adore me as her wonderful mother whatever dreadful things I did. I didn't realise that at the time, of course, because it was just how I was, how I am, my character. So I was utterly crushed when Clare turned out to love Mum more. All that's obvious' – Helen did not want to reminisce, even with Cecilia, about that dreadful night – 'but the interesting bit for now is that I have been trying to do it again. I wanted to be the preferred and glorious mother to Clare, now, effortlessly stealing her heart from the drab little adoptive mum. It's all about trumping and routing more deserving mums. That's not very good, is it?'

Cecilia went over to Helen and put her arms round her. 'You are such a good person,' she said.

'I was thinking just the opposite,' said Helen.

'No, you are. It's the way you face really difficult feelings. It's the way you can give up comfortable positions, just like that, see further, and sail into the unknown. My goodness.'

Morale rose for both of them, despite Helen's disappointment. Pleasure in understanding human nature was one of the things they had in common. Furthermore, Helen was delighted to be praised by Cecilia.

She went on: 'So now, the upshot of my visit to your dear bloody MMV isn't that I get a lovely brand-new daughter, in thrall to me, but that I traipse up to Sheffield to see Mum in her old folks' home.'

'Yes. But with exciting news for her.'

'There may be a novel in all this. *The Leaden Casket?*'

'There may well.'

'Shall I just write to Mum?'

'No. Go.'

~

The french doors to the garden were open. The herbaceous border was at its springtime best, and as Clare and Robert George looked out at it, they were both silent. They were silent because they were both thinking about Rita George. Each knew what the other was thinking. Clare voiced it.

'Mum would have loved to see this.'

Robert nodded.

'I'm so glad you've kept it lovely, Dad,' said Clare. 'Some people might have let it go. You haven't.'

'I've let the vegetables go,' said Dad.

'She did them,' said Clare. 'You never did.'

'Yes. I tried to keep them up, or at first I thought I would, but what's the point?'

'The strawberries have come back of their own accord,' said Clare. 'I had one.'

There was another silence. Perhaps Dad didn't feel like talking. But soon she said: 'I'm so glad Mum really liked David. And you do, too, don't you?'

'Yes, I do. We used to say we were glad you had met such a good man. We must talk about the wedding. There'll be a lot of arranging to do. The garden looks lovely in the autumn, if it's nice weather. And I must sort the house out, and the catering.'

'The house is fine. We don't need to do anything special to it.'

'You tell me what to do, darling, and I'll do it. If Mum was here, she'd have plenty of ideas. You'll have to be the boss.'

'Nearer the time.'

They were silent again, and then Clare said, 'I'm glad I decided against meeting my birth mother.'

'Ah,' said Dad. He was pleased, but did not want to make his daughter unfree.

'And there's something I want to talk to you about. David and I are thinking of moving down here. Then we'd be near you, and near Granny. She seems incredibly frail now.'

'She is. But you both work in London, how would you . . . ?'

'It takes us nearly as long to get to work in London in the traffic as it would to commute. David wants to be settled in the country before we have children. I agree. And this is the obvious place for us to move to. So . . .'

'It's a lovely idea, darling. But think carefully. Don't do it just for me. Or for Granny. I can look after Granny. And you can come down at weekends, as you do.'

'No, it's not just for you, it's better all round,' said Clare. 'Schools, and everything.' She knew her father was moved and happy at the idea, so she went on: 'We've looked at a few houses, and there's one we like, very near the sea, with a very unusual stained-glass front door, enough rooms, lots of light, and a huge wisteria all the way up the back. A south-facing garden. You must come and see it with me, but not today. Today we'll just have a cup of tea and sit in the garden.'

She entwined her fingers in her father's hand, and he accommodated them and put his other hand on hers. 'I love you very much, darling,' he said.

'Love you Daddy. Did you think any more about getting a dog?'

'But what would a dog do, all day, with me at work?'

'I know. That's the problem. Do you remember Renzo?'

'Of course I do. He was a dog and a half. I see him every day, when I look at the pictures of you, the ones on the piano. Yes. Do you remember the time he nearly drowned?'

'Yes. And the time he ate Mum's knitting, and she couldn't find it anywhere?'

'He was a puppy then.'

Clare had, or said she had, certain concerns about her car, and Robert examined the engine. He knew a lot about cars, and liked looking after them. Then he came out with a pail of warm water and carefully washed the windscreen.

'This time of year,' he said. 'Insects.' He finished the job with a chamois leather. 'Well,' he said, 'I can't see why there should be the funny noise, but get in, and drive me about a little, see if I hear it.'

So they did that. Then she made a meal from food that he had got in for them. In the evening, she drove home to Hackney.

As she left, she said, 'It's not really home, to me, this is.'

~

Cecilia was worried about Tim and sex. On her side, after all she had been through and the wound she was left with, she did not miss sex. Indeed, the thought of any penetration or touch in the affected area made her blood run cold. Her sexual life with Tim had always been very straightforward and unornamented, and she strongly suspected that Tim was not a dog to learn new tricks. Alternative intimacies would not have suggested themselves to his mind, and had not crossed Cecilia's lips. In their years together before cancer, Tim had never sought anything but a bit of foreplay followed by intercourse. Tim was a creature of habit, and Cecilia had followed his lead. They had settled for the brief, simple sex of people past youth whose working life meant more to each of them than the bedroom did, which is not to say that their relationship, nor their sexual life, were unimportant to either. They jogged along happily, taking each other for granted, and taking jolly, though not earth-moving sex for granted too, as a perhaps weekly event. Their marriage was the background to their separate lives, rather than what gave meaning to those lives.

Throughout her radiation treatment and afterwards, sex had been difficult, but at least at that time she still had an identifiable vagina. Then came the operation, and now her vagina seemed to have been subsumed into the wound. All this had been worrying at the time, and Tim had minded, though he was much too nice to say anything or to suggest, in any way, by word or omission of word, in a life and death situation for his wife, that sex was a priority for him. And it was not. But he did miss it. And Cecilia did worry.

But after the advent of Cephas, the worry receded. And this was not, as Cecilia knew, because the situation that aroused it was any less important in itself. But when she lay in the bath and peeled the onion of her worries, the most immediate, accessible skins belonged to herself and to Cephas. What would happen to Cephas if she died? Got ill? Was Ian, perhaps with Marina, ever going to reclaim Cephas? Was Tim as all right as he seemed to be about Cephas? Was the ache in her back a spread of the cancer, or ordinary wear and tear? Sex was one of the small inside bits of the onion now.

Of course Tim had not had her attention, either, any more than he had had sex. He did not mind this, because surrounded by his books, contributing still to learned journals, enthralled by his computer, and doing well at the tennis club, his life in retirement was full enough. In a way he thrived on the diminution of Cecilia's attention, because he need no longer feel guilty, or accused, when he neglected her. There was no longer the 'Couldn't we have a chat?' or the 'I haven't seen you all day', to tear him away from his many occupations. But Cecilia did not like to watch him becoming more and more self-sufficient; it was precisely this trait that, before Cephas, she had worked so hard to modify in him. She didn't like to see herself capitalising on it now.

In time gone by, if she had not been available for Fez, Tim would have cheerfully gone alone. Cecilia had worked hard to create a climate in which projects lost their appeal if she was not part of them. Now, perforce, she was welcoming the putting back of the clock.

But Cephas liked Tim. He held out his arms and laughed when Tim, passing, gave him a benign, abstracted smile. And then Tim would stop in his tracks and smile again, this time his face full of engagement. Even he, teeming with preoccupations from his desk, could not ignore or resist. Cephas would wave his fists. Tim would say 'Hullo'. Cecilia loved to watch this. Tim had even changed a nappy once, not with the sort of success to encourage much repetition; but they had all found it very amusing.

Cecilia slept in what had been the marital bedroom. Tim now slept next door. The shared bedroom had been a casualty of cancer. Cecilia had been up and down in those nights and had wanted to be left to herself. Cephas's carrycot was still in her bedroom, but he was almost too big for it now, and there was a plan to put him in a cot. Cecilia was postponing enacting this plan, because she did not want to speak to Tim about putting the cot in her bedroom, a further stage in the permanence of Cephas; and yet she was not sure she wanted Cephas to sleep in the small room, which was up a few stairs, where Cephas might feel isolated.

Tim sometimes came into Cecilia's bedroom in the morning with cups of tea for both, and slipped into his old place beside her. On one of these occasions, with Cephas fast asleep, he touched her lovingly, then desirously.

She whispered, 'It's lovely of you to want me when there's so much wrong with me.'

Holding her breast, breathing hard, he said: 'There's too much that's right.'

Cecilia was greatly touched by this exchange, and repeated it to herself several times on that day and successive days. It reminded her to think about how to have sex, but she had not yet got a plan.

～

Marina was still away when Ian received the envelope that obviously contained the results of the paternity test. He had decided not to pay the extra for the expedited service, partly to postpone knowing; partly in case things done quickly were done less thoroughly. He had not mentioned his venture to Marina, in the emails, texts and crackling phone calls that more and more seemed to be necessary to both of them when they were apart.

He put the envelope on his desk and went to make some coffee. He felt waves of anxiety pour through his body. Sweat broke out. His heart laboured. His guts writhed. He was used to being in situations most people would find fearsome, and often enough he found them so; but in those circumstances he never felt like this. This was not fear, he thought; this was dread. He was not used to this horrible loneliness; normally, when the adrenalin raced unpleasantly, he was part of a belea-guered camaraderie. His hand shook as he poured himself a cup of coffee. He sipped it in the kitchen, looking out of the window at the trees and at the windows of the flats opposite, seeing neither. He was in no hurry, it seemed, for the moment of truth.

He tried to reason with himself. Why was he frightened? Of course Cephas was his son. All probability, including Cephas's increasing crop of brown curly hair, pointed to it. Why had he doubted? That was the mystery. Why had uncer-tainty clutched his heart, and then pressed him into action?

He had a momentary sense that Marina was a bird of ill omen; would he have thought of a paternity test if she had not uttered those two terrible words? To defend her, he decided he would indeed have come to it himself in the end. But he was not sure.

He ran through the worst case, his mouth dry in spite of the coffee. It was a horrible thought that he would have to tell Cecilia. Cephas, presumably, would be given up for adoption. Cecilia would feel betrayed. She had accepted and loved Cephas as a grandson, and for love of Ian. She would lose Cephas, and whatever dream he meant to her. Ian would have to tell Marina, and give up the pleasure of seeing her doting on his son because he was his son. And the third element was this: without knowing that it was happening, he had learnt to rejoice in being a father. At the very first he had been consumed by annoyance, fear and regret; but once Cecilia had played her part and things had settled, he had begun to feel almost omnipotent about having so casually, so unintentionally, fathered a little creature everyone thought was wonderful. He soared. He felt a man, as never before. The women admired him and the men, perhaps, envied him. He enjoyed both those ideas. It would be a sad climbdown indeed if he were not the father; and, of course, if he had been too stupid to know that he wasn't. That was another problem. He had spread the story of his reluctant paternity far and wide among his friends and colleagues, of course as a story against himself; could they exchange the new news without a smirk?

Suddenly he could not endure the loneliness, ran to his desk, and rattled an email to Marina:

I have done the paternity test and am about to open the result. Feeling tense. Please ring when you can.

Then he picked up the envelope and tore it open. He was used to mastering information immediately and accurately. It was 99.9 per cent certain that he was not Cephas's father.

Chapter 11

It was on the day after the slightly tedious and, to her mind, long-drawn-out excitement of Cephas sitting unaided for the first time, that Helen took the train to see her mother in Sheffield. She had written her a letter that would arrive on the chosen day itself, to advertise her coming, and had telephoned the care home. These precautions were all she could do to forfend against coinciding with Marj or Harry. She did not want them to know she was planning a visit, or they would be sure to pop in to view her out of curiosity, or so she supposed; and she would have to be a more frequent visitor if they were to regard a visit scheduled by her as a reprieve to them, as they did with each other. Cannily, she chose a time in the middle of a weekday, before either of them would be likely to have finished work.

She expected her mother to be in the day room, but actually she was among a few who had been pushed in wheelchairs into the garden, where they were lined up on a patio in the shade. They were supposed to look at the trees and sky, and widen their horizons thereby, but there was nothing in their eyes to support the idea that they were so doing. Helen picked up a chair as she passed through the day room, but looking through the open french doors she was not sure that she could identify her mother from the back. Three little grey heads and a bald one. That narrowed it down. She walked round to the front of the row, dangling her hard chair, and recognised her mother.

Meg Gatehouse looked older and more vague than when Helen had last seen her, which was inexcusably long ago. Someone had fluffed up her hair in an unbecoming and unfamiliar white coif, presumably as a tribute to the visit of the daughter from London. Her head was bent forward as if half dozing, and her little hands were folded on the blanket on her lap. She did not see Helen as soon as Helen saw her.

Helen put the chair beside the wheelchair, sat down, and said, 'Mum.'

Meg came to, and focussed, and a beautiful smile, warm and intelligent, began to spread across her face. When it had reached its fullest extent she unclasped her hands and stretched one out to Helen. 'Hennie,' she said.

Tears began to course down Helen's face, but her mother's eyesight was not up to that sort of detail. Meg went on: 'How kind of you to come. I hope you are quite better now. I was so sorry you were ill.'

'Getting better,' said Helen, not wanting to disclaim incapacity completely while it could serve as a reason for absence. 'I am so happy to see you.' Then she added, insincerely, 'You look very well.'

'I can't complain,' said this woman who never had complained. 'They look after us very well here. Teresa. Gemma. They are all very nice. Perhaps one of them will bring you a cup of tea after your long journey.'

'I don't need tea,' said Helen. 'I've come now for two reasons. One is because I haven't seen you for so long, because of the cancer' – the word evoked the expression and nod of concerned acquiescence, as well as complete forgiveness, that Helen had hoped for – 'and to say I intend to visit you regularly from now on.' She had not planned to say this last, but it was done now. 'Monthly. The other reason is that I've got something important to tell you.'

It came into Meg's mind that Helen might be going to get married, which is what she had always hoped for. She knew exactly who Helen was, but it was more difficult to bear in mind that Helen was sixty-five now. She waited quietly.

Helen rattled in her handbag for her sunglasses and a tissue. The tears were still dripping down. 'Do you remember Clare?'

'Yes.' Meg's hand tightened on Helen's. Was she to be told of an accident? A death?

'Don't worry, it's good news. I put Clare up for adoption, and after that we did not know what had happened to her.'

'I know. But you never do. You only know they have been adopted.'

Or not, thought Helen, glad that her mother had never entertained that possibility. 'Yes. But recently I have found out that she was adopted by a wonderful couple and was loved and was happily brought up. Now she is thirty-two and has a good job and is getting married in the autumn to a nice bloke.'

'That is wonderful news, wonderful news,' Meg kept on murmuring, while Helen restated what she had already said in a variety of ways, letting it sink in, trying not to be hyperbolic, trying to say only what she knew as fact. Then Meg entered a different and busier emotional register: 'You must buy her something from me for a wedding present.' She looked at her handbag, which had come out to the patio with her.

'That's a lovely idea. But actually we don't know her. We only know about her. I have news of her, you see, but she doesn't want to meet me. That is all right.'

'Is it all right? I would have thought you might want . . .'

'I did, you are quite right. But it's for her to make the decision and she has decided against. But that's all right.'

Meg was looking back into the past. There was a silence.

Then Meg dragged her mind into the present and looked at Helen, with a smile. 'Well, darling, we must be very grateful.'

'Indeed.'

'And do you know what her job is?'

'Yes, she is an accountant.'

'A proper profession!' said Meg, thrilled

'A proper profession.'

'And you are a novelist, darling,' said Meg, not wanting to appear to take Helen's achievements more lightly than Clare's. 'That's very nice.'

'There's one other thing we know,' said Helen, 'and that's the birthmark on her forehead has been removed.'

'Birthmark,' Meg repeated reflectively in an undertone. What was a birthmark? A bathmat had come into her mind, but she knew it was wrong and tried to bat it away.

'Yes, that huge red birthmark on her forehead, when she was little, when we had her. Surely you remember.'

'Ah yes. It didn't matter. She was very pretty. But I'm glad it was removed. It didn't matter then, but for a young girl – well, you don't want it for a pretty young girl.'

Now Tony awoke, in the wheelchair next to Meg. He woke with a roar, which startled Helen, but no one else. Then he bellowed, 'Where are my teeth?'

'You've got them in, Tony,' shouted Meg, reassuringly.

'Mum, do you mind being here?' asked Helen.

'No, I'm very lucky. I'm glad your dad didn't have to come in here, though. It would never have suited him.'

'No.'

It had flashed into Helen's mind to offer to have Mum in her house in London, but she rejected the thought at once. She knew herself better, now. It would be just like keeping baby Clare: pleasant at first, and soon intolerable. Even in the interests of stealing the moral high ground from Marj and Harry, it must not be considered.

'Marj and Harry are near, and they are very good,' said Meg, as if telepathic. 'They try to visit me most days, one or the other. Then the grandchildren look in, when they can.'

Helen could see that her mother was gearing up to enunciate the names of her six grandchildren, counting them off on fingers, and she wanted to be spared that. 'Do you still do the crossword?' she asked. 'I've brought the newspaper.'

The crossword kept them occupied for a while. Helen was impressed by how smart her mother was at it. But time was hanging heavy by now for Helen. She was stealing glances at her watch, and longing to be on the train home.

'I brought you a book, Mum,' Helen then said. She had thought of flowers, or flowers too, but there would have been the problem of a vase, and, particularly being out of doors, she was glad she hadn't. 'You know you and Dad used to take us to castles? Well, I got this book for you, you might like to look at it.'

It was a big book called *Castles of the British Isles*, full of nice photographs. Helen tried to install it on her mother's lap, but it had no firm anchorage there. So Helen opened it at random, to see if her mother liked the idea of it, and held it open.

'Warwick Castle,' Helen read, but she was losing what little hope she had had for the book.

'I'd need my glasses,' said Meg, groping.

Helen put the book on the floor and said, 'Later, perhaps. I'm coming again in a month, Mum.'

'That's lovely. It's a pity you haven't seen Marj or Harry.'

'Yes, it is. Another time. Please tell them I came.'

Helen knelt on the patio and put her arms round her mother's bony shoulders. She gave her a careful, close, quite long hug, loving her more than she had since she was a child, and said: 'I'm off now. See you next month.' She wanted to say more, but she did not know how to put it, and that was enough for the time being.

So back to London. It was still a fine and sunny day, and Helen's spirits were sober, but good. She had not suffered consciously down the years from ignoring and discounting her mother, but now she felt her negligence might have been injurious to herself, unbeknown, rather as an unregarded hole below the waterline of a boat steadily chips water and causes unexplained malfunctions. Now she was on terms with her mother again, for the first time, really, for decades; and she was committed to that monthly visit, presumably for the rest of her mother's life, or her own, if the latter were to be the shorter. She would have to get used to mixing, a bit, with Marj and Harry. If Marj had had a breast operation, a fact that Helen had known but quite forgotten, and then reforgotten after her mother's letter, she and Marj might forge a rather dreary but viable cancer link. The feeling that was deepest, and which was offering Helen's restless heart an unfamiliar sense of peace, as she sat on the train, was gratitude to her mother, and love for her, and, yes, she could bear to feel even this now, admiration.

~

Ian had two phone conversations with Marina, but they were unsatisfactory. In the first, he was not sure that she registered the terrible news. She was distracted, and he could hear the kind of background noises that might well distract, although it was she who had rung him, which was their arrangement when one of them was working.

'Don't worry about it,' she kept on saying.

The second conversation was not much better. The essence clearly was that she could not bear him to be worried sick and her out of reach. And it was not fair to do this to her. He knew that on this tour she had seen Ali, an interpreter they both knew, killed by shrapnel.

Then Ian got an email from her:

135

I am certain sure, 100 not 99.9 per cent sure, that Cephas is yours. He is just like you. He reminds me of you all the time. It couldn't be coincidence. Everyone notices. These tests are probably scams. They are very new, you know. They won't have got the technology right yet. If it's possible they ever could. I bet you paid a fortune. It's probably just a racket. Somebody thought it up to make money – and it works, at least it has on you! Here everything is mayhem. I'm home on Tuesday, early pm. Don't worry. Love and a big hug. XXX

Initially there was a thrill of joy and relief for Ian in this note of airy cynicism. But then he knew it would not do. The second feeling was of increased loneliness, because Marina was not sharing, and hence not comforting, the anxiety and desolation into which he had plunged. The third feeling was of misery, because she obviously minded the changed state of affairs too much to believe it. Ian actually cried. The night was sleepless and the morning tormented. Then he pulled himself together and went to Cecilia's.

Cephas was at the kitchen table in a high chair having lunch. Cecilia was spooning him something out of a small tin. Every time his mouth opened, her mouth opened too. She had taken two seconds off to answer the door, leaving Ian to close it behind him, and gone straight back to spoon and tin. Everything seemed so normal in the kitchen, the sun coming in at the big window, the roses at the bottom of the garden, and Ian sat down and looked round, with a sense of leave-taking, like someone in a condemned cell. He wanted to avoid Tim at this point, if he could.

'Tim?' he said.

'British Library.'

Cephas spat out a mouthful of food. 'He's had enough,' said Cecilia.

She wiped his mouth with a flannel she had handy and then

wiped the tray of his high chair. She put a drinking beaker with a little spout within his reach. He brandished it, babbling loudly, and banging it on the tray. Cecilia took his bib off, that he might appear to better advantage to his father, who hated mess. He would also, she thought, hate the loud noise of the cup being banged on the tray, but that could not be helped.

Then Cecilia was able to look properly at Ian, with a welcoming smile, which stiffened and died as she saw from his face that something was wrong, indeed, very wrong. Her first idea was that Marina had left him. Then that he had leukaemia. Then that he'd lost his job.

'Ian,' she said.

'I've got something to tell you,' said Ian. 'Something that changes everything.'

Cecilia sat quiet, intent, and her hand came over her mouth.

'I am not Cephas's father.'

Whatever was going to happen in Cecilia's mind later, it was evident what her immediate and deepest response was. Her face became white. She stood up and went over to where Ian was sitting and put her hand on his shoulder, slightly gripping it. She said in a whisper: 'Don't tell anyone. They might try to take him away from us.'

Ian met her eye for the first time and stared. They stared into each other's faces.

Finally Ian spoke. 'Do you mean we are going to keep him on?'

Cecilia said nothing for the moment but sat down again. The banging of the drinking cup was reaching a crescendo. Cephas had discovered that the faster you did it, the more continuous the noise, and was capitalising on his finding. Little cries of triumph were now being added to the din.

Ian had never expected this response from Cecilia. What had he expected? He hardly knew. Tears; resolve; relinquishment of Cephas for adoption. That was the area he had assumed they would at this moment be in. But if Cephas was kept, whose project could he possibly be? Tim and Cecilia had had no intention, not the faintest thought, of taking on a baby in their retirement. There was no such twinkle in their eye. They wouldn't even, legally, have been allowed to, on grounds of age, let alone cancer. Ian himself had the wrong lifestyle for a baby; that had been plain from the first, even when he took for granted that the creature on the doorstep was his responsibility. If only, if only, thought Ian, he had taken that carrycot directly into care, and Cecilia had never known of its existence. Now he had something else to curse his stupidity for. Was it possible that he had landed his mother and stepfather with looking after a child into their late eighties which had nothing whatever to do with them?

'Mum,' he said, 'there's nothing for it. We're going to have to have Cephas adopted. Better late than never. Can't you stop him making that awful noise?'

Cecilia said nothing, but sat down again. 'We have to think,' she said.

'How can we, with that bloody noise?'

'Ignore it. Don't hear it. We have to see what's possible and what's impossible. Something impossible is that Cephas should go to strangers. Strangers to him. So, working within that, what is possible?'

'In that case, only that you keep him on. And you can't. Why would you? He's got as much to do with you as a baby you pass in the street.'

Cecilia's thoughts turned to Tim, and Ian could see from her face that they had. It was a moment he had anticipated and dreaded. Her face had an expression, not of indecision, but of someone beginning to plan a strategy. As she considered, she got up and went out into the hall, coming back with the pram. While she and Ian talked, she picked up Cephas, put him on the floor, changed his nappy, picked him up again and put him in the pram, which she began to push to and fro. She did these things, including making responses and asides to Cephas, without knowing she was doing them. Her mind was entirely engaged in the conversation with Ian.

'You'll never square this with Tim,' Ian was saying. 'And what will he think of me? The best thing is to have Cephas adopted. We should have done that in the first place.'

'Perhaps,' said Cecilia. 'But we didn't. We didn't, and we can't now.'

'Well? What can we do?'

Now he thought about it, he was impressed that Cecilia had not asked him how he knew that he was not Cephas's father. Most people would have demanded chapter and verse, finding out about the email from Leda, the paternity test, its result. He would have had to tolerate their astonishment, their gradual understanding, and certainly their views. Cecilia subjected him to none of this. He was grateful for her trust in him as a purveyor of facts.

But as Cecilia began to recover, and blood started to resume its ordinary routes through her brain, she did become curious. But that could wait. Ian was on a short fuse already, and this was no moment to look for anything other than headlines from him. She knew him well enough to be sure that his facts were well researched and proven, though she had no idea what they were.

'We need to work out why this should make a difference,' said Cecilia. 'Cephas is a child even if he is not your child.'

Her voice quivered. She was torn between her love for Cephas, who was at this moment trying to get her glasses off and beaming with mischief, and recognition that she had said goodbye to her quiet life of convalescence and retirement, which she had been enjoying and had deserved, to devote herself to a baby which had no claim on her. This was not a thought she wanted. Regret for those now impossible years of peace, nostalgia for what might have been if Cephas had not turned up, would be ably and vociferously represented on her behalf by Ian, by Tim probably, and by everyone in the world. Her own yearnings in that direction must be her secret.

She cleared her throat and went on: 'Whoever the father, whoever the mother, Cephas was a baby who needed a home. We have given him a home. This is his home. He is a person.' She stopped, and went on thinking. 'OK, so he isn't your son and he isn't my grandson. But he is exactly the person we have thought him to be, all along.'

'No, the whole point is, he isn't,' groaned Ian. 'He precisely isn't who we have thought him to be. That is exactly what he is not, and that is exactly the point.'

Silence again.

'Shall I push that bloody pram?' said Ian, starting up.

'No, it's OK.' Cecilia looked into the pram. 'He's nearly asleep.'

She adjusted the cat net. Thor materialised from somewhere and bounded on to it, thundering a purr. Cecilia pushed the pram to the other end of the kitchen, so that Ian should be troubled as little as possible by the mutual greetings of the small fry.

'If you had not thought he was mine, and your grandson,' said Ian, 'you would never have bonded with him.'

'Of course not. But I did, and I did, and he did, and that's where we are.' Then she said, 'Is Marina around?'

'Home tomorrow.'

Cecilia got up and went over to peer into the pram, where she could see, beyond and between Thor's black ears, the angelically sleeping face of the author of this anguish and soul-searching.

'Mum,' said Ian, 'sorry, but I don't want to meet Tim for the moment. I'll go now and leave you to break the news to him. Obviously I'll see you very soon. Phone me. I'll phone you. I'm away from Thursday. I'm going now.'

Cecilia was left to her reflections. She had been sad not to get a hug, but she realised Ian was at the end of his tether. She was still standing, and went back to look in the pram, to test her emotions, now she was on her own. Looking at Cephas's face, she could tell she had remained utterly loyal to him. But the word loyalty would not until now have found a place in her vocabulary about her feelings for him. Now the word loyalty came to mind. It would be over her dead body that Cephas would be banished from her house; but muscles of fidelity, foreign to her familiar, unambiguous love for him, were now exercising themselves. Did she feel differently towards him, now she knew he was not Ian's son and not her grandson? Yes, she found, there was a shift. He was still the baby she knew and loved, and had reared from two to seven months, a long time in a baby's life, a long time in her own. Yet there was a certain halo of meaning that he had lost. She would have to love him exactly as much as ever without that rich and golden halo of meaning to rejoice her heart. Perhaps, she thought, it was like the shift between being in love with someone and subsequently learning to love them. To cheer herself up, she tried to think of it as emotional progress rather than emotional impoverishment for her, but, whatever it was, she was not going to let him be taken to strangers.

What she had first said to Ian, 'Don't tell anybody, or they may try to take him away from us,' remained. That first response had, as one of its meanings, 'Let's go on as if we don't know this.'

But they could not go on as if they didn't know. People were going to be told. And then what? Cecilia would tell Tim, Ian would tell Marina. That would be the start of it. Suppose Ian were to decide to wash his hands of Cephas. In that case, even financially she and Tim would be in trouble. And what if she died? Tim would then indeed be in trouble, or Cephas would, in Tim's hands. Might Ian be so base as to say to her: 'Have him adopted, I am going to do nothing further for him'; and then, when help with him was needed by the old couple, might he be so base as to refuse it, on the grounds that the path of adoption had offered a perfectly good way forward, which they had refused to take? More likely, Ian would continue to fund Cephas, but more and more grudgingly, as the expenses mounted and perhaps as other dependants appeared in Ian's own life. And as for emotional support from Ian, that might be withdrawn altogether. Blame might take its place. All along, Ian had done what he had done for Cephas out of obligation and duty. Cephas had not won Ian's heart. Any corner of it that had warmed to Cephas in the past five months would chill to zero now. Cecilia faced the fact that for all Cephas's charm there was only one person in the world who loved him.

Ian would be within his legal rights to put Cephas into care now, tomorrow. Ian had registered the baby under his own surname and could do with Cephas what he judged best. Legally Ian was in charge. But surely he could not find it in his heart to do anything so terrible! Or could he, in order to avoid the future Cecilia had been imagining, which he might be imagining too? He might think it was kinder to Cecilia to take any choice out of her power. But Social Services and child protection would not be as heartless, as mechanical, as that would come to. They would listen to the grandmother, who had been the carer for five months. So Cecilia comforted herself, in these imaginary scenarios.

Now she heard Tim's key in the door. When she saw his big, familiar form in the kitchen doorway she began to cry, still standing by the pram. It was a familiar sight that met Tim's eyes, Thor on the cat net, Cecilia near the pram; but why the tears? He came over and put his arm round her. 'What?' he said.

'It's turned out,' said Cecilia, 'that Ian isn't Cephas's father.'

Tim's first feeling was of relief. His family was unburdened of a grave responsibility. Then he realised that it was not going to be as simple as that. 'Well,' he said. 'This is a surprise.' Then, after a moment's thought, he said, 'Why, has the real father turned up?'

'No, I'm sure it isn't that,' said Cecilia, who had not thought of this. Were it so, surely Ian would have said.

'Then how does Ian know?'

'I don't know, we can find out, but for the moment, I'm sure he does know. I'm sure it's true.'

'A bit of clarity would help. A bit of lunch would help.'

'We can heat up the rest of the food Eva made yesterday. I won't have any.'

'Oh yes you will.'

Tim heated the food in the microwave and put it on two plates. They sat at the table.

'I meant to have some salad with this,' said Cecilia.

'Too bad. What does Ian want to do?'

'I think he wants to put Cephas into care, to be adopted.'

'It's too late for that, now.'

'I know.' This response of Tim's heartened Cecilia enormously. 'I know. Of course it is.'

'That should have been done a long time ago, if it was going to be done.'

'I know. So what can we do?'

'Well,' said Tim, 'is Ian prepared to pay maintenance?'

'Probably he'll feel he must.'

'I think he should. And I think he'll have to keep parental responsibility. It's only a nominal thing. We would be too old for that, I think. We need to go into all this.'

Cecilia was ecstatic that Tim did not think of getting rid of Cephas. She put her hand on his arm. 'You are such a wonderful person,' she said. She kissed his sleeve.

'Not really.' He ate steadily, enjoying his food, his eye straying to the *Guardian*, which lay on the kitchen table. 'You do all the work, after all. The future is a bit of a worry, but we'll only have to live into our nineties, and we'll be fine.' He was not really cheerful about what had happened, but he saw it as no worse than what he had learnt to live with and come to expect. 'Don't be upset, it'll be all right. Anyway, we are used to Cephas now, and Thor would miss him.'

Cecilia was thinking no husband but Tim would be this wonderful. Tears were creeping down her face into her goulash, tears of relief. She was thinking about Tim. She was realising that the matter of Cephas's paternity meant much less to him than it did to her, albeit he loved Cephas as an external person much less than she did, if, indeed, he loved Cephas at all. A blood tie between Tim and Cephas had never existed, even as an illusion. The fascination of Cephas being Ian's son had not been a fascination for Tim. In any case, the matter of blood ties probably did not mean much to Tim, or at some time in his life he would have wanted a child. Cecilia understood that Tim remained more or less where he had been before this bombshell, dutiful, reluctant and resigned; forced by very odd circumstances to take on a child who otherwise would have had no appropriate provision.

Lunch came to a quick end, and Cephas woke up. Tim disappeared to his study. Cecilia went about the usual routine of putting Cephas on a rug in the garden, near where she could sit on a deckchair. He was grumpy after his sleep, but soon recovered, and sat straight-backed on his rug, putting one brick on top of another, and then trying a third, his chin wet with the dribble of concentration. Cecilia watched him, her unhealed wound smarting against the deckchair. She was glad Helen would soon breeze in. Freed by Tim from the intolerable anxiety of Cephas being torn from her, she was able to foresee the everyday reality of how difficult things were going to be. Scenes passed through her mind, in sombre guise: birthday parties, cake and candles; waiting among the other mothers in the school playground, she the antique; childhood illnesses, with their high temperatures and frightening coughing fits; child-friendly holidays. She received a brick from Cephas's hand, and, giving a whoop of delighted surprise, handed it back to him, with deliberate and stylised action. This game could go on for ever. Her most important task was to stay alive.

~

Ian met Marina at Heathrow. They were intensely happy to see each other, Marina as ever, Ian with a rush of joy he had not known before. They hugged. She smelt of aeroplane, and he breathed it in gratefully. He took her bag.

'You're being very nice to me these days,' she said. 'You took me to Heathrow and you are collecting me. Is this telling us something?'

'It certainly is,' he said. 'Quite what, I don't yet know. Do you?'

'Not yet.' They were both smiling uncontrollably.

In the car they talked about her trip. It had been a difficult one. She needed to talk about Ali's death. 'I held his hand. You remember him, don't you? The one with the flamboyant moustache.'

'Yes, of course I know Ali.'

'Ian, he called for his mum. I didn't know what to do. I said, "Ali, she would be here if she could." Then he died. We were all crying. This has decided me to give up the job. Not out of fear for myself. But in honour of Ali.'

'Why does that follow?'

'Don't make me explain. I haven't told you this before, because I thought you'd be upset, but I'm taking a home job. It's all happened very quickly, and I've been very lucky.'

There was a lot for Ian to learn, and he managed to stay with it until the environs of Hammersmith. There she picked up from his demeanour that he too needed to be heard. She stopped talking and said, 'I'm sorry, I know you've got news too.'

'Yes. I'm sorry. It must seem much less important.'

'All of it's important.'

'It was sweet of you to try to disbelieve the paternity test. But one can't, really. I'm sure you don't, really. So I've told Cecilia. She seems to want to keep Cephas. I don't know what will happen. The whole thing is a nightmare. And I leave for Syria tomorrow.'

'But how does the Leda side of things explain itself?'

'She must have already been pregnant by someone unknown – first stages of pregnancy – at the time of my godforsaken flingette.'

'You don't know who that someone unknown might possibly be? Legally they should pay maintenance.'

'No idea. I know nothing about her life. Absolutely nothing.'

'Now I'm home I can think about this properly,' said Marina. 'You know how one can't concentrate on home things while one's working. I've been thinking a bit, on the plane, but then Ali kept coming back into my mind. I had a little sleep, and dreamt Ali was Cephas, and he was dying.'

They arrived at Ian's flat, and he parked, and they walked to their restaurant. Ian was extraordinarily happy to be with Marina, in spite of the various distresses both were going through. They sat down at their usual table. The waiter greeted them as a couple, and this pleased them both. They chose their food.

'I love you,' said Ian. 'Have I ever said that before?'

'No. Not as such.'

'Well, I should have. It's been true, oh, probably for years. I'm just no good at thinking about these things.'

There was a short pause, then Marina said very seriously, 'And I love you.'

'Thank goodness for that,' said Ian. 'I don't see why you should.'

They held hands across the table. The wine came, and they touched glasses, and drank to themselves and to each other.

Ali was not forgotten, and neither was Cephas, nor Cecilia's bizarre predicament; but they talked about themselves, reminiscing about their relationship, about when she had known she loved him, about why he had stupidly ignored his love for her, and how selfishly he had fed upon her love and taken it for granted. There was much to say, and much to celebrate, and, in Ian's case, much he wanted to repent.

'As you won't be abroad,' he said, 'you'll always be in London when I get home. That's wonderful.'

At the end of the meal, Ian said, 'My place, because it's so near?'

'Right.'

'Let's live together. Will you?'

'Yes.'

Chapter 12

Cecilia had an appointment at the hospital. It was not one of Eva's times. She did not want to bother Tim, partly because she did not trust his competence, partly because, as he was so wonderful, he should not be asked for versions of the wonderful that were beyond him, or would tax him. It was the first time the need of a babysitter had arisen. Friends were working, except for Helen, who would be hopeless. Cecilia phoned Marina. Although Cecilia had been constrained by recent events to give up her precious hope of Cephas having a future with his father and Marina, she still liked the idea of Marina and Cephas being friends.

'Marina, it's Cecilia.'

'Oh. Hullo.'

'I'm just wondering if you could babysit this afternoon for a couple of hours while I'm at the hospital.'

'This afternoon. Yes, of course. It will be a pleasure. What time . . .?' Her voice sounded delighted.

'Come at two, and stay on afterwards – to supper if you can.'

'I'm seeing my parents tonight, so I'd have to go by, say, six.'

'Come to lunch, then, before I have to leave. Come at one.'

'Lovely, I'll look forward to it. I hope Cephas will be OK with me. Will Tim be in, if things get complicated?'

'Tennis, I think. They won't get complicated. I hope they won't. See you then.'

Sweet that Marina supposed Tim would be any good if Cephas got complicated. Cecilia made sure there was a tin of his favourite baby food in case Cephas wanted his tea before she got back. That shouldn't happen, but you could never tell with hospital appointments. With any luck a nappy change wouldn't be needed in the time. She would leave a drink ready in his beaker. He should wear a hat if he was going in the garden – it was summer now. Cecilia thought of and arranged all these things. Sometimes he didn't have an afternoon nap these days, but, if he did, the pram was there, and no doubt Thor would be there too.

It was going to be just Cecilia and Marina, for Tim had already gone to tennis. Cephas was asleep in the garden in his pram. Cecilia had laid the kitchen table for two and put out salad, olives, houmus, French bread. She was hoping Cephas would wake up before she had to leave for her appointment, so that she could deal with the post-nap grumpiness, before handing over to Marina.

Marina arrived, with tulips. 'Thank you, you shouldn't have!' Vase, brisk arrangement, position at the centre of the kitchen table. 'How lovely they look.'

'How lovely the food looks.'

Cecilia did not say, though she thought it, how lovely Marina looked. Cecilia had never seen her so beautiful. She also looked younger, and happier – more at peace. Perhaps something was going well between her and Ian. Cecilia remembered the lift to Heathrow. Then her mind misgave her, and she feared Marina had got fed up with his dithering, and moved on to happier times with someone else.

'Can I tell you about something that happened while I was away?' said Marina.

She told Cecilia about the death from shrapnel of Ali, that he had held her hand as he died and, though it made her cry to recount it, that he had called for his mother. Then she talked

149

about her previous acquaintance with Ali, which, though slight, had been significant, for interpreters are important. She talked about his cheerfulness and helpfulness, and the fact that he had two children. She talked about his moustache, his laugh, his cigarettes. She wished she had been able to visit his bereaved wife, but there was no way. Cecilia listened with the greatest attention and asked no questions, knowing that the story would unfold better without. Then Marina told Cecilia she was quitting her job. She told Cecilia about the new job, which would not require travel.

'I seem to be telling you everything,' said Marina. 'That must be because you are a psychotherapist. You must have been a very good one.'

She is not telling me everything, thought Cecilia, while she made appropriate responses. She is not telling me anything about Ian, or about love. At that moment Cephas's voice could be heard from the garden, and Cecilia went to bring him in.

'I haven't brought the pram,' she said, reappearing with him in her arms, 'but you can put it where you like. It goes up and down the steps quite easily.' Cephas was complaining, and Cecilia reached for his drink. Luckily she did not have to leave for the hospital straight away. He had time to get over this mood.

Cecilia was impressed that Marina did not approach him at this time. 'I'm keeping my head down till the sun comes out again on his face,' Marina said, in mock fear of Cephas.

But one of the satisfactory things about Cephas was that he was never crotchety for long. After five minutes he was usually all smiles again. Cecilia sat down at the table with him on her lap. Picking up and brandishing a fork was sufficient to restore his spirits, and soon he was interested enough in Marina to let her substitute a spoon for the fork, and to pass the spoon ceremoniously to and fro with her.

'To tell you something else,' said Marina, 'I so, so, so want a baby.'

'Do you?'

'Yes. And since I've known Cephas – well. Spoon! Spoon! Thank you. Or do we say ta? No, not in the salt, let's move the nasty salt. I never really knew a baby before. I'm thirty-five, nearly thirty-six, and the biological clock ticks away. That's a huge reason why I've left the job, actually, because I can't have a baby if I'm on the hoof all the time.'

Cecilia didn't know whether to say, 'And Ian?' or not. The hesitation was obvious on her face.

'I know what you're thinking,' said Marina, with a grin. 'We'll see.'

Cecilia felt entitled to give her a big hug before she left. Instructions had been given, and Marina had produced from her bag a wooden toy, obviously carefully chosen and held in reserve for this critical moment, involving putting shapes through shaped holes, which was making Cephas pant with excitement.

〜

Cecilia and Helen met often enough for Helen's visit to her mother, and the paternity of Cephas, to have been imparted and discussed and returned to. So the next time Helen dropped in, the first news was Cecilia's visit to the hospital.

'A terribly nice man,' she said. 'He looked at the wound very carefully with a speculum. It didn't hurt at all. Then he said: "Can you see the television screen?" I could, twisting my neck. "What do you see?" he said. "A red, shining circle," I said. "Your cervix," quoth he, "just where I wanted it to be." So the upshot is that the wound is healed. It hurts, because the tissues are all stiff and leathery – not his words – from the radiotherapy. But it's healed, and it's not that I haven't got a vagina, but that the wound has subsumed the vagina and is the vagina, a big, gaping vagina, but all clean and healed up. Of course the anatomy is quite different now, as he didn't scruple to point

151

out. I asked about sex. He said something could probably be managed and it would not do the wound – I must stop calling it the wound, but what can I call it? – any harm, but, in his words, it would feel very different to my husband.'

Helen had always wanted to know about Cecilia and Tim in bed, but she had not asked, for she had no language but ribaldry for sex, and that did not seem fitting. Now she was fascinated to have an insight without having to initiate the subject herself. One of her fantasies had been that sex had long been over in Cecilia and Tim's relationship. She was intrigued to infer that it had been a going concern until cancer.

Cecilia went on: 'It's different having a healed wound which hurts, from having an unhealed wound. If you have a healed wound which hurts, you are like an old soldier whose war wound still aches when the wind is in the east. An unhealed wound is a worry, could infect; any discharge from it could be pus. So I feel the better for that visit to the hospital. Marina babysat.'

'Ah, the broody Marina. It's a shame that young couple, if couple they be, won't take Cephas off your hands. That woman would be a good mother. But she probably wants a baby of her own.'

Inured to confidentiality, Cecilia said nothing.

Helen went on: 'What a pity Ian ever discovered that someone else is Cephas's father. Any idea who the culprit might be?' Cecilia shook her head. 'If that was known,' Helen went on, 'the blood dad would have to pay the maintenance. If Ian gets together with Marina, or someone else, and has a family of his own, he won't be wanting to go on bankrolling a child who is no relation of his, let alone of his partner's. Oh dear, what a coil. Still, you seem resigned.'

'All you say is true, and I am resigned because I have no choice, and, of course, because I love Cephas.'

'You're such a good person,' said Helen, repeating what Cecilia had said to her in another important conversation. Cecilia recognised the echo, and they smiled at each other, in intimacy and amity.

'I'm dying for a cigarette,' said Helen. 'Can we go in the garden?'

They went down the steps and sat in deckchairs, a few feet from Cephas in his pram, with Thor curled up on the net.

'What would happen if free colostomy supplies were cut?' said Helen, dreamily.

'We'd have to pay for them, I suppose.'

'But what about poor people?'

'We'd start a fund.'

'What if there were no colostomy supplies – if a volcano went off, or an H-bomb?'

'We'd probably have worse problems then than our stomas.'

'But we would have problems, with our stomas, that normal people wouldn't have.'

'Yes, we would.'

'Perhaps there'd be no food, so we wouldn't shit.'

Helen puffed peacefully on her cigarette. She had been enlivened, even entertained, she had to admit to herself, by the saga of Cephas and his paternity. She wondered if there was anyone in the world, the tale of whose misfortunes would not at least briefly cheer her. She probably liked Cecilia better than anyone she knew; but even Cecilia's troubles brightened a dull day for Helen. It would be different, of course, if something that risked Helen's own equilibrium happened to someone. If Cecilia had a bad scan, and her removal from Helen's life was threatened, Helen would be unequivocally distraught, and this, of course, she knew. She noticed, testing herself, that she would not welcome bad news of her mother's health. Marj's? That would be fine, except insofar as it upset Mum.

'I still hope Ian and Marina will get together, even though as things are now it wouldn't have anything to do with the fate of Cephas,' said Cecilia, whose mind had been ranging in a different direction.

'I agree. They're both very nice.'

~

Ian got back from Damascus looking browner and thinner, although he had not been away very long. Marina met him at the airport. They went to Ian's flat. Marina found herself tidying, and doing some abandoned washing-up, while he unpacked, showered, and put on the washing machine – the usual tasks of return. He whistled for joy all the time. How different, he reflected, from his last homecoming, bedevilled by Leda's garbled but fateful email, and by Marina's absence.

'What about coming in?' he called from the shower.

'No, because I want to talk.'

'We could talk in the shower.'

'We wouldn't.'

'I owe you so much,' he trumpeted from the washing machine.

'Nonsense. I'm making coffee, OK?'

He joined her, his curly hair still wet, a towel round his shoulders, his shirt unbuttoned.

'You look so lovely,' she said. It had to be said, although she wanted so much to be practical. She poured the coffee. When she had finished he took her hand.

'I love you,' he said.

'Good. I was going to ask you if that had lasted. That was part of the talk.'

'What are the other bits of the talk?'

'About living together. Has that whim lasted too?' She was confident, but at this moment a little anxious.

'It has, and is no whim. Even I have been thinking about that. The trouble is, this flat is a bit bachelory. Specially as you won't be going away. It's just a traveller's digs. Don't you think? And yours is lovely, but tiny.'

'Yes. And that's part of the talk too.'

'Go on. I'm liking this talk.'

'Good. So please listen to my plan unfold, and don't raise objections until—'

'—until it's fully unfolded.' He nodded obediently. 'I won't.'

'This is it. We both put our flats on the market. That can be done tomorrow. We house-hunt briskly and briefly – I'll do it – for a nice little house close to your mum's. You'll see why it's got to be near hers, just listen. Then we move in. Then we take Cephas over. That's why Cecilia's got to be close, so that he can see her every day, including bedtimes, until he accepts us as the main people. Next bit of the plan: we start trying for a baby of our own. Immediate projects: flats on the market; house-hunt; bridging loan probably; get Cephas more accustomed to us doing things for him; I come off the pill. So far so good?'

'Can I ask questions yet?'

'Yes.'

'Why are we taking Cephas? And why are you coming off the pill quite so quickly?'

'OK. We are taking Cephas for three reasons. One, I love him. Two, we have always thought him yours. Three, Cecilia and Tim at nearly seventy can't be responsible for a baby.'

'You love him. Of course I can't oppose that, if it's a fact. Two, we have thought him mine, but he is not. The fact that we thought he was doesn't constitute an obligation for us to take him. Number three is a sound reason, I see that. But that's just as much a reason to get him adopted by another nice couple, as it is a reason for us to take him.'

'Perhaps. But we can't get him adopted. It's too late; too late from his point of view. He knows us all, he thinks he belongs, he likes me, he's passionate about Cecilia, he's been carefully healed from whatever Leda and that separation meant. It would be hard to do it to a dog, but to a baby, no. Anyway Cecilia wouldn't agree, and you could scarcely steal him from her under cover of night and dump him on Social Services' doorstep.'

Ian blinked at this picture of him, in which there was just a hint of dislike. He was seeing the Marina who could get things done, who had risen in their shared profession, and now in a decisive and fuss-free way had eased herself out of it, into more stay-at-home roles that presently suited her better. Most people didn't make things happen without long indecision and discussion. She did. And in a more domestic context she was doing it again.

'OK, well,' said Ian, 'if we say there's no choice about us offering to have Cephas – Mum might refuse to part with him, mind you – that gives us no time living together, just as us. I thought that's how it would be, just us, me coming home and there would be you, and we would be alone together, in a shared place of our own.'

'You have to see it differently. We are alone together in a home of our own, and Cecilia and Cephas come round, and we get used to Cephas, and Cephas gets used to us and to our house, and he gradually becomes more and more of a resident, until he is one. It will take a long time. We will be nicely alone together quite a lot.'

'OK, that sounds better. I'm not really arguing. I know you will get your way, and in some sense I feel you are right. In fact I think you are rather wonderful. But, next question. Why do we have to start wanting a baby of our own quite so soon?'

'Yes, I thought we'd get to that. I'm nearly thirty-six.'

'Yes, but Mark and Amelia—'

'I know. But I don't want to risk it. My sister, younger than me, is on IVF. She's had two goes of it. If I had to have all that, I'd be over forty, with chances getting slimmer. And, anyway, if you've been on the pill for ages it takes a long time to wear off.'

'You've obviously thought about this.'

'Yes, all the time while you've been away.'

'Suppose I'm infertile? I've been worrying about that now that Cephas isn't my baby,' said Ian.

'That's a different subject and needn't come into the plan. If either of us is infertile we'll worry about it when it happens.'

'You won't leave me, will you?'

'No.'

'Should I have a fertility test? The internet probably does that test too.'

She giggled. 'You are very silly. Of course not.' But she liked it when he was humble and inglorious.

Ian sat thinking about the plan. 'Well,' he said, 'it doesn't seem too bad. At least I get to be with you.'

'And I get to be with you.'

'And with Cephas, damn it, who by then will be one of those tiresome toddlers that make me want to refuse Mark and Amelia's dinner invitations.'

'I know. He will be. He's absolutely wonderful. He's nearly crawling already.'

'He is a bad bet genetically. A mad mother, and father unknown, the choice of the mad mother.'

'Leda had good taste in men.'

He caught her meaning, and smiled acknowledgement. They both sat silently for a minute, looking at the plan. 'There's one thing missing,' said Ian.

'Oh. What have I forgotten?'

'Will you marry me?'

'Yes.'

~

The next day saw Ian and Marina at Tim and Cecilia's. Tim answered the door.

'They're in the garden,' he said. 'Shall I make some coffee?'

So Ian and Marina went down the steps into the sunny garden, a welcome sight for Cecilia. Cephas was on a rug, lying on his tummy, having what Cecilia called 'crawling practice', and, indeed, to the accompaniment of a groaning noise, he was managing to propel himself, nearly flat, but with his elbows and knees taking some weight, towards the edge of the rug. His head came up and he registered the arrival of Ian and Marina with an interested stare. Then his head went down again like a swimmer's, the better to manage crawling practice.

By tacit agreement Ian and Marina said nothing about the plan until Tim came out with a tray. But Cecilia could see from their demeanour that something was up, and she was privately excited. When Tim appeared, and the tray was on the garden table, the coffee poured, and everyone seated, Cecilia restored Cephas to his sitting position in the middle of the rug. Thor appeared and trotted, tail up, to sit on the rug with Cephas. He had not liked crawling practice, with its unfamiliar grunts and groans, and had briefly retired to a safe distance. Marina leant over to talk to Cephas. She held out her hands. He smiled, and passed her a small brick that was on his rug. He waited for her to give the brick back. The exchange persisted during the conversation.

'Marina and I are getting married,' said Ian.

There were exclamations of joy from Cecilia and a benign and interested smile from Tim, who stood up, as if something physical must be done to greet such news. Then he shook Ian's hand and came round the table to kiss the leaning Marina.

'Not exactly a whirlwind courtship,' said Ian. 'I feel now it should have been.'

The plan in its entirety was not divulged then. The part of it that Tim and Cecilia needed to know related to the house that was to be bought in their neighbourhood, and the offer gradually to adopt Cephas. Cecilia found tears falling down her cheeks. She looked at Marina and smiled. She knew it was Marina's plan, and Marina knew she knew.

'I don't know when I've been so happy in all my life,' Cecilia said. 'It's much the best thing that could happen to Cephas. I really will have to see him all the time at first, though.'

'Of course you will.'

'Then even after we've made the transition,' Cecilia went on, 'you must drop him off here all the time to be babysat, and I must often pop in.'

'Or he won't see Thor,' said Tim.

Coffee over, Tim went for glasses and champagne. The champagne was not cold, as no celebration had been expected. But it was welcome.

Tim was ashamed at the degree of selfish relief he was feeling. A great weight had tumbled from his shoulders. He breathed deeply and said to Ian: 'You still have parental responsibility for Cephas under the law, so nothing will have to be changed to make this new arrangement in order. He has your surname, as it is.'

'OK, right,' said Ian, who had not thought of the law.

Marina had, and gave Tim a quick smile. 'Yes,' she said. 'I looked it all up. Ian has been responsible for Cephas all along, since he was born, under parental responsibility. If you had kept him, you would have had to get a residence order, agreed by Ian. Only that doesn't have to happen now.'

Cecilia murmured, looking at Cephas and Marina, absorbed in each other, 'Such a huge change, in such a short time. My poor heart.'

The doorbell rang. Ian got up and came back with Helen. She was quickly told everything, and was amused and delighted by the news. The remains of the champagne fell to her. She became fascinated by the thought of house-hunting locally and promised to do so on Marina's behalf. She had some ideas already. Marina put up with this equably, hoping the enthusiasm would fade before it became intrusive.

'I'm drinking to happily ever after,' Helen said. 'Ian and Marina, you'll have to get a cat.'

'Aha,' said Marina to Ian, 'so the original plan was incomplete in two ways.'

Chapter 13

The height of summer passed, and the year was moving towards autumn. Projects for marriage, and for house moves, were edging steadily towards completion for Ian and Marina, and for Clare and David. Because of Helen's writer's block, and the consequent drop in her income, or her fear of it, she had taken a lodger, an Indian medical student, with whom, she assured Cecilia, the friendship was platonic, although Cecilia was not convinced that it would remain so.

Encouraged by the nice gynaecologist, Cecilia was taking tentative steps towards sex with Tim, which he was welcoming uncertainly. He was back in the marital bed now. Cephas had a cot in a room of his own, and was sleeping through the nights, tired out by vigorous crawling. His first birthday was not far away. It had been diplomatically easy for Cecilia to allow Cephas an increase of houseroom now he was only a temporary resident. Marina and Cephas were very close. He recognised her approaching footstep and looked expectantly towards the door, and it was alleged by his greatest fans that he said, 'Mina.' Even Ian was resigned to Cephas, and to quite liking him. The two of them played a Roaring Tiger game, which was very noisy, but which everyone but Thor found worth stopping what they were doing to watch for a few minutes.

Both Helen and Meg took pleasure in Helen's regular visits,

which had not dwindled. Bob George was doing bits of carpentry in the little house in Hastings with the stained-glass front door.

Perhaps it was the increasing chill in the weather that affected Diana's health. An able-bodied nun, Sister Nancy, once Mother Etheldreda, drove her to their doctors' surgery. The young GP listened to Diana's heart and lungs.

'I'd like you to go into hospital for a week or two to have a thorough check-up,' he said, slipping his stethoscope from his ears to his neck.

'I hardly think it's worth it,' said Diana, briskly hiding her withered breasts, 'particularly given the stretched resources of the NHS. I am ninety-one. How long is one expected to live?'

A difficult question, and one that defeated the pleasant young doctor. 'I'm only saying . . .' he said, and stopped.

'I will go to hospital,' said Diana, 'if it becomes difficult for the sisters to look after me at home. Then I shall be grateful for hospital provision. But that may not happen. Not all deaths are terribly complicated. We have had plenty, and many of us have managed to die in our own beds.'

~

They drove home, and Diana succeeded in getting out of the car unaided. But she knew she was ill. Soon she took to her bed. Once during the next couple of weeks she was rushed in an ambulance to A & E in the local town and came out alive, with a pharmacopoeia of pills. At home again, she was brought meals on trays, but she had no appetite. She wrote some letters, letters in which the friends subsequently realised there had been a hint of goodbye. But she did not really have the energy even for this. Her bed was near a window, and her eyes were drawn again and again, for longer and longer, to the sky and the branch of the pear tree that cut across it.

'Sister's just staring out of the window now,' was said of her. She had been much relied on, and the prospect of her loss was daunting. Women who had been her novices looked at each other with fear and courage in their eyes. She seemed to have given up reading. The gardener picked chrysanthemums to be put where she could see them. The sisters began to have morning and night prayer in her room, rather than in the chapel, and, few though they now were in comparison to what they had been, it was an uncomfortable fit. Once she was to be wheeled down for Mass, but her whiteness and gasping at being taken out of bed aborted the enterprise. The Blessed Sacrament was brought to her daily by Father Reg.

'How do you think you are doing?' he said.

'I think all right.'

'Is it possible to pray?'

'Probably no more impossible than it has always been.'

He understood this as a more mystical utterance than he had been aiming for. Twice now he had administered the Sacrament of the Sick to Diana. When he was ordained it had been called Extreme Unction, and he had a sinking feeling that this was the better name of the two where Diana was concerned. After he left the room she went back to looking at the window.

A night came when the sisters were worried enough to call the doctor out. Diana was asleep, breathing heavily. The doctor listened to her chest. Then he sat down beside the bed and took her hand, which she did not seem to notice. 'Pneumonia,' he said. 'I don't think she'd want to go to hospital for intravenous antibiotics. What do you think?' No one thought anything. 'I'm afraid she will probably pass away before morning. She is very poorly indeed.'

'Is she suffering?' asked Nancy.

'No, she's going peacefully.'

Someone hurried for the prayer book. Diana had assisted quite often, in her long life, at the Prayers for the Dying; and when they were being read now her eyelids flickered a little. Nancy thought to raise her voice, realising the hearing aid had been discarded, and when they got to 'Go forth, faithful Christian', Diana opened her eyes, and said with a look that was interested and almost mischievous, 'Ah, is it that time, now?' As the doctor had foreseen, by morning she was dead.

The sisters, and gradually a wider circle, were confronted afresh with the question mark a completed life imposes, perhaps especially a long life – what is a life? What was this person's life, now there is no more to be seen of it? The story is finished; and what was the story? There is so much to be done when someone dies. One of the tasks that fell to Nancy was to draw up a notice of the death and of the date of the funeral on the computer, and to duplicate it. Then she took possession of Diana's address book and began addressing envelopes.

She would miss Diana very much, but she did not think that was why she was crying. It was the worn, well-filled address book that was evoking the tears. Some of the names and addresses were written in a firm, neat, restrainedly flowing hand. Others were fainter and shaky. The address book had lasted an adult lifetime. In the vagaries of its owner's calligraphy, it told the story of a life, from its youth to its prime, from its prime to its old age. Quite a number of the entries had RIP written across them, mostly, of course, in the shakier handwriting. These entries had not been crossed out, nor eliminated to make room for later-comers, but kept, while being helpfully identified as dead.

'Cecilia Banks' was there, in the neat writing of vigorous maturity, and 'Clare George', in the tremulous, careful hand. Nancy wiped her glasses and went on with the job.

～

It was a Saturday. Clare, in her and David's flat in Hackney, heard the post drop on the doormat. She went to pick it up. There were some usual sorts of things, an important letter connected with their house move, and a mysterious letter, addressed to her. The name and address on the envelope of this last were handwritten, an intriguing rarity, in a neat, even hand that Clare did not know. She opened it at once.

'We are very sorry to have to tell you of the death of Sister Diana Clegg, formerly Mother Mary Vincent, CCHJ. She died peacefully' – the date of her death was given, and her birth date, and the date of the funeral. Underneath was written, 'Let perpetual light shine upon her.'

Clare read it twice. Then she pressed it to her lips and tears came to her eyes. Then she went into the sitting room and stood beside David, who was at the computer.

'David,' she said, 'look at this.'

He turned and took the sheet of paper from her. He had heard the break in her voice, and his hand went reassuringly to rest on her hip. His first thought was that it was something about her dad. He was very relieved to see that it was not.

'Sorry,' he said. 'It's your nice Sister Diana, isn't it. I'm sorry.'

'She was so . . .' Clare broke off. She was crying.

'So what, darling?'

'So . . . interested in me!' The words burst out, and she laughed, through tears, at hearing herself come out with something so selfish.

His arms went round her middle and his cheek against her tummy. Then he stood up and gave her a proper hug. 'I know you really liked her,' he said.

'Yes, and you were going to come with me next time.'

'Never mind, darling.' He didn't ask if there was any mail from the lawyer, though it did come into his mind. He began to sidle into the kitchen, holding Clare, to have a covert look. He saw the solicitor's letter, but was able to resist picking it up, yet.

'She helped me with all that stuff about the first two years of my life.'

'I know she did. She laid something to rest for you, I think.'

'And now she's simply dead.'

'Well, people do die. She was old.'

'Yes. I haven't seen her for, well, longer than usual, because of our move and our wedding. Do you think she understood . . .?'

'Of course she did.'

'I'm so sad.'

'I'm sorry.'

'Mum, then Sister Diana, soon it'll be Granny. Lucky Dad's well, and your parents.'

'Yes.'

'Our children will have two grandfathers.'

'They will.'

'And a grandmother. I'm so glad they'll have a grandmother.'

'Will you want to go to the funeral?'

This was a new idea for Clare, and she went back into the other room to look again at the notice. She was cheering up. 'A Thursday,' she said. 'Thursday week. I could. I can take it out of my annual leave.'

'We were saving annual leave for the move, but I suppose one day . . .'

'Only one day. Will you come with me?'

So it was settled.

~

Exactly the same letter, with just the same handwriting on the envelope, arrived at Cecilia's. Unlike Clare, Cecilia was able to sense that the hand was that of a nun, and she was puzzled. She had no premonition of what she was going to see. She read the message, and stood stock-still, looking at the paper.

'Well,' she said aloud, 'she had a good life.'

She felt her life reshuffle and arrange itself differently, adapting to the absence of a person who had been important, very important at one time, and always, whether important or not, there. At her age, Cecilia was experienced in death. Grandparents and parents in turn had all left their unique and unfillable gaps. A few friends had already predeceased her. Irreplaceable conversations had fallen silent for ever. She was hardened, but not indifferent.

She thought of MMV on the day she had last seen her, the momentous day of Cephas's arrival. She saw her in her mind's eye old and thin, but rather lovely, somewhat ethereal, and, as ever, very clean and tidy. Cecilia did not like to think of her having to go through the physical strenuousness of dying. Diana had always been very controlled, and death would have done away with that control. Cecilia sighed. She took comfort from a second look at the letter, and the word 'peaceful'.

She went to the calendar on the wall, to check the date of the funeral in relation to other things that were happening. She saw that she could go. Marina could have Cephas. Indeed Cephas in a brand-new pushchair was out with Marina now. Marina was having a month's holiday between her jobs, and was dividing it between Cephas and house-hunting, though sometimes these two occupations could be combined.

Tim was in his room, at the computer, but Cecilia had no strong impulse to tell him the strange news. The death of MMV felt very personal and she did not want to have to endure an absent-minded response to it.

Helen arrived, full of a house she had seen for sale. She wanted to show Cecilia the house agent's details, but Cecilia stopped her.

'Please listen,' Cecilia said. 'MMV, Diana Clegg, is dead.'

Helen was quiet at once and took Cecilia's hands. Helen always knew when something mattered, albeit sometimes she did not choose to act on that knowledge. 'A big thing,' she said. She was looking affectionately into Cecilia's eyes. 'Are you OK?'

'Yes. Yes. Thank you for understanding.'

They had a cup of tea and talked about death.

'No one I have loved has died,' said Helen. 'But that's because I've loved so few people. I hardly minded at all when my father died. And Gordon, I didn't feel a thing. Who else? No one, really. And Mum is still alive, thank God. I love her. Very much, oddly enough. Perhaps I haven't loved people, to save myself from the grief of their deaths.'

'Now that you love your mum, you'll be in for it when she dies.'

'I will. I'll suffer like mad. Don't you die.'

'I'll try not to. I suppose we are both on the front line, you and I.'

'Yes. Will we always be, now?'

'Well, for five years, anyway,' said Cecilia.

'Then we will be in the front line, either way, because of our age.'

'Ages, you mean. You're younger. And look at your mum's longevity.'

'I'm already older than Dickens, Trollope or George Eliot ever were, let alone the novelists whom we think of as dying young,' said Helen. They were silent, then Helen went on, 'I wouldn't have found Mum again, but for your MMV.'

Cecilia was ready for the estate agent's details now, and the excitement of possible properties engrossed her and Helen's attention.

∼

Ian, Marina and Cephas drew up outside a house with a 'For Sale' notice outside. The child seat was now a fixture in Marina's car, Cephas was strapped into it, and Ian, home in the earlier morning from Damascus, was in the back.

They got out. The estate agent was already parked, and jumped out of his car to meet them. Marina had viewed the house a few days before, and this time was bringing Ian to see what he thought of it.

They went through the rooms, Ian carrying Cephas, who was annoyingly stretching out his arms to Marina and complaining. Marina was explaining in an undertone to Ian, for some reason not wanting the estate agent to overhear, how she had designated the different rooms in her mind. There was no furniture, as the owners had moved out. No carpets had been left, and the rooms and the stairs echoed to their feet and voices. Marina liked this house, and was beginning to be afraid its apparent dereliction might put Ian off. She was able to clothe it imaginatively, in a way Ian was not, especially with Cephas grizzling.

They looked out of big windows on the first floor and saw the garden. It was a good size and grassy, with bushes round the edge and a big tree, some of whose leaves were still clinging to the branches. Marina thought the garden was wonderful. Downstairs, there were french doors to it from the kitchen, where she had imagined herself cooking, and children running in and out.

The estate agent left them to themselves, saying he wanted a cigarette and would wait for them outside. Marina sat on the hard floorboards, and Ian put Cephas down beside her. Cephas gripped Marina's leg and looked disapprovingly at Ian.

'We can't let him crawl because of splinters,' said Marina.

This did not matter because, of late, Cephas could pull himself up to a supported standing position, and, if there was a sequence of objects of the right height to hold on to, could actually walk. The first time this happened it had been a big event for his fan club. Now he stood and took some steps, with the help of the the window ledge and the cold radiator.

He first looked out of the window, then worryingly licked its dirty glass, then was fascinated by and babbling at the antics of two squirrels in the tree.

'Can you see us living here?' asked Ian, standing, looking out of the window.

'Well, I think so, can you?'

'I believe I can. Do you think that chap is really having a cigarette, or has he left us to fall in love with the property better without him?'

'Well, he does smoke, but probably both. And is it working? The love, I mean?'

Ian walked out of the room and could be heard echoing round that floor and then the floor above. He came back. 'He is smoking down there,' he said. 'I saw him out of the front window. Well, I like this better than the other one you brought me to.'

'And it's ten minutes walk from Cecilia's.'

'We'll have to buy everything. Carpets, curtains.'

'Yes, except they're leaving the kitchen stuff.'

'Are they? And between us we've got quite a bit of furniture ourselves.'

Marina was in a state of happy excitement. She was surprised Ian seemed to have discerned nothing out of the ordinary. She had been a few days late with her period, then a week. A week was very unusual. Unprecedented? She believed so. She had thought it might be due to the vagaries of coming off the pill. But her whole body was caught from time to time in an enormous exhilaration.

'Ian,' she said, 'I'm late with my period.'

Ian had been standing behind Cephas in case he fell backwards, but now turned and crouched in front of Marina. 'Really?' he said.

Marina had feared a touch of dismay, and then perhaps a grumble, half peevish, half humorous, about an inundation of children. She had not expected delight, which is what she saw now on Ian's face. 'Really?' he said again. 'And do you think . . .?'

'Well, it's unusual enough for me to think . . .' She mimicked his unfinished sentence.

'How wonderful,' said Ian. He took her hands.

'I was afraid you might feel overwhelmed.'

'I probably do, but so happy. Since the paternity test, I've been afraid I am infertile.'

'But that's mad, if Leda was pregnant already.'

'One can't help one's mad ideas.'

'I seem to be able to. Perhaps I don't get them.'

'I know. That's why I want you to be the mother of my children.' He looked round the room. 'This house is a nice size for a family house.'

'We've got another one to look at yet. But we'd better drop Cephas off first, he'll be needing his morning nap.'

Marina stood up. She was happy and relieved that Ian accepted the possibility that she was pregnant so gladly. However, she was dashed, even aggrieved, at the immediate reason he had given for his pleasure. That reaction had shown her an Ian involved with himself, rather than an Ian involved with the two of them as a couple. She did not want her pregnancy to give Ian the chance to be airily conceited and powerful, as he had been when he believed he had fathered Cephas.

They began to go downstairs. Ian did feel a bit overwhelmed, now he thought about it. But he reminded himself that he was forty-one, and that at forty-one it was time, if not high time, to be enterprising about life rather than timorous. The fear of being tied down, which had paralysed his capacity to make decisions based on love, and had blunted his awareness of what he really wanted, seemed to have disappeared. The memory of that fear, and of how unashamedly he used to air it, almost as if it was something to boast about, embarrassed him now. As he walked down the dusty staircase, he felt free and strong. He was very much aware of his body. Cephas was looking at him over Marina's shoulder, smug at being in her arms, rather than in his. Ian made a good-humoured, frightening face at him.

Chapter 14

'You are looking very smart,' said Helen.

'I've been at MMV's funeral.'

'Oh my dear. Was it today?'

'Yes. Sit down. Have a glass of wine. I'll tell you all about it.'

Helen accepted, and was ready for the story. 'But where's Cephas?' she said. She did not like to have to foresee interruptions.

'House-viewing with his parents. They do it all the time now. Well. It was a big funeral. They had it in the church next door to the convent and it was packed. I like a good send-off. There were two bishops there. In full regalia, and quite a lot of priests. MMV's nephew – I didn't even know she had one – did a tribute, and so did the convent chaplain, who obviously knew her well. I didn't cry until the coffin was carried down the aisle and came past me. I wasn't specially thinking about her. It was just death, and solemnity. Then we all turned silently and went out after the coffin. I was at the back of the church and so I was rather at the front of the graveside. We'd had to trail to the convent grounds through wet grass to get to the nuns' graveyard. It was beginning to rain. We sang the Salve Regina and the priest was saying some prayers you couldn't hear. Then the coffin was lowered into the grave.'

'Go on,' said Helen, fascinated.

'We were all getting wet, but no one seemed to mind or

notice. Most of us took a handful of earth and threw it on the coffin. I did not, because, of all things, the stoma had started going like an engine, and I didn't want to make any movement that would encourage it. A very old man – someone said he was the convent gardener – threw a lovely bunch of garden flowers on to the coffin. He was crying. Then we all headed slowly indoors. All the graves are the same. A simple wooden cross, and the nun's name and dates.'

'How many were already there?'

'Fifty-ish, probably.'

'Were there any names of nuns you had known?'

'Do you know, I forgot to wonder. What with the stoma, and the rain, and my smart shoes slipping on mud, I was intent on getting under cover. We headed for the convent refectory, which was quite a large room, icy, of course, but we all crowded in, and there were cups of tea and sandwiches.'

'No drink?'

'No. It was about three o'clock. They had wisely timed the funeral, perhaps, so as not to have to offer it. I talked to one of the bishops, who was very nice, and had known MMV very well in Rome during the Vatican Council. Then we split up because he desperately had to get outside for a cigarette. There were a lot of grey heads there, of course, as you'd expect, like my own. But there were young people too. There was a handsome young Polish priest, in tears. He told me she had given him some useful spiritual direction. There was the old gardener's grandson, about thirty, who said his grandad said MMV had a green finger. There were even some children. They played outside in the drizzle. There was a nice young couple in the middle of a house move – I thought of Ian and Marina, and we compared notes – and MMV had helped them in some major way they didn't want to talk about. The young GP looked in, which was good manners, and he said MMV was impressive. Then I talked to Father Reg, who was the convent chaplain, and had said the Requiem Mass.'

'Is he a grey-head?'

'Very much so, except bald as well. He said Diana was a great loss and had made a huge contribution.'

'It makes me think of the end of *Middlemarch*,' said Helen.

'Can you quote it?' Helen could often quote verbatim.

'"... that things are not so ill with you and me as they might have been, is half owing to the number who lived faithfully a hidden life, and rest in unvisited tombs".'

They were both silent. Then Cecilia sighed, and refilled their glasses.

'How was the stoma doing, by then?' asked Helen, zestfully.

'Ponderous. Protuberant. Preposterous. Luckily quiet, except for the occasional whisper and creak. I tried to pretend the noises were from my mobile. Heaven knows what people thought the bulge was, specially under this elegant jacket, which I had to button because of the terrible conventual cold, which I well remember.'

'Only at that time you would have welcomed it, as a mortification.'

'Yes. And now I just felt bloody freezing. I was glad to get home, change the bag, warm up, and now you're here, and we're having a drink, and it's lovely.'

'But aren't you still melancholy, from the funeral?'

Cecilia reflected. 'Not melancholy,' she said. 'Solemn. In a perfectly pleasant way.'

For the moment, the subject had come to a natural end. 'I may have got through the writer's block,' said Helen.

'Oh, how wonderful!'

'A novel provisionally called *Perdita and Hermione*. That won't be its title, but it keeps the theme in my mind.'

'I suppose you don't want to talk about it – but anything you did want to say . . .'

'Not yet. I have to admit, though, I have talked about it with Das.'

'Aha.'

'Not aha, really, though I do like him.'

There was a ring at the doorbell. 'Tim will get it.'

Tim did, and Ian, Marina, Cephas and Tim came into the room. The kitchen suddenly seemed very full. Cecilia felt too tired to get up. Cephas crawled over to her and pulled himself up on her knee, babbling cheerfully. She touched his cheek with rapt fondness, but hoped someone else would produce tea or wine or whatever was required. Marina noticed the lassitude, and knew Cecilia had been to a funeral. She set about providing what was wanted. Glasses and another bottle of wine were settled for, and Tim put out a bag of crisps. Helen headed for the garden and a cigarette.

Helen stood in the doorway, smoking and looking out at the drizzle and the autumnal garden. She was happy to have started writing again. It was as if a pair of wings in her, often spread, sometimes soaring, but furled now for too long, had begun to open again, feather by feather. She thought of Cecilia, and the pleasure of their friendship. She thought of her mother, in the home in Sheffield, who had accepted the renewal of Helen's visits as if they had never been broken off or begrudged.

She thought of Das, his devotion to his mother, his disbelief that Helen's could be in a home, the delicious meals he cooked, taking for granted that his landlady would share them. Her hand went to the colostomy, and she arranged the position of the bag, but without rancour and almost without advertence. She had a routine scan coming up in a few weeks, and of course hoped for the best. Pocketing the cigarette stub so that it could never annoy Tim, she turned and went back into the house.

Everyone had moved into the sitting room, and all were settled on various chairs and sofas. Helen joined them. Ian was weighing up the advantages and disadvantages of various houses, and there was talk about that, and about Cecilia's walking distance from each of them. Offers on the flats Ian and Marina were selling were coming in and were not too disappointing.

Someone suggested a takeaway, and Tim got a brochure from the local Indian restaurant out of a drawer, and began to ask for orders. All this took some time, as the brochure had to be passed from hand to hand, and Tim needed to write things down.

In the middle of this Cecilia's and Marina's eyes became riveted on Cephas. He had pulled himself on to his feet by means of a chair, and had picked up a set of keys that happened to have been put on the seat of it. He held the keys in one hand while he inspected them. But because they were rather heavy, he needed two hands to enjoy the full experience, and there he was, standing, unsupported, holding the keys with both hands. Marina and Cecilia exchanged glances, and the heightened emotion in the room caused a hush. Everyone stared.

Marina was the nearest. 'Cephas,' she said quietly, holding out her hands to him.

He dropped the keys on the floor and walked the three steps to Marina. He knew at once that he had done something wonderful. He held Marina's knee and looked all round, beaming. He saw Thor curled up on a distant sofa and seemed for a moment about to set out in his direction. But Cecilia said, 'Cephas,' and held out her hands to him. He took the four steps to her, staggered, and held on, laughing. He looked all round again. Everyone was smiling, everyone was still.

'Cephas,' said Marina again, holding out her hands welcomingly. Again he toddled to her. He looked at her, smiling, then he looked all round. Cecilia prepared herself to receive him again. But Cephas was looking at Ian, and seemed to be measuring the distance between them with his eyes. Then he set forth, and arrived between Ian's outstretched arms.

PART II
Shit Scared

Chapter 15

Cecilia felt it was a bit much to have to write a cheque for a hundred and fifty pounds to Mr P after what he had told her. She felt sardonic and injured as she looked at the bill, but recognised that there could be no cut price for bad news. She would have been shocked, after all, if fees were inflated when there was something reassuring to say. But how willingly she would have paid twice – three times, ten times a hundred and fifty pounds, oh, a king's ransom, she would have paid, to have heard: 'Well, Mrs Banks, we don't think you've got anything to worry about, what we think we were seeing was just . . .'

She had decided to see her consultant privately, to be more expeditiously told the result of an X-ray, the consequence of some hip pain she had been suffering. But there was no clear-cut result from the X-ray as yet, and the surgeon had told her this, expensively, in his Harley Street consulting room. Various colleagues, specialists, he said, had looked at her X-ray, and discussed, and come to no conclusion. There was a fracture, but the question was, why was there a fracture? More tests would have to be done, first of all an MRI. She would, of course, be given appointments immediately the tests had been booked, and he would mark the request urgent. And yes, of course she would be switched back to the NHS.

'Mr Pidantone,' said Cecilia, 'may I ask you whether, from

your long experience, you think this is the return of the cancer, or do you think it could be something else?'

'Cecilia,' he said, 'we go back a long way.' He was the person who had performed her operation three years before, so there was something in what he said, perhaps especially for him, who was so much the younger. 'Anything I know, I would tell you. But I don't know. That is why we are doing the tests.'

With which she had to be satisfied. Indeed the 'Cecilia', and the quiet acknowledgement of ignorance, raised him in her estimation. But as she went home, and in the days and nights that followed, she was intensely lonely and afraid. It was also difficult to get about, and she had been warned to keep as still as possible, to stop the fracture getting worse.

'I can walk a few hundred yards, slowly?' she asked, in desperation, and this was reluctantly agreed. She was thinking of the short walk to Ian's, which she had to be able to do.

Until she got the date for the MRI, she was in limbo, and in those days she looked eagerly for envelopes from the hospital, as familiar as they were hated. But when she did get the date, it became clear to her that there were only two possible paths out of her limbo. Then she felt that limbo life was more bearable than the sight of the crossroads that then appeared before her, the crossroads marked respectively Inferno and Paradiso. Which was it to be?

If the pain and fracture were a reappearance of the cancer, which seemed to Cecilia the likeliest outcome, she saw death along the Inferno path, indeed, but only at the end of that path, and that terminus was not what she most recoiled from. Three years ago, and two years ago, there had been hospital appointments regularly and frequently, taking over her life; and it was the prospect of a repetition of that pattern that appalled her. The bus journey, so familiar, usually with Tim; the endless waiting; the suspense; the overwhelming emotions, hidden or disguised, endured privately in crowded rooms, or in a cubicle with a doctor looking at his computer; the hopes and the disappointments. More than that, the subjugation to an alien world ruled by the medical profession; of floral garments that did up at the back, or didn't; of attempts to decode into common sense what was being muttered over the heavy wad of her notes; of the fact that strangers knew more about her body than she did, who had known it so long.

She knew Mr P thought he had extracted all the cancer in the long and complicated surgery. She had hesitantly come to believe that indeed he had. So if this new conundrum were cancer, it would give the lie to that hope, and in doing so would mean the cancer had survived, had survived both radiotherapy and the knife, and ensconced itself afresh somewhere in the pelvis, flesh or bone; and found a foothold, as Japanese knotweed does, where it was thought to be eradicated. And if it had managed to come back now, she must no longer think of herself, as she had done in her happier moments, as someone who had been cured of cancer, nor even, she suspected, as someone whose cancer was curable. Cancer had found an extraordinary affinity with the cells of her body, and those patient and innocent cells had inexplicably stood aside to give it houseroom again. Mr P did not know, for sure, and that was a ray of hope. But Cecilia could not feel optimistic. The pain and the fracture were so close to the site of the original tumour. She could too easily imagine a few stray spores that had dodged the might of modern medicine regrouping with a snuggle of satisfaction and setting up their colony. Nothing but her death would end their lives now. So Cecilia felt.

She couldn't settle to anything. She watched people go past in the street outside her house, with umbrellas in a summer shower, and thought that for them – she did not know, of course – these were ordinary days. They were days, for them, of normal preoccupations, not by any means all pleasant; but all belonging to a life that is expected to continue unchanged.

She felt very much alone, and this in spite of having a perfectly nice husband to whom she had told what had happened with Mr P. Tim's line was that what had been seen, indeed what she felt in her hip with every step she took, was probably not cancer, but a fracture from radiation. Sadly for this theory, Mr P had said they did not think it was that. Tim, with his scientific objections to radiotherapy, stuck to his guns. Perhaps his confidence kept him from having to make experimental journeys with Cecilia down the path marked Inferno. She had not told people other than Tim, on the grounds that there was nothing, as yet, to tell. She would broadcast her woes when there was a diagnosis. Or possibly it could be a reprieve that she would broadcast.

She had not lost weight and her face in the mirror did not seem peaky. Those should surely be good signs. But perhaps her general health being unimpaired as yet by this new inroad from cancer might merely mean her body was going to put up a struggle, was going to ignore the new malignancy for as long as it could, then go down fighting, system by system, chemotherapy by chemotherapy; and the whole process would be long drawn out and terrible, precisely because of her good constitution. She felt sorry for her body, in its valour and its defeat. But why had it succumbed? Was it betrayed, or was it treacherous?

She realised now that, without recognising it, she had become ready to install herself, with a sigh of relief, among the whole and the free, in a position to look down pityingly on the lower ranks, still enmeshed in the hospital. It seemed ironic that she, with a colostomy and a reinvented backside, should have managed to presume she could bloom afresh among the healthy, among the insouciant aristocrats of the body. But so it was. She had not noticed the transition. She had not known until now that she had come to see herself in that enviable light. She knew it only now that she was cast into outer darkness.

At times her spirits lightened. She hoped it was because she was getting used to being philosophical, fatalistic, and able to live a life of a sort despite the confines of a condemned cell. But really, and she knew this, it was because her eye had strayed to the Paradiso, rather than the Inferno, path.

'Well, I'm very glad to tell you, Mrs Banks . . .' What gesture would be enough to celebrate that moment? Would she kiss the floor of the doctor's cubicle, or throw her arms round the doctor, or both? Certainly, in the years suddenly left to her, she would never complain again, or be bored again, or find the repetitiveness of the daily round dull. She felt a passionate, tearful longing for ordinariness, for the ordinariness of so many past days she had taken for granted, and not thought to rejoice over.

She put it to herself how much worse things might be. Suppose this had happened forty years ago, and she had been forced to anticipate leaving Ian motherless. That gruesome picture made what was actually going on seem by contrast tame and orderly. And what if she were still the mainstay for Cephas? Things were better than they might be. Of course she would be missed, missed by people who in the past had depended on her: by Ian, by Cephas. But there was no one, now, who looked uniquely to her. That was something to be grateful for. Tim would be all right. And then there was the stoical train of thought. We all have to fail and die, at some point. Why did she feel that her time, in her late sixties, should not rightly have come? It was not particularly early, and certainly would not have appeared so in past centuries, and would not appear so today in most of the world, to begin the process that would culminate in death. Indeed, she might well see seventy.

Yes, but as an invalid. As someone in thrall to the hospital. As someone 'not dying of cancer but living with cancer', as a saying goes in cancer circles. As someone who was being brave and was an example to her friends. As someone who could not move freely, could never carry Cephas again, or even Ali. Could she bear it?

A year ago she would have worried about having to leave Helen. But Helen was more free-standing now. Helen was writing again, and seemed to have more people in her life. Her mother, certainly, but also her brother and sister and their families now had their places in Helen's affections. The epoch when Cecilia, Helen's colostomy friend, was all-important, had gradually come to an end. Cecilia and Helen still saw each other often and talked on the phone and were intimate, but the circumstances that had generated their mutual need were different now. Their contact was not daily. Helen had rung for a chat more than once since Cecilia had been in the clutch of mortal dread, and had apparently not heard anything noteworthy in Cecilia's voice. Don't let her know, thought Cecilia, until there is anything to know.

Nothing altered or was mitigated, in the days and nights leading up to the MRI, but Cecilia began to feel steadier. There were still vertiginous moments when she peered down the Inferno path, but she did so less often, and, when she did, saw nothing worse than what she had already seen. Her fears had become her familiars. That did not make them less real, nor, if she entered into them, less devastating; but it made them a little less pressing. She had become like those who plough again on the volcano slope or the earthquake fault on which they happen to live. The gravitational pull of ordinariness, as strong over all life as gravity itself, exerted its influence. She went to Ian's, she tried not to limp, she played with Cephas, who was now nearly two; she looked after Ali, aged ten weeks, and chatted with Marina when Marina got home from work. She paid Mr P's bill, cooked meals, had first thoughts about a seventieth birthday celebration for Tim. She also counted the days to the MRI, after which there would be more days to count, until the thumbs-up or thumbs-down of its result.

One evening in this period she was watching football on television with Tim. It was a pleasure to see the fit youngsters running and kicking, and it did not matter that she had never grasped the offside rule, nor, on this occasion, even grasped which goal was whose. It was pouring with rain at Wembley, as indeed it was locally, and there were crackles of thunder, both on the television and overhead. Cecilia welcomed the drama of the thunder and the rain. She watched. It was always soothing to be doing something with Tim. She was wondering whether her urine stream was slowing up, and, if it was, whether it was because a pelvic tumour was butting into the bladder. Perhaps it was, and might soon butt into the urethra as well, blocking it from functioning. She might become unable to pee. She imagined herself having to have an ostomy for pee as well as an ostomy for shit. Whereabouts would the second bag lie on her abdomen? Symmetrical, or at a jaunty angle to the other? Somebody on the television scored, and from Tim's demeanour it was a remarkable goal. Certainly the footballer seemed to think so. Did he feel, at this moment, she wondered, as she would feel, if the MRI result was good? She would not be able to run and leap and slide along on her knees. There would not be room, for one thing, and it would make her hip hurt. But the ecstatic expression on the footballer's face seemed to match the opening up of the Paradiso path.

At that moment the doorbell rang. Tim was absorbed, so Cecilia limped to the front door. Ian was there, holding an umbrella, and someone was with him, someone whom Cecilia for a moment took for Marina. So who was with the children? But it was not Marina. Before Ian had spoken or let down the umbrella, Cecilia recognised the drenched features of Leda.

'Come in.'

She took them into the kitchen. No point disturbing Tim

yet. She was too astonished to suggest a drink or tea, and stood looking at them, while they stood, dripping.

'Sit down.'

They all did. Ian was looking at her with a shocked, beseeching expression; Leda did not make eye contact.

'This is Leda,' said Ian.

'Yes, I recognise you,' said Cecilia, cheerily, still failing to catch Leda's eye. Leda's wet black hair was all over her cheeks and shoulders. Her face was still strikingly and unforgettably beautiful. She crouched on a chair.

Ian spoke to Cecilia in quiet, quick sentences, as if Leda was not present. 'Leda, Volumnia, sorry. Her name is Volumnia. Volumnia found my new address through work, and called on us this evening, an hour ago. She has nowhere to go tonight, and we can't put her up, not having a spare room.'

This was not strictly true, for although Ali had a room bespoken for him, he was not occupying it yet. Ian telegraphed Cecilia with his eyes not to say anything to that effect – as if she would.

'So we thought you might just possibly give her a bed and she can sort things out in the morning.'

'Yes, of course,' said Cecilia, who now had not thought about cancer for five minutes. 'I am so sorry you don't have anywhere to go. What's been happening?'

No answer. Leda looked at her feet, puddling rain on to the floor, glanced towards Cecilia, and looked away again.

'Can we go on calling you Leda?' Cecilia said.

Again, no answer. A little agitation of feet and fingers indicated that she had heard.

'Mum, is it OK if I go now?' said Ian. 'I'm wanted at home.'

His eyes were passing a message to Cecilia about the shock this encounter had been for him and Marina, and about his and Marina's urgent need to be together. Cecilia's eyes signalled an understanding. Ian left, bumping into Tim, who, having heard an arrival, was coming into the kitchen. In Ian's hurry he could say nothing to Tim, but only gestured despairingly towards the kitchen door. He did not attempt to take in Tim's greeting, which was, 'One all, so far,' and ran all the way home in the rain.

'OK, call me Leda,' Leda was saying as Tim came into the room. Cecilia was relieved to hear her voice.

'Tim,' said Cecilia, 'this is Leda.'

She hurried on talking, about the rain, the football match, the possibility of food or drink, to curb Tim from saying anything unguarded. An agreed strategy was needed about Cephas before anything was said to or in front of Leda that presupposed a link. She saw Tim having some such thought himself, and he looked enquiringly at Cecilia, as if seeking instructions. She closed her eyes and tightened her lips in his direction. Then she got rid of Tim by saying, 'If the match is over, could you sort out a bed for Leda?'

'The spare room, or the small room?'

'The spare room.'

The spare room had resumed its character as spare since Tim had moved back into Cecilia's bedroom, after his exile from the double bed during the worst of her cancer. The small room had been Cephas's for a few months before he was transferred to Ian's, and that made it out of bounds for Leda in Cecilia's mind, at least until the agreed strategy had been arrived at, and until it was clear how much Leda did and didn't remember.

Leda wanted nothing to eat or drink, and did not want to talk. She sat looking at the floor and twiddling her wet hair nervously. Surely she was at least thirty, but she seemed a child. Her only luggage was a small shoulder bag. Cecilia was failing to create a homely atmosphere. Leda declined any dry clothes but sat dripping in her wet ones. Her shoes squelched when she stood up, which she did as soon as Tim reappeared to say the bed was fixed. Cecilia insisted on collecting her wet sweater, trousers and shoes from outside the closed spare-room door after Leda had undressed. Leda complied, on condition she could know exactly where her clothes were to be, and Cecilia showed her the airing cupboard, and, in detail, where her clothes would spend the night. Cecilia called a hearty 'Sleep well!' through the door as she picked up the garments. No response. She supposed Leda's undies and socks would have to dry as best they could. Cecilia hoped she would not sleep in them. However, Leda had survived for nearly two years in whatever circumstances had been hers, and must, in some sense, know how to look after herself.

Tim had guiltily sneaked back to the TV, but now turned it off, and came into the kitchen for a conversation with Cecilia. They did not quite whisper, but talked in low voices.

'What on earth is happening?' asked Tim, coming close.

'Leda turned up on Ian and Marina and Ian has offloaded her on to us, but only for the night.'

'How do we know it's only the night?'

'True. The important thing is not to say anything about Cephas.'

'OK. Does it matter that she's mad?'

'How do you mean, matter?'

'Will things be queer? In the night?'

'I don't know, I hope not.'

'Is she in bed now?'

'Yes.'

'Would it be all right if I watch the end of the match?'

'Yes.'

Cecilia was left to her thoughts. She now felt a moral duty to examine her very strong impulse to keep Leda and Cephas apart, and to do nothing to jog Leda's memory. Was that fair? Was it not just the kind of crazy-making antic that would make a psychotic person tormented? Cecilia, who had spent the whole of her professional life unearthing buried pasts, realised that she was now taking it for granted that the right thing to do was to make sure the past stayed buried, or, even worse, to bury it deliberately. Then it struck her that she had no reason to suppose Leda did not know she had given birth to a baby nearly two years ago, and that the baby had been associated with Ian. How psychotic was she? Hard to tell. But indeed it might be precisely because that fact was lodged in her mind, a piece of history about themselves that few would forget, that she had sought Ian out. Everything in Cecilia cried out against this. She wondered uncomfortably whether Leda had set eyes on Cephas during her brief visit to Ian's house. All too likely.

She thought about 'Leda' and 'Volumnia'. She remembered her own immediate impulse to continue to call this person 'Leda', as she always had, although Leda Oubliette could not possibly be a real name, and to reject the imposition of a fresh alias. Cecilia's psychotherapist's sense of duty to internal continuity, continuity symbolised in this context by an unchangeable name, ran counter to her much stronger desire that Leda should be amnesiac where the self of two years ago was concerned. She thought back to how readily Ian, eager, no doubt, for any available discontinuity in Leda's mind, had accepted 'Volumnia'. Perhaps Cecilia should have done so too. Unfortunately, and in the heat of the moment Ian may have forgotten this, Volumnia was every inch a mother, and not an auspicious one.

However, if Leda had arrived on Ian's doorstep to reclaim Cephas, she wouldn't stand a chance of doing so, under the law. She had abandoned Cephas when he was merely weeks old, and hadn't seen him or looked for him ever since. And Ian had always had parental responsibility. The worry in Cecilia's mind was not that Cephas was in danger of being put into Leda's custody – look at her, anyway – but that her arrival would cause trouble in Ian's little family, and disconcert

Marina, who had been so wonderful in loving and accepting Cephas. And what about disconcerting Cephas? Cecilia's mind went back to the time when Cephas's eyes had raked every face he saw for the features of Leda.

The obvious person to talk to at this point was Ian, but Cecilia did not want to interrupt an important conversation between him and Marina.

It was good to have strong feelings about something other than cancer, and about people other than herself. She felt more human, at this stage in the evening, than she had felt since her ill-starred appointment with Mr P. She crept back into the sitting room, an ear cocked in Leda's direction, to watch the end of the penalty shoot-out with Tim, and then it felt like bedtime. Tim, as usual, fell asleep at once. As Cecilia lay awake, she could hear quiet activity next door.

~

Leda, beautiful but emaciated, was taking careful stock of her room. She had removed her socks, but was still wearing pants. A bra she neither possessed nor needed. She moved about softly, looking like an erotic model in a photo shoot, except for the expression of intense anguish and anxiety on her face, and the absence of bodily self-awareness in her demeanour.

She was checking out this new place for any sign that her arrival had been foreseen. She was looking for a telltale mark. The trouble was, the mark might be very small. She started with the windowsill, and worked her way along it, with eyes and very light fingers. Then she did the top of the bedside table, then the shelf below. Then she did the top of the chest of drawers. That was it, for the spare-room furniture. But she still had the floor to do. The floor was a fitted carpet that had not been very well vacuumed. She had a torch in her bag for use on these occasions, and shone it as best she could in the crevices of the carpet's dusty pile. No mark. No mark so far.

She was stronger than she looked, and was able to move the single bed fairly briskly and quietly, first one way, so that half the carpet underneath could be investigated, then the other, for the other half. It was much dustier under the bed than elsewhere; but to her practised eye dust could not of itself obscure a mark. No mark to be seen. Now she was exhausted and longing to get into bed. The bedding would not need to be done, because it was obvious from the conversation between Cecilia and Tim that it was fresh, and if her coming had been foreseen, the mark would have to have been put in place before Tim made up the bed. That was a relief. She left the light on, as usual, to be on the safe side, and climbed into bed. Her heart was racing, and so was her mind. Should she redo the windowsill? Had there been a doubtful area? No, she had been very careful. She began to relax. She began to feel dry, warm and drowsy. Tomorrow she must get new batteries for the torch. There had been a flicker.

She sat up with a start. She had been reminded that she had not done the drawers, but only the top surface. With any luck the drawers would be empty. They were not. There were three of them. The top one had a few pillowcases and towels in it. These articles had to be shaken out and inspected, of course on both sides. She could save the torch by doing this close underneath the ceiling light, for which she had to stand unsteadily on the bed. The second drawer was stuffed with papers, apparently old bills and bank statements, going back five and six years. It took a long time to check these, some by the torch, some by the overhead light. There was no mark. The third drawer had nothing in it but a pair of men's shoes. They could be easily checked, and Leda got back into bed, by now aching with fatigue.

She was about to fall asleep when the voice of one of Us reminded her that though she had done the contents of the drawers, she had not done the insides of the drawers themselves.

She was up in a trice, and hard at work, emptying the drawers again, and running fingers and eyes over the splintery wood. How could she have overlooked that? It was because she was tired. But one of Us could always be relied upon to remind her, and that was something to be thankful for. No mark was found.

It looked as if the vigilance of Them had failed to detect where she would be tonight. She got back into bed.

One of Us nudged her sleepy mind with the thought that she had not pulled out the chest of drawers and done the carpet underneath it. She was dutifully on the go again, but the piece of furniture was too heavy to pull out quietly until she had removed the papers from the middle drawer. She piled the papers on the bed. Now she was able to shift the chest of drawers and do underneath it, the carpet a darker colour not disclosed since Tim had bought the house forty-five years ago. The papers then had to be replaced in the drawer a second time, and the drawer stealthily closed. Dawn and its chorus were beginning before Leda got to bed and to sleep.

~

Ian ran home. He arrived to find Marina sitting in a low chair feeding Ali. It was a comforting sight. Instead of bursting into the room full of words and expostulations, he abated both his speed and his volume, and came gently and quietly over to stand next to Marina, his shins against her knee.

She looked up, and there was humour in her eyes. 'Well,' she said, 'So what now?'

'Mum took her in for the night. I'm sure Mum will help sort her out. We don't want her round here. What do you think was happening when she and Cephas saw each other?'

'There was nothing to be seen. Cephas looked round at her, then went straight back to the TV. She didn't even look at him. She didn't look at anyone, but she was at least aware of you and me. I don't think she was any more aware of Cephas than she was of, well, Benjy.' Marina indicated the sleeping cat. 'Or am I being very facile?'

Ian was silent, marshalling his thoughts, still standing, pressing his shins against Marina's leg. He put his hand on her head.

'I absolutely don't want her round here. Not at all. I probably should have taken her to Social Services, not to Mum's. We don't want her to think she has anything to do with us. I wish now I hadn't taken her to Mum's, but if I hadn't, we'd have had to have her for the night. Thank God I'm at home till the fifteenth. I wonder if we can get her into an institution before then.'

'Maybe she's not as mad as she was.'

'I think she's worse. She's much grimmer. More driven. Thinner.' Ian did not say, 'No one would want to have an affair with her as she is now,' but that's what he was thinking.

Marina said, 'But she didn't say anything mad.'

'She said she was called Volumnia, and wouldn't eat or drink anything, and wouldn't talk. She seemed to have no curiosity. She seemed completely preoccupied. Didn't you feel that? How she got it together to trace me, I can't imagine. But the worrying thing isn't how, but why.'

'Did you still think she was beautiful?'

'No! I thought she was terrifying.'

'I thought she was beautiful.'

Ian was not to be drawn in to the beauty question. His eyes were moving everywhere as he tried to work out a strategy. 'If we can't get rid of her before I go, perhaps you and the children had better stay with your parents while I'm away.'

'I can't. I've got work.'

'Be ill,' said Ian.

'I can't. You be ill.'

'Mum will be here tomorrow as it's a working day for you.

'OK. But she must not let Leda anywhere near here. I'm sure she wouldn't anyway. We must be very clear. I don't want any contact between Leda and Cephas.'

'She can't harm Cephas, you know,' said Marina. 'Can you imagine Child Protection giving him to her? There's nothing she can do. Cephas is completely safe.' She put an arm reassuringly round Ian's legs. 'In fact,' she went on, 'it doesn't actually matter if, or what, she remembers.'

'Maybe it's him I'm thinking of, more. What if she made a scene? And the fact is that we simply don't know what is in her mind. Does she remember she gave birth to Cephas? Does she know Cephas is the child she gave birth to? We have no idea, and we can't ask, or we might revive memories. Memories better unrevived. Which reminds me, no one must say the word Cephas in her presence. That's terribly important.'

There was a silence, while they thought. Marina felt sorry for Leda. Leda was being so completely unconsidered as an end in herself. But Marina did not care enough about this to want to alter the dynamics. Let Leda be kept at bay. Let her be institutionalised if possible. Let her disappear again. Let her forget. Let there be no link between her mind and the existence of Cephas. But in spite of these thoughts, Marina said, 'Perhaps Cecilia will get Leda to talk to her. I always think Cecilia must have been a very good psychotherapist.'

'I don't think she did nutters,' said Ian. 'Not real basket cases. It was more subtle than that, I got the impression. The important thing is I talk to Cecilia tomorrow morning early.'

Ali had fallen asleep at the breast. Ian leant over to look at the little face. 'Shall I put him in his cot?' he whispered.

He took Ali from Marina's lap. Ali's lips moved slightly as Ian's arms closed round him, and his eyes went slitty, then closed again. Ian went into his and Marina's bedroom and laid Ali carefully down in his carrycot. It was quite a warm evening, Ian thought, so he put only one woolly shawl on Ali. He tucked the light shawl well in, all round. Ali would probably sleep until about five. Ian looked down at him, satisfied. Then he went next door to check on Cephas, who had his own room. He was fast asleep, his big bear on top of him. He was pink and beautiful and sweating slightly, his brown curly hair damp on his forehead. Ian moved Big Bear to the side, in case he was making Cephas too hot. He picked up Small Bear and put him where Big Bear had been. Cephas usually liked both bears to be available at night.

Chapter 16

From time to time during the night Cecilia heard the furtive sounds from next door subside. Then she tried to sleep. But the noises started up again. She lay and stared into the dark, trying to understand what the movements might betoken. At the same time cancer and her personal future, so uncertain, were never out of her mind. She dozed off during a lull both of noises and of anxiety, and was woken at seven with tea.

'She was on the go all night,' Cecilia whispered to Tim, accepting her mug. Thor slipped into the room with Tim and leapt on to the bed. He walked up Cecilia's body and crouched, purring into her face.

'All's quiet now,' said Tim.

'You were asleep. It was soft, inexorable noises, going on and on.'

'Will you be able to have a word with her, I mean, do some psychotherapy?'

'Hardly. It isn't the setting. I don't know what to do. We need outside help. Organisations. We need to get rid of her. What about Cephas? He's got to be protected.'

'Well. It would be good to know what her motive is in chasing up Ian, after nearly two years.'

'What if she's chasing up Cephas? Never say that name in her hearing, by the way.'

'Need you be so scared of her? Even if she does see Cephas'

– he altered his tone to a stage whisper for the word – 'what can she do? She has no legal right to custody or care.'

'I don't know. Rock the boat. Grab Cephas and scream. Remind him of the first two months of his life, when we don't know how bad it was for him, with a mad mother.'

Cecilia's mobile rang. Of course it was Ian.

'How are we going to get rid of her?' he said. 'Thank God I'm home for a couple of weeks, but I've got a lot of work. You're going to have to keep Leda away from Cephas. Can you do that? You're having the children today, at our house. How can you be sure Leda won't come with you?'

'I don't know. She's fast asleep now, having been on the go all night.'

'Marina is going to work at nine. You'll probably be here about eight-thirty. And I'll be around, though I've got meetings. I'll have to be out for a couple of hours both morning and afternoon, but I'll come home at lunchtime, to see how things are going, and then as early as possible this afternoon. Don't take any risks.'

'It may not be as bad as we think,' said Cecilia, aware that Ian's panic was nudging her into a position more like Tim's.

'I've rung the police,' said Ian, 'as I have to do, every time I hear from her. I said I'd seen her. They wanted an address. I said I didn't know where she had gone for the night. A lie, I'm afraid. But I don't want the police visiting you and prodding her memory with having had a baby two years ago. They managed to trace her parents, by the way, I don't know how, when she has so many pseudonyms. I gave the police permission to give her parents my phone number. I don't know if that was a good move.'

'Well, surely the parents would have reported her disappearance from their lives at some point, and the police made a match. I always thought they must have got that missing persons photograph from the unfortunate parents.'

'OK, Mum, look, I don't care. All I want is for her to

disappear again. Will you try? Couldn't you get her into a mental hospital? She needs a psychiatric assessment.'

'Indeed she does. But one man may bring a horse to water—'

'My phone's going, I'll have to ring off. See you in an hour.'

Cecilia was tired. She had hardly slept, and had a day of childcare ahead of her. Although there was now a rich overgrowth of other anxieties, her private concern for herself was still there, able to make her heart turn over and sink when her thoughts took that direction.

'Can you cope with Leda?' she asked Tim. 'I'm minding the boys at Ian's today. What will happen when she wakes up?'

'Well, I thought I was going to tennis,' said Tim. 'I wonder if she plays. There are always spare people looking for a game, or for a fourth.'

This was a new idea indeed. It created a different Leda and one whom Cecilia was rather proud of Tim for having invented. Let him try it. And if not, and if Leda wandered round to Ian's, Ian would be there on and off, Cecilia all day, and Marina home about six. Whatever might be in Leda's mind, Cephas would not be at any risk.

Off went Cecilia, trying not to limp as she approached Ian's. Cephas recognised her knock and ran to the front door. 'Gran, Gran!' he was calling, and she waggled a finger through the letter box.

Ian opened the door. He looked relieved. 'At least she hasn't tagged along after you,' he said.

Cecilia crouched down, so that Cephas would not think it odd that she did not sweep him into her arms. They hugged.

'Gran cally,' he said; but she couldn't, and together they walked into the kitchen. Marina, who was feeding Ali there, looked up and smiled at Cecilia.

'I've left two bottles of expressed milk in the fridge,' she said. 'If he's hungry again, and he will be, he'll have to have formula. Is that OK?'

It was, and Cecilia knew the ropes.

'Cephas's lunch is in the covered dish in the fridge,' Marina went on, 'just to be microwaved. There's plenty of everything. The usual sort of thing for his tea.' And Marina always thought to cater for Cecilia's lunch: 'I hoped you might like what's left of the salmon and broccoli we had last night.'

Marina had noticed Cecilia's limp, but also that she was trying to conceal it. Cecilia registered that Marina did not bring up the subject of Leda, possibly because Cephas was present, possibly for some other reason, more to do with downgrading the status of an unwelcome problem, and she took Marina's cue. Cecilia had noticed in her daughter-in-law a knack for moral leadership, which she was not sure she entirely liked, though she had been grateful for it where Ian was concerned. At this moment she felt Marina was taking a position of wisdom and restraint, the kind of position that Cecilia had got used to occupying, or finding attributed to herself; and this put Cecilia's nose slightly out of joint.

Ali was in the big pram in the garden, and Cecilia and Cephas went outside as well. Cephas wanted to show Cecilia some little cars he had stabled under a bush. He was particularly pleased by the fact that they were impossible to see until you drew very close. Cecilia was adequately astonished. So the day of childcare started.

∼

Tim did not find it difficult to hang about, because he had so many indoor occupations, mostly at the computer. But when lunchtime came and went, and there had been no sound from Leda, he began to hanker for his tennis. It was a fine day now, but the forecast had suggested showers later. He looked out of the window at the sky. Eva arrived, to do the cleaning, and Tim told her there was a guest. Hanging about doing nothing was a bit more difficult for Tim with Eva being busy around him. He found the contrast rather strong. However, what with the sound of vacuuming, noises began to emerge from Leda's room. Tim waited, filling the kettle with a view to coffee or tea. Finally Leda emerged from her room, fully dressed, intent and wan. She did not meet Tim's eye or sit down, but she accepted a cup of tea. She drank it standing, her bag on her shoulder. The only moment she fleetingly focussed was on Thor, who was strolling about the kitchen, and prepared to be interested in her. She stooped to stroke him.

'Do you play tennis?' Tim asked. 'I often do, about this time, and you would be welcome.'

Leda took a long time to answer this question, and Tim sat down and began to be beguiled afresh by the newspaper. Leda was considering. There was very little chance that They would trace her to a tennis club, so this might be an occupation Us would approve of. On the other hand, was it safe to leave her bedroom, with the possibility that in her absence They would identify it as where she was staying? If she lay low all day in her bedroom, there was no chance They could slip in and place a mark. If she went out for a considerable length of time, They might invade, and she would have to do marks, all over again, this evening, as she had last night. She wasn't getting a clear directive from one of Us about what she should do, although she readied her brain, and listened. She knew the nature of her present task, which was to seek out Ian, for the word was that he had been recruited by Them. Because Leda was an agent of Us, her physical proximity to Ian would weaken the hold that They were able to exert over him, and with any luck he would become what Us called Ex-dangerous. Her task entailed seeing Ian every day for a week. That would be enough to detoxify him. Leda was rather humbly grateful to have been endowed with what Us termed Transformative Energy.

Presumably Ian was at work rather than at home at the

moment. She had successfully performed her yesterday's sighting of him. She must catch him again this evening. As time did not press, she decided to agree to play tennis. Tim was pleased and surprised, and found a pair of Cecilia's tennis shoes, which fitted well enough. Leda knew she would have to do marks later, having left her bedroom untenanted; but the attraction of tennis, in which sport she had represented both her school and her university, was strong.

~

Cecilia limped home at about five, leaving Ian with the little boys.

'Now I'm going to amaze you,' said Tim, coming out of his study. 'Leda is absolutely brilliant.'

'Brilliant?'

'At tennis.'

This was really interesting, but Cecilia was longing to sit down. They went into the kitchen and Tim put the kettle on. 'You must be tired,' he said.

'Yes, and a cup of tea will be nice, but do tell me about Leda and tennis.'

'Well, first she was a fourth in a fairly mediocre doubles, but soon everyone was staring. Then she played with me against the Greens, then in a singles that held everyone spellbound.'

'And what was she like, about it?'

'Took it in her stride. She must know she's near professional. What a surprise.'

'Indeed. Where is she now?'

'In the spare room. Has been since we got back.'

'What are we going to do about her?'

Tim took up the drift of the question, rather than the question itself. 'She didn't seem mad at all. Just deadly serious.'

'Do you mean because she's good at tennis, and can do that without seeming mad, we keep her indefinitely as a house guest?'

It occurred to Cecilia that Tim might have no objection to the continued residence of this beautiful and now, to him, interesting young woman. There was a look on Tim's face she did not quite like. He looked younger, brighter-eyed, liberated. She became aware of herself as a worn, untidy woman, getting on for seventy, with a full colostomy bag and a bad hip, who hadn't fully solved the problem of how to have post-operative sex with her husband. She wanted to say something blistering about Leda, but, on the other hand, if tennis took over, it would be a way of keeping Leda away from Cephas and his family. So she said nothing, and was a little comforted by Thor, who never failed in love.

Tim was not a person to read a mind. 'You should see her at the net,' he was saying. 'It's a pleasure to watch her.'

Cecilia was sure it was, and bitterly sipped her tea.

At that moment Leda came into the room, her bag on her shoulder, fresh from doing marks. It was on her mind that she had not yet seen Ian today and had to find a means of doing so. She stood, looking at the floor.

'I've been saying how splendid your tennis is,' said Tim. Leda did not respond. Cecilia was pleased. Surely Tim's enthusiasm would be discouraged. But he was busy offering her a cup of tea. 'Of course you must come again tomorrow.'

'OK,' Leda said, thinking that it would be a way of passing some time incognito again, before the daily rendezvous with Ian could be arranged. The thought had occurred to her that Ian might go abroad before the necessary week was up, and she did not know what Us would have to say about that.

'Do you know if Ian would be at home now?' she said to Cecilia.

Cecilia could not think of an answer. Taking silence as agreement, Leda slipped out of the room and the house. 'Now what?' wailed Cecilia, picking up the phone and dialling. 'Ian?'

'Yes.'

'She's on her way to you.'

'Why?'

'I don't know.'

'Why did you let her?'

'No stopping her.'

Ian rang off. She could imagine his stern, exasperated expression. As well as her fear of cancer, her anxiety about Cephas, and the shine in Tim's eye, Cecilia now had the feeling of having let Ian down.

Ian opened the door but did not ask Leda in. He stood on the doorstep. 'Sorry,' he said, 'we're rather busy.' It seemed better, with the use of 'we', to pretend Marina was within, and, indeed, she was expected home any minute.

Leda was glad it was Ian who had answered the door. That saved time. She could do Ian on the doorstep, and, in her consequently brief absence, a mark would have scant opportunity of creeping into her bedroom. After thirty seconds, in which both stood still, Leda exuding Transformative Energy, and Ian longing to close the door on her, she said, 'OK.' She turned to go and almost at once encountered Marina. Of this hurrying figure she took no notice.

Ian took Marina in his arms in the doorway. 'You're home, good, good, good,' he said.

'Why was she here?' asked Marina, too dismayed to give herself wholeheartedly to the hug.

Cephas heard his mother's voice and came out of the kitchen at top speed. 'Mummy.'

Marina picked him up and held him tight. 'Why was she here?'

'I don't know. I said she couldn't come in.'

'My mummy,' said Cephas.

He was rubbing his nose against her cheek. He glanced round, hoping to see Ali and lord it over him, but Ali was not in view. They went into the kitchen. Marina took everything in with a glance – the fact that Ali had had a formula feed; that Cephas had had fish fingers for tea; that Ali had a different babygro on, which probably meant he had been sick; that poor Ian had already had a glass of wine; that Cecilia had tried to leave everything shipshape.

'All well,' she said to Ian, 'but what was she doing here, and why were you staring raptly at each other in the porch?'

'Raptly?' Ian was astonished. 'Surely you realise I regard her as Cruella de Vil and Himmler rolled into one? Obviously I was keeping her out.'

Marina saw to the children for the next couple of hours, but was not easy in her mind. The set of Leda's head, seen from behind as Marina approached the house, had shown concentration and intent. Did Leda crave to see Cephas, or was it Ian she wanted? Marina did not forget that her husband had had a brief but passionate affair with this bizarre woman.

Ian was cooking, with Ali in a sling. He had meant to be ahead with the supper by the time Marina got in, but first he had been talking with Cecilia, then Cephas had peed all over the floor while running about with his potty on his head, then Ali had puked up most of the formula feed. But Ian was happy. His life was right for him. He loved Marina, and admired her. He was inclined to idealise her, and saw no disadvantage in that. Cephas he had grown to like very much. He had more to do with Cephas than he had with Ali, due to the ages of the children, and the natural way the family paired off on account of that. Ian carefully noticed Cephas's development, especially now, when he was beginning to put words together. And thoughts. They had been in the garden earlier, he and Cephas, and had watched Benjy sunning himself on the wall.

'Benjy,' Cephas said, then he looked at Ian and said, 'Thor.'

Ian was touched at Cephas linking the cat Benjy with the cat of Cecilia and Tim, who had actually meant much more to him than Benjy did, and at a more difficult time in his life. 'Yes,' said Ian, 'you will see Thor soon.'

'Soon,' said Cephas.

How did he know what 'soon' meant? Perhaps he didn't, but knew it was comforting. Cephas interested Ian more than Ali did, but because Ali was Ian's own flesh and blood he loved Ali in a more unquestionable way. Ian would have interposed his body between a bullet and either child, but with Cephas there would have been a tinge of duty about it. With Ali it would have been a reflex action.

Because of the nature of his work, Ian was abroad too much to be enslaved and ground down by his family, and enough to ensure that his homecoming was, every time, a hero's return. He enjoyed his work, and the family had no money worries. Ian was happy. Marina had devised for him a life that suited him, and he had trusted her enough to say yes to it. But now this Leda business was disturbing his contentment.

It was a priority to get rid of Leda before his next assignment, and Cecilia did not seem to be making much headway with this. He had vaguely hoped Cecilia might get Leda into an institution, but there seemed to be no talk of that. The bloody parents, whoever and wherever they were, to whom the police had given Ian's phone number, had shown no signs of life. Leda could not go on staying with Cecilia and Tim, a couple of streets away from Ian's. She mustn't be allowed to come round and bother Marina while he was away. His mistake had been to take her to Cecilia's, but the alternative was to turn her out into the rainstorm. He should have done that. He had lied to the police about where she had gone for the night, and that was probably an offence. He was not indifferent to the knowledge that hers was a body he had once, briefly, intensely loved, nor to the guilty wish for that body to disappear for ever without leaving a trace on the earth.

Chapter 17

I t was the morning of Cecilia's MRI and she was having breakfast before setting off for the hospital.

'Tim, an extraordinary thing,' she said, coming back into the bedroom, and speaking in a whisper. 'I found a copy of *The Lady* in the kitchen bin. Of course I've taken it out and put it in the recycling. And there was a crumpled-up envelope with it. Addressed to Volumnia Adjutant, at our address.'

'What lady?'

'It's a magazine.'

Tim was able do nothing with this, and Cecilia withdrew. She could make a few deductions. Leda had intercepted the post, but that was quite understandable, as the post usually arrived in the afternoon, when Leda might be about and Cecilia not. Evidently Leda had given her current alias, and the address of where she was staying, to someone unknown. Why should someone have sent a copy of *The Lady* to Leda? And, having received it, why should Leda have thrown it away, thrown it away almost on receipt?

Cecilia returned to the recycling box. She looked at the magazine, marked by kitchen waste, and flipped through it for any clue. There was material about children, which caused a certain disquiet to Cecilia; but on the whole it seemed to be aimed at the middle aged and elderly. There were advertisements for nannies – could Leda possibly have ambitions there, stemming perhaps from her truncated motherhood? Perish the thought. Now Cecilia picked out the envelope. 'Volumnia Adjutant', and Cecilia's familiar address, in a rather artistic, almost certainly feminine hand. A buff, good-quality envelope, not reused. She wasn't sure, but she thought it was rather wildly overstamped. She went to the window, but from any angle the postmark was illegible. She put the envelope back in the recycling.

Tim was not accompanying her to the MRI, because there would be no news, good or bad, that day. He would come to the next appointment, which would be for the result. As Cecilia limped from Reception to Waiting Room, from Waiting Room to Waiting Area where patients changed into hospital gowns, she felt the demeanour she assumed when in thrall to the hospital possessing her once again. She was pleasant, humorous, patient with the wait; a little ironic, as if not really ill, as these others were ill; and, under that veneer, abjectly yearning to be liked by these skilled adolescents from all the countries in the world, who held her fate in their hands. She spotted one or two other elderly middle-class women, whom the hospital seemed to affect in the same way as it did her. She saw the well-behaved, cooperative smile on their lips that she felt on her own, and detected in them the same private panic, which they, like she, had long been conditioned to hide. Cecilia always took a book with her to the hospital, but seldom read it. In the end her turn came to be escorted to the white tunnel where she must lie. When her time was up she felt as Thor did whenever he left the vet. But she had not really left the vet, or not as Thor did, with a routine return for injections in a year's time. She would be back in two weeks, to exchange limbo for Inferno or Paradiso.

She went straight from the hospital to Ian's, where she was to look after Cephas while Marina took Ali for injections. Ali, too, would be like a cat at the vet's, but not for long, and

Marina would certainly make it all right for him. When Cecilia arrived, Marina and Ali were ready to set forth, and Cephas was looking forward to having his grandmother to himself. The word 'my' had developed a big presence in his still small vocabulary since the birth of Ali.

'My gran,' he said, when he saw her.

Because Cecilia had been in full charge of Cephas for most of his first year, she had a special relationship with him. Cephas's transition to Ian and Marina had passed smoothly, largely owing to Cecilia's constant presence in his life during that time. But she was 'mine' to Cephas in a way she would never quite be to Ali, and she felt that it was not in her heart only that there was an abiding sense of their having survived, survived something that could have been fatal for him, and survived it together; and a sense that it was because of her that he was unscathed, and had a mind that was able lightly and joyously to fasten completely on his little cars, and how to make them run, one by one, down a tilted board, each in turn received by Cecilia.

Either she was soon going to be dead, she thought, or she was not. Whichever way, from Cephas's point of view, she must put her all into this sort of moment. If she was to disappear from him, their love and cooperation would be important to him for ever, as a memory, as an active benefit installed within him. That would make the grief worse, perhaps; but he would be the stronger for it. So she caught the cars and handed them back to him, and the game went on. Then she spotted that one of the cars had no roof, and she was disposed to make a little man out of plasticine to insert into the driver's seat.

'Now a little man is driving this one,' she said.

Cephas had not liked the interruption, although he had understood it, and had waited patiently. He considered the improved vehicle. 'No little man,' he said, and carefully detached the plasticine figure. Breathing hard with concentration, he transferred it on to a small plastic horse and put the equestrian figure at a safe distance from the game.

Cecilia arrived home to find Tim and Leda just in from tennis. Leda was wearing what appeared to be brand-new tennis clothes. She looked stunning. The short white skirt showed off her impeccable legs, and the socks and shoes contributed an athletic note. The white top was excessively becoming. Cecilia looked at Tim. Everything in his face and demeanour showed that none of this beauty was lost on him. Tim launched into a detailed description of the tennis, and of his partner's amazing prowess, and had clearly forgotten the MRI. Cecilia felt old and dejected, furious and self-pitying. Her unresponsiveness was not noticed. Soon, to Tim's disappointment, Leda left the room and her bedroom door could be heard closing behind her.

'What does she do, all those hours in the spare room?' said Cecilia. She was attempting to disregard Leda's wondrousness, and the question was designed to return her in Tim's mind to her correct status as a problem.

Cecilia's tone reminded Tim of the MRI, and, understandably, the fire went out of his eyes.

'Where does she get her money from? Those tennis clothes must have cost something,' carped Cecilia, with the same intent.

It struck her as ironic that she could honestly say she loved Tim, and yet she hated the look of happiness on his face. He seemed much handsomer than usual, and younger. His eyes shone. Even what remained of his hair seemed to rise more vigorously on his brow. And she, who loved him, was setting herself to remove these enhancements if she could, and looked forward to the return of his usual appearance, pleasant, absent, mildly haggard and burdened. Talk turned to the MRI, and Tim sagged immediately. Cecilia was being the bad witch at the christening, importing gloom and fear to replace festivity; and there was nothing she could do about it. She hated Tim's golden glow, and she hated Leda, the good fairy whose wand had evoked it.

~

Marina was becoming more and more sure that it was Ian, not Cephas, that Leda was after. Her evidence was that Leda would ring the doorbell, and, on the step, if Marina answered, was likely to ask: 'Is Ian in?' Sometimes she did not ask this, but stood on the step, peering over Marina's shoulder into the house. Sometimes Marina had Ali in her arms, and sometimes Cephas ran to the front door ahead of her; but Leda took no notice of either child. She peered wistfully for Ian, or sometimes muttered a request for him. Sometimes Ian would appear in the background, and then Leda's face came to life. She would call: 'Ian, here a minute,' and stare at him, as if mesmerised. Ian would ask her if she was all right, and if she had any plans for the future, holding Cephas's head rather firmly against his leg. She didn't answer, but turned and left. Something like this had happened every day Marina had spent at home. She had begun to wonder what happened when she was working and Ian was in sole charge. Did he invite her in? He said not, and she believed him. But she knew it would be difficult for Ian to bear such peculiar social moments as these visits created, without doing something polite to normalise the situation, even if he was not beguiled by Leda's beauty. This state of affairs had been going on for nearly a week. So Marina was uneasy. She was also cross with herself for her unease.

One day she got home to find Leda on the doorstep, the door open, and Ian framed in the doorway. Ian and Leda were silent, staring at each other. Marina's arrival seemed to break a spell, and Leda turned to leave, brushing past Marina with a face radiant with the beauty of relief and achievement. Marina felt that Ian looked confused. She came in as usual, and summed up the situation with regard to the children. Cephas was parked in front of the television, and Ali asleep when he shouldn't be if his parents were to have a half-decent night. Ian wanted to give her a hug, but she ignored him, and he trailed into the kitchen after her. He felt embarrassed, although he did not see what he could be doing differently with Leda.

'So what was happening out there?' asked Marina. Her voice was chilly.

'The usual. She just stared at me.'

'You seemed to be gazing back.'

'I've found that if I do, she buzzes off. It's as if she gets enough of something.'

'Yes, but of what?'

'I have no idea. She is a nutter. How can one know?'

'I think she's in love with you.'

Ian had harboured this thought himself, and was secretly flattered by it. He said, 'The good thing is she never takes any notice of Cephas.'

'I know she doesn't seem to, and we can hope that's genuine.'

'I don't think she's suddenly going to turn round now and remember she gave birth to him, if that's what you mean, and make a scene. A scene is all she could do, remember – she has no legal rights.'

'So she trots round every day from Cecilia's because she's besotted with you.'

Marina began to clatter accusingly in the sink and look around for evidence that her supper had been thought of. Cephas heard his mother's voice and now ran into the room. Marina stopped whatever she was doing and swept him up for a big hug.

Ian was aggrieved. He had done nothing to encourage Leda's attentions. When she had first reappeared, his only feeling had been fear that she wanted contact with Cephas. Time had allayed this fear. Leda had revealed herself as harmless. But now, it seemed, she was making Marina jealous. That was too mad. But, Ian thought guiltily, there was no denying that when he was at home without Marina, and he heard the doorbell, the thought that it might be Leda lifted his spirits. He enjoyed the brief and mysterious eye contact she sought with him. This didn't actually mean he thought about her between times. He was much too busy and cheerfully ensconced in his own life to have hankerings. But the beauty of her face and the intensity of her silent gaze was engaging at the moment it was happening.

'My greatest wish,' he said, 'is that she finds something else to do than hang round Cecilia's and visit us.'

'She plays tennis, too, with Tim.'

'Does she? What an extraordinary person.'

Marina was wrong to interpret this remark as approving. Ian was registering surprise that Leda's personality included areas of organisation when she was otherwise so delusional. Marina's misapprehension led her to say, 'I don't see any signs of supper. Perhaps these interactions with such an extraordinary person drive mundane matters out of your mind.'

'I'm sorry. I got behind with things. Darling Marina, I can't believe you mind, mind anything to do with me and Leda. Don't you know how much I love you?'

Cephas understood some of these words, and said, 'No!' to Ian. 'No,' he said, 'my mummy.' He gripped Marina's neck.

Ian came over and put his arms round them both. 'No more of this nonsense,' he said. Marina was pacified, but the idea of Leda remained a sore patch in her mind.

∽

Marina need not have worried. Leda did not come again. The reason for Leda's rapturous expression at the end of the visit that Marina had viewed from the pavement was that it was the final visit. Leda's mission to Ian was accomplished. Ian was still one of Them, nothing could stop that; but he was rendered innocuous by seven consecutive days of Leda's Transformative Energy. He was now designated Ex-dangerous. Leda would await instructions to move on to someone else.

The someone else was revealed the next day, and was Lewis Munro, the man in charge at Tim's tennis club. Lewis was cheerful, helpful and middle aged, not bad at tennis himself and often in demand as a coach. It is often the least likely people, thought Leda, who are agents for Them. They were constantly getting better at recruiting agents who were inconspicuous and could even be mistaken for the salt of the earth. Leda was pleased about her next mission: she had been enjoying tennis, and it should not be difficult to encounter Lewis daily for a week. So far, Leda had only been to the club with Tim. Now she would have to join, for there might be days he would not want to go. But that was all right, for plenty of money was arriving.

~

'Tim,' said Cecilia, on the morning of the appointment with the oncologist, 'the most extraordinary thing has happened again. Another copy of *The Lady* is in the rubbish.'

'How do you mean, the lady?'

'It's a magazine. It's a back copy, but not very far back. I had to fish it out to put it in the recycling, again. I can't possibly try to explain to her about rubbish collections, she'd attach a mad importance to the categories. With *The Lady* was a buff envelope again, crumpled up. This time it was addressed to "Medea Wimbledon".'

'Medea Wimbledon?'

'Yes. That'll be her new alias.' Cecilia was glad of this opportunity to present Leda to Tim in a madder light than the tennis court afforded. 'Medea. What do you say to that?'

'What time is our appointment?' asked Tim, wondering whether tennis could be fitted into the day.

Cecilia followed his train of thought, and was hurt, although she had liked 'our'. Inferno or Paradiso for her; for him, the club, with Leda. 'Ten-thirty,' she said. 'Plenty of time for tennis afterwards.' He did not recognise that she had read his mind, nor that she was attacking him.

That afternoon Helen came.

'I've missed you so much,' she said to Cecilia. 'It's ages since I saw you.' They hugged, then Helen stood Cecilia away from her to study her face. 'You look a bit pale. What is it? I know! Leda!' – which Helen knew about by phone.

'Medical stuff I didn't tell you,' said Cecilia. 'But I'll tell you now. I've had worries about a supposed pelvic fracture, and whether it was bone cancer or radiation damage, and I've had an X-ray and an MRI—'

'Good heavens, how ghastly, and you didn't tell me. I thought we always tell each other our cancer moments. I shall have no peace if you start hiding things from me.'

'I'm sorry. In a way this was too near the bone. Pun. I would have told you if there was a verdict, either way. Anyway, the news is that there still isn't. No verdict. The news is that there is no news. The MRI doesn't clarify which it is. And the wonderful thing is I don't have to do anything. Another MRI in December "when the picture will be clearer".'

'But Cecilia – it might be bone cancer.' A vicarious version of the Inferno or Paradiso landscape was coming into view for Helen. She was horrified.

Cecilia was disappointed at a reaction to the news, or the lack of news, so different from her own. 'It might. But this has shown me that I dread hospital, and treatment, even more than I dread illness and death.'

'But I don't, on your behalf.'

'Tim and I both felt better – liberated – when we walked out. Borrowed time, perhaps, but, who knows, my hip may have stopped hurting in three months.'

'But for now you are in limbo.'

'Yes. But I feel better for having an authorised place in limbo. Before this morning, I was just floating uncertified in limbo. Now limbo's my official habitat. It'll do me, for the moment.'

'Usually they're longing to do tests and biopsies.'

'That's what was so wonderful. I felt I was in the hands of Doctors Lydgate, Thorne and Gibson, not a twenty-first-century hospital in the Western world.'

'Yes, it is like that,' said Helen, who also liked nineteenth-century novels. But she was not exuberant, as Cecilia was. What if it was bone cancer? Would it not be on some runaway path to disaster during the next three months? But Cecilia was happy with the situation, and Helen did not want to mar that. Post-cancer, unworried periods were to be cherished. Helen herself had a scan coming up in three weeks.

'I've got a scan coming up in three weeks,' she said. 'Three weeks. It's about now that I enter the gravitational force field of worry.'

'I'll have to know all about everything,' said Cecilia. 'Don't treat me as I have treated you.'

'I never could.' Now Helen lowered her voice to a stage whisper. 'How about Leda?'

'Very strange.'

'Where is she now?'

'In the spare bedroom. She spends ages in there, quietly moving things about. She screams if Eva tries to go in there to clean. I try to have conversations about what she might do or where she might go, but she says nothing. I know she has parents, but she presumably wants to give them a wide berth.'

'Does she have meals?'

'Not with us, but I presume she must eat. She has money.'

'Where does she get it from?'

'I have no idea.'

'So she's not pursuing Cephas?'

'Apparently not. I thought at first she must be, because she trots round to Ian's. But they say not.'

'Has she got her eye on Ian, then?'

'Nothing is as straightforward as that. She plays a straight-forward game of tennis, however.'

'Tennis?'

'Yes. She goes to the club with Tim. Misery for me, to watch Tim fancying her.'

This last interested Helen enormously. She tried not to let her enjoyment show, but it was difficult. Poor Cecilia, Helen thought, but what an intriguing turn of events. Tim so staid, Leda so crazy, and neither understanding the other; and Cecilia looking on, jealous, and understanding both.

'Does she know he fancies her?' enquired Helen. She had decided against asking, 'Does she fancy him?' although it would be even more interesting if this, counter-intuitively, were to be so.

But Cecilia was regretting what she had said. She had thought to ease the sore in her heart by making light of it; but Helen's words chafed. 'Fancy is too strong,' she said, insincerely. 'But she is a very beautiful girl.'

'All this talk of her and I have never seen her,' said Helen.

'She's always in the spare room, at tennis, watching the news on TV, or out once a day for a ten-minute visit to Ian's.'

'Why? If she has no designs on Cephas? I can't think of any reason but Ian.'

'No one knows. She could be after Ian, but I doubt it. If you're psychotic, you see, what you do doesn't have meanings other people can recognise. What I hope is that she'll soon move on, again for reasons unknowable. My lack of real interest in what makes her tick shows me I was quite right to retire when I did. You'd expect a psychotherapist to want to under-stand her. I don't.'

'Of course you don't, with all these worries about cancer,' said Helen. 'And the worries about her getting too near Cephas. I suppose she's forgotten she ever had a baby.'

'She's probably turned the experience into something else, in her mind. The astonishing thing is that she actually looked after him for two months.'

'Yes. She must have been able to see him for what he really was, then.'

'Maybe. But possibly it was more that whatever the fantasy was, it did not involve starving him.'

At this moment the door opened and Leda came into the room. She stood looking at the floor. On her shoulder was her bag, and on her arm a large plastic carrier bag with her tennis racket sticking out of the top. Cecilia and Helen stared at her, both startled, Helen intent. So this was Leda. Well, it was true that she was beautiful. Helen's school of thought was that the right thing to do with mad people is to act as if they were normal, so she stood up and held out her hand. 'I'm Helen,' she said, 'a family friend. You must be Leda.'

Both Helen's overtures were ignored by Leda, who had unearthed a mark in the spare room. It was in the very corner of one of the drawers, and she was troubled because it might have been there unnoticed for some time. It was true that They could not undo the work she had done on Ian, but They might, now they had tracked her down, make it more difficult for her to depotentiate Lewis. Also, now that her whereabouts were pinpointed by Them, her life was in danger. She looked at Cecilia. 'Goodbye,' she said.

'Why, wherever are you going?'

No answer.

'Have you got somewhere to go?'

No answer again, then Helen spoke up. 'I've got a spare room,' she said. 'You can come to my house for a few nights, it's only just round the corner.'

Leda turnèd a radiant smile on Helen. Helen blinked. She had felt rebuffed when ignored by Leda, and her offer of hospitality was a child's impulse to turn rejection into approval, neglect into attention; but she had not hoped for approval or attention of this order, and she smiled unstintingly in response to the intimate, caressing loveliness of Leda's smile. Poor Cecilia, if Leda smiled on Tim in this way, thought Helen, while Cecilia understood for the first time what Ian had seen in Leda. There was an awed silence.

'What's the address?' Leda asked, and Helen told her. Leda disappeared in the direction of her bedroom again.

'Well!' said Helen. 'What an apparition.'

'I haven't seen her smile before,' said Cecilia. She remembered Cephas, eight weeks old. 'That could have been what Cephas used to search our faces for.'

Luckily Cecilia did not seem to have thought of Tim's being on the receiving end of that smile after a good shot on the tennis court. 'Am I crazy,' asked Helen, 'to have offered her a bed? Das has gone, the spare room's empty – I suppose it will be all right.'

'It sounds as if you're regretting it. I'm sorry. I must start working on how to move her on. You can't be landed with her indefinitely.'

'On?'

'Well, there are hostels. Farms. Therapeutic communities. The trouble is I don't know anything about them.'

'They're probably being cut, as we speak. Why did she suddenly decide to leave here?'

'We could have a hundred guesses and they'd all be wrong.'

Leda was in her bedroom texting. She texted the words 'Lancelot Centrecourt', and Helen's address. She sent the text.

Chapter 18

Lily Bridges was in her garden. It was her favourite time of day, and her favourite time of year. It was mid June and four in the morning. Luckily she slept so badly that she did not often have to miss this treasured moment. The birds were stirring. There was the untrodden glisten of dew on the lawn, trodden only where her bare feet had fallen. There was a magnificent dew-jewelled spider's web stretched between the honeysuckle and the lavatera, perfectly and quickly spun, and in the dead centre of it sat a fat black spider. The snails were still up, the large, established ones who had survived several winters; the smaller, excited ones whose first summer it was. She had brought with her a small bowl of porridge oats soaked in milk, which she scattered for the snails. She scattered the oats quite widely and thinly, so that there shouldn't be a conglomeration of hungry snails in any one spot, leading to excessive competition, or providing a larger target for any birds who might prefer a carnivorous breakfast. She had a basket of seeds and nuts with which she carefully refilled any of the bird feeders that needed it. Birds were flying down to see what she was doing. They liked her. She stood as still as she could for her various ministrations, to ensure that her foot would not slip on to an unsuspecting snail, slug or worm. Lily was absorbed and happy, and she would be neither again until this time tomorrow.

Her own breakfast, three hours later, was less cheerful. Guy

Bridges was looking at his wife with puzzled annoyance. Her face habitually wore an expression of anxiety and apprehension, and this annoyed him more than usual this morning.

'I cannot understand,' he said, unrolling his napkin from its ring, 'I just cannot understand why you did not tell me Jane is found.'

'I'm sorry,' said Lily. 'I thought I had.'

'You're talking as if it's something unimportant. Our daughter disappears. She is a missing person and the police are involved. You take a phone call from the police to say she is found, or at least has been reliably sighted, and you don't tell me. I just can't understand it. It's as if you don't live in the real world.'

'Perhaps I don't, any more.'

'That's not good enough. Imagine my feelings hearing it first in the shop. "So glad your daughter has been found," Ron said. And he showed me the paragraph in the *West Sussex*, with the photo of Jane. It made me feel a complete fool. There were other people in the shop. And all along, you knew.'

'She hadn't been found, you know, exactly, they still don't know where she is.'

'That's not the point. The point is, she hadn't been murdered. And you didn't bother to tell me.'

Lily had no answer for this. It was a just accusation. Her large, sad eyes became even more anxious and apprehensive, and the toast she had buttered for herself would have to become a snack for the birds.

Guy went on: 'Maybe you should have a test. For Alzheimer's. I could take you to Dr West. Shall I make an appointment?'

'Please don't. It might turn out I do have Alzheimer's. And there's nothing they can do about it. So what's the point of knowing?'

'But at least I'd be told what I'm up against.'

There was a silence. Then Lily thought of a stratagem. 'I think I did tell you,' she said.

'No you didn't.'

'I think I did. It was when we were on our way to the point-to-point.'

'No you didn't.'

'Yes, I think I did. I said, "The police have had information about Jane; she has been seen in London."'

'Nonsense. Would I have forgotten?'

'You were worrying about the horsebox.'

'Impossible. And anyway, what a moment to tell me, if you did. You knew I was thinking about the race.' He was silent again, crossly swallowing too-hot coffee. 'If you had told me, I would have rung the police back at once. I would have wanted all the details.'

'But we would have been late for the point-to-point. You wouldn't have wanted to risk that.'

'Well, what a moment to tell me, if you did.'

'I was surprised you didn't take more notice.' Lily was inventing freely now.

'I probably didn't hear.' The question of which of them might have Alzheimer's had arisen in his mind. 'This bacon isn't very good. Where did you get it?'

'At the shop.'

'I thought we'd agreed not to get our bacon at the shop, but at Robertson's.'

'I know, I'm sorry, I was in a hurry.'

Guy lifted a rasher on his fork. He whistled. Danny woke and bustled to the table. Guy shook the bacon off his fork and it fell into the dog's mouth. There was a brief snapping noise and Danny crouched near Guy's chair. There might be more.

'You did ring the police back, dear, and there weren't any details,' said Lily. 'And we rang that other number the police gave us, Mr and Mrs Forest, and there weren't any details there either.'

'Of course I know that! And of course we did. But that was

after I had heard about it in the shop, and I told you, and, I'll be damned, you already knew.'

'Yes. And what I think is that I had already told you.'

An angry silence. Then Guy said, 'It isn't the point that there weren't any details. Surely you can see that. The point is there might have been. And you didn't even ring the Forest people's number.'

Lily had been hoping Guy would not arrive at re-excavating this mystifying fact, and luckily he stopped there and changed tack. 'The police have been hopeless,' he said. Lily sighed with relief as always when the blowtorch of Guy's indignation turned outside the family. 'Why couldn't they have followed her up, once they got a sighting?'

'As you've said, the main thing is that she hasn't been murdered, or disappeared.'

'Yes, that's the main thing, certainly. But another thing is, why doesn't she want to see us? She could come, this is her home.'

This question had been so frequently asked, and was so unanswerable, that silence fell. It was a familiar silence, and had Lily and Guy each staring into space, staring into spaces that were quite separate from each other, though of the same origin. Lily was glad that a Jane conversation seemed to be settling into its usual repetitive sadness and bewilderment, rather than into something more threatening to herself. She knew that Guy was unhappy about Jane. There was a bristling, uncomprehending sorrow in him, which included feeling terrible about Jane in the village and with friends, and which had led him into prevarications about her whereabouts and activities. When Jane became a missing person, he could no longer prevaricate, and had to bear the pity and concern of his neighbours. His story about a high-flying job in New York was then exposed for what it was, to his intense humiliation. The family's being a subject of gossip was misery to him, and the silence that fell in the shop when he entered to pick up his copy of *The Times* made him wince. Lily knew all this, and also knew that underneath this surface layer of pain lay another, which consisted of lonelier, more sleepless anguish, and, potentially, though this did not quite translate into thoughts, guilt about what he might have got wrong in relation to his daughter.

Because the police, rather than Lily herself, had become Guy's target, Lily was able to eat one of her pieces of buttered toast before she went out to see the horses. She took the apple and carrot and stood at the fence. They spotted her at once and both cantered towards her. She loved the contrast between their size and their power, and the sensitivity of their soft, mobile mouths against her hands. On her way back to the house she had a word with Angus, the gardener, who also looked after the horses, and, in the kitchen, with his wife Greta.

Then she went into the room called her study, not that she had ever studied anything in it, nor, indeed, anywhere. She closed the door behind her and went to a shelf where back numbers of magazines were neatly piled. She picked a copy of *The Lady* from the top of a pile. She placed it on her desk, while she took a key from under a paperweight and unlocked and opened a drawer. She took out a wad of twenty-pound notes and turned to page twenty-nine in *The Lady*. She checked the page number a couple of times to make sure, for she knew the money would have to be burnt if it was between the wrong pages. Then she put the notes carefully into the magazine, backed well up against the spine. She checked a few times. Then she opened another drawer and disentangled a large buff envelope from a packet. She inserted the prepared copy of *The Lady* into the envelope and stuck it down. She reached in a pocket for her mobile phone, and for her reading glasses, which were strung round her neck. She reread a text and, while rereading it, wrote 'Lancelot Centrecourt', and, underneath, carefully transcribed a north London address. Then she affixed four or five first-class stamps to the envelope.

She never took her missives for Jane to the shop, which was also a post office, although that would have been the nearest. As usual, now, she said, 'Walkies,' to Danny and off they went together across the fields to the anonymity of the pillar box on the Chichester road. No one seeing her and Danny, respectively stumping and lolloping through the fields and beside the wood, would have imagined that this vague, fluttery, benign, elderly lady was thinking about the police. But she was. She was wondering whether concealing the fact that a missing person is not exactly missing is a crime, and, if so, whether it carries a prison sentence.

~

If Cecilia thought the absence of Leda from her house would remove her from the tennis court, she was to be disappointed. It was remarkable how tennis had taken hold of Leda. Cecilia and Tim both had their thoughts about this. Tim's habit was to go to the club every few days, not every day; and the next time he went he learnt that Leda had been without him. Indeed she had joined the club on her own account. These news items caused him involuntary jolts of dismay, especially when he realised that men he had thought his friends had vied to include her in sets or have her as their partner. And, indeed, why shouldn't they? But Tim felt sidelined, or worse than sidelined, ignored, or worse than ignored, rejected. It was crystal clear that Leda's involvement in tennis had actually had nothing to do with him, and now Tim understood for the first time how he had relished the idea that it had. Leda had been taken up by a group of players rather better than himself, and among them she had a starring role. He sneaked glances at her from time to time from the humdrum of his more ordinary game. He could not help these glances, and would have liked to have the freedom to allow them to become stares. But stares, if they threatened to begin, made him feel unfaithful to Cecilia, and ridiculous in the eyes of anyone who might be watching. Not that anybody would be likely to be watching him, when every eye, if disengaged from a tennis ball, moved naturally towards Leda, athletic and graceful, beautiful of face and body, extraordinary with racket, long and dark of swinging hair.

Now that she no longer belonged to him, he noticed her behaviour more. When she had been under his wing, he had not observed how taciturn and unresponsive her manner was. She seemed to come to the club to play tennis as a car comes to a petrol station to fill up. When she had finished, she picked up her sweater and left. She did not acknowledge Tim's smile and greeting. People tried in vain to start conversations with her. There was an exception to this lack of social involvement, and it was one that surprised Tim. She did not seem to mind passing the time of day with Lewis. Lewis was usually somewhere to be seen, perhaps doing some job about the place, possibly just hanging around, hoping to be part of things. Tim became increasingly sure that Leda liked Lewis. Why Lewis? Why not Tim? Tim chid himself for these painful feelings, rusted since adolescence.

But he would soon have reverted to ordinary life, immersed as he always was in his many interests and pursuits, if he had not had to see Leda every time he went to tennis. But the week went past, and suddenly she was no longer there. This disappearance created quite a major stir, and not solely in the equilibrium of Tim. Tim became visible to fellow players again, if only as a conduit for news of Leda. Tim told Cecilia that Leda had not been seen on the courts, in an attempt to find out if she or Helen could cast any light. They could not.

Meanwhile Cecilia was pleased to hear that Leda was at the club whether Tim went or not. It proved that Tim's enchantment with Leda was not mutual. It had not seemed likely that it was; but what was likelihood, with the likes of Leda? And Tim's sense of loss punished him for his boyish, inchoate hopes.

Cecilia couldn't find it in her heart to be sorry for him; but she did manage to resist making fun of him to Helen. She was pleased that Leda had vanished from tennis, and very pleased to see Tim's mild chagrin fade and pass, and soon he was once more the abstracted, rather crushed, elderly academic she knew and loved. The moment of shining plumage was over. It is possessiveness, thought Cecilia sadly, that prevents us from wanting those we love to be happy in their own way.

Apart from self-criticism, and even that was interesting and bearable, things were looking up for Cecilia. Leda was no longer under her roof, arousing concern and irritation as an alien presence, and disquiet where Tim was concerned. Tim's infatuation with her was dying from inanition. And Cecilia's hip was improving. Sometimes she could take a step without pain. There was discomfort, and it moved around her pelvis. But it was better than it had been. Perhaps she would turn out to be suffering from some non-fatal condition. She was cautiously rejoicing.

Things were looking up for Marina as well. Leda had stopped appearing on the doorstep as abruptly as she had started. At first it had felt unbelievable. But then several more days had passed and there had been no sign of her. Marina and Ian talked it over together. Interrogating the matter with Cecilia, they learnt that Leda was now at Helen's. More days passed. No Leda. Marina breathed easy again. If, for Ian, there was a tinge of regret buried in the shared relief, it was a pale one, and he concealed it. He had a tour of duty coming up, and he particularly did not want Marina to have to face Leda in his absence abroad. He did not want Cecilia to have to do so, either, on the days when Marina worked and Cecilia babysat.

'A bad idea,' he said to Marina, 'to have Leda at Helen's. However did that come about? That bloody woman has to be in on everything.'

'D'you mean Helen? But you like her.'

'Usually, I suppose, but why ever . . .?' He faded out.

'Leda must have had nowhere to go. What I don't understand is why she suddenly had to leave Cecilia's. Though I'm glad she did.'

'Anything to do with Tim?' Ian was being mischievous. 'All this so-called tennis—'

'Hardly.' Marina was refusing mischief. She could not countenance Leda's unfailing attractiveness to men as a joking matter, or not yet. Or not with Ian. Or not with Leda still in the neighbourhood.

'Hardly indeed.' Ian was serious again. He understood why Marina had declined to enter into his silly fantasy, and was sorry.

~

Helen and Marj were sitting one on each side of their mother's bed in the care home. It was afternoon, and by rights Meg Gatehouse should not have been in bed, but still sitting out in the day room or on the patio. But she had become very tired, and begged to lie down, and both Helen and Marj could be eloquent and forceful, and Gemma, in charge that day, had succumbed. Teresa might have held out against this piece of unorthodoxy, but she was not on duty. So Helen, sixty-five, and Marj, sixty-two, sat by the bed of their mother, ninety-three, all of them hot in the close cubicle, the July sunshine dancing outside.

'Express disapproval, three letters,' said Marj.

'Three letters,' Meg said thoughtfully. 'Well.'

'Treat unjustly,' went on Marj. 'Five letters.'

'Tut,' said Helen.

'No, five letters.'

'Disapproval,' said Helen. 'Tut.'

Marj wrote.

'Well, I don't think that clue is very good,' said Meg. 'Tut isn't a real word.'

Helen liked her mother's pedantry. 'No, but that's what they mean.'

Marj was waiting for her mother to say 'abuse', so repeated, 'Treat unjustly.'

'Abuse,' said Helen.

Marj said nothing to Helen, but wrote, again. Helen did not seem to realise that the crossword was for Meg. Marj tried to find a clue that Helen would not get before their mother. 'Sausages, slang,' she said.

'Bangers,' said Meg.

Marj wrote.

'I'm having a scan in a couple of weeks,' said Helen.

'What sort of scan?' asked Marj, who had also had cancer, though well in the past.

'Chest, abdo, pelvis.'

'Chest,' said Meg, cottoning on to the word of the three she knew. 'I wish you would give up smoking.'

'That's not the point, Mum,' said Marj. 'This is to see if Helen's cancer has spread. It's got nothing to do with smoking. Please drink your tea, Mum, or your juice.'

Meg was looking dreamily at Helen. Her tea was cold and her juice warm. 'We had an awful time with your TB when you were eight,' she said. 'What a worry. You were off school for two terms. That's when you started reading all the time. I've often thought you wouldn't be a writer but for that.'

'Yes, but TB isn't the point, Mum,' said Helen. 'That's nothing to do with it, any more than smoking is.' She wished she had not brought up the subject of her scan. She had wanted comfort, and comfort had not come.

'Well, let us know how you get on,' said Marj. Helen wondered whether Marj, probably without knowing it, hoped for the interest and excitement of a bad result. She knew she would so hope if the positions were reversed. She sighed for human nature.

'Very out of date,' said Marj. 'Seven letters.'

'Archaic,' said Helen.

'Give Mum a chance,' said Marj, writing.

Helen began to think about her mother's death. When she came in this afternoon, Gemma had intercepted her to say that Meg was not eating properly. Worse, it was difficult to get her to drink. She was dehydrated. They had thought of putting up a drip. They would see if the doctor authorised it, on Tuesday. Would Helen try to get her to drink? Of course she would. She tried, but it was uphill work. Meg's sips were so tiny, and her distaste so visible.

Would she die in this bed, with Helen on one side and Marj on the other, and Harry, perhaps, standing at the foot? Or would she have been hustled into hospital, and die among tubes and monitors, with her family trying to get a look-in? Helen, having neglected her mother for years, was, at least at moments, passionately fond of her. Marj, a faithful daughter down the decades, who had borne the brunt of the various stages and decisions that had brought Meg to where she was now, felt much less, and could look at the neatly folded hands, and see the occasional lost look in the eyes, without undergoing waves of love and tenderness, without, even, rehearsing death. Marj popped in nearly every day, having chosen a care home near her own house; Helen visited monthly. The carers and nurses looked to Marj for the practicalities, but it was for Helen's visits that they fluffed up Meg's hair and tried to get her to look more lively. Marj had coped remarkably well with the return of the prodigal in the shape of her older sister, partly from innate magnanimity, partly because she really did need help, and all help was welcome. Her three sons were rare sights in the care home, and her grandchildren, mostly late adolescent, nine-day wonders.

Objectively, Meg had not been a difficult mother. She was warm, busy, committed, stable, punctual with meals and thoughtful about her presence at home. She gave the impression, so cherished by children, of being just like the other mothers. Her husband had been cut from the same cloth, and there had been no rivalry with the children from him until they were too old to be affected. They were all adults by the time heart disease made him Meg's prime concern. Marj and Harry grew up and settled into lives rather like those of their parents. They had stayed in Sheffield, marrying local people. Helen was different, and had followed different stars, stars she had believed brighter by far, though she was not so sure now. Perhaps, she was thinking now, her development had indeed had something to do with her TB year. She remembered how steadily her mother had supplied her with books. She had never thanked her.

'Thank you for all the books you got me when I was ill,' she said now. 'It must have been a trouble for you. I never thought of that, then. I thought the books just appeared. Thank you.' She was not sure whether Meg had heard. 'How did you know so well what I was going to like?'

'Your hearing aid isn't in, Mum,' said Marj, after a quick look at Meg's not hearing face.

'It's being dried out,' said Meg.

'Dried out?'

'It came in the shower with me this morning by accident. Gemma was very worried. But we think it will be all right when it's dry.'

The shower was in compliment to Helen, and had perhaps been a mistake. More staff were drawn into it in the end than could well be spared. It would not be repeated. Meanwhile the hearing aid was in the airing cupboard, and Gemma hoped for the best.

The supper trays were heard distantly clinking, and then one came into the cubicle for Meg.

232

'I don't think I want anything,' said Meg.

Helen lifted a cover from its plate with the big gesture of a conjurer. 'There!' she said.

But Marj knew at once that the version of fish and chips revealed would be no good. She sat resignedly while Helen talked their mother through how delicious it would be. In the end Marj said, "Try the pudding, Hennie.'

Their mother took two mouthfuls of the spotted dog and custard. 'What a wicked waste of food,' said Meg. 'Won't either of you have any?' But distaste was contagious.

'You'll have the cup of tea,' said Helen. And Meg drank some of it.

Her daughters left together, Marj for her short walk home, Helen for the train. It never had occurred to either of them that Marj might invite Helen for supper, let alone for the night. Their relationship was circumscribed by their mother's situation. If either of them regretted this, the regret was not voiced.

'She's not eating,' said Helen.

'No. She can't go on long like this.'

'Do you mean she might die?'

'Of course she might die.'

Helen absorbed this as best she could. 'How will we know if she's dying?'

'The home will ring me and I'll ring you.'

'Straight away, please.'

'Of course.'

'Or even if they haven't said anything, but you've got suspicions.'

'Of course.'

'Tell you what. I think I'll start coming fortnightly.'

'Right. Might be a good idea.'

Chapter 19

L eda was aware that Helen was away for the day. That
gave her a chance to have a search for marks more
thorough than would otherwise have been possible. She was
at leisure, for Lewis was safely Ex-dangerous, and she had not
yet been issued with the next candidate for Transformative
Energy.

It was very quiet. Unlike Cecilia's house, Helen's was noisy.
Leda had liked the quiet at Cecilia's, but was getting used to
the different atmosphere at Helen's. Helen banged doors, talked
at full volume on the telephone, laughed loudly, coughed, played
the radio so that it could be heard from at least two rooms
away, sang. So, today, the quiet in Helen's house was striking.
Luckily, however many noises there were around her, Leda
could always hear the voices of Us.

She had her ears cocked, because she expected a message.
She was not usually left long before her next task was
announced. But she heard nothing, and continued to look for
marks.

She had done her bedroom thoroughly, more than once,
including a shelf at the top of a wardrobe that had needed her
athleticism, toned by recent tennis, to reach. It seemed that
They had not yet found her. Perhaps she had fooled them by
moving to somewhere so near where she had been before,
rather than at a distance. Now she moved around Helen's house,

in case a mark had been deposited somewhere other than in her bedroom, though that was fairly unlikely. That had only ever happened twice. But you could not be too careful. It was not always possible to check out an entire house, because of the danger of attracting the attention of its inmates. But with Helen away Leda had a rare opportunity.

The kitchen was quite messy, which made it more complicated. There were breakfast dishes to be washed up, and Leda looked carefully between stacked crockery for possible disturbance. There was a cyclamen on the windowsill, and its leaves and buds had to be examined. She did not wash up, nor water the plant, though both needed doing, because any household activity on her part, wherever she was, added to the possibility of her being spotted by the restless searchlight of Them. Her footprint must always be as light as possible, wherever she was staying. 'Be like a ghost, wherever you are,' the voice of one of Us reminded her. So Leda worked on, stealthily.

At one point she heard the post, and went to the front door, glad Helen was not there to laugh or question or puzzle over the envelope for Leda. She collected her packet and left the rest of the post on the floor, exactly as it had fallen, as a ghost would do. When she got hungry, she slipped out for fish and chips. Helen had supplied her with a key. It was important never to eat where she was domiciled, and better, really, not even to accept a cup of tea, though sometimes you had to. There must always be something from the sea in her meals. Her standard diet was cod and chips. Sandwiches with prawn or tuna were other staples.

~

After Helen arrived home, she went to see Cecilia. When they were sitting in the garden with glasses of wine, Helen lit a cigarette and said, 'I'm worried about Mum.'

'In what way?'

'She's not eating. I think she says different things to me from how she talks to Marj. Not this time, because Marj was there, but the last time I went, she said, "I could go on for ever. I don't want to. People always die of something. With your dad it was heart. I will have to find something to die of." Of course I made light of it, but what if she has hit upon starvation as her thing to die of?'

'I don't suppose it's as conscious as that. But, Helen, you have to face it. She may be on her last lap.' Cecilia was thinking about Helen's last-minute rediscovery of love for her mother. The renewed contact was precious, but, in the nature of things, would be brief.

Helen was quiet, thinking. Then she said, 'There are two people in the world I one hundred per cent don't want to be ill or die. One is you; one is Mum. Everyone else, well, there would be something a bit enlivening about hearing they were ill, or had some awful diagnosis. Perhaps because it would make me feel it wasn't me. This time.'

'What if it were Tim? Ian?'

'No, I always want them to be all right, and Marina, and the little boys. But that's for your sake, I think. Like I want Marj to be all right, but only for Mum's sake. If Mum was dead, I'd respond cheerfully, with sisterly involvement, but secret glee, to the drama of Marj being ill. I'm saying it how it is, because I'm always honest with you.'

'We've talked about this. Having cancer makes us want other people to have it too. There's that.'

'There is. But I see it on other people's faces. The hairdresser is a bit disappointed that I seem to have recovered. She wanted to be drawn into some unreal sorrow about my demise.'

'It's the same as wanting to stare at a traffic accident,' said Cecilia, who was always conscious of trying to stop herself from doing this.

'Yes. We all want excitement, but not danger.'

'It's the fact that it isn't oneself, or anyone one loves.'

'This time.'

'Yes.' Cecilia was pondering. 'It could also be useful as a free rehearsal for what is ahead for us all. Not for the traffic accident, specifically, but, more generally, for dying.'

'That's a nice idea.'

'Or,' went on Cecilia, 'a defence. Turning helplessness, because it's always events you have no power over, into excitement.'

'It would be good to think it's as benign as that.'

Thor appeared on the garden wall, and, seeing Cecilia, jumped down and ran to her with a greeting cry. He leapt on her lap, purring and treading.

'Does Thor miss Cephas?' asked Helen.

'Not a bit. Odd, isn't it? When they were so close.'

'What happens when Cephas is here?'

'Cephas pursues Thor, calling and grabbing, and in the end Thor jumps over the garden wall. He never scratches, luckily.'

'Does Thor like Ali? He must be just the age Cephas was when Thor met him.'

'Yes. But Thor doesn't take any notice of Ali.' After a few moments Cecilia asked, 'So when's the scan?'

'Next Wednesday.'

'Shall I come with you?'

'No, no point. But could you come with me to the results, a week later?'

'Of course. Why didn't I come to your last one – six months ago? I can't remember why.'

'Das came with me. I miss him, you know. Now what about Leda, the present occupant of Das's room? She is an odd bird.'

'What are you thinking of? Not that I disagree.'

'She's been in the stoma loo. I know she has. My stoma stuff is very slightly moved around. Now why would she do that? Curiosity? About colostomies, I mean.'

237

'I don't think it would be that. It would be something funny happening in her mind.' Cecilia was trying to address afresh, now guiltily because of Helen, the problem of what could be done about Leda. She needed to be persuaded to move on, but where, and how? Ian had a duty to be consulted, but he was abroad.

'Funny mind or not, I'm going to tell her what she can do and what she can't while she's in my house,' said Helen.

'That might be no bad thing. You are much braver than me.'

That was as far as they got in the bit of the conversation that was about Leda. They went on drinking their wine, and Cecilia went on stroking Thor. Tim now seemed to be moving about in the kitchen, perhaps doing something towards supper, and Cecilia wondered if they could run to inviting Helen to stay on. Cecilia couldn't remember what was in the fridge.

After a short silence Helen said, 'Have you noticed we don't talk about our colostomies much any more?'

'Yes, I have,' Cecilia answered. 'But that's because we did.'

'You mean we did talk about them, when we needed to?'

'Yes. When they were newer and more shocking.'

That was another nice thought. They dwelt on it. Then Tim appeared at the kitchen window.

'Are you girls coming in for something to eat?' he called jovially.

'Cecilia is,' said Helen. 'I am going home.'

'Do stay if you like,' said Tim, who had spotted some lamb chops he thought he would cook. 'There's plenty.'

'No,' said Helen, 'thanks. I'm going to go home and read the Riot Act to your tennis partner.'

~

'Blug,' said Cephas. He was holding Marina's knee with both hands and looking up into her face.

It had not been an easy afternoon for Marina. A visit to the playground with both children and the pram had been all right, but then there had been a complicated work phone call, and then a conversation with Ian who was in Somalia and had a bad line. She couldn't hear everything he said and she knew he was in a war zone. A chill had crept around her heart, and she wanted to ring him back, just to have another word. But that was not their custom. As he was the one who was working, it was for him to choose the moment to talk. If she phoned, it might be a bad time. And it might tell him she felt lonely without him, on only the second day of his absence, and in Marina's book that would not be fair. So she warmed the chill around her heart as best she could.

Then a friend phoned and wanted to come round with her two-year-old, and Marina had said yes, because Cephas seemed to like the idea, and went to get his bulldozer, which he took into the garden. Marina watched him walking busily through the french doors and remembered when it had made her dizzy with excitement to think of the french doors and the garden belonging to her and Ian, and the children running in and out. Was it as good as that vision had promised? Basically, yes. Basically, better. Only the dizziness had passed. But the friend's visit was not a success. The children fell out over the bulldozer, Benjy scratched the visitor, not without provocation; and each mother was too tired to pretend not to take her own child's part. Marina was glad to see the back of her friend.

She put scrambled egg in front of Cephas, and sat down to feed Ali. It crossed her mind to find out if Cecilia was free to pop round. But that would excite Cephas and delay bedtime. And Marina had to get some work done before tomorrow, when Cecilia was coming anyway, to babysit.

'Blug,' said Cephas, his eggy hands on Marina's knee.

'Yes,' said Marina. 'Lots of blood.'

She knew what he was referring to. That morning his nose

had bled, and the sight of the redness of the blood, and its copiousness, and the realisation that it came from himself, though not from a bit of himself that he could see, had been significant events. He had sat gravely through the cleaning-up process, offering his beautiful little face to the warm damp flannel. Marina knew to make that process take longer than it needed to. Perhaps this moment of special attention came back into Cephas's mind now to compensate himself for, or to distract his mother from, Ali's feed. Did it make it different, for Cephas, Marina wondered, that he had never been at her breast himself? Nor at anyone's? Or did those emotional irregularities iron out, in time, with enough love and care?

'Lots of blug,' said Cephas, with satisfaction.

'Gran is coming tomorrow,' said Marina. 'We can tell her about the nose-bleed.' She added, 'About the blood,' in case he had not recognised the blood under its changed terminology, but she need not have bothered. Cephas was clever as well as beautiful.

The feed was over and it was last play, Ali on a blanket on the floor, nappy off, kicking; Cephas, now unchallenged for its possession, rediscovering the bulldozer and pushing it a bit too close to Ali. Entertainment or aggression? Both, thought Marina, and was just about to suggest a story to Cephas when the phone rang. Marina knew it couldn't be Ian, because he always rang her mobile. It was Marina's mother, and they chatted, and then Cephas had to talk to Nan, though for him talking on the telephone consisted of remaining transfixed in expectant silence. So Nan talked. Then that finished, and Marina suggested a story, which sent Cephas running for a book. The phone rang again.

'Hullo,' said Marina.

'Hullo. Good evening. I hope I'm not disturbing you.'

'No.'

'This is Lily Bridges. I hope I'm speaking to Mrs Forest.'

'Yes, that's right.'

'We rang you a few weeks ago because we thought you might have information for us . . .' A male voice was to be heard in the background. 'Yes, about the whereabouts of our daughter. We telephoned you a few weeks ago, but . . .' Male voice in the background again, possibly hectoring. 'But you didn't have any information then, though you had seen her. We wondered if the picture had changed. We are sorry to . . . Yes. She might be under a different name.'

'I know who you mean,' said Marina. 'I don't have a phone number for where she is staying, but I have a phone number for someone who would be able to give it to you.'

Shufflings on the other end of the telephone, and then the male voice. 'Sorry, good evening. Did you say you might have a number we could telephone?'

'Yes.'

More shufflings, while Guy Bridges, who did not trust his wife's accuracy of transcription, prepared to write. Marina gave Cecilia's name and number, and the conversation ended.

Marina was uneasy. She knew that in the distant days when they had thought Leda was stalking Cephas, Ian had not told the police and her parents where Leda was staying. Marina had regretted this prevarication and would not have done it herself, but she understood Ian's defensiveness and fluster. Her conscience had taken refuge in the fact that the sighting of Leda would suffice to reassure the parents about the very worst possibilities. She hoped enough stages and uncertainties had crept in by now to obscure the fact that she and Ian had wilfully withheld information.

'The kind donkey said, "Would you like a ride on my back?"' she said, holding the picture of the kind donkey so that Cephas could see it. She had no doubt that she was duty-bound to give what facts she could to this unfortunate couple. It would be immoral to do otherwise. '"Yes please," said the cat, and the kind donkey went down on his knees.'

'Benjy,' said Cephas, for the cat was tabby. He looked earnestly at Marina and marshalled his words. 'Not Thor,' he said.

'No,' said Marina. 'Thor is black and white.' They often had this conversation when they got to this page.

'"Hold on tight," said the kind donkey, "but don't scratch with your claws."' She could tell that Ali's cheerful kicking was not going to last and scooped him up from the floor into her other arm. But for the phone calls, she would have had Cephas in bed before Ali's cries threatened to turn plaintive. Her mobile rang. She got a hand free. 'Ian,' she said.

'I'm sorry. You must be in the thick of bedtime.' He was always good at time difference. 'I can't talk, but I just wanted to say goodnight.'

'I am. But goodnight. And lovely to hear you.'

'Daddy,' said Cephas, going by Marina's voice. 'Talk to Daddy.'

'Not just now, Daddy's busy.' Cephas accepted this, and Marina pursued bedtimes, her heart light.

~

Cecilia and Tim were having their lamb chops when the phone went. Tim got up to answer it. He announced his phone number, as was his way.

'Hullo,' said the other voice, quiet and tentative. 'This is Lily Bridges. I hope I'm not disturbing you.'

'No,' said Tim.

'We've been told you might have a phone number where our daughter is staying.'

'Who is your daughter?'

'Oh golly, it'll be Leda,' said Cecilia.

'We don't quite know her name,' said the voice on the telephone. A raised male voice could be heard in the background. Then the female voice went on, 'We are not sure what name . . .' Now Tim could clearly hear the male voice shouting, 'Of course we know her name, we are her parents.'

'It's about Leda,' said Cecilia. 'Better give them poor Helen's phone number.' She wrested Tim's attention from the distant fracas and dictated Helen's number, which Tim transmitted. He was thanked and rang off.

'They must have been on to poor Marina,' said Cecilia. 'And now they are going to ring Helen. Should we ring her first? Or ring Marina to see what happened?'

'We could let it be,' suggested Tim, 'and get on with our supper.'

That was all very well, thought Cecilia, eating chop, but something really must be done about Leda. The present situation wasn't fair on Helen and wasn't fair on Leda's parents. And what about Leda herself, left alone to grapple with her mysterious madness? There was no reason why Cecilia should feel responsible, but responsible she felt. She would talk to Marina about it in the morning. Tim was no help. The poetry of his crush on Leda having faded, chiefly because he never saw her now, it was impossible for Cecilia to interest him in the mere prose of Leda as a problem and a puzzle.

After supper she sat down alone to unravel why she was so reluctant to try to bring in health professionals. Certainly Leda would hate it, and would oppose it at every move. But that certainty was Cecilia's excuse, now she looked closely at her conscience, rather than her reason. The real reason concerned Cephas. Any mental health professional trying to work with Leda would want to bring back into her mind the fact that she had given birth to a baby. It would be considered vital to Leda's recovery that she should become conscious of that. Then she could grieve that she had given him up, or undergo whatever would be considered appropriate. It might involve meeting Cephas as his birth mother. It might involve keeping in touch with him. It would certainly not involve reclaiming him, nor knowing that Ian was not the natural father. So what would it mean, of such dread to Cecilia? She realised that what she was afraid of was losing the simplicity, the apparent ordinariness, of Cephas's place in his happy, normal family. There had been moments in Cephas's short life when, unknown to him, all might have been lost. But his little boat had righted itself each time, and had kept him warm and dry and unaware of danger. That magic was very precious to Cecilia, and she had been part of it. She did not want that little boat rocked again.

She realised that she felt protective also of Marina. Cecilia had loved and admired Marina's determination to adopt Cephas. She had rejoiced to behold Ian swept up by that determination and fledged into a father. She had watched thankfully as Cephas became securely attached to Marina. She had inwardly applauded his robustness and Marina's sensitivity as the relationship established itself. It had been a thing of beauty for Cecilia. And what if Leda were to flash one of those rare, bewitching smiles at Cephas, perhaps not and never to be forgotten in his earlier self; and what if, after that, Marina's frequent but tamer smiles were dust and ashes? Cecilia quaked at this thought.

But what about Leda? She had rights too. She had needs. The strategy, if you could call it that, which Cecilia, Ian and Marina had put in place, more in a spirit of manning the barricades than of thoughtfulness, had ignored Leda. They had acted, or reacted, in shock, rather than sagacity, at the moment of Leda's sudden arrival. And that was understandable. Now it was time to think again. The strategy had obliterated Leda as a human being. She was merely a dangerous force, to be damage-limited, depotentiated, and got rid of as soon as possible. Now Cecilia realised, painfully, penitently, that this would not do.

Cecilia remembered that she had managed to have some of these trains of thought when Leda first came. Such constructive thoughts had existed, but been buried and forgotten. Cecilia had to face the fact that this was because she did not like Leda. Dislike, more than anything, was what had discouraged Cecilia from having any serious desire to help. Leda was hard work and offered no reward. She was not interesting. But much worse, and provoking real hatred, and this Cecilia was loath to admit to herself, was that she had had to watch Leda bring sweetness and light, joy and youth, to Tim.

She limped to the telephone to dial 1471. It might be convenient at some unforeseeable point to have Leda's parents' phone number.

~

Helen arrived home. She could hear that Leda was in, as she nearly always was, because of the spare room TV steadily muttering a news channel. Helen had another glass of wine, and several pieces of crispbread with butter and Brie, the crispbread designed to eliminate calories. She was about to knock on Leda's door when she heard the front doorbell. Standing outside was a pleasant-looking plump fifty-year-old, with balding but newly combed hair, smiling shyly. He held a small bunch of wrapped-up flowers.

'Sorry to disturb,' he said. 'I am Lewis Munro. I wonder if you have a Margaret Clitherow here?'

Helen thought quickly. 'May I ask how you know this person?' she said. 'Come in.' She led him into the kitchen where she had been having her meal.

'I run the tennis club,' he said. 'Margaret came every day for several weeks. She came as a guest at first. Then she joined, and she gave this as her address. The thing is we haven't seen her since. I thought I might take the liberty of ringing the doorbell as I walked past on my way home. Just to check that nothing, you know, that nothing is wrong.'

'She's OK,' said Helen. 'She's here. I'll see if she's free.'

Helen was enjoying this. Any intrigue was the spice of life to her. She was already looking forward to telling Cecilia. A voice from the spare room answered Helen's knock and explanation.

'I don't have to see him,' called Leda quietly.

Helen rejoined Lewis. 'She's busy, she says. Sorry,' she added, for Lewis looked very disappointed. 'Have a glass of wine. Or I've got beer.'

Lewis was happy to accept a glass of beer from this nice and very unexpected lady. They chatted about the weather, about their mutual friend Tim, and about Helen's indifference to sport. They even got on to mothers.

'Drop in again,' said Helen. 'You might be luckier.'

He thanked her for the beer, and the hospitality. 'Perhaps you could tell Margaret we all miss her,' he said, 'and we hope she'll be back soon.' He proffered his flowers. 'I was going to . . . in case she was ill. May I give them to you, instead?'

Helen liked that. Not 'Will you give them to her?' but 'May I give them to you?' She thanked him, and Lewis was on his way. Helen felt slightly energised, as she always did when she met a new man, however trivial the contact. On his way home, my foot, she thought, lighting a cigarette. The poor thing is smitten. Leda must have smiled at him. She found a vase for the small bunch and put it in the middle of the kitchen table. Then she knocked on Leda's door.

Silence greeted her, but instead of creeping away, as Cecilia would have done, she opened the door and looked in. The television was on, News 24. But the television was not on the table designated for it. It was on the floor, and the table it had sat on for years was pulled out into the centre of the room. Leda was on her hands and knees, her nose to the floor, examining the area of carpet the table no longer covered. At Helen's intrusion she sprang into a kneeling position.

'What are you doing, my poor girl?' said Helen, astonished. 'Have you lost something?'

Leda looked away from Helen and didn't answer.

Helen was undeterred. 'What in the world is going on?'

'I thought I lost . . .' began Leda. She could not think what to say. She had gone white. This had never happened before. 'I think I dropped . . .'

'You're looking as if I'd found you disposing of a corpse,' said Helen. 'Sit up and tell me what on earth is going on.'

Leda did not move. There was nothing she could say. She stared hauntingly back at Helen.

'I'm disturbing you, I'll go,' said Helen, and withdrew, closing the door quietly. 'Phew,' she said aloud, as she sat down again at the kitchen table. 'Phew.' She refilled her glass. 'Just as well Lewis didn't see that.'

But seriously, what was she to do? Her impulse was to ring Cecilia. But something held her back. She had interrupted something so private, so intense, so personal, that it defied Helen's usual recourses to anecdote and humour. To know in a general way that Leda was psychotic was one thing. To see it with her own eyes was quite another. Helen felt uneasy, alone and sad.

The door opened and Leda came in, jacket on, with bag and baggage, not much of either. 'I've got to go,' she said. 'Thanks. Goodbye.'

'But,' said Helen, 'where are you going? Have you anywhere to go?' Leda said nothing and immediately the front door could be heard closing behind her.

Helen sat on, troubled. Then she went to have a look at the spare bedroom. The TV had been turned off but was still on the floor, its table had not been put back in place, and the bedside table was upended. None of that mattered. More striking was the tennis racket abandoned on the bed, which, even Helen could see, was, for a tennis racket, grand. Beside it was a copy of *The Lady*, whose frequency as a surprising arrival Helen knew about from Cecilia.

Helen did ring Cecilia, who had been in the throes of her long and sobering train of thought about Leda. Helen needed to talk, but was not disposed to be either humorous or anecdotal about the figure kneeling on the carpet, a sight she could not get out of her mind. Their conversation was subdued and concerned, albeit with an edge of relief that, for all they knew, they might never see Leda again.

But Helen did see Leda, fleetingly, the next day. There was a ring at the bell, and there Leda stood. 'Did I get anything in the post?' she asked, and Helen handed her a packet addressed to Miss Flyte. The next moment Helen shouted after her to offer the tennis racket; but Leda neither answered nor delayed.

Chapter 20

'We'll never have grandchildren,' said Guy Bridges, staring out of the window into the summer rain. 'Bruce is as queer as a coot and Jane is off her head.'

Lily regretted the rain. It always lowered Guy's spirits. They were going to a wedding, and, although there would be a marquee in the garden, the sense of festivity would suffer. Lily's friend, the mother of the bride, had passionately hoped for fine weather. And here was Guy, getting into a gloom already.

'Well, do you really want grandchildren, dear?' asked Lily.

'No,' said Guy. 'But you should.' He stood up to get a better view of the rainy garden, the fields and woods beyond, and, beyond again, the downs. 'Who are we going to leave all this to?'

'Half each, I suppose.'

'A poofter and a nutcase,' murmured Guy, knowing how much Lily minded this sort of talk. 'Anyway, we've got to ring that other number. About Jane.'

'I know,' said Lily. 'I was waiting till nine.'

Guy stared at the rain. He wondered what Angus would do with the horses. Probably he'd bring them out into the field if it wasn't too wet. As soon as Guy stood, Danny got up, yawned and scratched his way across the wooden floor to sit beside his master. He was hoping for a walk and the rain meant nothing to him.

Guy had taken early retirement from the army. He had

become more and more discouraged by its failure to promote him beyond the status of major, especially as, in the course of time, his son became the Colonel Bridges that Guy thought he should himself have been. This beautiful place had belonged to Lily's parents, and to her grandparents and great-grandparents, going back a hundred years. When Lily inherited it, at her parents' death, Lily and Guy had decided to move in. She had been born in the house, and had always passionately loved it. She knew every tree and every blade of grass. Guy had a reasonable pension; Lily the remains of family money.

'Nine o'clock,' said Guy. 'We'd better make that phone call.'

These phone calls fell to Lily, and she picked up the receiver and looked at the number she had written down last night, which lay beside the telephone. She dialled.

'Hullo,' said a woman's voice.

'Oh, good morning. I hope I'm not disturbing you. We think you might know the whereabouts of our daughter. We were given your number as a possibility . . .'

'Yes,' said the brisk and resonant voice on the other end. 'I know who you mean, because my friend rang up and said you might phone, having already tried her. In vain, I'm afraid. Well, your daughter was here for a little while, but she's left, and I have no idea where she's gone. She didn't say.'

'Thank you so much for . . . . Well.' Lily looked at Guy to check if she was doing all right.

'Ask if she knows where Jane went when she left,' said Guy, having overheard some but not all.

'I have, and she doesn't. Sorry, I'm just talking to my husband.'

'Ask her to phone us if she sees her again,' said Guy, in a whisper audible in London.

So Lily asked that, and gave Helen the telephone number, and the conversation ended.

'She seems to be able to find people to help her, still,' said Lily.

Guy left this, not wanting to be positive, and turned back to the rain. His bacon and eggs had left him with a stomach ache. 'I've got a stomach ache,' he said. 'Where did that bacon come from?'

'Robertson's. Unsmoked back. That's what you like.'

Guy pondered gloomily. 'I think I'll walk now, even though it's raining.' Danny's tail wagged.

'Don't forget we're due at the church at eleven,' said Lily.

'I know we are. Neither of our children will get married. I knew you and your mother would turn Bruce into a queer, fussing over him.'

Lily said, 'Perhaps he'll have a civil contract, one day.' Her waspish moments were infrequent, for, in her way, she loved Guy very much; but his last remark had goaded her.

'This rain will bring out slugs and snails all over the flower beds,' Guy reflected, retaliating immediately, as a soldier will. 'Will you put down Slug Death?'

'Yes, all right.'

Guy put on a big black mac and wellies and whistled for the dog. Lily raised a brolly and picked her way across the lawn to the shed, where she found a jar marked Slug Death, half full of cake-topping hundreds-and-thousands. The hundreds-and-thousands looked colourful and convincing as Slug Death pellets, she thought, on the earth of the flower beds, though the rain might soon wash them away.

~

It was with a rather festive feeling that Helen and Cecilia set off for the hospital. It had not been part of their friendship so far to go out together. So although the occasion was not festive, and from time to time Helen's heart knocked uncomfortably in her throat, there was a sense of outing, and truancy, as they jumped on the bus. Cecilia did not jump, exactly, because of her leg, but it was as near a jump as ever happened to her now.

'Seat at the back,' said Helen.

They sat down. 'This familiar route,' said Cecilia, and, 'Will we ever be free of this bloody trip,' said Helen, together.

'Who are you seeing?' Cecilia asked.

'It's Dr Z's clinic. Of course it may not be him.'

'It might be an underling.'

'Yes.'

'I hope it is.'

'Why? I rather like Dr Z.'

'He's one I hardly know. But I always think when it's delegated to an underling it's not going to be bad news.'

'Don't you believe it. They don't even look at the results until you appear in the flesh before them.'

'Ah. So I've been wasting my time studying their faces as they call our names from the doorway. When they are summoning someone else and they catch sight of me, I've always tried to guess whether they are appalled or delighted by what they have up their sleeve to tell me when my turn comes.'

'They've got nothing up their sleeve for you until you go into the room and they bring up you and your results on the computer.'

They were silent, thinking about doctors, so alien to both of them, but, for both of them, masters of their fate.

'I wish I ever got a woman,' said Cecilia.

'I know what you mean. Our department – you'd think Elizabeth Garrett Anderson had never existed.'

'Perhaps women don't go in for guts.'

They arrived, and soon were in the crowded waiting room. In spite of herself, Cecilia savoured the consciousness of not being the patient. She felt like the big sister, who had left school the term before, returning to watch her younger sister's netball match. But she knew too well that she had left the school only for this one occasion. She was on its register still, as much as she had ever been.

They had not brought books, intending to talk; but it was difficult to talk in such a crowd, and they both picked up papers, *Metro* and the *Sun*, and idly flipped through them. Helen took a faint interest in celebrities she had never heard of being suspected of putting on weight, and Cecilia turned to the football.

'I'm scared,' said Helen.

'Don't be. These scans are routine. They call them staging scans. And after five years we don't have to have them.'

'And then we can get back to dying of old age. Like Mum.'

'Exactly.'

'But I'm scared.'

'Of course you are.' Cecilia took Helen's hand in a firm grip.

Whether it meant something, or nothing, it was indeed Dr Z. At the cry from the door of 'Helen Gatehouse' both women were afoot with obsequious haste. They followed Dr Z along the corridor. Helen was pale. She sat down. There was a chair for Cecilia, too. Dr Z had his chair, and studied the computer.

Cecilia had not considered Inferno, nor indeed Paradiso, for Helen, because neither she nor Helen, so far, had been condemned or even placed under suspicion by the results of their routine staging scans. Now she did consider Inferno, and her own heart pounded. Dr Z seemed to be taking a long time. Helen sat absolutely still with closed eyes. She was trying to make herself not exist.

'Just a bit of trouble with the computer,' muttered Dr Z.

This was true, but it was not his only trouble. He read the radiologist's report, and did not like what he saw. So he brought up the scan itself, and zeroed in on Helen's left lung. He was very conscious of not being a radiologist himself, and if the report was fine, his habit was to give the good news without tracking down the scan, as it had always been reported on by someone more professionally scan-literate than himself. He noted the name of the radiologist who had written this report, and registered that he was a new acquisition and a bright young thing. Dr Z sighed, and brought up the report of the previous scan, six months before. He observed that the radiologist then was a senior and eminent colleague who had now retired. In that report all was well with Helen's left lung. Had Bertie missed something that his replacement, with the eye of youth, of science, of state-of-the-art training, had spotted? Dr Z tried and failed to bring on to the screen the previous scan, as reported on by Bertie. He wanted to see whether an inexpert but not uneducated eye, such as his own, could discern any change in the left lung between its image six months ago and its image now. But as the computer would not bring up the January scan, he made his decision, and turned to Helen.

'Everything fine,' he said, 'except something we're not very sure about in one of your lungs. I'm sorry.' His large, expressionless face veered from Helen to Cecilia and back again. Both women looked horrified, as he had expected. 'Don't worry,' he went on. 'What we'll do is have an MRI of the area, and that will clarify the picture.'

Helen was beyond speech and was swallowing noisily. Cecilia said, 'Are you saying there's a chance the cancer has spread to a lung?'

'That's what the radiologist thinks,' said Dr Z. 'I'll read you the report, just as it is in front of me.' He did so.

'He says it's small,' said Cecilia, who was trying to keep her wits about her.

The stated smallness was a concern, not a relief, for Dr Z, in connection with Bertie's failing eyesight.

'Will I die?' asked Helen.

'Oh, don't worry about that,' said Dr Z. 'We've got plenty of treatment ideas for this sort of thing.'

'I never expected . . .' began Helen. She started to cry, even slightly to whimper, and Cecilia took her hand.

'I'll book an MRI urgently,' said Dr Z.

'Will Helen get the date in the post?' Cecilia did not want loose ends. 'When?'

'Yes. In the next few days. Could be a phone call, could be a letter. I'll book it now.' He turned back to the computer. 'Now you two lovely ladies go and have a nice cup of coffee and don't worry. You are in very good hands.'

The two lovely ladies shuffled out.

'You'll come home with me, of course,' said Cecilia. 'Have lunch and a bottle of wine.'

'I just can't believe this,' Helen was saying. 'I just can't believe it. I think I'm dreaming.'

At home a sympathetic Tim made lunch and opened a bottle. 'Bad luck, Helen,' he said.

'Well, we don't know yet,' said Cecilia, who found herself taking an optimistic line. 'There's got to be an MRI, it could say something different.'

'No, it won't,' said Helen. 'It's obvious I've had it.' She began to cry. 'Why?' she shouted. 'I haven't got a cough, or no more than the usual smoker's cough, or any pain.'

'Breathlessness, I believe,' contributed Tim, who was always more interested in a topic than in a person's feelings about it.

'Well, I'm breathless now,' wailed Helen, assailed by a new worry. 'Who wouldn't be?'

'This'll calm down,' said Cecilia. 'Like my bone stuff. It's bad at first. Humans get used to anything. And then the MRI, and its result, and things may be perfectly all right. They wouldn't be doing an MRI if they were certain sure this was cancer. You're in just the same position as me.'

This helped Helen. 'We're like two soldiers in the front line,' she said. 'Tim's nowhere,' she added, with a quick scowl at him. The 'breathlessness' still rankled.

'We all die, though,' said Tim, serving salad.

'Cecilia,' said Helen, 'are you secretly glad it's me rather than you?'

'Can't answer that,' said Cecilia, 'because it is me, too.'

Silence. The wine was helping. 'I never thought . . .' said Helen. 'I mean of course I was terrified of my scan result. But I never thought I would really have to hear those words. Cecilia, what did that report actually say?'

'I should have made notes, I was too shocked. Something about a small area . . .'

'The word deposit . . .'

'Possibly.'

Helen shuddered. 'The words they use,' she said. 'The words make everything worse.'

In the early evening Helen went home. The sunlight was beautiful and familiar, even though it glowed on and warmed scenes not beautiful in themselves. I will miss evening light, thought Helen. Better think of things I won't miss. She would not miss washing her hair, changing the colostomy bag, sitting alone of an evening hoping the phone would ring. She would not miss pens that didn't work, her face ageing in the mirror, ironing. She would not miss computer breakdown, cold weather, wanting sex. She would not miss taking the car to the garage, wrangling with her publisher, hangovers. She would miss the occasional inexplicable sense of well-being, a feeling she still sometimes got, in spite of her illness, though less often now. She would miss writing, when it was going well. She would miss Cecilia. She would miss her mum.

And the thought of her mum, as she let herself into her house and sat down, made the tears flow as no other thought yet had. She would have to tell her. Perhaps she might become unable to visit as regularly as she had been, or as frequently as of late. Having found herself as a daughter, late in the day, she might have to lose that self again, and not by her mother's death. She moaned at the thought.

Before long she telephoned Cecilia to share that thought with her. Then she phoned a couple of other friends. Talking was helping. So was another bottle of wine. So was crying. So was smoking, though that she did not notice doing. But her left hand went often to the left side of her chest, to where she thought her left lung would be. Nothing hurt. She took a few deep breaths to check that she was not breathless. What was her lung doing to her, so secretly, and why? She forgot to have anything to eat. The stoma sighed, gasped and whispered like a companion, like a Greek chorus. She phoned Cecilia again, to ask her whether it would be a good idea to Google 'lung cancer treatment', or 'lung cancer secondary', and Cecilia most definitely thought not. Cecilia made her promise not to. She knew Cecilia would realise she was tipsy, but that didn't matter. Why shouldn't she be? She rang Marj. Marj was sympathetic and concerned, and in the course of the conversation reported that Mum was no worse. Marj suggested that nothing about Helen's plight be told Mum until things were more definite. In the end Helen got to bed and scrambled into some sleep, dreaming of trains that did not come and countries in which she was lost.

∼

When Cecilia woke the next morning she immediately knew that something was on her mind. It took a second to find it. It was Helen.

Cecilia had not expected this to happen to Helen. For one thing, Helen's personality did not consort with death, as, Cecilia felt, her own did, much more readily. More important, Helen's operation had always seemed to Cecilia rather straightforward, perhaps by comparison with her own. She had always supposed Helen's long-term chances were the better.

Cecilia contrasted what she felt this morning with how it had been with her after her hapless visit to Dr P in his Harley Street consulting room. She felt gloomy and apprehensive on Helen's behalf, and braced for trouble, as she had been for herself. What she did not feel, as she had a month ago, was the pounding and the sinking heart, the sweats, the visceral involvement and the primitive terror. Those feelings, she thought, were unique to a mortal threat to one's own body. Or to the body of one's child.

So that was interesting, she was able to think, as she got up, her leg still hurting, though less. She was looking after her grandchildren this morning. Ian was abroad; Marina off to work. She made cups of tea for herself and Tim, wondering how she would feel if it were Tim in the firing line. Essential though he was to her, she would not feel at gunpoint, physically, as she had for herself. Which would be just as well, for, with steadier nerves, she would be more use. As she hoped to be to Helen.

She had arranged on the telephone last night to drop in on Helen on her way back from Ian's this afternoon. She was not confident that Helen would remember that engagement. She could text to remind her. Cecilia did not want to telephone in case Helen was managing to sleep.

She rang the doorbell and heard Cephas's running steps and cry of 'Gran!' Then Marina could be heard, and appeared. Cecilia and Marina smiled, and Cecilia crouched down to give Cephas a big hug.

'Daddy phone,' said Cephas, arranging the words intently, and looking straight into Cecilia's eyes to confirm she had understood.

'Yes, Ian has just rung,' Marina said. Her smile changed from a greeting one to a happy one.

'Good. All well?'

'All well,' said Marina and Cephas together.

It was an effort for Cecilia to spend time with her grandchildren. Part of her dreaded it every time. The noise, the physical activity, and, in a way, the boredom. But it was also the most important and sustaining joy of her life.

Marina left, having given instructions. It was a sunny day again, and possible for all three to be in the garden. Ali was in his pram, making little noises preliminary to going to sleep, and Cecilia and Cephas played with cars. There was a paved area outside the door from the kitchen, and this was good for cars, or better for them than the lawn. Cephas no longer cared for cars in grass, as his taste for realism had grown. He liked the road Cecilia drew on the paving stones with a piece of chalk.

'More road,' he said, and Cecilia obliged.

'Vroom vroom,' both said.

The game ended when Cephas grazed a knuckle, and then they had the interest of finding sticking plaster. Cecilia was glad to go indoors, and had a cup of coffee while Cephas had juice. Marina had asked her to buy some strawberries if it turned out to be convenient to have an outing. So Cecilia brought the pram in and through the house, and they set forth for the shop.

Annoyingly, Cephas wanted to push the pram. Cecilia let him come in front of her, so that he could feel he was pushing it while she really did the work. Cephas objected to this, and shouted, 'Me push, me push.' But the pram could not be moved by his strength alone. Cecilia was being reasonable, and letting him find out for himself what was possible and impossible. But he was frustrated and she was irritated. He changed his mind and decided he wanted to ride in the pram. He turned to Cecilia with his arms stretched up and a pouting expression. He whimpered. But she could not trust herself to lift him. This was worrying for both of them. Momentarily, it was a stalemate.

Then a young man, passing, said, 'You want to get in the pram? OK!' He lifted Cephas in, smiling at Cecilia, and immediately hurrying on. Cecilia settled Cephas, at the opposite end of the pram from Ali.

This sudden encounter with the outside world made Cephas first chastened, then reflective. 'Want to get in pram, OK!' he could be heard murmuring.

'Yes,' said Cecilia. 'A kind passer-by lifted you in.'

'Kind passer-by,' said Cephas.

'Shall we tell Mummy?'

Cecilia had to bring the large, heavy pram into the shop, but that was managed. Cephas spotted a bag of crisps that he wanted, and started pointing and grizzling and bouncing up and down. Tired, thought Cecilia, as many a loyal ancestress before her. She was determined not to give him the crisps, as it would put him off the wholesome lunch Marina left for him, and was not family policy. But now Cephas was angry, and yelled, and, despairing, put his face down among the shawls and shook with sobs.

'Remember the kind passer-by?' said Cecilia, when they were clear of the shop.

But Cephas could not be distracted, and would only say, 'Want crisps!', and they got home crestfallen. However, he was cheered up by the feat of climbing out of the pram, Cecilia's arms there in case he fell, which he did not. Cecilia wanted to have Cephas sitting down to his lunch before Ali woke, so she set to work quickly. Luckily Cephas enjoyed washing the strawberries in a basin on the floor.

After lunch, and a suggestion of his potty, quickly defeated and followed by a standard nappy change, Cephas was installed for his nap on the sofa in the sitting room, with a rug and Small Teddy. Cecilia sang a couple of the songs she had always sung to him. Then he slept. Meanwhile Ali was waking up, and Cecilia quickly warmed a bottle from the fridge. Routines were synchronising rather well today. She sat on a low chair feeding Ali, still crooning the song she had been singing to Cephas. She did not know Ali very well. He was so much his mother's. But now he was looking at Cecilia over the bottle with a clear, interested gaze, frowning slightly. She turned the bottle a little, to break the airlock in the teat, and felt how firmly Ali was holding on. She felt him as a person more strongly than she ever had before, and bowed acceptance to the lifelong love this engendered.

But she was thinking about Cephas as well as about Ali. She thought about the morning. Cephas had not been able to push the pram; he had not been lifted into the pram by her as he had wished; he had not got round her for the crisps. These setbacks were so ordinary, and he had responded to them so ordinarily. Cecilia's spirits rose at the recollection. You can tell by a child's sorrows, she thought, even more than by his joys, that he has survived.

He had survived. And this took Cecilia'a thoughts back to Leda. What had she and Cephas done together, mad as Leda was, in the first two months of his life, that had put down firm foundations for him, or, at least, not destroyed beyond repair his innate ones? She would never know.

After his feed Ali was easily lured to smile, and he and Cecilia were smiling alternately and in unison when Marina walked in. Cecilia was glad Marina came on a scene so peaceful – Cephas asleep, as expected at this time of day; Ali fed and happy. Marina had high standards, and Cecilia wasn't surprised that she couldn't resist doing the small amount of tidying and washing-up, quickly and efficiently, almost before saying hullo to Cecilia or greeting Ali. Once things were orderly enough for her to feel settled, and each adult had a cup of coffee, she could join in smiling with Ali, and then took him, and danced with him, and changed his nappy, and put him in the sling on her chest. She went on smiling with Ali from that closer vantage point, while she and Cecilia chatted. Cecilia had not forgotten she was going to call on Helen. At some point during the car game Cecilia had sent her a reminder, and Helen had texted back.

'Two things I wanted to talk to you about,' said Marina. 'One is, you are limping. I haven't asked you so far, because if you wanted me to know you would have said. But now I am asking.'

So Cecilia recounted the bone saga, Marina listening intently.

'Why didn't you tell us?' asked Marina. 'Here's me piling grandmother duties on you . . .'

This is what Cecilia had feared. She expostulated and re-assured. Marina asked more questions, including whether she could tell Ian, which in Cecilia's view was now up to her.

'And what's the other thing?' Cecilia asked.

'About Leda. Any news?'

'None. She left Helen's in a cloud of dust and hasn't been seen or heard of since.'

'That's what I thought. Are you worried about her?'

'Yes. And I feel we were unfairly phobic about her.'

'I feel that, too. Ian doesn't.'

'No, he wouldn't. But I'm glad you do.'

'Of course I do. After all, she is Cephas's—'

Her sentence remained unfinished because at that moment Cephas himself appeared in the doorway, pink with sleep, holding Small Teddy. 'Mummy!' he said. She put her arms round him. That was the advantage of the sling. Then he pulled back and looked at Cecilia, urgently. 'Kind passer-by,' he said, and they told Marina the story.

Chapter 21

Dr Z stuck his head out of his cubicle. 'Bertie! Dr Hertzel!' he called. A stooping figure stopped and turned, not sure where the summons was coming from. Now Dr Z burst into the corridor and Dr Hertzel was enlightened. Dr Z took both his hands.

'What brings you in?' asked Dr Z. 'It's so good to see you.'

'Good to see you, too,' said Bertie Hertzel. 'I'm sitting in on a meeting. They are starting a clinical trial on Crohn's disease, and they asked me to join the steering group. I don't know what sort of help I can be. I knew Burrill Crohn, years and years ago, and they found that out somehow, and that's probably why they have invited me, rather than for any wisdom of my own.' The old, seamed face beamed at Dr Z. 'I knew Bernie Sachs, Jesse Shapiro – Burrill's wonderful team, I was privileged to sit at their feet.'

'Could you step into my room for a moment? There's something I want to ask you. I hope it won't make you late.'

So they stepped into Dr Z's cubicle. Dr Z brought up Helen on the computer, and the report on her recent scan, and the scan itself. Dr Hertzel nodded and understood.

'Now here's your report on her previous scan, in January,' said Dr Z, glad the computer was working so well.

Bertie Hertzel went on nodding and smiling, but something was making him a bit impatient.

'These young people,' he said. 'They are so cocky, so full of themselves. He's obviously never seen childhood TB on a scan before. That's what he was looking at, and he mistook it for a secondary carcinoma.'

'Is it childhood TB?'

'Yes, and very typical. Barn-door obvious.'

'Well I'm . . . May I ask why you didn't mention it as such in your report?'

'Turn up my report on this patient's first scan, and you'll find I did. You don't have to mention something every time you report, if it's irrelevant. But have a word with your bright young thing. He should get back to his books. That generation haven't seen childhood TB.'

'He thought it was cancer,' said Dr Z.

'These days they think everything's cancer,' said Dr H. 'Now, if you'll excuse me, old chap . . .' And he was on his way.

∼

Cecilia arrived at Helen's. They hugged.

'How have you been?' Cecilia asked.

'Not too bad. Considering.'

'I thought you might ring this morning.'

'No, I remembered you were looking after the boys. I remembered you were coming round this afternoon, too. How could I forget that, drunk or sober?'

Cecilia was surprised to see Helen was in almost high spirits. She said nothing, to offer Helen the floor. They sat.

'I woke up this morning,' said Helen, 'and I went down and down. Then down further. I got dressed, in utter misery, and sat in this chair. Down further. Staring out of the window. Death, pain, misery, suspense, loneliness.'

'I know,' said Cecilia.

'I got a cup of coffee and some toast, but I was thinking, bitterly, why should I feed myself, why am I feeding this doomed creature. Let it starve. I sat on, doing nothing. Then after a couple of hours three things happened.'

'Go on.'

'One was I realised we are all programmed to die. All animals are. This doesn't sound very profound, but it was. And it still is, hours later. What it comes to is that perhaps deep down we don't actually fear death. We just think we do. The convention is we do. The reality is we take it in our stride.'

Cecilia was silent, intent.

'The next thing that happened was I realised that nothing bad is actually happening to me now. This minute. Of course I am terribly afraid it will. Fear of the unknown. But at the moment, nothing is actually happening. I feel well. What I am agonising with is the pain of fear of pain, not the pain of pain itself. And who knows but what it goes on like that, each day? Each day, of itself, bearable. That's not new or profound, either. But both those thoughts did the work in me as if they were. As if they were illuminations, inspirations. No, those words are too fancy. Something much more mundane and solid. I felt myself calming and expanding. Not drowning but waving. Almost.'

'My goodness,' said Cecilia, listening and learning.

'Yes, who would have thought it. The next thing that happened was I wanted to go on with the novel. When that happened I was stunned and impressed that the writing urge should be strong enough to counteract the panic urge. But it was. And the fact that it was, was in itself emboldening. The novel had frozen stiff in me with Dr Z's words. Yesterday I never expected to touch it again. But it struggled to life. It was alive again. And I sat down to it. And it went well. It's because I was working that I haven't rung you.'

'Well,' said Cecilia.

'And I thought: I want to finish this before I die. Like a proper writer.'

'Like a very proper writer. Helen, you always amaze me.'

'Of course I might go down again.'

'You may go up and down. But the dry land of these two thoughts, and the experience of the writing urge triumphing, they will be there, whatever.'

'I hope so. How did you manage your time of fear? You didn't even tell me about it at the time. And until I had it myself, I didn't really imagine how awful it must have been for you.'

'Not as well as you, I don't think.' Cecilia was being very careful with what she said. She didn't want to disturb Helen's new equilibrium, or to tamper with it. It didn't matter, at this point, how little she spoke.

Helen was thoughtful. 'Sometimes today I've wondered whether my feeling strong is only because, deep down, below consciousness, I've forgotten I'm supposed to be ill and die. That it's a sense of myself I simply can't hold on to. I'd hate it if it was only that.'

'Just hang on to the strong feeling. No need to doubt or modify it.'

Cecilia had not had time to eat the nice plateful Marina had put in the fridge for her, and Helen hadn't had lunch either; so now Helen produced a collection of exotic but slightly stale foods in delicatessen plastic, and a bottle of wine, and they had a meal together.

'D'you think this is a punishment for smoking?' asked Helen, lighting a cigarette.

The phone rang, and Cecilia did not have to try to answer this complicated question. It was Marj, asking how Helen was. The conversation ended with, 'See you on Tuesday,' and Cecilia asked after Marj and then after their mother, and then fell silent, so that Helen could revert smoothly to the main news.

The phone rang again. 'Hullo,' said Helen, then, 'Yes?' She executed a silent pantomime of amazed excitement or terror in Cecilia's direction. 'Yes,' she said several times. Then, 'Yes,

yes I did. When I was about ten.' Then, 'Yes, I see. Well, that's . . .' Then a beaming smile to Cecilia, and a few dance steps. 'Thank you so much for ringing.'

She came back to her chair. 'That was Dr Z,' she said. She lay back smiling ecstatically and tears crept down her cheeks. 'It isn't cancer. It's the childhood TB.'

'Oh Helen. How wonderful.' If Cecilia felt at that moment more alone with her own condition than she had, she did not show it.

'All that thinking,' said Helen. 'The strong, brave, grown-up feeling. All that. I don't need it after all.' She tapped the left side of her chest. 'You are perfectly all right,' she said to it. Then she went on: 'Do people feel like this when they win the lottery? It's called over the moon. It's called tickled pink.' After a moment she said, 'A tiny bit of me feels cheated. Cheated of being that bigger person. I was doing so well.'

'You certainly were,' said Cecilia. 'But the strong feeling and the writing feeling and the two thoughts aren't wasted, and you can't stop being that bigger person.'

'No. It's a rehearsal.'

'Yes. And a help for me.'

Helen opened her eyes and slowly stood up. She came to Cecilia and stooped to put her arms round her. They were both crying.

~

It was a bad line again. 'I guess you're between teatime and bedtime,' said Ian. 'Friday, so Cephas must be watching *Look at Big Ships*.'

'Yes. Right on all counts.'

'Good to hear your voice. Longing to be home.' The words crackled and receded. Marina couldn't help shaking the telephone, though she knew it would do no good. Now Ian was saying something about Ali.

'I hear Ali,' said Marina, 'but not what you're saying about him.'

'Not our Ali.'

'What?'

'I'll go somewhere else . . . Is that any better?'

'Yes.'

'I tracked down Ali's wife and told him we have called our baby after Ali. That's what I wanted to tell you.'

'Oh good.' Tears came to Marina's eyes. 'How wonderful. How was she?'

'Brave. I took sweets for the children.' Crackle and hiss. Pause. 'In half an hour I'm interviewing Bruce Bridges.'

'Oh good, I'll be watching. But I've forgotten who he is. I know the name.'

'Can't hear.'

'Forgotten who he is.'

'A colonel in the Black and Blues and a lovely man.'

'Ah yes, I remember him.'

'Are you OK?'

'Well, not quite. Will you hear if I say something?'

'Yes, fine.'

'Cecilia's got a cancer threat. It may be cancer. It may not.'

'Oh God.'

'I can't talk about it now, can I, and maybe I shouldn't have mentioned it at all. But—'

'Of course you should have. Are you working tomorrow?'

'No.'

'I'll ring you from the airport, the signal is always good there.'

'And don't worry. It may well be nothing.'

'I shan't worry, yet. But I'm glad to know. I'll phone her.'

'Goodbye and love.'

'Goodbye and love. Kisses to them.'

~

Cecilia and Tim.

'Splendid news,' cried Cecilia, on seeing Tim and Thor come out of his study to greet her. 'It's not cancer.'

'How wonderful. Thank God. What a relief. How do you know?'

'No, I mean Helen.'

Pause. 'Oh. Well. Good news anyway.'

'She had TB when she was a child, and whatever is left over from that was mistaken for lung cancer on the X-ray. The doctor phoned her. While I was there.'

'She must be over the moon.'

'She is.'

'And you must be quite tired. The little boys this morning, Helen this afternoon.'

'Yes. And I told Marina about my own scare.'

'For the first time?' Tim was surprised. His impression was that women always told each other everything at the first possible moment.

'Yes. I hadn't wanted to worry them. Until there's anything definite. By the way, you sounded very relieved, when you thought I meant me, not Helen, at the beginning of this conversation. Very relieved for someone who is convinced that mine is radiation damage.'

'Yes, well, it's nice to have something one's sure of confirmed. I'll have to wait a bit longer for that.'

Cecilia liked this answer, but was not satisfied. 'How could I have suddenly found out? You must know I haven't had an appointment today.'

'The doctor might have rung you,' said Tim, thinking fast.

'Unlikely, when . . .' Cecilia decided to let it go. 'Marina was concerned and wants to tell Ian and oh dear, I regret telling her.'

'Yes. She didn't have to know, probably, ever.'

Cecilia liked this answer too. 'We talked about something

else, as well. We are both a bit worried about Leda. Disappearing like that. And we treated her so terribly. Just wanting to eliminate her. Make her not dangerous. Not thinking about her, as her, at all.'

'Well, she had tennis, and everyone liked her.' Now that Tim no longer saw Leda, she was scarcely a memory, though what there was of it remained a sweet one.

'I know you adored her. That and Cephas were what made me desperate to be rid of her. Did you know I hated you adoring her?' Cecilia had not been so forthright with Tim about his feeling for Leda before. Enough time had passed to make it possible for her to be open with him. It was a relief.

'I wouldn't say adored.' There was a silence, while they both thought.

'Do you see what I mean about being worried about her?' asked Cecilia, for whom Tim was now, possibly, someone with whom she could approach the subject of her version of Leda, rather than having to ignore, or attempt to depotentiate, his.

'Well. I wouldn't be sure what to worry about. She seems to get on all right in the world. I didn't really see her mad side.'

'Oh yes you did. You just didn't notice it, because of beauty and tennis. No one could fail to see what you call her mad side. It wasn't a side, it was her.'

'Well, there's nothing much you can do about her, is there, now that she's disappeared. It may be sad, but there it is. No point feeling guilty.'

'People always say that. But I'm not so sure. There may be quite a bit to be said for feeling guilty, and what can come of it.'

~

Helen made a number of phone calls, and told her story several times, with unflagging verve, and to each listener's congratulatory response. Although elated, Helen grieved for the loss of her high seriousness. She found she had settled back immediately into life as usual, and wasn't sure that this was what she most wanted. There had been a gritty reality about the two hours on her chair this morning, and their consequences in her mind and heart. Could it really have been as recently as this morning? She had gone down indeed, and then down further; but in the process had discovered deep waters in herself she could not have foreseen were there. Part of her wanted to feel these waters around her again, buoying her up, buoying her up in defiance of any known hope or expectation. But there was no escaping the joy of ordinariness. That joy could not be resisted. The high seriousness would wait, she hoped, and be there, still costing no less than everything, when she next needed it.

The doorbell rang and Helen answered it. On the threshold stood Lewis, he of the tennis club, smiling and shy.

'Oh,' said Helen. 'Hullo.'

'I just wondered whether Margaret is in. And would like to see me. Lewis.'

'Of course I know who you are. Come in.' Helen felt warm and hospitable towards him – towards anyone, really, at this moment. 'Sit down.'

'Well, I'm just on my way home, but I thought . . . Thank you.' They sat.

'Margaret isn't here any more, I'm afraid,' said Helen.

'Oh. Do you know where she has gone?'

'No, sorry. She moved out rather suddenly and left no details.'

'No bad news, I hope?'

'None she told me. Would you like a glass of wine? I'm having one. Beer?'

He accepted, and smiled more intimately at Helen, for both knew they were remembering from last time that it was beer for him.

'It's obvious you were very taken with her,' said Helen. 'And I'm not surprised.'

'It was funny. She didn't take any notice of anyone. Just played tennis. But suddenly she started coming to find me. Me of all people. There are some good-looking blokes her sort of age in and out of the club. But she ignored them. She used to come and find me, even when I was in the – well, we've got a sort of glorified pavilion we call the clubhouse where I do paperwork, computer nowadays of course, and mend rackets, which is my hobby. I might be in there, and there'd be a little knock. And it was her. She didn't say anything, she'd just come to see me. She must have liked me. I don't know what she could have seen in me. And then, from one day to the next, she completely disappeared.' He made a gesture and a hissing noise suggestive of evaporation. 'She'd paid her six months' sub. No one could understand it.'

'She's an unusual person.'

He needed to puzzle over the mystery of what had happened to him several times more, adding details, and Helen listened sympathetically. She did not want to point out that Margaret was psychotic, from reluctance to spoil a dream that might otherwise stay intact for all time. That wonderful week, when Margaret was his secret admirer and he, her speechlessly worshipping friend. Perhaps the best week of his life, thought Helen, assessing this ordinary-looking man, his undistinguished physique, his balding head, his lack of eloquence, his unassuming manner. He revealed himself as a smoker when she lit a cigarette, and she liked him for it.

'Tell me a bit about yourself,' she said.

But the further bit about Lewis had to wait till later in the evening, for Helen, of course, was still full of her own news, which burst into the baffled silence she had created by her request. Interested and entertained, Lewis listened to what Helen had already honed into anecdote. He was reasonably informed, having had a prostate scare himself, and Helen found him a worthy audience. Finally they had exhausted that.

'Now,' she said, 'tell me the best and the worst things in your life at the moment.'

By now Lewis was not baffled nor even hesitant. 'Best,' he said. 'The best was Margaret liking me. But I don't know if she really did. Worst, that's easy – never seeing my daughters and knowing my wife is putting them off me.'

'How old are they?'

'Twenty and eighteen.'

'I'm sorry.'

Helen felt they were old enough to make up their own minds, and said so. She ascertained that Lewis and his wife had broken up ten years ago and that she had taken the children and the house. He now rented a small flat. Helen was vigorous on his behalf. He was pleased with her support, and he warmed to her invective against Lisa, but didn't feel he could do anything about anything. She was frustrated, but managed not to bully him.

'Lives!' she said. 'They don't work out that well, do they?'

'I bet yours has.'

'Why do you say that?'

'Well, you are beautiful, not so young, I know that, but beautiful. Attractive. Interesting. Outgoing. Lovely to talk to. I wouldn't expect you to be single.'

'Ah well, I am.'

'You know what my job is,' said Lewis. 'What do you do? Or perhaps you are retired.'

Helen didn't like the fact that she looked retired. She told him she wrote novels. He was impressed, and more so when she showed him the short bookshelf devoted to herself. She might not have succumbed to pointing this shelf out to him if it had not been for the word 'retired'.

They picked an evening when he would drop in again, and he went off into the night, light of heart, forgetful of Margaret, and thrilled with his new friend. Helen sat and thought about him. Lover? She wondered. She definitely liked him. She liked the look of the cushion he had dented. He was not sexy in an obvious way, but she found she had experienced him as a physical and male presence. That said, in her late sixties, perhaps sex was not the point. He could be a friend. Perhaps she could give him good advice about his daughters. However, if they were going to have sex, she would have to warn him about the colostomy. Her heart sank at that thought. She loved to appear glamorous, and she guessed she had done so to him. A glamorous older woman. But there was nothing glamorous about the colostomy. She realised her fantasies and speculations were bounding ahead, but then they always did; and she rightly guessed that they were not bounding more spryly than his were. That was what she liked about him. He was emotionally available. He was romantic. He had used the word 'beautiful'.

Chapter 22

The phone went in the night to tell Marina that Ian had been abducted. He had been exploring by himself – not advised – and, according to witnesses, had been grabbed from a car that had sped away, knocking down a woman and two children. It was the Foreign Office that rang Marina, and, immediately, with cold and shaking fingers, she rang work. The night desk knew, of course, but had no further details. She turned on the radio. The item was not there yet. Now walking up and down her bedroom in the excess of agitation, she phoned his mobile, which was not switched off, but rang and rang. At least she heard his voice. But at the sound of his voice, sobbing replaced terror. It did not replace it. There were both.

She dressed, still walking. Her thought was to go out there. Knowing the terrain, she might be able to do something. She rang the Foreign Office. They were against her going. It could do no good. She finished getting dressed and went on walking up and down. She rang his mobile again, to hear his voice, but now it was disconnected. She rang the Foreign Office to tell them the exact time the mobile had been disconnected, and that before that it had still been on. She rang work and told them the same. She had not used her mobile for these calls, for it was her mobile that Ian always used to call her, and she must keep it free. Now she made sure that it was on and charged. She looked at her watch again. She had just checked it for the

Foreign Office call, but could not remember what it was. Four-sixteen. About nine-thirty there. He must have been on an early reconnoitre. Thinking of what he must have been doing, what he must have planned and decided to do, his mind working in ways so familiar to her, made her think of him, his character, his body, his face, his self, the blessed ordinariness of his presence. She could not do without him. And then she thought of him thinking of her. He would be thinking he would probably never see her again, as she was thinking she would probably never see him again.

There was a cry from Ali, and this brought her back to the children. She picked him up and held him close. He was teething. A picture came into her mind from a few days ago; Ian dancing him in his arms, singing, 'That tooth, that tooth is bitterly uncouth, the curse of youth, forsooth, forsooth,' a chant that Cephas had taken up. Her tears poured on to Ali's head and down both their faces. She began to feed him. She would have to go on doing this, and doing everything, with Ian dead.

Dead or disappeared? Held hostage? How would she know? When would she know? Perhaps he was dead now. Perhaps even now she was on a planet on which there was no Ian. If there was no Ian, there was no one. Yes, there were the children. There had to be. Feeding Ali, she rang Ian again. Nothing. She looked at her mobile. No text from him – obviously. She held her mobile to her cheek, then to her lips. She thought again about going out there, getting on the next plane. The Foreign Office could not stop her. She could not bear to feel so far away. Cecilia could look after the children. She turned on the radio. Yes, they had it now. Correspondent Ian Forest abducted. Don't say our thoughts are with his family. They did.

Best ring Cecilia soon, or she would hear it first from the radio.

~

Tim, restless, with the World Service on quietly, heard it before Cecilia did. He was listening in a dreamy way, thinking to find the news soporific, and hoping to get back to sleep. The name of Ian Forest hit him physically. It was a sensation before it was a thought. He was not sure what he had heard, so he slipped quietly out of bed and went to his computer. Thor, intrigued and pleased to have someone up so early, purred and wreathed around his bare legs. Yes. Abducted. Tim was trying to take in what had happened. The message was clear enough.

Cecilia. It was for Cecilia, not for himself, that Tim was thunderstruck. He went back to the bedroom. Cecilia was awake, upright in bed, sensing something. The news on the radio had moved on. He would have to break it to her.

'Ian,' he said.

'Yes?'

'Ian has been abducted.'

Silence. Then, 'Tell me what's known so far.'

Tim gave the scrap of information, which was all there was. Cecilia instantly started to get dressed. Tim went to make tea. It was still only just after five. The birds and the sunshine were busy outside.

Now it has happened, Cecilia thought, wordlessly. The one thing that must never happen has happened. This was what she had feared more than she could possibly have feared anything else, and the fear within her now was not like any other fear she had known. This fear was like a bolting horse, galloping, plunging, panting. She wanted to run and scream. Instead, she was quietly putting on her shoes. I can bear this, she told herself. Other mothers have. I must be strong, for Marina, for the children. And I will. She did her hair – she had nearly forgotten to – hoping to appear a normal, not a deranged, Cecilia, for Marina and the boys.

She saw Ian in a foreign dungeon, sitting waiting, waiting for he knew not what, one foot on top of the other, as in scaring situations when he was little. If I could offer myself in his place . . .

Tim came in with a cup of tea for her. 'It may be all right,' he said. He didn't know what else to say.

She drank her tea. 'It may be,' she said.

The phone rang. It was Marina.

'I know,' said Cecilia. 'I'm coming over.'

'Now?'

'Now.'

'Good.'

Cecilia felt nothing of the many pains that now attended her walking, as she speeded to Ian and Marina's door. Her heart thumped, what was left of her guts seethed. She was up against something as solid as a brick wall, a fact not patient of mitigation or insight. It had not crept nearer and nearer, as her own death-dealing fates had; she had hit it, without knowing it was there. It had hit her. And there it was. She was not optimistic. How could she be? And yet hope had a hold. It may be all right. It may be all right. Sometimes it was. Meanwhile she must be strong.

Marina opened the door. They did not hug, but looked into each other's faces. Each had the comfort, if comfort it was, of knowing they minded equally. With no one else in the world would they have had that satisfaction. Both wanted to be strong, and strong for the other, not competitively, but Cecilia because she was the senior, and Marina because it was her character.

'It may be all right,' Cecilia said.

'Yes. It may be.'

Cecilia was in the house, but immediately the doorbell rang again. It was a courier from the Foreign Office.

'They are giving me a phone,' said Marina. 'They don't want me to use the house phone or my mobile. I wouldn't use my mobile anyway, because . . .' Her eyes met Cecilia's and filled

278

with tears. Cecilia's filled too. What moved her was the stead-
fast childishness of the hope that one day the phone would
ring and it would be Ian.

But of course all the phones were soon ringing all the time,
and Marina choked callers off the mobile immediately. As
friends and colleagues heard the news, they phoned. Marina's
mum and dad phoned. Her sister phoned. Marina could not
resist calling the Foreign Office and work. People phoned
Cecilia too, hearing the news. Any conversation Cecilia and
Marina had was constantly interrupted.

The phones woke Cephas. He found Ali on Cecilia's lap
and turned to his mum. She laid her hand gently on his head,
but was walking up and down, talking on the phone.

'No Ali,' suggested Cephas to Cecilia, beginning to climb
up the side of her chair. Seeing how it was, Marina scooped
up Ali, and Cecilia took charge of Cephas. First he sat on her
knee, establishing supremacy over Ali, and they chatted, Cecilia
hoped normally. Then they started thinking about his breakfast.
Cecilia set his cereal on the table and sat down beside him. He
attempted gusto, but could not really eat. How much did he
know? wondered Cecilia.

'Shall I put the news on?' she asked Marina, in the next lull.
'The TV?'

'Don't. It's announced on every bulletin, but anything that
happens we'll know first, and they show a boxed picture of . . .
a boxed picture that I don't want . . .' She gestured towards
Cephas.

'Quite right,' said Cecilia. She felt foolish for asking.

But Cephas suddenly wanted TV, and Cecilia put a children's
programme on for him. She came back to the kitchen.

'He doesn't usually watch TV at this time,' said Marina. 'I
wonder if he senses . . .'

The phone rang again. Cecilia washed up Cephas's breakfast
and made cups of tea. She made toast and buttered it and cut

the slices in four and put the plate and the cup near where Marina was standing.

Activity was fostering hope and ordinariness for both of them. Both knew that the slight rise in well-being, the slight lowering of foreboding, made no difference. They knew that whatever was externally true was unchanged by it. But they were glad to be able to use it, the better to hide their fear.

Ali had been whimpering unnoticed and was screaming now. Cecilia took him and walked him up and down. 'He's hungry,' said Marina, 'I'll feed him in a minute.'

'Have your tea and toast,' said Cecilia, who was managing to reduce the screams back to whimpers. 'You have to look after yourself. For the sake of . . . for the sake of all of us and everything.'

Marina quickly ate two pieces of toast and drank her tea. 'Come on, little one,' she said to Ali, taking him from Cecilia. She sank down into her feeding chair.

Cephas ran back into the room. His wet night nappy had slipped down and his pyjama legs were sodden.

'Come and let's change you,' said Cecilia. 'And you aren't dressed yet! Silly Gran.'

'Cars,' said Cephas. 'Cars and cars. Two cars.'

'Two' was his current word for anything more than one. He got hold of Cecilia's hand to lead her to the sitting room.

'Oh God, it'll be the press,' said poor Marina. 'It doesn't matter. We don't have to go out.'

The press it was, as Cecilia saw. For Cephas the spectacle was fascinating. Cecilia persuaded him to get changed and dressed on condition he could come straight back and watch. All the papers' front pages were to carry photographs the next morning of Cephas looking out of the window.

Marina kept trying to clear enough space in her mind to go through the many abductions that were well known, some of which, indeed, she had herself presented to the public on the news. She was assessing the likelihood of Ian's survival. She went round and round. There was that story, but then again there was that one. Her thoughts returned to this activity in every gap. She knew it was no help, and, on balance, it was depressing; but it was what she could not help doing. Cecilia did not know Marina was doing this. Neither knew where the other's mind was. Cecilia's was with the boy sitting with one foot on top of the other. She could almost see Ian, and almost smell his hair. Perhaps Marina was using her memory and her statistics to keep the physical sense of Ian at bay.

Cecilia began to understand what Marina was driving at, or, rather, circling round, when Marina began to ring colleagues to ask them what exactly they remembered of various cases, thus adding to, and sharpening up her store of memories. Cecilia overheard, and was drawn into the highs and lows. It was not heartening. She could hear Marina trying to make it so, and, in most of the exchanges, could deduce the interlocutor's stress and tact. Cecilia went into the sitting room to be with Cephas. The TV was still showing its cartoons, but Cephas was ignoring them, and had eyes only for the cameras and the cars. Cecilia watched them with him, well shielded by the curtain. Cephas did not need her, so she went back into the kitchen, in case Marina missed her presence, and in case Ali could do with anything she might be able to offer. There was now a big atlas on the kitchen table, open at the right page. She did not look at it. The morning went on.

Marina's mother rang again. Cecilia could tell from Marina's side of the conversation that she was undertaking to commit her life savings and sell the family's country cottage in the event of a ransom being demanded. Marina was touched, for her father and her sister would also have been involved in this commitment, and the phones would have been busy. She tried to be grateful, while explaining that ransoms were not paid.

'I understood that conversation,' Cecilia said when Marina rang off. 'How sweet of them.'

Cephas appeared in the doorway. 'Tim,' he announced, and Cecilia went to look.

Tim was battling through the reporters. He worked his way to the front door, which Cecilia opened a chink to let him in. 'I never thought of that,' he said, shaken. 'I've brought you girls some lunch.'

He had made a chicken casserole, and he, Cecilia and Cephas sat down to something like a normal meal. Marina could not look at food. Cecilia put a helping in the fridge for her. She must eat. She was breastfeeding.

Because he could not leave, Tim was added to the company in the afternoon and tried to teach Cephas Snakes and Ladders. Ali slept. Cecilia was at a loose end. She watched Snakes and Ladders, which alternated for Cephas with staring out of the window, and felt a little supported by Tim's presence. Marina was on the phone, either the house phone or the one the Foreign Office had issued. Only her mobile had fallen silent. At one point Helen was to be seen outside, tangling with reporters, but she did not have Tim's persistence, and left, to eat her cargo of fishy delicacies alone at home. Cecilia talked to her on the telephone, and to others; but nothing had any reality for her, except that beloved body, somewhere, alive or dead.

Time passed slowly. Around sundown the press faded away. Cephas became crotchety, which Marina put down to his not having been out all day. Tim played football with him in the garden to give him some fresh air. It didn't last long. Cephas came indoors claiming he had hurt his foot. But it was his whole self that hurt, and he didn't know why. He put his face down in Big Teddy, and cried quietly.

Tim went home, due to pop back later with Cecilia's stoma away-bag. People, including Helen and Marina's parents, asked if a visit would be welcome and if there was anything they could do. Marina parried these phone calls. For the moment she wanted only Cecilia, who minded as much as she did. She did not want people who minded for her sake. What would she have in common with them?

'I don't believe this is happening,' Cecilia muttered at one moment.

She was expressing something both women felt, but Marina disowned it. 'Why?' she said. 'It's not a surprising thing to happen. It's a risk that goes with the job.'

'Yes,' said Cecilia. She felt rebuked, but strengthened. If it was a risk that went with the job, Ian must have thought about that risk, and must have decided long ago that he could face whatever he was facing – was facing, or had faced. 'Yes.' Then she said, 'Has anything happened, in the phone calls, which offers any information?'

'Not yet, there's nothing. But no one is despairing.'

'And we won't either. And I'm going to heat up some food for you.'

Marina tried to eat. She agreed that she should. Cecilia and Cephas fed the cat, then Cecilia began to put Cephas to bed. He had a bath, with his boats floating in it. She was trying to make things feel ordinary. Usually he liked to submerge his boats and give them a rough time; but tonight he took them carefully out of the water and put them on the side of the bath. 'Safe boats, now,' he said. Cecilia's tears mingled with the bathwater.

After Cephas was asleep Ali had a long playtime. He did not usually have both his mother and his grandmother hovering over him, and he liked it very much. He lay on a blanket on the floor in a patch of sunlight, and the cat, Benjy, came to sit near him. Ali's nappy was off, and he was kicking vigorously. His mouth tensed whenever the kicking intensified. Cecilia crouched uncomfortably beside him, absorbed in him, offering

283

rattles, and beaming in response to his smiles. Marina came and went. Cecilia had always wished she knew Ali better, and this was an opportunity. She did not want Marina to guess that she was having the thought that Ali might be all there was left, biologically, of Ian. She did not want Marina to think she was paying special attention to Ali for that reason, and indeed that was not the reason.

Cecilia bathed Ali and brought him, beautiful and fragrant, his hair standing on end, to his mother for his last feed. Marina sank into the feeding chair and received him. She was very tired. While Marina was feeding Ali, Tim came back to the house with Cecilia's overnight stoma supplies. Tim and Cecilia went into the sitting room. They sat down. She ached in every limb.

'I'm so sorry,' Tim said. 'You must have had an awful day.' No answer was necessary.

Soon Cecilia said, 'Marina must eat. Oh dear.'

Tim turned on the TV.

'Turn it down,' said Cecilia, in case the news, with its lack of newness, would bother Marina. They watched the bulletin through, and saw the picture of Ian. They switched off and sat in silence.

'I suppose neither of you wants a drink?' asked Tim. 'I could get . . .' His sentence petered out.

'I keep wondering what might be happening.'

'Yes, of course.'

But conjecture was not Tim's thing, even at the best of times. Nor, actually, was reassurance. He liked action. He always rose to a task. Realising this frustration in him, Cecilia said, 'Thank you for bringing the stoma things.'

'You'll be staying here all night, I suppose.'

'Oh yes.'

'Not a lot I can do,' he said, unhappily. 'I think I'll go home. By the way, I've fed Thor.' He left.

Cecilia did not attempt to hide from herself the discrepancy between what she felt and what Tim felt. She would suffer, steadily or less steadily, until Ian was recovered, and, if he was never recovered, for ever. Tim would sleep well tonight, and in the morning the calamity would come back into his mind, probably because Cecilia was not in the bed beside him. She did not hold this against Tim, though it made her sad, and, inevitably, increased the distance between them. People were entitled to feel what they felt. Sitting in her chair, she breathed deeply. She was trying to calm herself and ready herself for the night. Soon she heard Marina moving about and putting Ali in his cot. She could hear her singing. Then she heard her tidying up in the kitchen. Then she came into the sitting room holding two mugs of tea.

'I've sugared them,' she said, attempting a smile.

'Sugar in a crisis,' agreed Cecilia. 'Eight-thirty,' she commented.

'It's one in the morning there.'

'I heard you singing to Ali.'

'Of course. You want to do what you usually do.'

'The phones have gone quiet.'

'For the moment.'

It was still light and, outside the house, an ordinary day. 'Will you sleep?' asked Cecilia.

'No. Will you?'

'No. Shall I ask Tim to pop round with sleeping pills? I've got some.'

'No. What's the point? Well, you have them, if you like, of course.'

'Could you eat anything?'

'Not just now. Sorry. Thanks.'

Cecilia did not mention food again. The Foreign Office phone rang a few times, and Marina briefly conversed. The house phone rang; it was Marina's mother. Cecilia was wondering whether to hope Ian was alive or dead. She could imagine circumstances where it might be better for him to be already dead. Might what happened to him never be known? It might only ever be known to him, to him, and to whoever held him. It didn't matter that she could think of nothing to say to Marina. And Marina knew that she didn't have to speak to Cecilia. They sat in the darkening room, each with her thoughts, minding equally and totally. An hour passed.

Marina's mobile rang.

~

When a car drew up beside Ian and he was quickly hauled into it, he instantly faced the worst. This was it. Exactly this had been it for others, and now it would be it for him. There were three men in the car, the driver, someone beside the driver who had leapt out to help tug Ian in, and the one sitting beside Ian who had tugged him in and was engaged in tying his hands and blindfolding him. Before the blindfold went on he snatched a glance at his watch. No one spoke. The car was close and hot. Ian was trying to estimate how long the journey was, to see if he could tell anything about his location. Before long they drew up and parked. He thought they had been driving south-west. These were the thoughts he was having, thoughts definitely connected with survival, if not escape, although he was pretty sure he had had it.

He was manhandled out of the car and made to stumble up a brief approach and into a house. What felt like a gun was pressed against his kidneys, but, of course, it could have been anything. The house felt like an ordinary house, not like any sort of stronghold. One man was in the house and now the captors all spoke to each other. Four of them now, he thought. He felt they were young or, at least, that two of them were. The one who had been already in the house seemed almost a boy from his voice; the one beside Ian in the car had seemed young. Ian's knowledge of the language was not as good as it should have been. He could not understand what they were saying to each other.

He was pushed into a room by two of them, the contents of his pockets removed and his watch unstrapped. His mobile phone and all identification was gone. Then one of them left the room. Ian's feet were now tied, he thought by one of the younger ones. It took a comparatively long time to get the knots right, and Ian could hear what he thought was nervous breathing. Then he was left alone, and a key turned in a lock. But it sounded like an ordinary key and an ordinary lock. His guess was that this was a temporary stop on a longer journey.

He could hear the voices of his captors, talking, arguing, possibly. He took the argumentative tone as a good sign. Now he sank into a sitting position, and found he had a wall to lean against.

Now he thought of Marina. His head went down between his knees. When would Marina hear? Would she have heard already? Would she berate him in her mind for carelessness? She would not. She should but she would not. He remembered that she had arranged kidnap insurance for both of them. He was grateful now. At the time he had scoffed. Perhaps someone was going to negotiate for him. He raised his arms to feel the wall with the back of his hands. He stood up and tried to inch his way along the wall. But with his feet tied moving was too difficult. He crouched against the wall again.

How lucky that he had had a good breakfast. It might have to last him a while. Although he believed, in one part of himself, that he had had it, yet his minute-to-minute thinking assumed he would soon be free. He thought of the children. At home it would still be night. He could not take in the possibility that he would never see Marina or his children again, although he was capable of putting that idea to himself.

He wanted to write something to Marina. I love you, would

be enough. But, if he died, how would the message be conveyed? It would not, of course. However, when he heard someone come into the room, he said the words for 'write' and 'wife', but there was no answer. A cup of water was put to his lips. He hoped it was water. He drank it. Don't annoy them. 'Thank you,' he said.

He rehearsed another sentence for when he was next visited. It was more difficult, but working it out passed the time. When someone else, or possibly the same one, came in, he said, 'I am a man, like you.' Then he said it again. No answer. Obviously their policy was not to speak to him. Not even when they realised that he knew at least a little bit of the language. 'Wife,' he said. 'Children.' Why should this young man care? Everyone this young man knew must have had more losses than this stray Englishman was self-centredly anticipating. But still Ian said, 'Children. Two.' Then he tried again, 'I am a man, like you.'

Later he found himself saying, 'I love your beautiful country,' and felt like a phrase book, although it was true. Flies buzzed. His wrists and ankles ached. He wanted to see.

He tried to transfer love mentally to Marina, and wondered if she might be doing the same to him, at the same time. He thought of Cecilia, and what she must be going through today. But she would say, 'Don't worry about me, darling, I am as strong as a horse,' as she had when he spoke to her about her possible bone cancer. He thought of Cephas, and wondered how they would explain to him, if they had to, that Daddy was gone. Ali would not need to understand. He was too little.

He dozed. He awoke to eat some food that a different one of the four custodians brought him. This one had rougher hands and a different way of breathing. He smelt of cigarettes, actual tobacco. Eat everything, the advice was; you don't know when you'll get anything else. There was something touching about being fed with a spoon. 'Thank you,' he said. He indicated that he wanted to pee, and for this his hands were undone and a receptacle placed in them. He made no effort to capitalise on his hands' brief freedom. He longed to wrench off his blindfold, but the word was that it was better to conform.

He did not despair. He saw every reason to despair, but he did not. This was partly temperament, partly kidnap insurance, partly that he could not dislike his kidnappers, partly that he had not been killed at once. None of what was happening, he thought, would be too bad, if he did not love people. If he was now as he had been a few years ago, unattached, all this would be different, and not nearly so bad. There were moments when he wished he had never married, and that he had no children. He felt intense love for Marina. If he could get a message to her, he would die happy. He could see her face very clearly. He carefully imagined in turn each one of the rooms in their home. His mind was a jumble, his senses alert.

The room darkened through the blindfold and he realised that night was falling. For the first time, he cried. He heard voices, possibly arguing. One voice appeared to be dominant. They might just be talking. Or it could be the TV. It might be an altercation about his fate. He had no sense of how much time was passing. There must be a window in his room, or he would not apprehend the darkening. That was consoling. He was in the same world as everyone else.

Two men came in. They hauled Ian to his feet and removed the bands round his ankles. They prodded him to walk. He was taken through the doorway of his room, and then a doorway to the outer air. The evening smelt fresh. He stumbled on. Now three men – he thought it was three – were trying to put him into the boot of a car. Ian was tall, and did not fold easily. But they squeezed him in, and the lid came down. He was uncomfortable, even at first; he became much more so. He felt the odds were that he was being taken to a place of execution. The drive took a long time.

Then the car stopped. Surprisingly, its engine was still running when the boot opened. Two men were pulling him out. He groaned with pain as his limbs and neck straightened. Now he was standing, his hands still bound, his eyes still blindfolded. Probably this was it. He expected a bullet in the back of his head.

There seemed to be only one man now. The other must have got back into the car. He felt the lapels of his shirt tugged straight a couple of times, to equalise them, as a schoolteacher might prepare an untidy child for assembly. Something was dropped into his breast pocket. Then the bands around his wrists were cut away. He stretched his hands out. The car door slammed and the car roared away. Ian waited.

Nothing happened. It was absolutely quiet. He was alone. Slowly he raised his hands to his blindfold. His cramped fingers tussled with it. It took a while to get it off. He was in darkness. The darkness was almost as black without the blindfold as with it. But he looked up and saw a sky full of stars. He felt his shirt pocket, to discover what had been slipped into it. It was his mobile. Of course it would not work, out here.

It did.

Chapter 23

In spite of her mounting anxiety, Lily Bridges fed the birds and the horses as usual. It was an activity usually associated with peace of mind, but no longer. She had a care for the snails, as always; but today this was dictated by habit rather than empathy. The beauty of the early morning garden struck her with melancholy, not with joy. She came back into the house to the smell of breakfast. She drifted into the kitchen.

'Good morning, Greta dear,' she said. 'Do you happen to know if there have been any telephone calls?'

'Not that I know of, Mrs Bridges. The major is in the dining room, waiting for you. He can probably tell you more than I can.' Greta smiled at Lily, looking up from the Aga. The smell of bacon made Lily hungry in spite of herself.

'Thank you.' Lily wandered off.

'There you are,' said Guy. 'There you are at last. That chappie's been found.'

'A chappie?'

'The one that was kidnapped yesterday. He interviewed Bruce a couple of times. You know. That chappie. A journalist.'

'Oh yes.' Lily was checking the laying of the table. Guy would worry if everything was not in order. 'He seems to have been let out very quickly.'

'Amateurs, probably. An impromptu kidnapping. That's what they think.'

'That could be just as bad.'

'How do you mean, just as bad?'

'They still could kill someone.'

This was unanswerable, though Guy tried to find a retort. Because he wanted to put Lily in the wrong, he took notice of her, which entailed looking at her. Doing so, he was struck by her appearance. 'You don't look very well,' he said. 'Do you feel all right?'

'Yes,' said Lily. 'I hope I'm not coming down with something.'

'Coming down with something? Like what?'

'Well, cancer, I suppose, is what you always think of at my age.'

Guy was taken aback. He had been thinking of a cold, and was going to say, as he often did, that he himself did not catch colds, and how lucky he was to have that sort of constitution. Now he said, 'You don't come down with cancer. Cancer isn't something you come down with. I've not heard that before.'

Lily had kindly not said, 'at our age'. She did not believe she had cancer, but wanted to deflect Guy's attention from her appearance. She knew roughly what she looked like, and exactly why.

Breakfast came in. Danny stirred in his corner, but knew it would be wrong to approach the table. He stirred and sniffed, but did not stand up or allow his tail to thump.

The prospect of breakfast was always a treat for Guy, and he never expected breakfast to be a disappointment, though more often than not it was. 'Bacon,' he said. 'Eggs. Sausages.' He loved the look of the chafing dishes that kept the different things warm. He loved the noise of the dumb waiter being wheeled in. 'Thank you, Greta,' he said to her retreating form. He shook out his napkin.

'Try to have a good breakfast,' he said to Lily. 'It'll make you feel better.' He helped himself and tucked in.

Lily took a rasher of bacon and a piece of toast. Her mind

began to do the rounds again. Which day was it when . . . If it was the last time she did the flowers for church, which it felt as if it was, then it was a whole fortnight ago. It had never been that long before. She shivered. She pulled herself together and tried to eat.

'The sausages are underdone,' said Guy. 'It makes them spongy. They should be crisp.'

After breakfast Guy went out with the dog and Lily retreated to her study. She sat down. Waves of anxiety were running through her body. Please, please, please, please, if I could only get a text. Please, please, please.

~

'Well,' said Marina's mother, 'Dad and I certainly opened a bottle of champagne for you last night.' She and Marina were talking on the telephone.

'Good. You deserved it.'

'How do you feel today?'

'Happy.'

Marina's mum had hoped for a bit more, but settled for that. 'So how did they pick him up? Do you know any details?'

'His mobile was working, as you know, so they incredibly quickly got a fix on where he was, and a jeep came out for him. Where he was dropped was less than five miles from a small American base, out in the desert. It's because he was so near the base that his mobile had a signal.'

'That was lucky.'

'He thinks it was intentional.'

'You don't mean the gang purposely chose a place he could be rescued from?'

'He thinks so. He won't let anyone say a word against the men who took him. Haven't you heard him talking on TV? It's positively embarrassing.' Marina laughed. She didn't think it was at all embarrassing.

'When will he be home?'

'Soon, I don't quite know when. Tomorrow or the next day. You and Dad are coming this afternoon, aren't you? Cephas can't wait.'

'Yes, we'll be with you about four.'

'Good. And Mum . . .'

'Yes?'

'You know I'm just as grateful for all you offered as I would be if you'd given it. Oh, wait a minute, Cephas wants to speak.' Cephas took the receiver and waited.

His other grandmother knew to expect silence, so started talking at once. 'Hullo, darling. See you this afternoon,' she said, and Cephas speechlessly handed the receiver back to Marina. After a few more words, they rang off.

'Nanny bring me a present,' said Cephas, with quiet confidence.

'Extremely likely,' said Marina.

~

'A terrible day,' Helen was telling Lewis.

'You know his mother, I know that,' said Lewis.

'She's my best friend and my colostomy friend,' said Helen. 'Imagine what she was going through.'

'All's well that ends well,' said Lewis.

He was wearing long brown shorts. Helen hoped he just happened to be wearing them. It would be sad if he thought they enhanced his appearance. In fact he had so hoped. When he came to see Helen now, it was not truthfully on the way home. He left work early, went to his flat, changed and showered and returned. She on her side made certain preparations for his advent, including making sure she was wearing an opaque colostomy bag, because you never knew; buying beer as well as wine, tidying the sitting room, and putting a bit of discreet make-up on.

'Cecilia's told me Ian's wife was being wonderful,' said Helen. 'They've got two children.'

Little did Lewis know, thought Helen, that one of those children was the natural son of the woman he knew and adored as Margaret Clitherow. Helen had not had enough glasses of wine to be tempted into conversational unreserve of that order. And it was a long time, indeed, since Lewis had harked back to Margaret.

'I saw him on TV,' said Lewis. 'I didn't know he had anything to do with you.' He was pleased it was a small world, and he liked to feel that Helen was at the heart of it. He had a present for Helen, and was trying to find a way of introducing it. 'You've been so kind to me,' he said, 'giving me so much drink and hospitality. I have brought something to give you. I hope you will accept it.' He produced a small parcel. 'I haven't gift-wrapped it,' he said, 'because if I did you might feel you had to accept it whether you liked it or not. So you could just have a look at it, see if you could fancy it, and if you do, it's yours.' He drew a Kindle from its box. 'A must-have for a twenty-first-century literary lady,' he said. Helen winced at that expression, but excused him.

Helen had not had a Kindle in her hand before, and how to work it took a lot of explanation. Their heads were close. Helen was overwhelmed at his kindness and this moment raised the voltage of their relationship. In all honesty, she did not think she would use it, and could not feel it to be an improvement on books. However, she could not bear to disappoint him. They agreed she would try it and see how she got on. He felt that his idea had been half a success and he was satisfied with that.

'The things they think of,' said Helen. 'I can't keep up. The world changes so fast now. An example: who, forty years ago, would have thought that by now telephone boxes would be obsolete, and condoms in high demand?'

She had thought out this sentence before, and Lewis was as pleased with it as she had hoped someone would one day be. Once he had enjoyed it, however, it presented him with a new and private thought. If he was to have sex with Helen, she would probably expect him to have a condom to hand. He registered this. He liked Helen very much, and loved the relationship as it was. However, he had his fantasies. He had caught himself hoping that romance would one day come into the picture. More than likely it was only in his mind, and she had never even thought of it. She had once said that she missed sex, though. Had that been a hint? Was the condom reference a hint?

'Do you think this little object will make books obsolete?' wondered Helen. 'I think that would be a pity. Books look so nice on walls.'

'Specially your books,' Lewis said. Then he added, shyly, 'I've put one of your books on the Kindle. The most recent.'

He was really getting very keen on her, thought Helen, seeing the shine in his eye, but there was no harm in that. She had never felt there was any harm in people being keen on her. And it was particularly charming now, in view of the comparative dearth of keenness these days.

They talked about their mothers. Helen now went to Sheffield one day a week, which was a big encroachment on her time, and made her feel saintly, but she would not have wanted it otherwise. She loved sitting by her mother, boring though it was. Lewis's mother was only eighty, but was becoming more and more confused and forgetful. Odd things happened. Was she safe on her own? Lewis had found her hairbrush in the fridge last time he visited, and the electric kettle on the gas stove. The time before, the hoover had been left running and it was as well he turned up when he did. Helen enjoyed these stories, and admired the total lack of humour and anecdotal pleasure with which Lewis recounted them. They moved back to the Kindle before long, with ineptness from Helen, know-how from Lewis, and much laughter.

~

It took Cecilia longer than anyone else to recover from the day – it was a Thursday – during which Ian was in custody. Both Marina and Tim seemed to have got over it. They were in high spirits. What each and either had been through on that day had healed well. They were young, thought Cecilia. They were also not the mother. Marina appeared unchanged, though happier, if you could go by smiles and beauty; Ian seemed more in love with her, and had more energy for his little boys. These were not changes so much as augmentations. Ian now had three weeks off work and they were thinking of their first family holiday. There had been talk of Cecilia and Tim going as well; the young parents would be freer in the evenings. Cecilia preferred to stay at home, and made that clear. She did not want to drag her complicated and attention-seeking body to foreign parts, and she did not want to leave the cat. Pros and cons about holidays and venues were the current subject of discussion in Ian and Marina's house. Cephas, let alone Ali, had never seen the sea, and it was important to put that right. Cecilia was glad to think of all this activity, but she was tired. That was one of the ways in which she had not recovered from that day.

She had become accustomed to a sense of her own vulnerability. She was very likely 'living with cancer', as the oncologists cheerfully put it. She was used to the emotion this evoked for her, and because she was used to it, it was an emotion that loomed less large than she might have expected. She could be cavalier towards it. She went on from one day to the next, making the best of her aches and pains; and, if, apprehensively, she compared a source of discomfort unfavourably with what it had been the week before, this was a private matter. It was a private matter, not because she did not have people to talk to who would listen, nor because she did not respect her doctors; but because it was boring for her. It was monotonous. Most pains righted themselves after a few days to a bearable level. She accepted that she would never be the woman she had been, and that this was a pity.

Such were her feelings about herself, though she knew this balance would shift if she was forced into a fresh scare. Her feelings about Ian's vulnerability were very different. She knew, of course, that people do get kidnapped, and die, horribly, far from those who love them. This she knew. Furthermore, she was fair-minded on this count. When a one-year-old had been murdered, and it had dominated the news, Cecilia had said to Marina, who had, naturally enough, agreed: 'It's not better that this is happening to another little boy, and not to Cephas. It's just better for us.'

The loss, pain and bewilderment that Cecilia had undergone when Ian disappeared was such as to make her cancer cosy. That is the trouble with love, she thought. She had always known that Ian lived a fairly dangerous life. She had not allowed herself to think that the worst possibilities such a life offered might actually happen to him. Because they had happened, albeit briefly, Cecilia now lived in a changed world. She could not bounce back to where she had been before, as, it seemed, Ian and Marina had been able to do. That day had hollowed out a space in Cecilia, a space that had not refilled since the unspeakable joy of his release. That moment of relief had probably brought her heart nearer to stopping for ever than had those hours of tension. But the residue of the hours of tension remained. She was marked. She was not a mother who had lost a child in a terrible way, but she was a mother who knew what it was to lose a child in a terrible way.

Some dying soldiers, she knew, call on their mothers. Would Ian have? It broke her heart to wonder. It had not come to that, in his case. She would never have known if he had or not. But what was sure was that she would have spent the rest of her life calling on him, in case, at that moment, he had needed her in vain.

~

'We haven't had a proper catch-up,' Helen was saying to Cecilia.

This was true. In Cecilia's new, removed existence, she had not really wanted to catch up with anybody. But now she felt she must rally.

'No,' said Cecilia. 'Tell me about everything.'

'But first,' said Helen, 'we haven't talked properly since last Thursday.'

'No. Well, it was awful. But it's over.'

'Not quite, in you,' said Helen shrewdly.

'No.' Cecilia was grateful, but did not want to tell Helen more, or not now. 'It's all holiday talk for the young people.'

'Where are they going?'

'Ithaca is the most recent favourite.'

'The isle of return.'

'I'm not sure if they've thought of it like that.'

'They must have. Anyway, I know someone who has a friend who has, or anyway used to have, a wonderful holiday house in Ithaca, I'm sure it was Ithaca, right on the sea . . .' Helen always had friends who could help, be it with holidays or anything else; and Cecilia felt tired. Helen extorted an undertaking that Marina should be referred to her if she and Ian could not accommodate themselves unaided.

'Have a look at this,' said Helen, producing her Kindle.

Cecilia looked. 'Is it yours?'

'Lewis gave it to me,' said Helen. 'And do you know what – he's put *Flies to Wanton Boys* on it.'

Now Cecilia was really impressed. 'He must be in love with you.'

'There is something between us, but I don't know what it is. He isn't really my type at all. Too nice, too plain, too conventional, too bald, too – well, ordinary, I suppose. And now, of course, I have to say too young, though it seems no time since I would have had to say too old.'

'How old?'

'Fifty-three.'

'That's OK. You don't look a day older than that. Does he know your age?'

'Of course,' said Helen, not disclosing that she had knocked five years off. 'What's more, he knows about the colostomy. Apparently he thinks nothing of it, except bad luck for me. He may not understand what it is, of course.'

'He could always Google it. He's obviously electronically minded. As with your little machine. I wonder what it cost.'

'Yes, that worries me, too. Enough of him. Mum.'

'Yes.'

'One stage worse every time I go up. They don't make her sit out any more. She lies in bed propped up. Her face is transparent.'

'She still knows you?'

'Yes. And she takes my hands in her little warm ones.' Helen was tearful at the memory, or perhaps at her own words. 'She looks lovely, and she is adorable. It's very dull, but I wouldn't be anywhere else.'

'Does Marj come in?'

'Occasionally. But she usually takes the afternoon off, gratefully, unless there's something we need to talk about.'

'You can show your mum your Kindle next time, and read aloud to her from it.'

'She's past being read to. She's waiting. That's what she's doing. She sees things we don't see.'

'It sounds peaceful.'

'Yes. It is peaceful. But boring too, if you're someone like

300

me. I'm just so glad I'm doing this, instead of trying to ignore Mum, as I did for years. It turns out I really love her, you know.'

'Good.' Cecilia was pensive. 'I wish now . . . I wish now I could have been better with my mother. She wasn't ever as old as your mother, and she wasn't ill for nearly as long. For the last months she had a live-in carer. So she was well looked after. But when the carer had time off Mum would get in a state and phone, imploring one of us to go round. I wish I had, now. I did go, often, on ordinary visits. But I didn't respond to the loneliness. I think I was immature enough to feel, defiantly, I need freedom, I'm entitled to a life. You know.'

'Did she have her marbles?'

'She did. But I think, now, that there are ways age affects the brain that aren't cognitive, and that you can apparently have a full set of marbles, as she had, but something has been lost emotionally. In my mother's case the capacity to be alone. We don't think of that as a marble. But it may be one. And I wasn't sympathetic. That makes me very sad, now.'

They were silent. 'Mothers,' said Helen.

'I know.' More silence. Then Cecilia said, 'What is a life?' Neither ventured an answer.

'Health?' said Helen. An easier topic, although not unconnected.

'No change for me. Still uncertainty. But I don't mind. I really don't. Specially since . . .'

'Since Ian was abducted.'

'Yes. And you are well?'

'The stoma's bulgy. Perhaps I need to see Hyacinth.' Hyacinth was the stoma nurse, in whose waiting room Cecilia and Helen had first met.

'More bulgy than it has always been?'

'Yes, I think so. Don't forget I can't see it, except in a mirror. I'm not skinny like you.'

'No harm getting an appointment with Hyacinth.'

'No. Specially now I see her privately and don't have to wait ages.' Soon Helen said, 'Any news of Leda?'

'None.'

Though true at that time, this last was soon to prove otherwise. After Helen had gone, and when Tim and Cecilia and Thor were in easy chairs in the sitting room after supper, the phone rang. Cecilia answered.

'Hullo.'

'Good evening. Is that Mrs Banks?'

'Yes.'

'I'm so sorry to disturb you again.' By this point Cecilia had realised three things: one, that she was speaking to Leda's mother; two, that the voice on the phone was hushed, as if not to be overheard; three, that the woman speaking was in a state of intense, mouth-stiffening anxiety.

'No disturbance.'

'This is Lily Bridges. I am trying to find information about my daughter, whom you kindly sheltered not very long ago. She uses various names so you may not know her under her real one.'

'Which is?' Cecilia could not resist asking.

'Jane Bridges.'

Jane Bridges! Poor Leda. 'I know who you mean,' said Cecilia. 'But I'm afraid we have no news of her. I'm very sorry. What's the position?'

'She is a missing person.'

'How do you mean?' Silence. 'I know she was a missing person for quite a long time, and then we saw her, for a couple of weeks, and then she moved on, first to a friend of ours, briefly, then, I'm afraid, to we don't know where.'

'She is a missing person. She is a really missing person.' Lily was breathing hard, and Cecilia could tell she was trying not to cry.

302

'Say more.'

'This is the first time she hasn't kept in touch with me.'

'With you.' Cecilia was puzzled, then said slowly, 'You mean – all the time she was a missing person officially, she was really in regular touch with you?'

Silence.

'Look, please don't worry, I won't tell anyone,' Cecilia went on. 'This is just between ourselves. I completely understand, and sympathise, if you had your own reasons, good ones I'm sure, why you had to keep her contact with you a secret.'

'Secret. That was it. I must go now. All I wanted was to ask . . . And thank you.'

'I've got your number, and I'll ring soon, hoping you will have heard from her—'

But Lily had put the phone down.

Luckily Tim was too absorbed in the TV news, which had just started, for Cecilia to be tempted to break her word to Lily. Blind and deaf to the programme, she sat and thought.

Chapter 24

There was a touch of autumn in the air. Everyone was noticing it. Cecilia announced it to Tim; Guy told Lily; Helen bemoaned it in her mind. Ian and Marina, in Ithaca, were unaware of it. The touch of autumn crept into Meg Gatehouse's nursing home, and illumined the little patio. The sun was very bright, and its light very lovely, but the nip in the air had an unmistakable character. Yet the atmosphere was bracing, in spite of its gentle melancholy; and spoke of beginnings as well as endings, as the first day of autumn always does.

Helen had come to her mother's bedside a day earlier than had been arranged, alerted by Marj. 'It may be nothing,' Marj had said. 'But they're getting the doctor in, and Gemma thinks she's poorly. I know you'd want to know.'

'Yes indeed,' Helen had said. 'To know, and to come.'

So she sat by Meg Gatehouse's bed, the cool sunshine patterning the cubicle furniture, though not greatly, for the window was small. Meg was asleep. Helen took her hand. Meg slept on. Helen did not want to wake her while she was peaceful, but found herself not seeing much point in being there if her presence was unnoticed. 'Mum,' she said quietly, as a compromise between these two feelings. No response. So Helen took the newspaper out of her bag.

She glanced at it, but was not reading. She was wondering

when her mother was going to die. What if it was today? Yet it seemed so unlikely that any change would take place. The ancient face was so settled. Helen looked at the date on the newspaper. Would this be the date that she, Marj and Harry would have to have engraved on their mother's tombstone? She put the newspaper down, thinking she had heard a tremor in the breathing. Would her mother die, now, this afternoon, with only Helen present? Helen quite liked that idea, but thought it unfair, when Marj, certainly, and Harry, probably, had been so much more involved with, and present for, their mother's declining years than Helen herself had. She might be seen as sweeping in to collect unearned glory. Perhaps her mother would sleep throughout Helen's entire visit, all three hours of it, and never know that Helen had patiently sat by her.

Helen wanted a cigarette, and thought longingly of the patio. Yet she liked it by the bedside. Her place there had become a home. It had come more and more, over the past months, to be the right place for her; and when she was in London, she often felt homesick, she fretted. She was fretting now, too, but only out of boredom. Boredom and loneliness. Time went past. She tried to read the paper, but found herself wondering what sort of a gap in her life her mother's death would create. She was certainly not company, nor someone to talk to; and, for Helen, she probably never had been, or not since childhood. Their differences had emerged strongly in Helen's adolescence, in a way differences had not appeared between Mum and Marj. And then Marj had a family, and the existence of the boys had bonded Marj with Mum, in an everyday, unspoken way, as had the fact that Marj had settled in Sheffield. Helen suspected, and now feared, that her mother was a huge part of the continent that was herself, and she wondered how that huge component of herself would fare when it could no longer be named. It never had been named. She had not known that certain solid and familiar mountains and valleys that she took for granted as her own derived from her mother.

She tried to predict her feelings when her mother died. There would be the loss of someone who loved her as no one else ever had. She would lose that love, and she did not know how much the live presence of that love throughout her life, un-acknowledged and unthanked, had bolstered and strengthened her. Perhaps its loss was dangerous for her – that she didn't know. Then there was guilt. She had treated her mother so badly, not responding, ignoring, despising. That had been the way of it for decades. But in the past year, that had changed. Surely the guilt would be somewhat eased by that. She would be able to dwell in memory on her recent monthly visits, her now weekly visits, and could set them, in the ledger, against those years of neglect and ingratitude.

The quiet, even breathing fluttered a little. Might she wake? Helen wanted her attention. 'Mum,' she said, 'Mum. Do you know Hennie is here?' But sleep took over again. Might she have been put on drugs? Helen felt like a child, pestering, wanting to jolt and jog her sleeping mum.

Teresa looked into the cubicle. 'Peaceful, isn't she?' she said. 'Bless.'

'Can I ask you something?' said Helen. 'It's just . . . Do you have any idea when she might be going to die?'

Teresa was often asked this question, and she always saw the other struggling to phrase it. 'I never guess,' said Teresa. 'She could slip away any time.'

'Could she slip away today?'

'Yes. Or in a few weeks, or in a few months. The great thing is that she is not in pain.'

'Yes, indeed. But I can't imagine her being like this for as much as a few months.'

'You'd be surprised, we've seen it often.'

Both knew, and neither wanted to say, that it would be more

306

convenient to know. Teresa had brought a drink, with a straw. 'You can try this, if she wakes up.' She put the beaker on the tray that lay across the bed, smiled at Helen, looked indulgently again at Meg and withdrew.

The next person to come into the cubicle was Harry, much more noisily. 'Harry!' said Helen, delighted.

He looked pleased to see her. 'Marj told me you were coming,' he said, leaning over to kiss her. She smelt aftershave and felt shaved cheek – her spirits lifted. Harry was holding a bunch of flowers in cellophane. It would be a long time before someone found a vase. He realised this now, and put them unobtrusively on the chest of drawers in the corner. He sat on the end of the bed.

They caught up a bit – his children, his coming retirement, her last novel. He groped for the right thing to say about her cancer, but gave up. She was relieved. Harry was six years younger than Helen. He had known her as a bully and a tyrant, while she did not feel she had known him at all. They were getting on better at their mother's bedside now than they ever had before. Both cared about appearance. Helen thought Harry quite handsome, tall and ginger-haired like Dad, with a nice smile; Harry thought Helen attractive and well preserved. Each confessed to wanting a cigarette, and that made a giggly bond.

But there lay their mother. It was easy to ignore her, as if she were an effigy of herself. It had never been difficult for any of her children to engage her interest. Even recently, even since she had been bedridden, she had always been delighted to see them. They had taken for granted that their presence would perk her up, and invariably their presences had. Each managed various adult emotions about this, but underneath each felt puzzled and rejected.

Marj arrived. 'How is she?' she asked, directing the question mostly at Helen.

'Like this,' said Helen.

Marj left the cubicle and came back with another chair. She knew where to find things. Sitting down, she leant over their mother and spoke to her, her face close. 'Mum,' she said, 'we are all here. Marj, Hennie, Harry. Wake up. You should have your drink.'

Meg seemed to make an effort to repeat her children's names and to smile. Marj inserted the straw into her mouth. Her mouth evinced no interest, but gaped. Marj desisted. 'Unless she drinks . . .' Marj said.

Now the doctor pushed his way into the crowded cubicle. 'You're having a party,' he exclaimed to Meg. He turned to the others. 'Perhaps you could just pop outside while I examine her.'

'It's because there are so many of us,' whispered Marj. 'When it's just me he lets me stay.' Helen and Harry took advantage of the moment to head for the patio, and, indeed, Marj went back into the cubicle.

'She's gone down since I saw her a couple of days ago,' the doctor told Marj. 'I can't be sure, but I think she's had a stroke. I have to tell you she could go any time.'

Marj found herself crying uncontrollably. When Helen and Harry returned, they said, 'Marj!' and 'What is it?'

'She may have had a stroke and she could go any time.'

A stroke, thought Helen. That explained her new unavailability.

'Could you stay the night?' Marj was asking her.

This was more than Helen had bargained for. But she could hardly say no. 'Of course we don't know for sure that she will die tonight,' she ventured.

'Of course we don't. But if she does, I'd like you to be with me.'

'Yes, I will stay.'

It was when Helen was looking for her mobile phone, to cancel an evening arrangement, that she realised she had no colostomy supplies with her. Of course she had not. She had been expecting to go home. Her hand went to her colostomy bag. The stoma had been active. No doubt it would be more so. The bag would need to be changed this evening. And she had not brought a spare.

She didn't want to say anything about this new worry in front of Harry, so she panicked privately for a while. Then she went in search of Teresa or Gemma. She found Gemma, who was catching up on the computer and did not want to be disturbed. Helen explained the problem. 'Have you got any supplies here?'

Gemma was nonplussed. No one in the care home at the moment had a colostomy.

'But haven't you got anything,' pleaded Helen, 'left over from someone who did, sometime?'

Gemma hadn't.

'But what would you do,' Helen asked, 'if a new person arrived with a colostomy?'

'Then we would have the supplies,' Gemma answered. 'The supplies follow the patient.'

Helen went back to the cubicle to find Harry leaving. He would come back tomorrow. Marj was to keep in touch. Helen said goodbye to him and then, when they were alone, explained the predicament to Marj.

'Can't you improvise?' asked Marj.

'You can't,' said Helen. 'It isn't like that.' She added bitterly, 'What would you do? If shit is pushing its way out of the front of your midriff, uncontrollably, you have to have something purpose-built for it to go into.'

This Marj could not gainsay. 'But do you mean you are going to have to go all the way home,' she said, 'just because of this? Couldn't you try a chemist?' But they realised it was well past chemists' closing time.

Helen did go home, as the stoma purred and sizzled into further action. At half past eleven, Marj phoned.

'Mum's perked up,' she said. 'Cup of tea. Knew me.'

Helen cried with relief. It was partly the primitive relief every creature feels on knowing that its mother is still alive; partly satisfaction at not having, after all, let Marj down. 'So no stroke,' she said.

'The doctor's not sure.'

'Shall I come back tomorrow?'

'Not necessarily. I'll let you know how we get on. I'm going home now, myself.'

It was not for three more days that Helen was called on to set forth again, taking the familiar train from St Pancras to Sheffield. Mum's perking up had been real, but not lasting. She had been incredulous to learn that she had slept through Hennie's whole visit, and sent love and regret via Marj's frequent phone calls. Helen had stoma supplies in plenty on board the train this time. But they were not needed, for Mum died quietly that day, with Marj and Helen beside her, and Helen came home.

~

Lily was imagining the worst. She saw her daughter in all different stages of being kidnapped, raped and murdered, and decomposing in a shallow grave. Unfortunately for her, she had a lively, detailed imagination.

She no longer visited the garden in the early morning. Anything that used to give her joy was now infused with agony. She walked the silent rooms, not the garden, listening for the house telephone. Her mobile was always in her hand. Guy thought she must be coming down with cancer, or Alzheimer's. He summoned the doctor, who prescribed tranquillisers and sleeping pills, neither of which Lily took, for fear of missing a phone call, or a text.

In her exhaustion, she sometimes did not care when she thought that her daughter was dead. She saw her in her shallow grave, or lapped to a skeleton by the waters of a stream, and by the waters' inquisitive wildlife. So be it. She had been a burden to her mother in her life; let her rest. This train of thought evoked harsh guilt, and Lily felt like a murderess; but it meant a brief respite from anxiety.

Only brief. For Lily did not really believe her daughter was dead. She believed she was helpless and suffering. It was those images that her mind probed, again and again. She knew Jane was mad, though she did not like the word. What might she have got herself into? It could be anything. And where was she? She could be abroad, where anything might happen, especially to a mad and pretty woman. When she got to this point in the circuit of her ruminations, Lily was liable to moan and wring her hands.

She did not contact the police, for two reasons. One was that she did not think it would be any good. The other was that she was afraid for herself. All the time Jane had officially been a missing person, Lily had been hearing from her every few days, and despatching money to designated addresses. That would be seen as wrong, in the eyes of the police, and in the eyes of Guy, should he come to know it. He had suffered horribly, in his own ways, while he thought Jane was missing, and in that period Lily could at any moment have enlightened him. She did not, could not, because of Jane's threats of suicide if her mother spilt the beans.

To Guy, Jane had been lost, been a missing person, and then been found, and heard of from various respectable-sounding people. Since that stage, Guy had not thought of her as lost or endangered, any more than the police had, though he had no notion where she was. He had her in mind as making her own way in the world, as well she might, at thirty, and for all he knew no longer mentally ill. Presumably she had a job, or preferably a husband; or how was she managing for money? She had never been slow to come to her parents when she was broke. He was sad and puzzled when he thought of her, but not frightened. He hated being sad and puzzled, so he preferred not to think of her, and gradually thought of her less and less. Lily knew all this about Guy. She did not feel she could confide her new terrors to him.

Meanwhile, Cecilia worried about Lily. She had assured Lily that she wouldn't talk to anyone about their phone conversation, and she reluctantly kept her word. She had also told Lily that she would soon ring her to get an update. This she knew she must do. A mother who had been through what Cecilia had been through could not leave another mother in that same state if there was anything she could do to alleviate it. From what she had understood from Lily, and from her own knowledge of Leda, whom she must now think of as Jane, it seemed likely that Lily's anxiety was not irrational. Cecilia kept an eye out for female corpses on the news. Cavalier in spite of herself towards Jane's fate, Cecilia was emotionally involved in Lily's.

The telephone conversation was not satisfactory. Lily was in her study. She had been looking at the wad of money in her desk drawer, and at the stack of copies of *The Lady*. She had been looking at her mobile phone. She picked up the house phone almost before it had rung.

'Hullo?'

'Hullo. This is Cecilia Banks. I wonder if you have heard anything about your daughter.'

'No.'

'Have you told the police?'

'No.'

'I'm afraid you were disappointed when you picked up the phone. When it rings you always hope it will be news.'

'Yes.'

'I'm so sorry.' Cecilia did not know what to say. The other woman's voice was soft, almost pleading; but firm in its reserve. 'I'm so sorry,' Cecilia said again.

'Thank you, that's very kind of you.'

'Do you want to talk about it?'

'There isn't anything to say.'

'Do you speak about it with anyone – your husband?' asked Cecilia, knowing the answer would be no.

'Not at the moment. Excuse me, but I want to leave the telephone line free.'

'Please let me know if you hear anything.'

'Yes, indeed, and thank you. Goodbye.'

So much for that, they both thought in their different ways. Cecilia was thinking she had tried and failed, but that she would certainly keep trying. She was afraid Lily was heading for a breakdown. Lily was still physically racked with disappointment that the call had not given her news of Jane.

~

Helen was sitting in the chair where she had sat when she thought she had lung cancer. She was unrolling her feelings about her mother's death. In the first place there was a weight off her shoulders. What had to happen had happened. And it had been all right. It had been all right, for a death. Death did not come much better than that. But she could not feel death was all right. Her mother's heart had been beating for ninety-three years, and it had stopped beating. Her body had been warm for ninety-three years, and was now cold. These mysterious realities swam in Helen's mind.

Marj and Harry were organising the funeral. They knew the church, they knew the cemetery. They had grown-up children, most of whom were taking views about, and parts in, the ceremonial. Helen was not needed, and would go up for the funeral, like any other guest. This made her feel left out, but she reckoned it was better to feel left out in her absence than in her presence. She had sent money.

After the funeral, she needn't ever go to Sheffield again.

That realisation contributed to the weight off her mind. That fixture in her monthly, then her weekly timetable had disappeared. She felt released. But at the same time she felt too free, too weightless, utterly unmoored. Those had been important days in her calendar. Very little had happened in them. But they had mattered more than any other days. They would be missed.

She remembered all those years when she had not bothered about her mother. She had turned up for her father's funeral, tipsy, with a tipsy man who was a stranger to the family. She had not joined in family Christmases. She had not been part of selling her parents' house, getting rid of their possessions, or putting her mother in the care home. She had visited the care home, but rarely, fleetingly, and in a self-laudatory spirit. Cancer had afforded an excuse to put an end to those infrequent visits. How would she be feeling now, she wondered, if that attitude and pattern had never changed? She recoiled from the thought, and allowed herself to be happy that she had taken her mother on, taken her on fully, in the last period of that long life. She felt like the labourer who signs on for work at the eleventh hour, and, when night falls, is paid as much as those who have toiled in the vineyard in the heat of the day. The love between her mother and herself had survived the long interruption, and, indeed, when Helen took up the relationship again, seemed to have deepened. For her mother's love, there had not been an interruption. Helen remembered the faithful letters, the occasional phone calls, the birthday presents; and the opportunities these had offered Helen for moments of contempt and negligence. None of that mattered now, because of the past year. A bit more than a year, actually, she was pleased to remind herself.

She thought how typical it was of her mother's emotional restraint that, when contact was resumed, she never said anything about Helen's long alienation, nor even asked why it ended. She accepted Helen's return without wonder or question, let alone recrimination, greeting her as if she had seen her yesterday. It was forgiveness, but forgiveness of the highest order, for no wrong was acknowledged. When she came to this thought, Helen put her head down on her arms, and cried.

Chapter 25

Jane was in the psychiatric unit of a London hospital. She had been an in-patient for three weeks. After she was sectioned and brought in, this was the conversation that took place between the social worker and the psychiatrist. The social worker was looking at papers from a file, the psychiatrist studying her computer.

'Something a bit complicated for a late Friday afternoon, Gloria,' said the social worker, Mel. 'But rather up your street.' They knew each other and got on well.

'Go ahead,' said Gloria. 'I've got some of it here. Virginia Woolf. That can't be her real name.'

'We're sure it's not, but they're working on that. They'll come up with her real name. Give them time.'

'OK. What exactly happened?'

'She's been following the Archbishop of Canterbury. She must have looked up his engagements, because she's attended them daily for the past week or so. She seems to need to be close to him. She must be in love with him, I suppose. She burst into the vestry at – where? – here we are, Salisbury Cathedral. Three times in different venues she's been hurried off and cautioned, but has been determined and quite wily about getting back. He's been incredibly nice about it. He didn't want her arrested, and she hasn't been, although there has been police involvement. The police are looking into her identity, as well.'

'So what happened today?'

'It was a church in London. The Brompton Oratory.'

'A Catholic church. An ecumenical do, no doubt.' Gloria was more interested than Mel in church matters.

'She ran up the aisle and jumped the altar rail, leapt over it. There was a bit of a fracas, and members of the congregation got involved. Social Services took over, then their psychiatric team. She was interviewed and has been sectioned for her own protection.'

'Have you met her?'

'Yes. She's very good-looking, very thin. Striking. Certainly schizophrenic. She doesn't say much. We've all got the impression she was listening to voices. All the reports say that.'

'Ah.' Gloria had been working on the computer, entering this information, under the provisional heading of 'Virginia Woolf'. 'How old is she? I need a date of birth.'

'She looks about thirty, but she wouldn't give her age.'

'It says no fixed address here. Is that right?'

'Yes. It gives you the wrong idea, though. She's definitely, well, posh.' Mel did not like using this word, but could not think of any other way to put it.

'Family?'

'We're working on it.'

'Not very communicative, by the sound of it. Well, I'll see her now, and almost certainly prescribe, and we'll take it further forward tomorrow, as and how we need to. Thanks, Mel. Have a good weekend.'

~

Lily was with Greta, talking bacon and sausages, when she heard Guy bellow for her. She excused herself to Greta. Guy stood at the foot of the stairs, holding an envelope in one hand and its contents in the other, calling Lily's name in an upwards direction. Then he saw her appear on the steps up from the kitchen.

'Oh, there you are. We've had this letter – come in here.' He backed into the drawing room with her following, then he closed the door, and stood, consulting the letter. Its envelope fluttered to the floor. 'We've got this letter from – from the Kensington and Chelsea Health something. Jane is in hospital.'

Guy was unprepared for Lily's reaction. She emitted an inarticulate sound, and grabbed the back of an armchair to steady herself. 'It's not that bad, is it?' he said, coming close to her. He put his hand under her elbow. Their eyes met, but he did not discern that what was on her white face was unspeakable joy, the lightning bolt of peace of mind. 'Sit down. You've had a shock,' he said.

'Yes,' agreed Lily, as soon as she could speak. 'I'm sitting now, and I'm perfectly all right. Thank you, dear. What else does the letter say?'·

Guy read as he spoke, looking down at the letter, then at Lily, then at the letter again. 'She's been sectioned again. Remember, sectioned – like she was before. She is being treated. She doesn't want us to visit. They think she is settling down. She has been very agitated.'

'Poor girl,' murmured Lily.

Guy was quiet, and reading. 'There's another bit,' he said. 'It says here that she had a baby. Yes. The year before last. I can't believe that. We've heard nothing about that. They refer to it here as if we already know. You didn't know, did you?'

'No,' said Lily, amazed, but not too amazed to be relieved that there was something she could be truthful about. 'Of course not.'

'For which the father has parental responsibility. It says that. The father has parental responsibility. Well, I suppose that's as it should be. Certainly Jane would be in no state—'

'Does the letter give the address where she is? We can write to her.'

'Yes, it does. You can write to her. I wouldn't know what to say.'

Guy passed the letter to Lily. Lily really wanted to be alone to unpack and jettison the terrible fantasies of the past weeks, and revel in the happiness of the present moment. But this would be unshared with Guy, and she appreciated the feeling that they were facing something together, and that he was letting it be like that. So for the moment, she revelled in this, instead. Together they went into the kitchen to get coffee and came back into the drawing room, Guy carrying the tray.

'Now we can talk it over,' said Guy, the coffee making their sitting down together a conversational occasion. 'At least we know she's being looked after,' he went on. 'Sometimes I'm afraid – well, we never know what's happening to her, because she doesn't keep in touch. And now this child. Can you believe she's had a child?'

'I've never known what to believe, with Jane. Nothing surprises me. That's not true. This has.'

'You mean the baby.'

'Yes.'

'Yes.' He was silent, then he said, 'Shall we ring up those numbers we've got – the people who put Jane up, whom she stayed with – and see whether they know anything about a baby?'

Lily was pleased with this suggestion, for she had suspected Guy might want to keep Jane's possible baby secret, as something shameful. She suddenly realised that Guy need never know of her deception of him in Jane's 'missing person' period. No one need ever know. That nightmare was over. But the greatest source of pleasure within her at this particular moment was the one that caused her to say, now, 'You are being so nice.' Her eyes filled with tears.

'Don't cry about it, then,' he said, trying to be hearty, but his own face was crumpling.

~

319

Now Lily had to write her letter to Jane.

Dear Jane,

We are sorry to hear that you are not so well again, but glad that you are in good hands. The letter from the hospital tells us that you do not want us to visit, but if you change your mind on that, you only have to let us know. You know we love you.

Now Lily wished she was writing a nice card, not a letter, for she found she had nothing more to say. You are entitled to say less on a card.

She went on:

The garden is looking lovely, though Angus is having to rake leaves already. Autumn seems to have come early this year!

This was ridiculous.

I hope you have not been too unhappy. I think of you, as you will know. So does Dad.

Love,
Mum

Because she and Guy were being a team, rather than, as was usual for them, each a person in isolation, she showed him the letter. He interested himself in it, it passed muster, and it was he who gummed down the envelope. She posted it at the shop, freed of the walk to the pillar box on the Chichester Road.

~

Cecilia had hovered over the telephone a few times in the last days, wondering whether to ring Lily Bridges. If she did, the poor woman would certainly think the call was about, or from, her daughter, and the wave of disappointment would be crushing. So Cecilia hovered.

This came to an end when the telephone rang and it was Lily, with Guy, as usual, audibly in the background. 'Good morning, Mrs Banks.' Cecilia recognised the voice, and knew, from the sound of it, that things were better.

'I was going to ring you,' she said. 'I hope you have some news.'

'Yes. I do have a little news. We know that Jane is alive and well.'

'That's wonderful.'

'There's something we would like to ask you, if you don't mind,' went on Lily.

'Ask me anything,' said Cecilia.

'When you were kind enough to have Jane to stay with you . . .'

'Yes?' said Cecilia, as silence had supervened.

'I wonder whether she said anything about a child?'

For a moment Cecilia did not know what Lily meant. 'A child?' she asked. Then she felt something like a net beginning to close about her.

The male voice could be heard, and then Lily went on, 'It's come to our attention that Jane may have had a child. I'm just wondering if you are able to throw any light on that. You see, we know nothing about it.'

'She certainly didn't mention it,' said Cecilia. She tried to gather herself together. She felt shaken and shocked, and that Cephas was imperilled. She needed time, she needed to think, she needed to consult. She did not want to lie, but she definitely did not want to tell the truth. 'Look,' she said, 'there are some other people who saw your daughter at that stage, and I want to have a word with them. I'll ring you if I find anything out. Meanwhile, it's wonderful that she's safe and sound.'

If Lily wanted to say more, if Guy wanted to chip in, they did not get a chance. Cecilia had rung off.

She walked up and down the room, her face in her hands. She hated, and she recoiled from, the idea of Leda and her parents knowing Cephas. And yet, what was the threat? There was no threat. Morally, legally, emotionally, Cephas was the child of Ian and Marina. So why did Cecilia's blood curdle at the picture of Mr and Mrs Bridges and Leda – Jane, rather – perching excitedly, with cups of tea, in Ian and Marina's sitting room? They could do no harm. Yet how much better would it be if they knew nothing of Cephas, and could be held at bay from that sitting room? How had they found out? From Leda? That chilled Cecilia further, as she had always been cheered by the thought that Leda had forgotten or repudiated Cephas. But in the hospital, people would be working on her to get her to remember and yearn for that significant past. Of course they would. Cecilia sighed and sat down. This was the sleeping dogs, awake. So far, they had only opened their eyes. Soon they would be in full cry.

Now Cecilia began to criticise herself. She was too much in love, she forced herself to realise, with Cephas's life as a myth, as an idyll. He had been rescued, he had been transplanted, he was thriving. He had a little brother. Order had come out of chaos. Blessed ordinariness had evolved from the bizarre. That nuclear family was so dear to Cecilia, not only in itself, but as a symbol of the victory of light over darkness. She did not want the edges of that icon to be frayed by the intrusion of other, messier worlds. But it was unfair, she knew, to foist her own idealisations on Cephas. He might like his birth grandparents, his birth mother! Why shouldn't he? Cecilia did not want him to like them. She now identified this as one of her most significant fears. If Cephas went gladly, curiously, endearingly, to Mr and Mrs Bridges, enchanted by the pretentious gifts they would certainly unload, she knew her heart would turn to dust, and that she would cool towards Cephas, poor child, as someone who was fraternising with the enemy. For the enemy itself, her hatred would be murderous. And the grandparents were far from being the only enemies. What if a siren song from Leda rendered Cephas deaf to Marina's voice?

The important thing was to see what Ian and Marina said. If they had an impulse as strong as hers to refuse entry to the blood relations, it would be easy. Cecilia would no longer have to wrestle with her conscience. She need not take a view; it was, after all, their responsibility. It occurred to her, fleetingly, that if she said nothing to them, the dogs might go back to sleep. Ian and Marina perhaps need never know of Mr and Mrs Bridges' questions. But conscience forbade. She mused a little on the intensity of her feelings. They were not good feelings, she knew that. In them lay traces of the same psychic element as exists in ethnic cleansing and genocide. Was that possible? Yes. The quantity was less, to the point of comparative invisibility; the chemical composition, the same.

Yes. But, much more simply, she must not lose sight of her jealousy and possessiveness – the fact that she was mortally scared that Mr and Mrs Bridges would beglamour Cephas, and Cecilia would be displaced from her precious position in his affections. Perhaps blood, after all, is thicker than water. She had never experienced Marina's nice parents as rivals. They had their place, but with Cephas their place was secondary to hers.

Tim came into the room.

'Who was that on the telephone?'

Cecilia explained, and said something about her consequent trains of thought.

'Nothing dangerous can actually come of this,' Tim said. 'And you don't even know that they'd want to meet Cephas. And if they did, so what?'

'Yes, I know all that.'

'Also, it's not our worry. It's Ian and Marina's worry, not ours.'

'I know that.'

'Shall we both go over and see them? Shall I come with you?'

So it was quickly arranged. It was past the children's bedtime, which was as well, and Tim and Cecilia strolled over to Ian and Marina's house in the autumnal dusk. Over glasses of wine, Cecilia gave an exact account of her conversation with Lily Bridges.

Ian and Marina were fairly newly home from their Greek island, and still brown and fit. Cecilia had seen them several times already since their return, so photographs had been shown, and the success or otherwise of taking such young children so far away had been canvassed and adjudicated. Tim would not have minded seeing photos of monuments, if any; but knew it was not the right time to enquire.

Ian and Marina sat close together on the sofa, their hands entangled. Tim and Cecilia had armchairs. On the floor were Cephas's handsome metal trucks, presents from Marina's parents to mark the safety of Ian, Ali's changing mat, a couple of children's books, recognisable to Cecilia as favourites, and the cat, Benjy.

'So what are you going to say to Leda's mother?' was Ian's question.

'That's what I want agreement on,' said Cecilia.

'You could just not ring her back, actually,' said Ian. There was a silence, while this option was contemplated – by Cecilia, not for the first time. Then Ian resumed: 'It all depends how honest we need to be. I'd be most comfortable with the minimum. But this moral giant,' indicating his wife, 'will probably recommend the whole truth and nothing but the truth.'

Marina disclaimed being a moral giant. Tim got his glasses

out of his pocket, then a pen and an envelope. He put his glasses on and crossed his legs to make a better backing to write on. He was going to take notes. Cecilia loved him when he was like this.

Ian went on: 'Look at it from Cephas's point of view. He doesn't need these people. He's got two perfectly good sets of grandparents already. Our children are very lucky with their grandparents. These Bridges are sure to want to meet Cephas, if they manage to locate him. Then they'll bring Leda, mad as a hatter, and what if she says, "I am your mother," fixing Cephas with her intent stare? He doesn't need that. Nor do we.'

Cecilia was secretly gratified to hear her viewpoint expressed so vividly. But Tim put in: 'For all we know, Mr and Mrs B will not want to meet Cephas. You are jumping the gun. It might be enough for them to know he is adopted, settled, and OK.'

'Not adopted,' said Marina. 'We aren't adoptive parents. What we have is parental responsibility.'

'What used to be called care and custody,' Cecilia put in.

'Need that be a distinction?' said Ian, ignoring his mother's historical footnote. 'Everyone official assumes I am Cephas's natural father. I registered his birth. I am his father, under the law.'

'Yes,' said Tim. 'I think we can leave that out of it. Cephas is with his natural father and his natural father's wife. That's what is presumed, and that, I think, we needn't unravel. After all, no one purporting to be the natural father has come forward.'

'We needn't actually lie, you see,' said Ian to the moral giant, who was looking dubious.

'Yes, but it seems we do have to be economical with the truth,' she said. 'I suppose that's OK. But we shouldn't be afraid of the truth coming out, because, well, because there is nothing wrong with the truth.'

'Can we leave that?' asked Cecilia, pleased that she and Ian could retain a supposed blood-link with Cephas. 'Can we just do ifs and options? As Tim says, Mr and Mrs Bridges may be satisfied to know Leda's – Jane's – child is safe and well. They may not want to go further. If they ask to visit, you can say yes or no. If you say yes, once may be enough.'

'Or they may want to keep in touch, visit from time to time,' said Marina. 'I think it would be wrong to say no to that. We must try not to be tribal. We don't want to fall into an us and them mentality.'

'OK,' said Tim, writing. 'Three possibilities. One, they don't want to pursue the contact. Two, they do, just the once. Three, they want to be people in Cephas's life.'

Ian groaned. 'That's the one I fear,' he said, 'and the fourth possibility is that it's not just them, but Leda as well. If the third possibility applies, the fourth is almost inevitable. How can we keep her at bay, if her parents are allowed in?'

'Perhaps we don't have to keep her at bay,' suggested Marina. 'We and Cephas are under no threat.'

'It depends what you call a threat.'

'Say what you mean,' said Cecilia, who could not help being partial to Ian's argument, and could not resist hoping it would expand until it became persuasive.

'Well,' said Ian, talking mostly in Marina's direction, but his eyes taking in Cecilia and Tim as well, 'Say I am away, and Leda comes to the door, and makes a scene, and grabs at Cephas, and yells that she is his mother – you can imagine it without me describing. I don't want that for Cephas, I don't want it for you. If you mean by there not being a threat, that Leda couldn't get charge of Cephas under the law, of course she couldn't. But ghastly, uncontrollable things could happen. They could. Or maybe when you're working and Mum's got the kids. Or there could be an incident in the street, when one of you has your hands full with both kids.

I mean, imagine if Leda got Cephas into a car. She can drive, you know.' Ian paused, embarrassed by the lurid pictures he had drawn. 'I'm not saying this would happen. But it could. It could.'

There was a silence, because indeed it could.

'Do you think we need legal advice?' said Tim. 'Or social workers – Child Protection? They must be used to this sort of thing.'

'The thing is,' said Marina, 'we're not there yet. I think we should take it one stage at a time. We don't know whether Mr and Mrs B will want to meet Cephas, or what sort of relationship with him they would envisage. They probably don't know, yet. And we know nothing about Leda's, sorry, Jane's, wishes or intentions. She took absolutely no notice of either child when she was here. She paid a bit of attention to Benjy, but the boys might not have existed as far as she was concerned. We might be getting legal or Social Services advice for situations that don't arise.'

'I agree with that,' said Tim.

Warmed by his agreement, Marina went on: 'At the risk of being called a moral giant, I think we should be careful not to think of these people as a dangerous, alien force, to be eliminated. That's the thinking that starts wars.'

Ian and Cecilia both felt implicated in this criticism, and Cecilia, at least, was half in agreement with Marina. Ian rallied. 'I'm sorry, but I'd sooner indulge the sort of thinking that starts wars than have Cephas abducted by a maniac.'

'There again, you're jumping the gun.'

'You're saying don't let's plan now, this evening, for what might not happen,' said Cecilia. 'We don't need strategies for remote eventualities. We can see what happens and, when it happens, plan accordingly.'

'Exactly,' said Tim and Marina together. Ian did a pantomime of despair.

'So what's the next step?' asked Cecilia.

It was decided that Cecilia should ring Lily Bridges back, as promised. If they probed, she would refer them to Ian and Marina. Should she say Ian was her son? That she had always known Jane had a child, and that the child was her grandson, too? Grey areas, to be played by ear.

Chapter 26

Guy and Lily were enjoying getting on well together. This always happened when they could make common cause. It had been the same when the garden room ceiling fell in, when Angus's predecessor stole a horse, and when Jane last stayed at home.

'We have to decide what to say to Mrs Banks,' said Guy at breakfast, cheerfully uncritical of the quality of the bacon and the state of the sausages.

'Yes,' said Lily, who was feasting happily on toast and butter. 'That's if she rings back.'

'If she doesn't,' said Guy, 'we can start enquiries through the hospital. Someone they could put us on to must know something.'

'So we have got a grandchild, dear,' said Lily. 'Remember when you said we never would have?'

Guy did remember.

'We should think about when Jane leaves hospital,' said Lily. 'Perhaps we should have her here.'

'We did last time she left hospital. When would that have been?'

'Five years ago. Or a bit more.'

'That wasn't a great success.'

'She wouldn't take her medication.'

'No. That was the trouble. What if we had all that again?'

'I know.'

There was a silence, while both remembered scenes and episodes they would rather forget. Guy shook his head, as a dog shakes off water. Lily stared sadly.

They did not have to wait more than a day or two for Cecilia's phone call. Cecilia foresaw she was going to find it very difficult to know where to draw lines, and had endured a very troubled night. But she picked up the phone and dialled the Bridges' number.

'Hullo?' said Lily's voice.

'Hullo. Cecilia Banks. We were talking about your daughter's child, and the possibility that we at this end might know something about that child.' That sentence had been rehearsed.

Lily could be heard whispering or motioning Guy to come close to her. 'Yes,' said Lily. 'We have been wondering.'

'I know that this child exists, and that he is now two years old, and is very settled and happy in a good family, with a little brother.'

'Oh! You must excuse me – you must excuse my amazement. I am very happy.' Lily was as uncertain as Cecilia.

'Excuse me butting in,' said the next voice, Guy's. 'If you could give us any more details, we would be very grateful. Is the child a son?'

'Yes,' said Cecilia, and tears came to her eyes, being forced to think of Cephas so objectively.

'We understand he is living with his father.'

'That is correct. He is settled happily with his father and his father's wife. That is the legal position.'

There was a silence, and clearly Guy was thinking. 'May I ask how you know all this, Mrs Banks?'

Cecilia felt she was for it now. 'I know it because my son is the father.' What else could she say?

Stunned silence. Then Lily came on again. 'It is hard for us to understand so much, so quickly.'

Guy's voice could be heard asserting, 'No, it isn't, Lils. It's all quite straightforward.'

Then Lily again, piecing it together: 'So you are the little boy's grandmother?'

Cecilia was even more tearful at the words 'little boy', precisely because they were less objective. 'Yes,' she said.

'So of course you know where he lives,' said Lily.

'Yes.'

Brief conversation between Guy and Lily. Guy again: 'If we wanted to see him, would that be possible?'

Cecilia felt that her brushwood barriers against this moment had gone down one by one, or had never been there. 'As to that,' she said, 'you would have to ask the child's parents. Perhaps you would like to think and talk about that, and about how you would feel if the request was refused. And ring me back later. Goodbye.'

Guy was forced to put the phone down. 'That's that, then,' he said.

'Not necessarily,' said Lily.

'She didn't sound welcoming.'

'It's a difficult situation. Jane probably hasn't come over very well, to Mrs Banks, if you think about it.'

'No. She probably hasn't,' said Guy gloomily.

'They might think,' said Lily, 'that if we visit the little boy, Jane will come and make trouble.'

'We need to make it clear that we would visit without her, and without her knowledge.'

'So do you want to visit?'

Guy was silent. He didn't know. 'Well,' he said, 'you must want us to. You're his grandmother.'

~

In a conversation with Marina, Cecilia gave a blow-by-blow account of her telephone call with Lily Bridges. There was

331

then a further telephone conversation, the next day, when Guy and Lily told Cecilia they had decided they would like to ask to visit Cephas. Suggested by Marina, Cecilia supplied them with Marina's email, but, immediately, no telephone number or address for Cephas's home. The email from the Bridges came through to Marina the next day, and, after a brief storm between her and Ian, a teatime meeting was arranged brusquely on the telephone by Ian, resigned rather than converted.

It had to be quite soon, for reasons on both sides. Marina and Ian needed it to precede the date on which Ian was scheduled to be abroad again. Guy and Lily were anxious that it should happen before there was any question of Jane being discharged from hospital, in the first instance, and, almost certainly, discharged on to them. So it was arranged. Tim and Cecilia were also to be present.

'My word,' said Helen to Cecilia, 'that will be a dramatic event.'

'It might be. I hope it will be very tame.'

'I wouldn't mind being a fly on the wall.'

'Of course I'll tell you all about it, afterwards.' Cecilia sighed. She was still tired. 'Actually I'm dreading it.'

'I'm so sorry to be frivolous.'

'That's OK. How was your visit to Hyacinth?'

'Yes, I was going to tell you. I was right, the stoma's bulgier than it was, though goodness knows how I knew that, when I can hardly see it for bosom and rolls of fat. The stoma has a hernia, and it's got bigger. I have to see a surgeon.'

'Mr Z?'

'No, a different one. A specialist in stoma hernias. Stoma hernias are very common, I'm relieved to say. But she thinks I should get a specialist's opinion. I'm doing it privately.'

'Have you got the appointment?'

'Yes.'

'Shall I come with you?'

Helen actually went a bit pink. 'Thank you,' she said. 'You don't need to.' Her eyes shone. 'Lewis is coming with me.'

'Lewis? Oh Helen. I didn't know . . .'

'You didn't know he was such a pal. Well, he is.'

'Only a pal?' Cecilia asked.

'No comment for the moment.' Helen was smiling broadly.

'Well!' said Cecilia.

~

'We must take him a present,' said Guy.

Lily wasn't sure. It was hard to know the etiquette for such an unusual situation. A present might seem to be staking a claim. 'I'm not sure,' she said.

'Yes. On our way to the station we can find a toyshop in Chichester . . .'

'How will we find one?'

'Ask Greta. She's got grandchildren.'

Lily was impressed by Guy's ingenuity. He was in good spirits. It was Lily who was the more apprehensive. Lily did ask Greta. Pushing open the door of the toyshop when the day came, Guy and Lily were rather like children themselves, speechless, shy and important, clothed for an occasion, awed by the toys.

'Look at those tanks,' whispered Guy. 'That one is a Challenger 2. I must have a look at it. Yes. Very good.'

'He's only two. They are too old for him.'

'The army is in his blood.'

'Oh dear . . .' It was not the mention of the army, but of blood, that flustered Lily. Was Guy going to strike the wrong note with Mr and Mrs Forest? 'If we are taking a present for the child, I think we should take one for the younger one too.' That suggestion obliquely modified the significance of blood, Lily cleverly thought.

'That's a good idea. You choose that.'

So Guy was examining the war toys and Lily the teddies. Guy gained some help from the nice lady. War toys for two-year-olds. She suggested a much simpler tank, which Guy did not like because it was not a replica.

'How could they shoot straight from that?' he muttered. 'Look at that!'

She produced Action Man and some of his outfits. Guy was enchanted. He wanted to add a jeep. Lily was doubtful. 'Whatever we buy, we'll have to carry, all the way to London, and then to the address.'

'We can take a taxi,' said Guy, disposed to throw his usual caution to the winds.

The nice lady wrapped Action Man, his jeep, and his various accoutrements in bright paper, and put the whole in a carrier bag with the shop's name on it. She wrapped a particularly nice teddy, of medium size and pleading eyes, in the same paper, and that too was placed in a large carrier bag. Even after all this, Guy and Lily were early for the train, and stood, excitedly, Guy holding a bag in each hand, on the station platform.

~

'It isn't such a big thing,' said Marina.

'Yes, it is.' Ian was slicing a dark cake from the health food shop. 'This'll do them, for eats.'

'Yes, that looks nice.'

'Shall I get down the proper cups, wedding-present tea set, or shall we have mugs? We'd better have the cups. We don't want to be reported to Social Services for squalor.'

'Don't have the proper cups. What if Cephas asked, "What's that?" if he sees a saucer?'

'Mugs.'

There was a ring at the doorbell, and Ian went to answer, feeling that a male presence would keep the guests in their place – whatever their very odd place was. However, it was only Cecilia and Tim, tidy and expectant.

'No, they haven't arrived yet,' said Ian, in a mock stage whisper.

Tim and Cecilia relaxed and came in. Cephas, at the television, had recognised his gran's ring at the doorbell immediately, and ran out to her. 'Gran, Gran, Gran,' he said. She was still unable to snatch him into her arms, and stooped to him instead, enduring the faint look of disappointment, or was it anxiety, even? that this brought to his face. The two of them went into the sitting room to an armchair in front of the TV, he on her lap, which she could manage comfortably. 'Dinosaurs,' said Cephas.

'Yes, I see them,' said Cecilia. 'Do you like them?'

Cephas considered. 'Not all of them.' Then he said, 'Do you?'

She gave him an extra hug. It was not a question every child would ask. 'As long as they are safely on the TV, I do,' she said. He rather liked that answer. After a bit of thought, she said, 'Have Mummy and Daddy told you some people are coming to tea?'

This was not quite interesting enough for Cephas to answer, though it would have been, had he known that the two big toyshop bags were inching their way by taxi towards his house.

'Aren't you coming into the kitchen for the council of war?' asked Ian, putting his head round the door.

'I'm denying we need one,' said Cecilia.

'What war?' Cephas asked, but soon lost interest, as a tyrannosaurus devoured prey.

In the kitchen Tim was saying, 'It isn't such a big thing. Mr and Mrs Bridges are visiting to recognise their relationship with Cephas.'

'They haven't got one,' put in Ian.

'They want to establish one, an incredibly minor one,' said Marina, standing over the teapot and the tray. Ali was in the sling. 'Or maybe they just want to set eyes on him.'

'They may have several children and numerous grandchildren already,' said Tim.

'We don't know what they want, that's the trouble,' Ian said. 'Nor do we know whether Leda will be hot on their heels.'

'If poor Leda is off her head,' said Tim, privately reminiscing about the glory of her forehand drive, 'they may be as reluctant as we are to have her anywhere near Cephas. There seems to be a tendency to think this harmless old couple have no sensible thoughts of their own.'

'There certainly is in Ian,' said Marina, from her end of the room. 'It's us versus them, for him.'

'We'll see what happens,' said Ian. 'You're hoping for the best, I'm preparing for the worst.'

It was he who went to the door again when the bell rang. He saw a handsome elderly man in a suit, rather flustered and boyish, with a sweating forehead, holding two large bags; and a pretty, faded, hesitant woman, doing her best in purple and grey cashmere. 'Mr and Mrs Bridges,' said Ian, taking Lily's jacket. 'Ian Forest.'

The guests looked shy and grateful, but seemed to be bereft of words.

'Come in,' said Ian. There had been a council of war, perhaps; but he felt a lack of immediate tactics. Where to put the new arrivals? He hesitated a minute, then showed them into the sitting room, where they surprised Cephas, Cecilia and the dinosaurs. Cecilia stood up, unseating Cephas, who stared at the strangers, and at their bags. 'This is my mother, Cecilia Banks,' said Ian. 'You know her from the telephone. Mum, this is Mr and Mrs Bridges.'

'Guy and Lily,' whispered Lily.

'Guy and Lily.' Tim appeared in the doorway. He shook hands, which neither Ian nor Cecilia had done. 'This is Tim Banks, my stepfather,' said Ian. 'Guy and Lily Bridges. Please sit down. I am just going to help my wife bring in tea.'

They sat, except for Cephas. Tim switched off the TV, with a quelling look in Cephas's direction, not needed because of the eye catching nature of the carrier bags. There was a brief silence. Then Cecilia said, 'And this is Cephas.' It was, to be fair to her, partly the oddity of the name that made him difficult to introduce.

Guy held out his hand in a jolly way, and chuckled a greeting in a false voice. Cecilia's heart sank. But Cephas rose to the occasion, and solemnly shook hands. Then he shook hands with Lily, which was more alarming, because she took his hand in both of hers, and attempted to retain it, putting her face near his. He recoiled. Seeing she had failed to establish intimacy, or even chumminess, she said, 'We've got something for you.'

A huge and rustling unwrapping started, first the carrier bag, then the colourful paper. Cephas was in his element. Marina and Ian came in with trays. Marina felt that present-opening, which she had reluctantly foreseen, had begun rather prematurely; but perhaps this was inevitable, with the splendid toyshop bags on display. Marina was introduced and shook hands in her friendly, relaxed way. She it was who thanked for and marvelled at Cephas's presents.

'He'll think it's Christmas!'

With a little help from Ian, Cephas uncovered Action Man and the jeep, and was pleased and absorbed, running the jeep back and forth at the other end of the room. There was a parental prompt to say thank you, and he abstractedly did so. Tea was dispensed, cake offered. There need have been no apprehension about saucers, for Cephas was too engrossed in his new toys to notice the doings of the grown-ups. Guy was beaming, Lily fluttering, as they saw their gifts a success.

It felt to everyone that the conversation was heavily compromised by Cephas's presence. But each began to realise that actually it was not.

'How is your daughter?' Cecilia asked.

'She is in hospital,' said Lily. 'She is undergoing psychiatric treatment.'

'I'm sorry,' said Cecilia.

'She doesn't know we are here,' Lily said. Cecilia thought it was tactful of Lily to understand this might be a concern.

Guy looked at Lily disapprovingly. Was she going to say the wrong thing? What was the wrong thing? What was the right thing? He had no idea. He had turned his chair, so that he could easily watch Cephas without being obviously anti-social. 'My grandson', he was trying to make himself feel. He could not provide a sensation concomitant with this phrase. He had never really warmed to little kids. They had not warmed to him. 'My own flesh and blood', he tried on himself, but they were only words. Still, he watched Cephas. He now had the urge to say, 'How like Jane he looks', but in fact he had noted no resemblance, nor sought one. Perhaps he could say it to Lily. He caught her eye.

'Just thinking,' he said.

'What, dear?'

'Very like Jane at that age.'

This was so untrue that Lily was lost for an answer. 'I was thinking he favours his father,' said Lily, smiling towards Ian.

Cecilia did not like these comments, and was afraid Cephas might pick something up. She was relieved to remind herself that although all the cards about blood were in the hands of the Bridges, they did not know it, and could not play them. As far as they were aware, blood was equally matched.

No one knew where to steer the conversation. The Bridges had decided they wanted to meet Cephas, but did not know now what to do with the occasion. They were beginning to feel that this was all it was. They arrived; they saw a very nice little boy; they gave him a present. What else was supposed to happen?

Lily tried a new conversational tack. 'You have another child,' she said, looking towards the beslung Ali. 'Very nice. How old?'

'Four months,' said Marina. 'He's asleep.'

'That's a natty contraption,' said Guy.

'The sling? Yes. Cecilia says they didn't have them when Ian was a baby.'

'What's his name?' asked Lily.

'Ali.'

'Makes it easier for you to carry him about,' said Guy, looking appreciatively at Marina.

'Alexander, I suppose?' queried Lily, unheard.

'Do you have other children besides Jane?' asked Marina.

'Yes,' said Guy. 'We have a son. He is in Afghanistan.'

'That must be a worry for you,' said Cecilia.

'Yes it is,' said Lily.

It occurred to Guy to say that they were a military family and, with a laugh, that he hoped the army would not come out in Cephas's blood. He drew a breath to speak, but Lily, who knew what was in his mind, caught his eye. The words died on his lips.

No topic flourished. The cake went round again. Now Cephas ran up to Marina, and whispered, 'Another bag. Two bags.'

'The other present is for the other little boy,' said Lily. She turned to Cephas. 'For your brother. Would you like to give it to him?'

'Ali's asleep,' said Cephas, but actually Ali was waking up. He cried, and was carried off by Marina, who said he was hungry. For a moment Guy had hoped she might be the sort of woman he had read about in the paper, who breastfeeds in public.

Tim engaged Guy in a conversation about Sussex, and which village was near what, and what was a brown and what a green belt. Ian made a pretence of involvement in this exchange, but was more interested in policing Cephas, who was starting work on the bag in which Ali's teddy lay. Ian had a premonition of trouble. Meanwhile Cecilia was managing to draw Lily out on Jane – she had had her first breakdown at fifteen; she had been odd before that; she had always been very clever, and had done well at university, in spite of further breakdowns there. She had also been very good at sport. Lily didn't know why all this had happened to her. It was such a pity. Cecilia told Lily she was a psychotherapist, and sensed that this loosened Lily's tongue. Cecilia felt sorry for this nice, rather feeble woman, confronted with raw psychosis in the home.

'None of this can be easy for you,' she said.

'No,' said Lily. 'And the worst of it is – well, not the worst, I shouldn't have said that – is that she will probably come home soon, when she is discharged. I am not sure how we'll cope. But we have a very good GP, and a nice vicar, and they may be a help. But actually she always refuses to speak to either of them.' What was preoccupying Lily was that Jane must have had an affair with this tall and apparently normal man who was such a good father and carried tea trays, and why ever could Jane not have married him?

'They may be able to help you, though, even if not her,' Cecilia suggested. 'The more people you can talk to, the better.'

Her attention strayed now to Cephas's raised voice. He had been unwrapping the second parcel, as Lily had indicated to him that he might; and now was clutching a teddy clearly intended for Ali, and denying to Ian that it was Ali's teddy. Why, thought Cecilia, had Ian got into a confrontation now? It could have waited till the guests had left. By the time Marina came back into the room with a now alert, cheerful and adorable Ali, the teddy was having goes in the jeep at the other end of the room, on the shaky basis that it would be given to Ali the moment he appeared.

'Now,' said Ian, 'give Ali his teddy.' Conversations fell silent.

'I can't,' said Cephas. He ran out of the room. Ian pursued him, instead of more wisely giving the point up. The new teddy already sat between Big Teddy and Small Teddy on Cephas's bed. It was evident to Ian, in spite of his sense of justice, that the new teddy, as Cephas had foreseen, was exactly the right size for its intermediate position. 'My teddies,' said Cephas happily.

'Give Ali his teddy,' said Ian, audible to everyone.

'No!' yelled Cephas. There was a stifled cry from Lily and a tut from Guy.

Meanwhile Ali was intensely happy with the wrapping paper. Sitting in his baby-chair, he had seized the paper and was battling with it, hugging it, licking it, kicking it, and then starting all over again, with mounting excitement and cries of joy and effort. He disappeared behind a rustling, quaking mound of shine and colour. Everyone laughed. It was the best moment of the afternoon.

Ian, defeated, left Cephas in his bedroom with the three teddies. He came back into the sitting room, glanced at the clock, and offered drinks. This acted on the Bridges as a signal to talk about their homeward train, as Ian had hoped it might. Goodbyes were a muddle, with everybody crowded on the narrow threshold. Cecilia and Lily agreed to keep in touch; Guy offered Ian an invitation to bring the family to lunch, then regretted it, due to qualms about Jane; Marina stood and smiled, holding Ali, whom she had prised from the wrapping paper. Tim produced Lily's jacket, and offered a brolly that was not hers. It was in everybody's mind that Cephas was absent from the group, but for differing reasons no one commented. The front door closed.

Chapter 27

Jane feared all the nurses, and, more than anyone, the psychiatrist. She was supposed to call the psychiatrist Gloria.

'What can I do to get out of this place, Gloria?' she had said.

'Try to be happy here, and make the best of it. Have a good rest, and allow your medication to do its work.'

'It's Clozaril, isn't it?'

'Well, yes, it is. But I think you should relax and let us take care of that side of things.'

'I suppose you realise Clozaril can cause agranulocytosis? Myocarditis?'

'Very, very rarely. And the benefits outweigh—'

'But I'm shit scared.'

'No need to be, I promise you. I'll look up the statistics, if you like. You are probably likelier to win the lottery.'

Jane wanted to say she was not scared of side effects of medication, only because she no longer heard voices, so never knew what she was supposed to do. But it was better not to tell these people anything. They were probably Them. But without guidance, how could she be certain?

The only person who was obviously one of Us was the cat, a tabby from a rescue home. The psychiatric wing of the hospital had recently acquired her as an experiment. She was called Daisy, a stupid name according to Jane, but that didn't matter.

It was not her real name, obviously. Daisy liked Jane, and usually chose Jane's room to sleep in.

'Without Daisy,' thought Jane, speaking the words aloud in her mind, 'I might have gone mad.'

At first she had tried not to swallow the tablets, but the nurses were watchful, and they had fetched Gloria, who threatened her with injections. As had happened the last time she was on medication, gradually the voices faded. It felt as if they were struggling to be heard, and then they seemed to despair and drown. In the ensuing silence was a terrifying rushing noise. She asked the nurses about it, but no nurse could hear it. It was continuous and steady. Jane thought Daisy could hear it, for she often twitched her ears; cats' hearing is more acute than ours. Jane sat with her head in her hands. She had become useless to Us. Was she a traitor? Not a traitor, surely, for in her heart she was anything but unfaithful. But it had been very stupid to get caught. And now, in consequence of that one mistake, she was out of earshot of her mentors and the team.

She was going to and from the toilet because she was so scared. She was a lost soul. Being a soldier for Us was difficult and wearing. But it made life worthwhile. She tried to feel that she had done good work, and now, perhaps, had been retired with honour. But it was not so. She was useless and forgotten. She wished she was dead, as she used to wish before she was recruited by Us, before her life took on shape and meaning, became a matter of tasks and of achievements. It was unbearable to be in this terrible room, with its bed, its chair, its window that looked out on to a wall, its bedside table, its pastel colours, and its frightening, incessant noise. Everyone behaved as if there was no Us and Them. That was a trick of Theirs she was familiar with.

She no longer had fish at every meal. She had tried to be true to that important sign of loyalty and zeal, that commitment to the sea that was an emblem of her calling. Initially, as if to humour her, a sardine was put on the side of her plate, but only for the first week, and only at supper. After that week, it was implied that she would be discharged sooner if she was not faddy about food. Faddy! Thus she had lost another thread that linked her to her old, her real life. She no longer looked for marks. She could not even remember, now, how to recognise a mark. She wrung her hands as she walked.

'She's still very agitated,' Gloria said. 'Is she sleeping?' One of the night nurses replied that she was not. Sleeping pills were prescribed.

More and more often, as the days passed, it occurred to Jane that perhaps there was no Us and Them. Maybe there never had been. Perhaps there was just nothing. Perhaps the firm, instructive voices of Us were an illusion, an attempt to make order out of chaos. Perhaps the true noise was nothing but this dreadful inarticulate hissing, a travesty, a parody of the sound of the sea, a noise that only death could stop.

~

'Lewis has asked me to marry him,' Helen told Cecilia.

Cecilia looked up from coffee-making with a wondering stare. She did not speak, for if she had spoken her thoughts, her initial astonishment might have been uncomplimentary, either to Helen, on the basis of her age, or to Lewis, on the basis of his insignificance. Not that Cecilia had met Lewis. She had merely taken for granted that, in the person of Lewis, Helen had taken up with someone beneath her.

'You probably think I am much too old and he is much too dim,' went on Helen.

'I don't think any such thing on either count, if he has asked you to marry him,' said Cecilia, for whom this was at least partly true. At Helen's announcement Lewis had rocketed in Cecilia's estimation.

'We've been carrying on, in a gentle way, for quite a while,' said Helen. 'But I never expected this. No one has ever asked me to marry him before. I've just never moved in those sorts of circles, I suppose. He is divorced; I've never been married. So there are no complications.'

'It sounds as if you are thinking of doing it.' Irrepressible joy had crept into Cecilia's stare.

'Playing with the idea. It might be rather fun. OK, he's not an intellectual, but so what? I am not one really, either. He is very easy to be with, very kind, and he doesn't annoy me at all. He is taking my drinking in hand, which no one ever has before; they have all just gone on drinking even more than I do. Do you know what upsets me about it?'

Cecilia pondered. 'No.'

'That Mum isn't here. She would be so pleased. She always wanted me to be respectable.'

~

Mel, the social worker, was involved in the procedure of discharging Jane Bridges from hospital. 'The pharmacist is doing your medications,' said Mel. 'They'll be here in a minute. Gloria will go through them with you when she pops in to say goodbye.'

'All right,' said Jane.

'What time is your father coming for you?'

'I don't know.'

'How do you feel about going home?'

'All right.'

'I do know it's not easy.'

Jane had nothing to say to this.

'I must say Daisy has taken a liking to you,' said Mel. Daisy was asleep on Jane's bed. 'She's going to miss you.'

Jane smiled.

'Well, that got a smile out of you,' said Mel. 'Now, you've

got my phone number. I'm your social worker, don't forget, until we've transferred you to West Sussex.'

'Yes. All right,' said Jane.

Mel left. The pharmacist knocked and came in, smiling. There was a big packet of tablets. 'Gloria will take you through these. Goodbye and good luck.'

Gloria was next, and took Jane through the tablets.

'You needn't bother,' said Jane. 'All the instructions are on the labels.'

Gloria did not feel the hospital's contact with Jane had been a great success.

~

Guy arrived, bustling, harassed, and smelling of the outside world. It was a long time since he and his daughter had met. He pecked Jane's cheek. 'Very good,' he said. 'Well done. Your mum is looking forward to seeing you.'

'Cup of coffee, Mr Bridges?' said a head round the door.

'No thank you. We had better get on.' The head disappeared. 'Have you packed up, dear?'

'Yes.'

'I'll take your bags. The car's outside.' Jane picked up one small bag and handed it to him. 'Is this all?'

'Yes.'

'Do you have to check out?'

'They've all said goodbye to me.'

'Off we go then.'

'We're going to need something to wrap up the cat in.'

'Wrap up the cat?'

'Yes. We have to take the cat.'

'Take the cat?'

'Yes.'

'We can't possibly. Does anyone know?'

'Of course not.'

Guy stared. 'Then it would be theft. I refuse.'

Jane stood, body motionless, face stony. She said quietly, 'We are not going without the cat. Your jacket would do.'

'Of course not. I can't walk out of the hospital in my shirt-sleeves. Anyway—'

'We are not leaving without the cat.'

Guy was silent. He did not want a confrontation. He did not want to have come all this way and go home without Jane. He did not want to be involved in a robbery. He wanted to phone Lily to ask what to do. Then he lit on another thought. 'We can't do it, anyway. The cat would miaow probably, and be taken off you.'

'No, that won't happen. I have given the cat an eighth of a sleeping pill.'

'This is dreadful.' Guy was speaking to himself. He realised Jane had said her last word on the matter, and he remembered too well that in this mood she never budged. Horrible memories crowded into his mind. Having her at home was going to be awful. The hospital stay had obviously been useless. Slowly he took his jacket off, and smartened up what was left of his apparel as best he could.

Jane carefully wrapped Daisy's inert form in the jacket, arranged the bundle so that Daisy was completely concealed, and stood ready to leave. They hurried out of the hospital to the car. Guy was smiling and sweating with guilt and embarrassment, uttering unheeded goodbyes to porters and portresses; but Jane walked steadily, her face expressionless.

～

Lily wandered round the house, waiting for their arrival. It was five years since Jane had been home. Lily wanted the return to be a good experience for Jane, if possible; and first impressions mattered. She checked the bedroom she had designated for Jane, a large, airy room on the first floor. She had put flowers from the garden in a vase on the table. She wanted everything to strike Jane as pretty and homelike. With another part of her mind she knew that Jane was indifferent to prettiness and disliked the homelike. She hoped to lure Jane into improved relations with both by the quiet beauty of her bedroom. The days had lengthened, but the sun still came in, and shone on the beeswax polish of the table and floorboards. All the furniture was old and what Lily's grandmother had called 'good'. This room had been Lily's when she was a child. She loved it.

Then she looked at the first-floor bathroom. It had once been a bedroom, so it was big, with a huge, old bath, somewhat discoloured. Lily opened the window. Then she closed it. Would Jane be warm enough? Lily had put the central heating on early this year, to welcome Jane. Or she thought she had. Angus must have a look at it. She noticed a spider in the bath, and, though she knew this was not the sort of thing Jane minded at all, she removed it carefully and reopened the window to let it out. She decided to leave the window open after all. The clematis leaves wandered round the window frame into the room in a way that Jane might like. Lily proceeded downstairs to have a further look there. She had not decided yet what to have for supper, for traditionally Jane was a faddy eater, and it would be important to find out what, at this moment, was acceptable. She would have to get a list, and talk it over with Greta. Actually, Lily was afraid. She was afraid of Jane, and afraid of her presence in the house.

She heard the car, and went to the front door. She had chosen her clothes carefully that day, in an attempt to strike the right note for Jane, without knowing what that note was; so she stood at the top of the front steps in dull pinks and mauves and a matching silk scarf. She watched Guy get out of the car, and knew from the angle of his back that things had not gone well. And why had he discarded his jacket? His first gesture was to look imploringly towards the steps. He saw Lily, and was comforted enough to shrug helplessly. Now Jane was emerging.

It had not been an easy journey. Daisy had revived quite quickly, and was on the loose in the car. Finally she came to rest across Guy's shoulders, purring, and he drove as best he could. He and Jane did not exchange a word, once he realised it was no good exhorting her to restrain Daisy, which she could only do for five minutes at a time. He was furious with Jane, but you weren't supposed to feel that. He had hoped she would be all right after her sojourn in the hospital, at least for a little while; so he was also furious with the mental health professionals. But he did a good job, and they arrived in one piece at their destination.

The first thing Lily noticed about Jane, before even seeing how thin and worn she had become, was that she was carrying a full-grown tabby cat. Holding Daisy tight, Jane came towards the house and up the steps. 'Where am I sleeping?' she asked Lily. 'I need to put the cat in that room. At once.' Her tone was commanding.

Lily had not expected this to be the vein in which Jane was shown upstairs, but she accepted it, as she had to. She opened the bedroom door, and saw the pretty window, the flowers, the patchwork quilt and curtains, the dull shine of the good wood. Jane saw none of these things. 'Leave me alone, Mummy, to settle the cat in,' she said. Chilled and terrified, Lily left her.

But what alienated them both from Jane drew Guy and Lily together. They stood in the sitting room whispering like anxious children. Guy told Lily how he had been forced to connive at a felony over the abduction of the hospital cat. 'I suppose I'll have to write to them and explain,' he said. 'I suppose if I make a donation it will be all right.' They looked at each other with wide eyes, both measuring for the first time the enormity of the problem on their hands, and both sensing their scant resources.

Lily was the first to speak this thought. 'We're not cut out for this sort of thing,' she said.

'No,' he said. 'It brings it all back to me. I hoped it would be better.'

Lily thought of her life – of the garden, the early mornings, the dew, the birds, the snails, the spiders' webs, which, not there yesterday, were slung intricately from shrub to shrub, the horses' soft mouths, the unhurried consultations with Greta about lunch and with Angus about pruning the roses, the choosing of flowers for church, the familiar altercations with Guy. She felt as if she was losing everything, that all she was losing was lovely, and that she was not supposed to mind. She was supposed to be pleased. Imagine: 'Jane is with us at the moment.'

'Oh how lovely for you, after all this time. You must bring her to tea at the rectory.'

Guy did not look into the future so much as endure the present – that adamantine and unreasonable presence upstairs in the house, the emotional after-effects of the preliminary skirmish he had fought and lost, the shame of his unconditional surrender. Lily, often irritating, struck him as adorably harmless and predictable. 'Lilykins,' he said.

She put both her hands on his forearm and he put a hand on hers. They stood, listening. Voices were coming from the kitchen. 'It's Jane and Greta,' said Lily. 'Of course Greta doesn't know Jane.'

'Weren't Angus and Greta here when—?'

'No. Jane hasn't been home for five years, and—'

'But you must have told Greta about her.'

'Yes, of course. And Greta helped with the bedroom.'

They listened. Jane's commanding tones were easy to overhear.

'I need some meat,' she was saying. 'Or some fish.'

Greta could be heard saying something about suppertime.

'No, immediately,' said Jane. 'What have you got?'

Noises now, and more conversation, less audible. Then, 'The tuna will do,' from Jane, and she could be heard going upstairs.

'It's for that cat,' whispered Lily.

Later, under orders, Lily and Greta improvised a litter tray from a large baking dish, and provided ash for litter. 'We'll get cat food, tomorrow,' said Jane. 'Now all we need is a water bowl. Remember, the cat mustn't be let out of my bedroom for a fortnight. She'll have everything she needs there.' She disappeared upstairs with her equipment.

'Lily told me Jane's got psychiatric problems,' said Greta to Angus. 'But I never expected her to be such a handful. Wait till you meet her. I'm really sorry for Lily.'

Jane did not appear for supper. 'We'll let it go tonight,' Lily said to Guy, as they faced each other over fish cakes and mashed potato. 'Tomorrow we must start feeding her up. Have you noticed how thin she is?'

'Yes,' said Guy sadly.

Later, Lily heard Jane in the bath, and tiptoed to her bedroom door. She opened it just a chink, and craned her head in. Cat bowls had scattered their contents on the floor, the vase was upset and the flowers lay in a puddle on the table, water soaking into the good oak. The litter tray had evidently been used already. In the middle of the bed lay Daisy, a fine figure of a tabby cat, reclining happily and washing a paw.

Early the next morning Lily's mobile rang. She was awake, of course, but wasn't in the garden, for Jane's presence in the house made her unfree. 'Who can this be?' she murmured. 'It's half past six.'

It was Jane. 'I'm just taking your car to go to Tesco. Is that all right?'

'Yes, of course,' said Lily automatically, although questions and doubts were welling up in her mind, of which she voiced a few. 'What do you need to get? Are you sure you are all right to drive? Will Tesco be open? Do you know where the car keys are? Have you had breakfast?'

'Five questions, which I shall answer in order,' said the stern voice. 'Cat food. Yes; certainly, open twenty-four hours, if I remember right. Yes, on the hooks in the hall. Not yet.'

Jane rang off, leaving Lily to explain what had happened to the awakening Guy, who told her she should not have let Jane take her car. This from the person whom Jane had easily induced to steal a cat, thought Lily. It was not a simple matter to stand up to Jane.

Lily and Guy were breakfasting when Jane returned. She had been longer than expected, and they had begun to worry. They heard her go upstairs, and, presumably, feed the cat. Then she came into the dining room.

'There was a notice on the Chichester road about kittens,' she said.

'Yes, I've seen that,' said Guy, hoping to be chatty. 'Come and have breakfast. It says six kittens need homes. It's Bartons Farm.' He added this last for Lily.

'They don't need homes any more,' said Jane. 'They're in the car. No one wanted to adopt them and the woman was about to drown them. They are in a bad way. A fox got their mother. I'm taking over the long shed in the second field for them. I can't have them in my room because they would upset Daisy.'

'The long shed? But Angus keeps the—' wailed Lily.

'Look, Jane, dear,' said Guy. But she had gone. Guy and Lily looked at each other. 'I hope she hasn't stolen Fanny Barton's kittens,' said Guy. 'That would take some explaining.'

～

A few days later, in the psychiatric department, Gloria found Mel.

'Look at this,' she said.

Mel leant over a letter, written in longhand, the calligraphy clear and handsome, under a West Sussex address.

To whom it may concern:

When I left the hospital last Tuesday, I took with me the cat, Daisy. My sense was that she would be happier with me than in the bleak surroundings that were then hers. You will be glad to know that she is settling in well.

Should you want another cat to replace Daisy in your department, I will gladly pay any costs. I have no intention of returning Daisy.

Yours,
Jane Bridges

'Well!' said Mel. 'Did you notice the cat had gone missing?'

'No, and nobody's mentioned it, at least not to me. But that's not the point.'

'No, indeed.'

Mel reread the letter, then Gloria took it and reread it. She looked up and smiled. 'Just thought you'd be interested,' she said.

'She sounds amazingly together. Who would think it's the same person?'

'I know. That's what I wanted you to see. Well. You never know, do you?'

Chapter 28

London, again. Cecilia, Tim, Ian and Cephas in Cecilia's kitchen. Rain, and the early dusk of late autumn. Marina was working, and Ian had brought Cephas to tea with Cecilia because by afternoon both he and Cephas were ready for a change of scene. Ali was spending the day with his other grandmother, who had discovered a neighbour with a grandchild of Ali's age. They would play together. Or would they? thought Ian. However, he was glad to lessen his own duties. He and Marina could not help noticing that, try as she might, Marina's mother was more passionate about Ali than about Cephas. This could not be helped. Marina, particularly, did not like it, and felt let down by it; but she accepted that love falls where it falls and, like other rare and precious commodities, it must be appreciated and cherished wherever it is found.

'What's this about Helen getting married?' asked Ian.

'Well, she hasn't made her mind up yet. It's not as clear-cut as that.'

'I haven't heard about this,' called Tim from the teapot.

'There's nothing to hear, yet.'

'You told Marina,' put in Ian.

'Yes. By way of chat.'

'Don't you chat to me?' asked Tim.

'No point, often you're not interested.' As Cecilia said this she realised she was being a damsel in distress towards Ian, and felt ashamed. Ian's easy engagement and curiosity often showed her something she lacked in her domestic life, and that she missed it.

Tim laughed and said 'Touché,' but Ian was alert to this being no joke and looked sympathetically at Cecilia. 'Tell both of us everything you know,' he said gently. 'Hearsay, conjecture, the few known facts, everything.'

'Have you met the possible bridegroom?' Tim asked.

'I haven't.' Cecilia was not quite happy about discussing the affairs of Helen's heart in this rather frivolous way. However, she had got into it now. 'I don't know him, but you do.'

'I do?' Tim distributed tea. He was incredulous.

'He runs your tennis club.'

Tim hesitated. 'You don't mean Lewis Munro?'

'Yes, I do, and perhaps I shouldn't have said.'

'Well,' said Tim. 'But he's only in his fifties.'

'However,' said Ian, who was enjoying the conversation, particularly after eight hours tête-à-tête with Cephas, 'if that's all that's wrong with him, stranger things have happened.'

'Actually,' said Tim, 'he's a very decent chap. I've known him for years. But you wouldn't think he was right for Helen.'

'Is he the same chap as was there when I used to go to tennis?' asked Ian, groping in his memory.

'Yes. He's been there for years. He mends rackets, as well. Some people want to play with their father's racket, or people get hold of some champion's racket and want to play with that, and apparently he does a beautiful job. That's quite a lucrative sideline.'

'So we needn't presume he's marrying Helen for her money,' said Ian.

'What an idea,' said Cecilia, who hadn't thought of this.

'Well,' said Tim to Cecilia, 'perhaps you'd better probe that side of things before Helen commits herself.'

'What does she see in him, I wonder,' said Ian.

Cephas ran in and put his hands on Cecilia's lap. He looked into her face. 'Dinosaurs again, Gran, you like it,' he said, gripping Cecilia's skirt and beginning to pull on it, and with that earnest, exquisite face beseeching her, how could she not go next door, interesting though the grown-up conversation was? When she sat down, with Cephas on her lap, she understood that Cephas's need for her had arisen from troubled as well as companionable feelings, for a tyrannosaurus was chomping his way through a litter, while the mother dinosaur of the less predatory species watched and groaned. Cecilia was too tired to find a way of explaining that this footage was computer-generated, and indeed its being so might not make any difference. So she merely hugged Cephas more closely, and said, 'It's only a film.' But she could tell by the continued tension of his body that he knew such things really happen. This should not be on children's hour, she reflected. Then she realised it was probably not children's hour, but an obscure channel Ian had excavated for Cephas in the hopes of keeping him occupied. Cecilia loved Cephas intensely, and quietly kissed the back of his head. She was thinking that she had another MRI next month, and that what it revealed might wrest her from him, and him from her.

Next door, Tim was answering Ian's question. 'Hard to imagine what Helen sees in him,' he said. 'But there must be something about him women like. Leda took a shine to him when she used to play tennis with me. I don't know if anything came of it, but it was very noticeable.'

'And he to her?' Ian asked, curious about Leda's private life in spite of himself. 'The shine?'

'I don't know.'

Cecilia had prised Cephas from the television, and they came into the kitchen. 'OK if I fix scrambled egg for Cephas?' she said to Ian.

'He had that for lunch,' said Ian. 'He'll be clucking.'

'I don't mind clucking,' said Cephas. 'I'll cluck now.' He started.

'Don't cluck, darling,' said Ian.

'Beans on toast!' cried Cecilia, and this was agreed.

'Where's Thor?' Cephas asked.

'If you look round,' said Cecilia, with the air of a conjuror, 'you'll see him.' To give Cephas a clue, she looked at the kitchen's high places, and Cephas, following her gaze, spotted Thor in Cecilia's shopping basket on a shelf.

'Will he come down?' Cephas wondered.

'Maybe not.'

But Thor did come down, and was less reserved towards Cephas than had become usual. Cephas no longer grabbed Thor and tried to carry him, so Thor had regained some of his former benignity towards Cephas. He purred round Cephas's legs. 'Thor likes me again,' said Cephas excitedly.

Even Ian was touched by this. 'The two of them go back a long way,' he said quietly, to no one in particular.

'He wants you to feed him,' said Cecilia. 'Will you?' She cut the top off a cat food sachet and handed it to Cephas. Crouching, breathing hard with concentration and care, Cephas squeezed the contents into Thor's plate. Then he watched proudly as Thor tucked in.

Later that evening, Cecilia telephoned Lily. She had undertaken to keep in touch.

'Hullo?' said Lily. The way Lily answered the telephone always took Cecilia back to grown-ups answering the telephone in the war, when she was a child. The tone bespoke both certainty that it would be bad news, and apprehension that the line would be poor.

'Lily, it is Cecilia, Cecilia Banks,' she said reassuringly.

'Oh, hullo.' Lily sounded stronger.

'I'm just wondering how you are getting on. Perhaps you have good news of Jane.'

'Well, yes. Jane is out of hospital. She is here.'

'That's good, probably, but it may be a bit difficult for you.'

Silence. Then, 'Well, I think we are all getting used to the new arrangements. It takes a bit of getting used to, for everyone.'

Cecilia didn't feel Lily wished to unburden herself. They said goodbye, and reiterated that they would keep in touch. A minute later the phone rang. It was Lily again.

'I'm so sorry I forgot to mention how very kind you were that day we came to London and Mr and Mrs Forest very kindly . . .' Lily's sentence petered out.

'No, it's you who were kind. Think of the lovely things you brought for the little boys.'

'I hope Cephas is well, and Alex.'

Cecilia could not resist. 'Has Jane mentioned Cephas?'

'Oh no. She doesn't talk much. I was wondering, was it Jane who gave him that unusual name, or . . .?'

'It was Jane. That is a pet name. His real names are Julius Perdito. That's what's on his birth certificate. Julius Perdito Forest.' Cecilia was glad to get the 'Forest' in.

'Julius Perdito Forest,' said Lily, with wondering pride.

'Known as Cephas. All names given him by Jane when he was born.'

'Julius Perdito Forest, known as Cephas,' said Lily. After she had rung off she repeated the name in her mind several times, and, for some reason, went to bed happier.

~

'Have you talked to Cecilia, about us?' Lewis asked Helen. She was lying on the sofa. A recumbent position minimised the slight discomfort of the stoma hernia. Lewis sat on the floor beside her, his head resting on her breast. He had one of her hands in his.

'Yes,' said Helen.

'What did she say?'

'She was happy. Amused, I think.'

'Amused?'

'Yes, in a nice, loving way.'

'Good. I was afraid she might disapprove, and I know what her opinion means to you.'

'I suppose it does. Anyway, yesterday she said something else.'

'Yes?'

'She said, "Helen, I'm saying this because I love you. Are you sure he doesn't have any mercenary intentions in wanting you to marry him?" She said, "Probably I wouldn't say this if I had ever met him, because I would no doubt like him too much."'

'Well,' said Lewis, 'it's natural your best friend should say that. I respect her for it.'

There was a silence, and then Lewis spoke again. 'Of course I want to live in your nice house. But I've always thought I love this house because it is like you. Ever since I first stepped into it, it's been glamorous to me.'

'But that's not why you love me,' asked Helen anxiously.

'No, the other way round. I love the house because it's you.' He paused. 'But being honest I do like the idea of living in it, instead of my poky flat. But that's because you're here. At least partly. Or, anyway, I know I wouldn't have any interest in living here without you. Is that mercenary?'

'No, it's complicated, and rather nice.'

He kissed her hand. 'And there's advantages for you too. Are they mercenary? I can take care of you. If anything happens to the stoma because of the hernia, like that consultant was saying it could, I'll be here, to drive you anywhere and make it all right for you, or get an ambulance or whatever we need to do. Is that mercenary, of you, to be pleased about that?'

'Good question.'

'And things you don't like so much, like watching your

alcohol intake, and your calories.' He paused, and then said thoughtfully, 'I will be good for you.'

Helen relished this last sentence. She was also moved that he had used the word 'stoma'. Only initiates, be they sufferers or medical, use that word. Anyone else says 'colostomy'. She felt he was an insider, and had affectionately allowed himself to become one. They were silent, and then she said, 'The first time you saw the stoma bag, there were tears in your eyes.'

'Were there?'

'Yes. Do you know why?

'Because you are beautiful. And it was the first time I saw you naked. And there was the stoma bag, looking so . . .'

'So what?'

'Irrelevant. Silly, in a way. Like when someone puts a comic hat on an elephant. Against nature. Tamed. Modernised.'

'I know what you mean.'

He looked at her large white hand, with its rings and its wrinkles. It excited him. Would his ring ever slip on to that bare finger? He gently touched the place where it might sit. 'I'm not sure why I like your hands so much,' he said. He enjoyed this sort of talk. He had never had to ferret out his feelings before, and had not known it could be fun. As he was thoroughly in love with Helen, he did not have to draw back from or dissemble any emotion he might stumble on. He liked trying to find words for things. 'Loving you has made a person of me,' he said. 'You have taught me everything I know.'

'Not how to mend tennis rackets, for example,' said Helen, to keep the conversation light.

His intensities had a way of embarrassing her. They also alarmed her. If she believed that a man loved her, it had always been axiomatic to her that he would soon stop; and experience had not belied this enough to banish it. Yet she was coming round to the idea of marrying Lewis, ridiculous though it was. In his company she felt loved, cheerful, at home, unanxious.

Did that mean she loved him? She didn't know. He was not much good at sex, she thought, disloyally. Was that inexperience, or was it nervousness about potency? The latter was certainly true, and their lovemaking often ended in failure on his part and giggles on hers. But that was all right, although up to now she had thought sex all-important. She was probably a mother figure, though certainly an incestuous one. That was all right, too. At sixty-seven, you did not expect things to be more than all right, and you could count yourself very lucky if you got that.

~

Ian and Marina's. Much bustle, for Ian was off abroad next morning, and was busy at the computer; Cephas had a friend to play, and after two hours they were annoying each other. Ali had rolled and struggled off his rug, in his preliminaries to crawling, and was overexposed on the carpet. Marina had an eye to all these situations, and was also clearing children's tea and cooking grown-ups' supper. She scooped Ali into his sling, frustrating for him at first, because trying to crawl had been exciting; but the sound and sight of vegetables being chopped was soon a comfort. The friend's mother arrived to fetch the friend, and Marina managed not to ask her in for a drink, politer though it would have been to do so. His friend's departure unleashed Cephas on to Marina's legs, but she was ready for that, for it was Cephas's usual response to the sight of Ali in the sling; and she stood square and steady, continuing to chop. 'Just doing the veggies,' she said to Cephas, 'then we'll have bath, story and bed.'

'Will the veggies be cooking, meanwhile?' asked Cephas. He had recently learnt 'meanwhile', and liked it.

'They will,' said Marina.

'I don't like Toby,' Cephas reflected.

'That's only because of the jeep and the digger, I think.'

'He can't have them both.'

'Well, no, but it sometimes seemed as if he couldn't have either.'

'He can't.'

Marina said, 'Why don't you take teddies to your bedroom now, so that they'll be waiting for us when we do bedtime?' The pressure of Cephas's arms around her thighs, and his weight against her knees was heavy, and, anyway, she wanted to get on, so that she and Ian could have time together. She had to feed Ali, yet.

Later, over supper and a bottle of wine, after they had talked about work and how long Ian would be likely to be away, Marina said, 'I got a card from Lily Bridges.'

'What did she say?'

'Just thank you, and . . . I'll get it.'

'Tell me where it is, I'll get it, you must be tired.'

But Marina had returned with it already. She handed it across the table. Ian looked carefully at the rambler rose depicted on the front, then opened it and read it aloud.

Dear Marina and Ian,

I am disgracefully tardy in writing to thank you for the pleasant afternoon we spent at your house. You made us very welcome. Guy would like his thanks conveyed as well. We were both grateful to have a chance to see Cephas. It was a pleasure to meet him and Alex too. Thank you for inviting your mother, to whom I had spoken on the phone, and your stepfather to meet us. Possibly we might at some point be able to pursue the acquaintance, as we have a lovely home in Sussex where children can play, and you would be very welcome.

Yours sincerely,
Lily Bridges

'"Disgracefully tardy",' said Ian. 'That's of its time. Let's look at these crossings out. "Asking" is crossed out, and "inviting" substituted. Well, that's stylistic. But it shows she bothered with this card, and carefully reread what she had written. I think that's a bad sign. But then it might be just the kind of woman she is. "Meet", presumably aiming at "meet again", is crossed out, and we have "pursue the acquaintance" instead. Possibly a good sign – it sounds vaguer. I like "Alex"! "Your mother", "your stepfather" – as if at that point she is addressing herself uniquely to me.'

'Or it might be – like in Jane Austen – you take on your spouse's relations as your own. You know, "his sister" when it's his wife's sister.'

'True.'

'I rather like "where children can play".'

'I think it's sinister,' said Ian. 'She's trying to inveigle Cephas. Oh, and on second thoughts "pursue the acquaintance" might be there to avoid repetition of "meet". So it may not be a good sign after all. What do you think of "see" Cephas?'

'Well, she wouldn't have wanted "meet" yet again.'

'She hasn't used "meet" yet at this point.'

'Maybe she knew she was going to. Maybe she wrote the whole thing out first, then copied it on to the card.'

'The crossings out tell against that.'

'Not necessarily.'

'No, not necessarily. There's second thoughts and there's third thoughts.' Ian looked at the front of the card again. 'What do you think of the rose?'

'Peaceful. Static. Non-controversial. A card she happened to have in her drawer.'

Ian passed the card back to Marina to have a further look at, after their findings. 'We know from Mum that Leda – Jane – is back at home now,' he said. 'No mention of that on the card, in terms of the suitability or otherwise of Cephas playing in their garden.'

'She might not suppose Jane will stay.'

'Possible, but otherwise slightly sinister.'

'"Lily Bridges", not "Lily", though we are supposed to be on first-name terms,' said Marina, looking at the card. 'What about that?'

'It could just be age, or class. But if not, a good sign, I should say, as being more distant. You didn't say what you think about "see" Cephas?'

'Yes, it's rather odd, as if he was a monument.'

'A good sign, I think. You only have to see a monument once. Then you have seen it.'

'We shouldn't be so paranoid.'

'Shouldn't we? Anyway, you aren't. Only I am.'

'Cephas said "meanwhile" again today,' said Marina.

'"Meanwhile". That's very good.'

Distant cries showed them that Ali had woken. 'I thought this might happen,' said Marina. 'It's because I rushed his evening feed.'

'I'll go, you sit down,' said Ian. 'It'll be you he wants, but I'll try to settle him, and if I can't, I'll bring him in.'

Chapter 29

Jane was sleeping better, perhaps because she was occupied. After two weeks, Daisy was freed from Jane's bedroom, and became simply the cat, accepted even by Danny, who barked and got his nose scratched. Greta was pleased, as she had been suspecting the presence of mice, and in Daisy's first week of liberty two little corpses were presented to Jane. Jane was proud of Daisy for remembering to whom her first loyalty was due. So it was not Daisy who created an occupation for Jane. It was the feline life in the shed in the second field. Not only were the six kittens now thriving, and taking their first steps out into grass and thistles; but there were two other cats, strays, introduced by the vicar's wife, a woman of more understanding than Lily credited her with.

Once it is known locally that a welcoming cat shelter exists, numbers build up fast; and after a few weeks another litter of orphan kittens needed to be taken in, then a bedraggled tabby, hardly more than a kitten herself, pregnant and on the point of delivery. Jane was busy indeed.

She enjoyed naming the cats. Sibling groups shared a surname. The two sets of kittens were the Wordsworths and the Coleridges. Fortunately, the shed in the second field, known as the long shed, was not only long but very roomy, and the cats were able to find favourite places for themselves. They roosted like owls on rafters and promontories. They snuggled in strawy beds. They leapt gracefully from improbable places when Jane seemed likely to serve meals. A place was kept sacrosanct for the cat about to give birth, a place she had chosen for herself, which Jane had then screened off and provided with bedding.

As Jane toiled, planned and ministered, she realised that the terrible noise, which had replaced the voices of Us, had abated, or, which was as good, that she had become too used to it to notice. She decided to continue taking her medication. There was no word from Us to instruct her to stop. But all the same, it was a hard decision, for it went against her principles. It smacked of submission, submission to authorities that were not arcane and invisible. She had to accept a certain ordinariness in her mind. She had always known how to organise herself in respect of what needed to be done, but the present tasks were more mundane than were the tasks she had become used to. They were considerably less risky. She accommodated herself to this development, for she felt that rescue of cats was a worthy cause, albeit a cause on a smaller scale than the scale of her previous ambitions and voluntary servitudes. She had always relied on adult disapproval and misunderstanding to imbue her purposes with steel, but this seemed less important now. And, in any case, there was a modicum of parental disapproval, even of her present doings.

The displacement of Angus's rotavator had been the worst thing so far. There were apprehensions about the future.

'It's only been five weeks,' muttered Guy to Lily. 'She's already got about ten cats. What will happen if she wants more space? Or another shed?'

Lily knew the tally was seventeen, not ten. She knew, because Jane kept a list of the cats' names pinned to her bedroom wall, and Lily sneaked in to have a look round. There was no point in Guy having to face how rapidly the enterprise was escalating. For Lily, having her daughter at home was extremely trying and

366

unpleasant, but she only had to remember the period when she had imagined Jane captive or murdered, to be willing to settle for anything other than that. As Lily knew of old, Jane ignored opposition, or flourished on it; so she didn't have to fear that the reproofs Guy occasionally nerved himself to administer would put Jane to flight.

'Angus says you want the windows in the long shed boarded up,' said Guy. 'Why's that, then?'

'Foxes,' said Jane.

'You've got him working down there when he should be in the garden.'

'It's a matter of priorities.'

It was difficult for Guy to hold his ground. 'The wood will cost something.'

'He's found some old boards nobody wants. He's been a great help.' Of course Angus was bewitched by Jane. 'He's going to put in electricity, and in the winter we may need some heating as well.'

'First I've heard of it.'

'They're all simple jobs. They won't keep him long from the garden.' Guy did not hear the inflection of patience and mockery in his daughter's voice, but Lily did, and intervened.

'Are you having them neutered, dear?' she asked. 'If not . . .' She didn't finish her sentence.

'I haven't decided yet what's best for them,' said Jane. 'I can always try to find homes for my kittens.'

'Fanny Barton didn't have much success,' put in Guy, spotting a possible advantage.

'She did,' said Jane. 'And the kittens have done very well. You can come down and look at them, if you like.'

Electricity was hastily installed in the shed by Angus, bringing with it some forms of heating that made Guy wring his hands at the expense. 'Never mind,' said Lily. 'Think how much worse it could be.' They thought, and remembered; and in the end made no serious demur against this new pastime of Jane's, which was, when you come down to it, no worse than eccentric.

Early one morning, when Jane was giving the cats their breakfast, she noticed that the sides of the pregnant tabby, which had been bulging, were now as thin as the rest of her. Leaving her to eat with the other cats, Jane peered into the pen contrived to accommodate the birth. Half hidden in the bloodstained straw and crumpled newspaper she could see a small furry tangle of newborn kittens. Jane knew not to approach too closely, and very soon some tiny mews brought the mother leaping back. She settled among her kittens and began to lick them. With this new perspective, Jane could see that there were three kittens, two tabbies and a black. Jane felt rapture. She watched.

'Mrs Gaskell, Mrs Gaskell,' she said, 'you have done brilliantly.'

It struck her that Mrs Gaskell's breakfast had been rushed and scanty. Jane had always intended to feed her within her pen, once the kittens were born. A dedicated dish stood ready, and Jane spooned a generous helping on to it. She put it within the birth precinct. All the cats were well and frequently fed, and hence were unlikely to maraud the Gaskells' privacy. For now, Mrs Gaskell stayed where she was, among her kittens, purring and licking; but Jane was confident that she had noted her loaded dish. At this point Jane had another thought, and texted Lily. 'Please bring a bowl and some milk to the cats shed.'

Lily had observed Jane heading for the field, and, sure that Jane would be with the cats for a long time, had been trying to enjoy her early morning in the garden, as she used to. But it had not been possible. Jane seemed to be omnipresent, and this sense of her daughter's omnipresence disquieted Lily. The peace and solitude among the waking creatures, which had been the greatest pleasures of her life, were lost. So she trailed back into the house, noticing Jane's firm footprints in the dew that used to be all her own. As she entered the house she heard her mobile, found it, read the text, and hurried to the kitchen. A minute later, carrying a bowl and a jug, she was making her way to the cats' shed. It was not a completely easy walk for an elderly woman with neither hand free, and there were two gates to negotiate; but she arrived. Jane was waiting, and nodded acknowledgement. She poured some milk into the bowl and put it down beside the dish within the Gaskells' sanctuary.

'She's feeding them, you see,' Jane said. 'Milk might be a good idea.'

Fascinated, Lily tiptoed forward and looked. Mrs Gaskell lay on her side, an eye half open, a front paw in the air, her belly offered to the kittens, a little row of three, all sucking. Lily and Jane stood still and silent, side by side, watching.

~

Mid December. A cold, dark day for Helen's wedding. The weather did not matter. It was register office, followed by the upper room of an adjacent pub. No photos, except ones that could be informally snatched; no hanging about; no unseasonally thin clothes. No unacceptable wait, indeed, for the first drink. And it was champagne throughout, so, though worth waiting for, even better without the wait. There was a rich supply of finger foods, provided by a caterer friend of Lewis's who was there as a guest. Young people in his employ, though that day not under his direct orders, carried trays through the thick crowd.

There were numbers of old friends of Helen's, many of them writers or publishers. Marj and her husband were there, with one of their teenage grandsons; and Harry, without his wife, who had long since taken a dislike to Helen. Tim and Cecilia were there, of course, and Ian, Marina, Cephas and Ali. There was a group from the tennis club, which was nice for Tim. Other friends of Lewis's stood around cheerfully. Lewis's friends generally had got over their initial surprise or shock, and become delighted. They all agreed that he was happy. He was wearing a bright red velvet waistcoat and a gold tie, and had a yellow rose in his buttonhole, and his eyes sparkled. He was very pleased that his daughters, Millie and Tania, had been eager to come, having learnt from somewhere that this handsome elderly woman with the loud laugh was quite well known. 'Good on Dad!'

Helen wore a silvery two-piece dress, which she had selected to hide her overweight from those who had not met her before, and simultaneously to display her mild weight loss to friends, whilst camouflaging the stoma bag should it bulge. It was a fine balance; but Cecilia, who had been in on the deliberations, though not the shopping expedition, whispered to her that it was working well, and, anyway, looked lovely. Unexpectedly, and no one knew how, the local paper turned up, but luckily had finished and departed before those who were going to get extremely drunk had done so. The only ones to become prostrate and incapable were one of the publishers, one of the tennis club, and, more surprisingly, Harry.

'Well,' said Helen to Marj, 'at least that means he threw himself into it'. Marj and Derek, who had the task of conveying Harry home to Sheffield, took a sterner view.

Ali, in his sling on Ian's chest, was much talked to and admired, and, to his parents' relief, remained in a good mood throughout. Cephas fared less well, was bored and cross during the ceremony, and could be heard asking repeatedly, 'What is a wedding?' and making people frown or titter. Later he was happy, standing on the pub balcony with Helen's shy great-nephew and Lewis's pretty daughters who were all having cigarettes. Without knowing it, Cephas made it easier for the ice to break between them. Millie particularly took charge of Cephas, and he ended the day in love with her. There were speeches from Lewis and Helen. Lewis had kept his speech secret from Helen, and brought tears to her eyes by saying there was a poem about a Helen that began, 'Is this the face that launched a thousand ships?' and that her face, at every minute, inside him, launched the thousand ships of his love for her. This sentence was much dwelt on in conversations, drunk or sober, in the room afterwards, evoking as it did memories of, or aspirations to, emotional states we all respect, and, perhaps, desire. Coming after this, Helen regretted that her speech was jokey, beginning, 'Unaccustomed as I am to getting married . . .'

Cecilia found a chair at the edge of the room near the balcony on which Cephas was lodged, and chatted with the various people who came to sit beside her. She thought she was going to get stuck with the garrulous caterer, but off he went before very long to track down his staff, wondering why champagne was not circulating into Cecilia's corner. Helen tried to take a moment for what she called 'real talk', but was too much in demand to be able to settle. Having been carried off by Lewis, she rushed back with Marj and sat her beside Cecilia. Cecilia enjoyed meeting Marj for the first time, tracing facial resemblances, and hearing about Helen's family in a way she had not from Helen. Soon after that ended, Ian came, and asked Cecilia why she was sitting down. She said it was to be near the window to Cephas's balcony, in case he needed an eye kept on him, and this was partly true. She was tired, and Ian knew it, and he was worried; but he could not bear to make the concern more real by talking about it. Ali held out his arms when he saw her, beaming and bouncing, and there was a word about the possibility of her taking him; but none of the three really wanted that, and Ian wandered off. Then Marina came up with a selection of foods she thought Cecilia

371

might like. Marina had never particularly taken to Helen, probably because of Helen's indifference to children; but she found the occasion interesting. It is not every day that a woman in her late sixties gets married, and, when she does, it is not always to a husband so much younger.

'Do you think they will be happy?' Marina asked Cecilia.

'They may well be. I don't know.'

This made Cecilia think about Marina and Ian. She thought they were happy, and it was not something she usually doubted, partly, as she recognised, because it was so important to her that they should be. But happiness in marriage did not usually come up between them as a topic, as it had now. Marina had introduced it, and was there more in that than met the eye? Cecilia pondered. Marina, on her side, had no doubt about her own happiness and Ian's; and what had come into her mind was to speculate, not for the first time, about whether Cecilia and Tim were happy. So they sat, mother and daughter-in-law, close associates, friends indeed; but drawn together less by personal affinity than by the fact that the people they loved more than anyone in the world were the same people. They nibbled Cecilia's finger foods, each conjecturing about the other's marriage but saying nothing. This lasted a good half-minute, then they talked of other matters.

Marina left early with Ali, who was getting hungry, as she had foreseen he would. This left Ian with the task of prising Cephas away from Millie. But the party generally was breaking up, coats were on and the caterers were beginning to collect glasses. There was much seeking out and hugging of Helen and Lewis, who were the last to leave. They were off to Brighton for a week, where Lewis had roots; and some of the foolish jokes in Helen's speech had been about their far-flung and exotic honeymoon. At last they were left alone together, and Helen, spotting a bottle that was not quite empty, poured herself yet another glass of champagne.

'All right, Mrs Munro?' asked Lewis, holding her close.

'I think so. I don't know yet.'

He moved the glass as she leant to pick it up. 'No need for that now,' he said, and she realised he was right.

~

It seemed very quiet to Cecilia and Tim in the days after Helen's wedding. They both got colds. There had been a build-up of amazement, laughter, expectation, preparation and support, and now it was over. Christmas was coming. Marina and Ian were going to do Christmas, and Marina's parents as well as Cecilia and Tim were to be there. Marina's sister and husband were going to his parents this year. Cecilia was trying to decide what presents to get for the little boys, and also, less agreeably, for the adults. She needed a conversation with Marina about what food she and Tim should provide. Before Christmas something else loomed – Cecilia's next MRI.

'You know I've got my MRI on the twenty-second,' she said to Tim, coming into his study. 'It seems surprisingly near Christmas, but so it is.' She had the hospital's form in her hand, and was looking at it.

Tim took it from her. 'Yes,' he said. 'Shall I come with you? I mean, of course I'll come with you for the results, but . . .' They were old hands now and she did not always need to be accompanied unless news was to be imparted.

Unusually, terror rampaged through his body. He had got used to the medical limbo they had inhabited for the last months. It had been possible to put on hold the sense that cancer was lurking. Perhaps he had even forgotten that another day of reckoning would ever fall due.

His eyes went from the piece of hospital paper to Cecilia. She noticed his expression, and knew he was scared. She shrugged. 'It is as it is.'

He was left alone, but his computer did not exercise its

usual attraction. He went to the window and looked out. He realised his head had been in the sand over these last months, and that hers had not. He understood that she had been slowly metabolising the fear over time, while he, to be honest, had thought of other matters. It was a simple and a straight-forward fear, and a not uncommon one. His wife might be soon going to die.

He had not reflected, yet, on what this might mean for him, and, as he did so, he swayed and gasped. His fingers went out to cling on to the window frame. He felt the selfish panic that can betray us into grotesque acts of self-preservation, self-preservation at the expense of other people. Me first on the lifeboat! He was not afraid for her. He was afraid for himself.

She was his companion, his context, the air he breathed. Often he wanted to get away from her, back to the computer or his books, but there she always was. What would he be if she were not? What did he have? It seemed ignoble to try to shore up what would remain to him if she disappeared, but, when he ignobly tried to, he could see nothing. He had no family, few friends. No friends, indeed, in the sense that Cecilia had friends. Tennis? It would mean nothing. A feeling of vertigo seized him. It would be him and Thor.

He went to find her. The sight of her, so ordinary and familiar, calmed him. 'I haven't been worried enough about this,' he said. From the look on her face, he saw that it was his selfishness speaking. He should be containing fear for her, not suddenly escalating it.

He put his arms round her, but she was irritated, not comforted. 'No need to be elegaic,' she said. 'I'm not dead yet.'

'Can I come to the MRI?'

'No point. Come to the results.'

Both were frightened, but they were at different stages, and their fear did not bring them together. Tim went back to his study. Why am I so suddenly so shit scared? he asked himself. All may be well.

The next day the post brought Cecilia a card from Helen. On one side was Brighton Pavilion. On the other, in tiny writing to cram enough in, was the following:

L's mum totally Alzy but v sweet. Beyond speech. Points, but at what? Sad. Touching. Nice home, jolly nurses, sea through window. Held my hand. L lovely with her. Hotel comfy, wind cold. Hear sea in bed. Saw house L was born. Us both light-hearted. Hastings for day – chatted w nice young couple in garden of 'my' house. She pregnant – hope her exp. of maternity better than mine! Charleston tomorrow. See you soon, love H. L sends love.

Cecilia propped the postcard on the kitchen mantelpiece.

Her own predicament was more and more on her mind as the date for the MRI came closer. One of the things that occurred to her was that she might have options. It had been difficult, since her cancer had been first diagnosed, to see that. An option had been as hard to discern as is a narrow and nameless road off a motorway. The speed, noise and traffic had always taken her one way only, and it had been almost impossible to detect a turning, let alone to take it. Yet all along, hidden from sight, there had been options. When she had been detailed for chemotherapy and radiotherapy, she could have said, 'What if I had an operation and colostomy instead?' She had not. It did not cross her mind, nor Tim's. And it was not the doctors' fault. Their standard treatment usually saw her sort of cancer off permanently. They had built their motorway and they believed in it. But the fact was that it would have been better for her if she had said that. Her tissues would have been in better shape to heal if they had not been irradiated, and her cancer would have been nipped in an earlier bud.

She had understood from Mr P that the fracture in her

pubic bone could be either bone cancer or radiotherapy necrosis. She had also understood that there was nothing the hospital could do about either. If it was bone cancer, the treatment should be radiotherapy, and this, in her case, could not be, as she had already undergone a human body's full quota. If it was radiotherapy damage, 'damage' being a word she preferred to the 'necrosis' favoured by the oncologists, it would slowly get better by itself, or wouldn't; and would lead to other fractures, or wouldn't. In any case, no intervention would help. The MRI whose date was upon her now was expected to reveal which of the two likelihoods was the true one. If the fracture was bone cancer, one set of things was likely to have ensued and become visible to imaging; if radiotherapy residue, another.

But if nothing could be done, why was there a need to know? Was this a moment to perceive an option? She could cancel the MRI. She could continue in her limbo state, where she had been comfortable, or, at least, able to think of other matters. The nature of the condition that afflicted her bones would reveal itself, as conditions do, dramatically or otherwise, in the course of time. Leave it to time.

Somehow the thought of this option made her sweat with fear. There was something inherently terrifying about the minor road, the untravelled path, off the motorway, where things suddenly went quiet and you were on your own, in unknown territory. The doctors were no longer your travelling companions, because you had not done their bidding. Cecilia had never been a rebel, as so many like to designate themselves. This would be rebellion indeed, and the idea of it made her shiver.

And yet it was attractive. Cancer is so subjugating, subjugating us both to itself and to the medical profession. In order to combat that humiliation, in order to hang on to choice and autonomy, some sufferers set out to walk the world, some join Buddhist communities, some eat nothing but dandelion leaves. They defy conventional medicine. Cecilia had done none of these things. She had put herself under the hospital. But perhaps now, at last, she could fly a little flag carrying a subdued version of rebel colours.

Cecilia had always wanted to be brave. As a child, courage was her favourite virtue. Now she wondered which was the braver option – to have the MRI, and sit for at least a week, maybe nearer two, at the Paradiso or Inferno crossroad; or not to have it, and continue, now voluntarily, to travel the path of not knowing. She could stall, of course, saying she was ill, and postpone the MRI. That was tempting, but weak. As she thought the matter over, she began to feel there was an element of narcissistic triumph in cancelling the MRI. Perhaps there was too much bravado in it for true bravery. Perhaps, disguised in a certain grandiosity, it was a craven escape from the terror of being told the worst. Also, she realised more and more, it would not be a popular decision. Everyone would be against it. She could face Tim, but would she be able to face Ian? She suspected not.

But, on the other hand, if she had the MRI, it would be tacit consent to the medical wish to know for knowing's sake. She was not sure that she wanted to be signed up to that. There was something old-fashioned, or ancient, or oriental, or – she did not quite know what, but she knew she was drawn to it – about acceptance of not knowing. It seemed to smack of wisdom and peace, of humility, of acceptance of mortality, of what in some civilisations would have been expressed as being in God's hands. For all the excellent qualities she had encountered in the hospital, she had not encountered these. She had missed them.

She took stock of her physical condition, as she experienced it. She had her familiar aches and pains, some days worse than others. She was tired, yes, but that had only started when Ian was abducted. She still could not pick up Cephas, but a lot of grandmothers might be like that, even without cancer. She ate, she got about, she looked normal. If she were going to die, her body would have a lot of dying to do before the last breath.

~

Cecilia did not cancel the MRI. Tim accompanied her to it. But as she sat among the other gowned figures, waiting, she felt different from the time before. She felt she had made a choice. The decision had been inconspicuous and, to anyone else, invisible; for here she sat again, on time as ever, disguising her fears as ever, in the familiar area. Two weeks of suspense, sleeplessness and repetitive fantasies later, she was with Dr P and Tim in Dr P's narrow office.

'You're still a conundrum to us,' said Dr P, looking from her to his computer, then back at her and Tim. He said it in a hearty way, with a hint almost of congratulation, though defensiveness was underneath. 'We still don't know what's going on. There's nothing much for us to see. I'm glad you're walking better.'

'Surely that must be a good sign, that she's walking better,' said Tim. Cecilia was so relieved she could not speak. 'And probably a good sign too,' went on Tim, 'that there's nothing much for you to see.'

'I hope so. I'm afraid I have to send you away in the same uncertainty as you were before. We've had all the top radiologists look at it.'

Dr P was ashamed of his uncertainty, and expected Cecilia and Tim to be critical of it. Tim may have been. Cecilia was not. She was used to uncertainty now. It may be too strong to say that she throve on it, but it served to remind her daily that the comfortable certainty we are all expected to strive for is not a necessary or natural state for the human heart.